NICK SNAPE

A CITY OF ASHES

WARRIORS OF SPIRIT AND BONE BOOK TWO

For all those who stood by me
Each milestone is thanks to you

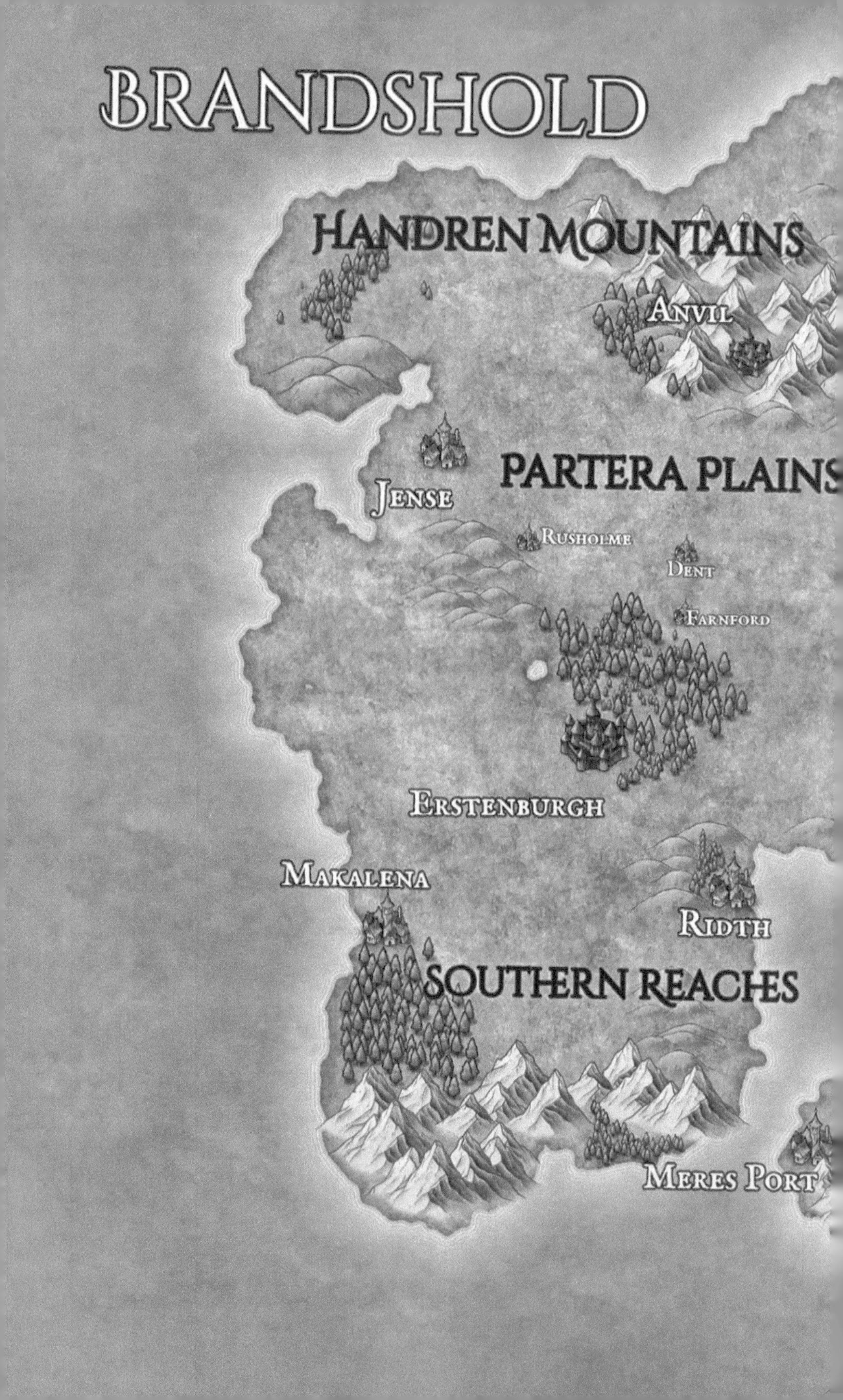
BRANDSHOLD
HANDREN MOUNTAINS
ANVIL
PARTERA PLAINS
JENSE
RUSHOLME
DENT
FARNFORD
ERSTENBURGH
MAKALENA
RIDTH
SOUTHERN REACHES
MERES PORT

Valley of the Unspoken
Pantsil
Khund
Karak
Isles of Tees
Isle of Meres
Shelby

CAST OF CHARACTERS

THE MAJOR PLAYERS

Ecne: an acolyte of Meister Kinst, the alchemical specialist, she has limited training in combat. Ecne has a sharp mind and is struggling to come to terms with the Seven's scriptures as their lies emerge. She carries Wisdom's crossbow.

Gowan: Laoch's First Ranger, who developed a hatred for him after he spurned her advances. Killed by an errant pot bomb, her spirit bonded with Fate's weapon. She kept Laoch alive during the battle with Nathair, though her spirit was weak when she returned to Leront's heartstone.

Laoch: a Queen's Ranger who fought in the Unbeliever Crusade. He rescued Captain Rakslin from a prison encampment, but at the cost of his Spear and brother. A drunkard, barely holding on to his commission. He now carries the weapons of Honour, Justice and Fate.

Oisin: a Handren, a human born of the mountains, and an Elite First Ranger. Burned in the fight with Nathair, he barely survived.

Sura: a Schenterenta, a female elven warrior, dishonoured by her suicide attempt and banished from her tribe. A Queen's Ranger and loved by Laoch. She died, though her connection with Honour's spear and her sheer will have maintained her in spirit form.

The Captain/Keran: a sea-captain from the realm of Mondrein. His spirit was tasked with riding the Wyrm Ship to search for the dragons of the veil and potentially use them as a weapon against the Constructors. Tricked by the Wyrm Ship and the Schenterenta shaman of his realm, he was forced to animate the body and armour of an ancient Inhibitor to aide the Sealgair. Later, his memories return, including remembering his name.

The Unspoken, or the Eighth: an Inhibitor, one of the three that rode An Chéad. She turned traitor, murdering her fellow Constructors and overpowering the dragon's Spirit Walker. She attacked and helped entrap Nathair, later entering scripture to become the Seven's false enemy, thus encouraging the people to prayer. Queen of the Unbelievers, she wears a spiritfire glamour.

COURT

Prime Jacka Vardrin: advisor to the queen and master of her spy network, he harbours a love for her. He is now aware of the Seven's deception, and wary of Lord Penance's power despite his protestations.

Prince Consort Adama: injured during the retreat from the Crusade and now a shell of the man he was. Unloved by the queen, she and Lord Penance contrived to have him falsely accused of conspiring with the Unspoken and placed under arrest in the High Lord's House.

Queen Erin Weister: became queen under the direction of the Seven Houses after King Panset's abdication and disappearance. Chosen specifically by Lady Fate, and married to Prince Consort Adama. She is aware of the Seven Houses' deceptions over the last thousand years.

LEADERS OF THE SEVEN HOUSES

Lady Death: her House symbol is the hourglass, and the God's weapon, a scythe. Lady Death fought at Lord Penance's side against Nathair, and was severely injured.

Lady Fate: her House symbol is the spindle, and the God's weapon, a bow. She acts as Lord Penance's most senior partner in the Gods' Council, though she does not always agree with his actions.

Lady Honour: her House symbol is the scroll, and the God's weapon, a spear. Lady Honour was injured by the tainted Wyrding that acted as a beacon to the Constructors.

Lord Hope: his House symbol is a set of scales, and the God's weapon, a sword. Fought by Lord Penance's side against Nathair, and was also injured.

Lord Justice: quick to anger, slow to forgive, and the youngest on the Council. The God's weapon is a maul, and his House's symbol, a crossed maul and quill.

Lord Penance: High Lord, Overseer being an older title. His House's symbol is a plate bearing the God's weapon – a scourge – lain at the feet of a penitent worshipper. Lord Penance is a manipulator of the Court, the Gods' Council and the flocks.

Lord Wisdom: an enigma, strong-willed in his oversight of the university and the meisters, but weak within the Council. His house symbol is a tome or book, and the God's weapon, a crossbow.

Sneed: a servant to High Lord Penance, and the former High Lord. He acts as a sounding board and is close to the queen, having championed her to Lady Fate before relinquishing the role of High Lord.

UNIVERSITY MEISTERS

Grand Meister Arknold: head of the university, an *engineer*, though she rarely uses that title due to the Houses' dislike for *science*. Inventor of the trebuchet, the ballistae, battlecarts and other devices, that challenge the tenets of scripture.

Meister Kinst: alchemical specialist, invented flash (gun) powder and Erin's Wrath, a high explosive. She is feisty and rails against the constraints that scripture and Lord Wisdom's oversight place on learning. Ecne serves as her acolyte.

Meister Yanpet: cartographer and mathematician, *persuaded* by Lord Penance to remain quiet about the source of the Soul Tear.

DRAGONS OF THE VEIL

An Chéad: the Unspoken's scarlet-scaled artifice dragon, and the symbol of evil used by the Seven Houses to persuade people to prayer. Newly awakened, she flies again, as the danger of the Constructors' imminent arrival threatens the Unspoken's peace.

Leront: the metal dragon who first chased the Seven Magi down, beaten and dismembered by the Magi. Leront's Spirit Walker remains within the heartstone, where Gowan also resides.

Nathair: the artifice dragon that rose after being fully awakened by the Captain. Intact and trapped after the Unspoken and An Chéad's intervention a thousand years ago, she fought Laoch and the others until the Captain and Sura's spirit subdued the Spirit Walker.

RANGERS

Captain Rakslin: commander of the Queen's Rangers, a hero of the Unbeliever crusade, and beholden to Laoch for his rescue. Killed at Smerral Clearing by the Sealgair.

Conch: Elite Ranger under Oisin's command. Infected with an ancient Inhibitor spirit that rode the Captain's armour, her tainted soul entered Lady Honour's prayer stone, and from there, her Wyrding. This tore through the veils and acted as a beacon to the Constructors.

Tanka and Felecia: Elite Rangers killed by the Captain.

Tappin and Kerund: new Rangers under Laoch's stewardship, died at Smerral Clearing.

OTHER CHARACTERS

Captain Mordant: captain of the City Guard.

Delish: a Handren guide during the Unbeliever Crusades.

Láidir: Laoch's brother, whom he was forced to kill, along with the rest of his Spear, after he was caught in a banefire trap.

Naru: Sura's twin brother, died when rescuing a wild horse herd from the Handren.

Nesca: a priest-in-waiting who served Honour's House, severely injured during the Wyrding infected by Conch.

GENERAL TERMINOLOGY

Dragons of the veil: artifice dragons built from cogs, metal and wire, powered by a heartstone. This contains a Spirit Walker, the twisted soul of a Schenterenta shaman that hungers for souls and the spiritfire they are made up of. They are hunters for the Constructors, and can fly between realms and slide through veils unnoticed. Also called veil dragons.

Gods' Council: the meeting of the Seven Leaders of the Houses.

Inhibitor: generalised term for a Constructor soldier.

Journey: the escape from the Constructors, though scripture describes this as a journey across the sea.

Learned: a person of learning, be it a meister, an acolyte or other such role.

Priests-in-Waiting: senior priests from whom the Lord or Lady of the House will choose a future leader. Sometimes shortened to "the waiting".

Schenterenta: labelled elves by humans, they are a people with cat-like eyes, pointed ears and dappled ebony skin. They are short in stature and powerfully built, yet retain a grace to their movements. They engage in an ancient form of spirit worship; however, their shamans lost their powers after the arrival of the humans.

Sealgair: hunters sent by the realm of Mondrein, with the Captain, to seek the dragons. Twin-souled warrior magi who wear an armour much like the Inhibitors', to reflect spiritfire.

Spear: Rangers are arranged into Spears, usually of five or six, who act as scouts behind enemy lines.

Spiritfire: soul magic. The act of using either one's own spirit or that of another, in the form of energy, to affect the world around one. This energy lies in all living things and can be retained in the bonds of certain crystals. The Magi were specialists, and their spiritfire was coloured by this, and savoured by the Constructors.

The Constructors: a race of soul-eaters and decadent artificers against whom the Seven Magi led a rebellion, escaping and taking thousands of the Constructors' spirit-dolls and menageries – humans – with them. It is believed they will hunt down and subjugate the descendants of those who fled.

The Patterning: Schenterenta warrior training.

The Seven Gods/Magi: The Seven were powerful Magi within the menageries of the Constructors. They escaped, taking as many humans as they could with them. On landing upon Brandshold, they wrote the scripture by which they expected the survivors to live. This forbade the study of science and demanded prayer at one of the Seven Houses. After the fight with the dragon Leront, four sacrificed themselves to form the structure of the first veils, only for Nathair to slip through. After her entrapment, with the Unspoken's help, the remaining Magi repeated the sacrifice to form the final three veils.

The Unbelievers: those who turned away from the Seven Gods and the constraints of scripture. Often the thinkers and the mavericks, many turned to the Unspoken in the mountains and formed an enclave at Anvil, under her protection. They regard her as a queen rather than a goddess.

Veils: a layer of spiritfire wrapped about a realm, designed to contain all magic and ensure it is undetected by the Constructors. Brandshold's veils are particularly strong, fed and maintained by the siphoning of portions of souls from those at prayer.

Veil curtain: the protective layer between veils.

Veil glyph: a detection magic that hides within a veil, releasing contained spiritfire should something come through.

Whitefire: spiritfire, but wilder. It can also be tainted by the Constructors.

Wyrding: the Seven bequeathed the Houses a Wyrding Stone, a means by which they can send the drained souls or spirits from their people to the correct veil. The Wyrding Stone is the conduit for this act.

Wyrm Ship: Wyrms are creatures that inhabit the space between realms, feeding off spiritfire that is naturally released. A favourite food of the veil dragons, they were hunted close to extinction. After the Journey, they found many realms were *veiled* and inaccessible. The Wyrm Ship is one such creature that allowed the carving of quarters to house the Sealgair and to protect the Captain on their hunt.

THE RISE OF THE FLESHMASTER

CITY OF SIGHS, THE REALM OF REPANTI

Wind brushed the silvered helm. Tendrils of smoke, caressing the intricate metalwork from the acrid fire that wafted below, flared dead nostrils and rode the numb breath that drew it inwards. The charred air swirled inside cracked and creaking lungs – purposeless. An age-old repetitive act that was little more than a body's memory. Leathered muscles squeezed, compressing lungs, and the air, its oxygen unused and dust-filled, exhaled back out into the night.

Fleshmaster Tarin let his hands rest against the brass rail that wrapped the polished, domed hull he stood upon. It reflected the flame of conquest, but not the light of the shrouded moons, as he stared down upon the field of battle below. The problem always remained the same: how to conquer, to crush your enemy, without killing too many.

Shock and awe. Create inevitability. Enable them to see they are truly just food and no more. End the concept of free will and freedom, as fast and as triumphantly as possible.

The *Kraken* floated high above the burning wasteland, its long-chained tendrils flowing beneath the hull. Each one pulsed and twitched, grasping at any life its tip came across, draining the souls of the living and the dead, and feeding the energy to the circle of crystal eyes embedded in the base of the mighty soulship. Each crystal shone with the whitefire his kind fed upon. Meanwhile, its officers directed the Inhibitor army across the plains and towards the city, their wheeled and multi-legged machines carrying death and subjugation before them.

The magi in the besieged city still wielded their powers, their spiritfire coloured by their faith; rainbows of light that washed the city walls, lashing outwards as they drew on their people to defend the city.

Tarin let a dust-filled laugh slip from ancient blue lips.

Fools, wasting good food.

The magi always tasted the sweetest, and the Inhibitors would fight for the right to present the best at their emperor's feet, hope in their white eyes that the scraps would elevate them another notch towards the *Kraken*'s power base. And it worked. That inner drive to please while being pleasured had fed the war machine for all the ages since the Sundering, the time when the menageries of the choicest spirit-dolls had fled their masters. No longer riding the luxury and decadence the dragons provided, the Constructors had fallen to being the bringers of war – hundreds of years, with their once-proud Inhibitors lowered to mere foot soldiers, spent in the struggle to regain that which had been lost. Though a step up from the chaos that had first ensued.

And we are close. Soon, we may be able to return home, replenished, and awaken our brethren. Then the hunt for my dragons and their prey can truly begin.

The Fleshmaster's muscles twitched, signalling his body's demand, and he reached out, placing an exposed hand upon the nape of the human at his side. His skeletal fingers danced, expectant, and he sensed the spirit surge towards their tips. The sweet warmth leeched from the human's skin, spreading through his own. A sigh slipped from his lips, the energy coursing into his atrophied heart and beyond, streaming throughout his body. The uplift melded with his own detached spirit, leaving him soaring.

It was this moment, this drug, an addiction way beyond mere food, that had brought the Constructors low. The strongest of their spirit-dolls had become corrupted, their slaved minds poisoned by the Seven Magi of his personal menagerie. The choicest, most unique of spirits on Innealtóir – and the corruptors of others.

Tarin sensed the change just as the *Kraken*'s mighty engine missed a beat. The battle below paused, artifice legs frozen as if his mind held time still. It was *that* moment, a pause in existence when fate took a hand. The shift rippled through him again, and the Inhibitors struck out once more. The *Kraken* turned to face the walls of a city he did not know the name of, nor did he care to know.

An ornithopter dropped in at his side, its dragonfly wings spread wide, matching the beat of the mighty *Kraken*'s movement. The time shift was due to its arrival. The moment of respite had been its slide through Repanti's failing veils. But it was also a portent, coinciding, as it had, with his musings about past failings.

There were no coincidences.

The pilot Inhibitor lifted the bug-eyed cockpit hood of the ornithopter and rose to grasp the brass gantry protruding from the *Kraken*'s deck. Tarin paused, admiring the pilot's lithe motion as he leapt aboard, his stride confident as he approached the Fleshmaster, his emperor. Tarin sensed the power residing within the blackened armour – their latest innovation, polished to a shine. The new crystal plates were thinner, lighter, the joints powered by their white spiritfire. The artificers had surpassed themselves again. They were capable of wonders once they could focus their butterfly minds on something *useful*.

The pilot dropped to one knee and held up the glowing message tube in both hands. "My Emperor, this spirit trace was intercepted. A beacon the young wyrms brought to our attention." The voice was hoarse, yet full of pride.

Tarin grasped the tube and pulled it close with the taste of anticipation dancing along his tongue. He opened the cylinder's stoppered end and allowed the whitefire to flow into his helm. Whispers crept into his mind, images seeping in like a still-wet painting of blood and fire.

Forgotten muscles eased his blue lips into a smile. "You have done well, pilot. Feed from my menagerie within, and we will talk again."

Tarin turned back to the city walls and watched as spiritfire lashed outwards, whipping against the approaching siege machine. The artifice brushed the attack off, trundling over the fallen bodies of the city's defenders. Its mighty ladders spewed heat and white flame as engines spurred the machine onwards. The *Kraken* could burn the city to the ground, eradicate any life below.

But if the message rang true, and the ancient Inhibitor spirit's call was not of desperation *but of redemption*, they would need the spiritfire stored below. For it painted the picture of a realm that worshipped Seven Gods and reviled the evil of dragons.

"There are no coincidences. The Seven have been found."

I

A WORLD UNBIDDEN

Innealtóir, The Realm of the Constructors

Laoch crouched at the tower's edge, mindful of the crumbling concrete and rusting metal that lay between him and the dizzying hundred-yard drop to the road below. He adjusted his sword, feeling Justice stir uneasily as the sigil sensed the strange atmosphere – the strands of spiritfire that were both unusual and familiar. The sliver of his God fretted in its setting, and Laoch picked up the sigil's unease; the waves of stress touched his mind, feeding his agitation. Time had seemed to stand still in the dragon's pocket, as if stretching out forever. Yet, paradoxically, it seemed the journey had lasted a mere instant. Laoch found the experience disconcerting, leaving him out of tune with his surroundings. It didn't help his unusual anxiety about the building's edge and the potential fall to the street below.

"Just another day in the Rangers. Nothing weird or strange happening here. No."

Laoch shuffled a little further forwards, edging next to Sura, who stood fearless, peering over the edge of the ageing tower. Elven eyes drank in the city that lay, still and empty, below. Birds flew in and out of the tall, twisting columns that punctuated the air, whirling between cold chimneys protruding out of the stern brick buildings. Keran had called these buildings *foundries*. Huge workshops, larger even than Ecne could wish for, these were the places where the Constructors had built their maniacal visions of machines. Akin to a smithy or an armoury, they should be teeming with people beating metal and smelting iron. Instead, they lay empty, stark. Life had insinuated its way into the abandoned buildings, weeds and vermin on the hunt for food amid the inert mechanisms and cold forges.

"It is not as empty as it looks. I think some of the foundries could be functioning, or are at least occupied," said Keran. The scaled spirit knelt, arms crossed, on the tower's edge. "I can taste some life, though old and bitter."

"Not quite what you warned us about, Keran," said Sura, taking an unmindful step outwards to hover above the huge drop. Laoch's heart thudded, encased in a cold grip. Sura's unnatural act struck a chord of grief laced with dread.

Laoch spun away, trying to ignore Sura, as an icy, metallic taste invaded his mouth. Muttering to himself, a prayer or two released to Justice as his hand rested on the pommel of his sword, he walked over to the strange contraption that lay half broken against the tower's central chimney, its feather-like wings fluttering in the breeze. Its wire frame was bent and twisted where the crash, and weather, had warped the golden-coloured metal. Its central core of stretched metallic skin lay torn, and inside, whatever mechanisms the winged vehicle still bore had Ecne's curious hands all over them, her eyes glimmering with wonder.

"Any thoughts, Acolyte? Is it some form of mechanical bird?" First Ranger Oisin asked. He stood at the machine's side, his burnt facial skin rapidly healing. His hair, though, remained absent.

"Dragonfly," Ecne replied, her feet playing against a pair of pedals as she squirmed in the seat's threadbare frame. "And I think the wings beat rather than soared. All these wires appear to have been linked to whatever's missing in the central body. Like Nathair's heart."

"I have little idea of what's going on, Ecne, but we're going to need that learning of yours here. So keep sharp. We've lucked out where we've ended up. It won't last." Oisin caught Laoch's gaze as he spoke, and he allowed himself an acknowledging nod. They'd talked briefly of the end – of the dragon's fire, and the battle in which they'd saved each other's lives. A soldier's bond, forged in heat and flame.

Laoch let his eyes drift to the enormous dragon, wrapped in on itself and lying inert on the other side of the cylindrical chimney, tail tucked beneath its silver-scaled chin. His breath caught, a moment of incredulity as the dragon's aura swept over him. It instilled a dread in his heart, a spike that lodged deep, despite knowing its menace was restrained. For now, at least. With it motionless, he could survey the joints and rivets driven into the mechanical beast, the horns from which lightning sparked, the scarlet eyes that were a portent of its purpose – to hunt, to feed. Nathair raised her chin, adjusting her metal forelegs, her talons scraping into the dirt of the roof before settling down again. Those scarlet eyes now set on him.

Ridden, but not broken.

Laoch turned at Sura's call, and watched as the spirit stepped back onto the tower's edge. Her eyes fell upon his, locking in. A smile leapt unbidden to his lips, returned in full, and his heart reared, shattering the cold that had wrapped around it. Moments of contrast that Justice tried to smooth as Laoch's fingers alighted on the sword's sigil.

Whatever chaos is to come, we are side by side, Sura.

———

Laoch entered the first chamber off the tower's stairwell. Sensing a change, a shift in the musty air, he spun to face the fungi-covered wall. A pulse beat at its centre, the movement highlighted by the briefest flash of a faded white light that shadowed the surrounding growths. The old Laoch would have lashed out, cracking whatever in the Seven Veils it was across the floor, before stomping upon it, just in bloody case.

The *new* Laoch – the calm and considered warrior he now needed to be – contemplated his actions, and brushed his sword sideways along the wall. The tip scraped against the bulge, and it sailed across the room. Oisin watched the sludge flying towards him before it splattered on the wooden floor near his boot. The lump of green and yellow sprouted legs, six incongruous sets on either side of the gelatinous mass. They waggled vainly in the air, the bulbous material bouncing with each movement. Laoch chose that moment to crash his boot heel into the centre of the legs, assuming the body beneath would crack and spill its contents upon the stone floor. Instead, his foot smashed into something hard, resistant. The twelve legs latched on, their sharpened tips digging into the sole.

"For Justice's sake," he cried, bouncing on one foot as he levered the other up.

Oisin grabbed the Ranger's arm. "Don't panic, Laoch. Calm. It's just an insect."

The mountain man prodded his sword tip towards it. The pulsing mass split, and a set of vicious bronzed pincers emerged to latch on.

"Shit!" shouted Laoch. "Shit, shit, shit! Get it off!"

He was about to stamp again when the pincers released Oisin's sword. The newly cleaned blades gleamed, and a dim white light penetrated the outer layer of the fungi covering the torso.

Oisin kicked Laoch's standing leg away, forcing the Ranger to drop on his backside, and struck at the raised boot with his pommel. Oisin was rewarded with a crack, followed by a deep hiss. A powder filled the air around the squealing creature. Another strike, and a leg sprang back, metal joints wavering before opening wide. As it fell, the First Ranger scanned the darkened room before selecting a chair to smash into the beast in a rare bout of fury. When he was done, an assortment of springs and wires protruded, exposed cogs slowing in a final whirr of life before the machine gave up the ghost.

"Welcome to bloody Innealtóir, realm of freaks and madness," said Laoch, staring at the dead clockwork artifact. "Nice place to visit. Wouldn't want to stay too bloody long." He glanced up at the mountain man, his reddened face grim as he prodded at the mechanical monstrosity with his sword tip.

"And this is just the beginning." Oisin lifted the combination of shattered legs and steel pincers, eyes wide as he took in the complex innards spilling across the blade's edge. "Keran and Sura talked of creations much bigger than this."

"Like dragons—" Laoch stood and eyed the rest of the artificer's room, the worktables and piles of wire clippings all under a layer of dust. "—and the like. How many people do they need to feed off to empower each one?"

"I fear we will soon find out, to our detriment. Check the next room, Laoch."

He nodded, deciding Justice's sword was best left unsheathed as he approached the open doorway. The architrave appeared to be made of wood, but was barely marked by age or any boring insects. Still true and precision-built, like the one they'd entered through on the tower roof. No hastily built castle, this. A building constructed, storey upon storey, to stretch skywards and challenge the sun itself. In his own realm – which he called Brandshold, now that he had reason to – a building such as this was beyond the meisters' skills. An attempt to construct one would have been labelled a challenge to the Seven. Here, this building had been the tallest, and the easiest for Nathair to access. The crashed mechanical dragonfly was a welcome sign of abandonment. They had time to come to terms with this strange city. Yet, the hairs at his nape were permanently on end. This first level was empty except for the moulds and growths upon one wall. Perhaps the artifact had leaked, as Keran had before his amalgamation with Nathair, and the surrounding mulch had thrived upon that?

Something to ask Ecne.

The sword lit the next room, the soft glow emanating from Justice's sigil. Back when he'd battled Nathair, the maul had appeared in his hand, first as a sword, and later, a shield, his survival dependent on his God's will. Laoch sensed the connection deepening, so his wish for low light created something akin to what he'd imagined.

The room he stood in had served as some form of quarters, though here were more signs of age – bedsheets faded and chewed, most lost to whatever vermin dared inhabit the space. There appeared to be a food preparation area, and a sealed cupboard which, on opening it, he immediately regretted. The stink washed over him as the inrushing air mixed with the fetid residue of once-fresh food. The central table displayed a sense of organisation, matching that in the artificer's workroom next door. The only sign of disorder was a set of haphazardly piled books.

Laoch touched the binding of the topmost one, only for it to decompress. A soft pop preceded the disintegration of the entire spine, though the shiny, woven paper within remained untouched.

"Damn."

Laoch blew the dust away and glanced over the first page. He had no words, a regret he only felt when selecting a brew from his frequent attendance at bottle shops.

A scrape of boots on the hardened floor warned of Oisin's arrival. "Found anything?"

"Nothing of use except these old books."

Oisin glanced over them. The smile that crossed his blistered lips produced a regretful wince. He moved Laoch's hand aside with a gloved hand, and his eyes ran over the words. "A simple recipe. For cooking."

"But you can read it?" Ecne asked on entering. The acolyte held the splattered artifice in one hand and some form of tool in the other. "Yes? Now that is a find."

Oisin leant back, keeping his distance from the insect-like creature, whose legs twitched as Ecne prodded at it. "Why?"

"Because, in all likelihood, it means that most of the Constructors' books will be readable, that we have a commonality of language. Possibly because we brought the written word with us when the Seven led us from here. Without it, we would be crippled, with only the sword and fist to glean learning with. If we are looking for a way to bring them down or fight back, I doubt they will *tell* us."

"I may be able to persuade them," replied Laoch, a wicked grin splashed across his face.

"Then see it *another* way," said Ecne, a sigh upon her lips and more than a little despair in her eyes, "that we should use both the quill *and* the sword in the fight to come."

"And the meisters' tools," added Sura, her feet barely gracing the floor as she swept in. "And the spirits, where we can. But remember, the Constructors are eaters of spirit and soul, not of proper food. This is likely a spirit-doll's space – a human collaborator after *subjugation*."

Honour's orange flared in Sura's eyes. Laoch looked away.

Sura continued, unaware, "Keran suggests we allow Nathair to rest, to absorb whatever spiritfire he can from the surroundings, while we search for a way to power the mechanical beast. It will not move far until it can feed on something."

Oisin and Laoch both flinched, the threat implied by the dragon's feeding as much a portent of their future as a concern now. Keran's perception of Nathair as a mighty weapon would be dipped in blood somewhere, in what was to come. Hopefully in whatever enemy the Constructors turned out to be.

"Do we have a next move?" asked Ecne. "Because if I'm not needed, I could explore this meister's workroom, get a feel for how things work."

"Not yet," replied Oisin. "We need eyes and ears until we know who, or what, lives below. And we require food and water of our own. This expedition is very underprepared. We search this tower first, then perhaps the streets below. In the old mountain ruins of my home, wildlife soon returned. Perhaps we can hunt or set a few traps. In fact, Acolyte, string, or at least a piece of rope, is the first thing I want you to find."

"Aha," said Ecne. "Now, I spotted those somewhere."

Distracted, Ecne wandered back into the other room. Oisin joined her to outline his needs.

"Will I be carrying Honour's spear?" asked Laoch, spinning to survey the room before settling on pulling open another set of cupboards, regret written across his face.

"Yes, if you would. Honour and Wisdom converse, though I cannot hear their words," replied Sura. "I am new to them, an avatar formed from death while holding the sigil. My creation fascinates them both, and they are exploring the potential. But for now, I cannot be far from the spear, and therefore its wielder. I would want that to be you." Sura's eyes locked onto Laoch's, who could do little but hold her gaze despite Honour's glow. "This is not easy for either of us. I find what I am fascinating, yet at the same time, I yearn for what I was. What I have lost. You."

"Lost? You requested I stand by your side. That will never change." Laoch firmed up his gaze, squeezing every ounce of belief into his eyes. His hand reached out, its tremble quelled by sheer will, to lace Sura's ethereal fingers.

"Thank you."

2

AN AMBITION UNFOLDS

CITY OF SIGHS, REPANTI

Smoke wreathed the brass rail, weaving its way over the black, gauntleted hands. A snake of ash and heat entangled the forearm, writhing as it rolled upwards to the armoured shoulder before tendrils were sucked into dry, leathery lungs. The Fleshmaster inhaled deep, the withered tongue tasting the memory of the pain held within.

A resultant smile cracked dried lips. "Ah, I do so enjoy these moments."

He pressed his fingers into the brass rail, squeezing tight. White eyes wandered over the shattered, blackened wall as the first of the Inhibitor machines dragged its many legs over the fallen stone. Bulbous eye-shields shone with power, and two jointed claws snapped at the defenders, who threw little more than arrows and stones at the 12-foot-high artifice.

"Dance, little ones, but not too hard. The adrenaline makes you taste that much sweeter, but not too much."

A claw lashed out. Hydraulics snapped the serrated edges shut about a female warrior, her leather-and-metal jerkin slicing in two. The two halves of her body flew in opposite directions. A second claw, attached to the next machine that clambered through the charred gap in the wall, whipped towards the defenders. The glinting edges caught an archer across the throat. The spurt of blood enthralled and annoyed the Fleshmaster emperor in equal measure.

"Popsilin!" he bellowed, and awaited the presence of the captain of the Mechanised Inhibitors at his side. It took a little longer than he liked – a point noted for another time.

The clomp of armour on the hardened wooden deck blotted out the cries from below as Popsilin appeared. "My Emperor," said the captain, though she did not drop to her knee. This was a battle; such extravagances were hated by the Fleshmaster when time was important.

"You told them? To hold back, keep as many alive as we can?" The hoarse, dust-shrouded words flew between ancient, metal-shod teeth.

"Yes, Fleshmaster, of course."

Tarin lashed out. Catching the captain behind her head, he shoved the woman towards the brass balustrade. "Then tell me why they are cutting down all before them. They have soul-lust, Popsilin. You told me the Vanguard were our finest soldiers. I see little evidence of that."

Popsilin stared down at the battlefield, thirty yards below the *Kraken*. The first eight Scorpion artifices were crawling over the rocks strewn before the newly created hole. A pulse of fear entered her throat, stretching the ancient, leathered tube. Below, her second-in-command held a pair of defenders, one in each pincer, and smashed them against the city tower.

"Let me deal with this, Fleshmaster. Personally."

Another smile encroaching on his day, Tarin pulled his captain back from the brass rail. "I shall enjoy watching your efforts, Captain. Make it quick."

Popsilin nodded, casting her eyes to the floor in acceptance of her dismissal, then pivoted, instantly on the run. She pushed aside the human spirit-doll, waiting for his master's bidding, and drew her keen-edged soulreaver from its scabbard. Without pause, she leapt from the deck, dropping through the battle hatch riven into the wood. Spreading her arms wide, the wind filled the armour's membrane between her underarms and torso, yanking her to the left. She caught a metal chain, which rattled like the *Kraken*'s tentacles that hung mercilessly over the burning battlefield. Inhuman strength, a pulse of retained spiritfire enhancing muscle and bone, stopped her dead as she held on tight. The chain links clattered as its controller responded to her mental call and released the flesh-hooked links to tumble down towards the ground before the city walls. Her muscles complained, eased by a thought as she watched the embittered, burnt earth close in.

Leaping the last five yards to the rock-strewn floor, she flipped once to land unsteadily upon her feet. It had been a while since her last face-to-face engagement, and the soul-rush surged through her, the smell of fear and dread upon the wind sending her mind into a whirl. The Mechanised Inhibitor captain shoved the addiction down, locking it away as duty to her emperor and her people demanded. Armour-clad boots shoved her clear of the charred landing spot and she charged upwards, jumping from precision-cut stone to charred rock, seeking her target.

A human groaned, the wisp of pain sliding out above them, a whirling cloud of spirit that drew her eye. Why waste the opportunity? Popsilin brought the soulreaver down, slashing the shattered man's throat. But with intent. The sword snagged the departing spirit and drew it inwards, feeding her body. The fresh energy surged through her arm and washed down to her legs as she spurred herself onwards, eyes catching the raised, barbed tail of the rearmost Scorpion.

"Hear me," she said, her words low and hard. "When I give an order, I speak with the Fleshmaster's tongue."

Spiritfire-infused legs kept her moving, shifting from a fallen pile to a shattered wall as she overtook the more cumbersome Mechanised Vanguard. Each jointed, powered leg had to drag itself upwards and over the stone. The multi-legged structure enabled the Scorpions to access the most difficult of places. The complexity of movement required, however, added to their weight and reduced speed.

A response flashed into her mind from the rearmost artifice, and the rest came tumbling in, the thrum of the soul-lust entwined in some, though not all. Her presence suppressed the desire, speaking to their duty, and the consequences of not obeying.

On reaching the lead mechanised artifice, Popsilin didn't wait. Unfurling the whip from around her waist, she lashed upwards; metal wires threaded with flesh hooks wrapped about the rearmost leg. Motors whirred and the leg shifted, its topmost joint rising above the Scorpion's brass-coloured torso. Popsilin leapt, her wrist flicking the handle in the hope the weapon would release. Its resistance was a loss of pride rather than failure. She let go and hit the metal-ribbed body, rolling on her shoulders to rise, soulreaver drawn.

"Now, the test of loyalty." She strode along the brass body, each booted step greeted by a clattering screech of two materials – one designed to grip, the other smoothed to prevent it. From behind, she sensed the 12-foot-long tail rising as the tip curled in on itself. If it lashed out, arrowing towards her back, then Schendrick, her lieutenant, had refused to accept his fate, eschewing the opportunity of a one-to-one challenge and the rise in status it offered.

The tail whipped from side to side behind her, curling in and out, its tip constantly pointing her way. She knew this, sensed the movements despite the jerk of each mechanised footstep over the broken and charred wall. Ignoring it, not letting the threat creep in and smother her resolve, she took the last four steps to the hatchway. It was sealed tight, with no gap for tools to wheedle the steel and brass ring open. She placed her open palm upon the central bulge and let a tendril of her whitefire seethe against the metal, forging the spirit energy into the key sequence of her command. The hatch clicked upwards. The tip of her sword slid beneath, releasing the catch, and with the toe of her boot, she lifted it open.

"Schendrick, by order of the emperor, you are to relinquish command of the Vanguard." Popsilin knew the Fleshmaster watched from above, could sense the pulse of his power tens of yards away, over her shoulder. The mighty *Kraken* loomed, and those in the Ornithopter Core and the Inhibitor Infantry would lap up what was to come. For them, this challenge was all about status. Bring the rising star down or solidify a key ally in the never-ending dance for the Fleshmaster's favour.

When you are so long-lived, time and patience intertwine.

The Scorpion heaved to a halt mid-stride, three legs raised while the rest held the artifice still. Two of the Mechanised Vanguard moved past, claws poised, tails wavering as they stood guard. The others circled in, bulbous white eye-shields staring inwards at the spectacle about to begin. Popsilin stepped back, wishing for her whip only briefly before steeling her husked heart as Schendrick's helm appeared above the hatchway. His broad shoulders followed, and as he took the last step off the internal ladder, he drew his whip and soulreaver simultaneously.

He does so love theatrics.

Whether in the right or the wrong, the winner would retain command of the Mechanised Inhibitors. That was the way when the emperor demanded loyalty. A rarity amid a battle, but ferocity and guile were needed to sustain their future, and the Fleshmaster demanded his commanders retain both. Besides, the rumours were rife about what was to come – that the dragons of the veil may have been found – and the glory that would accrue to those who retrieved them. Perhaps even a place at the Fleshmaster's side.

And her lieutenant's ambition was only matched by his ego.

Schendrick's elbow twitched, his armoured wrist bending as he laid the whip out in front of him. A threat. His affectation for large hooks and the splayed tip, one he spent hours droning on about, were on full display. The action delayed his first move, a wasted second – a sign of the man's confidence, perhaps. A thought flickered across Popsilin's mind. Had he contrived this moment, deliberately goading the emperor, and therefore her, into this challenge? A spectacle for the commanders and their army?

"Child," she said, her aged tongue clicking against the dry roof of her mouth. "Schendrick, Lieutenant of the Mechanised Vanguard, you are challenged for your disobedience. How say you?"

The helm turned, lifting to gaze at the *Kraken*. A gloved fist struck the armoured plate below the shoulder and above a dead heart, a gesture directed towards the brass rail where the Fleshmaster watched on. "I accept," he replied, and lined up the whip at his side, its barbed tip gleaming out front as he took a fighting stance.

Popsilin flipped her helm visor up, clicking her fingers inside to undo the buckle before dropping the helm.

Let them see.

She held her soulreaver up high and behind her, other hand palm out towards Schendrick. With her feet settled, light upon her toes, she waited. But not for long.

Her second-in-command drew his whip back, then slashed out low as he stepped in, sword cutting through the heat-driven wind towards Popsilin's outstretched hand. She slapped the blade aside and twisted her front leg away from the splayed tip and hooks, allowing them to scrape along the Scorpion's hull. Patient, she stepped to the side to await the next attack. Schendrick liked to dominate, to overwhelm.

This time he led with the sword, slashing at her side. Popsilin flashed her short blade to deflect the attack, then withdrew quickly and spun away left, preventing the whip from fully encircling her wrist. The hooks gouged into the dried skin beneath, tearing, parting husked flesh as they ripped clear.

Schendrick drew the handle back, and the whip's metallic thong whirled behind before he lashed out again, repeating the attack on her sword arm. Popsilin slapped her off-hand outwards, trying to snag the hooked chains. She failed. The links wrapped around her hand and, accompanied by a cry of glee, Schendrick pulled. Popsilin spun inwards, hooks tearing at the corners of her armour, and brought her hands together. As Schendrick drew back his sword to strike, she swapped the soulreaver to her left hand, tip down, and drove the blade into his exposed hip, then upwards into his torso. The man's scream sang in her ears. She continued the spin, slicing his inner armour before momentum carried her through the stroke, ripping the sword out of his cloven chest.

Her gauntleted hand slapped against his helm, the echoes bringing the wounded man to his knees before she sliced the buckle and cast the symbol of his position aside. A shock of black hair sprang out, spiked above the pure-white eyes. His skin flaked, and his twisted mouth bore witness to the agony coursing through his body. The Constructors had never been able to disassociate the physical pain of the bodies they possessed, a spirit memory perhaps, but it was a burden they forever sought to negate. And still they searched.

"Concede," spat Popsilin, the heat of battle raging through her shrivelled veins. It was an order.

Schendrick, eyes downcast upon the riven armour, guts splayed on the floor before him, coughed. "Concede."

She let the smile flicker. The thought of cutting Schendrick's spirit free to inhabit another body galled her. But it was tradition. Without it, their numbers would dwindle, their society would end as a people without children. But when you are immortal, feeding off a forever-breeding prey, what did it matter?

"Ferocity and guile, you bastard." She lifted the soulreaver, blade towards the man's neck, before she dropped her elbow, letting the tip waver. Popsilin lowered herself and whispered, "Never show your hand, understand? Always hold back when you spar. Never let others know your true capability." She plunged the soulreaver upwards, severing the throat and splitting the vertebrae as the blade continued its pathway up into the Constructor's one vital organ. The metal tore into Schendrick's brain, giving him a mere glimpse of terror, his white eyes upon the abyss. The sword drank his spirit whole – an ending.

The Fleshmaster grasped the rail tight, fascinated by the Inhibitor's final moments. A precious soul, lost to him now. One less tool with which to bring their full glory back, struck down and spirit consumed before his army.

A smile graced his lips before he opened his mouth. A mighty roar emanated from the dry throat, echoing off the shattered walls. The sound twisted, the guttural noise stuttering, peppered with a staccato bark as the emperor eyed the victorious captain. "Yes. You we will need, Popsilin. Win me this pitiful city. I want the magi alive at whatever cost. Bring me enough live souls to feed an army."

3
A Spirit's Tale Shared

Ersten Forest, The Realm of Brandshold

Lord Penance squirmed in the shoddy, ancient chair, eyes locked on the mosaic the meister and her acolytes had fussed over. The pieces had been meticulously cleaned, and each section reset after the wall had been sealed against further water ingress. The final layer of protective paste was due to be administered. The High Lord was taking this lull in the works to drink in the scene while Meister Trizone wove her magic in the far section of the domed room. The candles flared briefly as Sneed entered. The servant and confidant stood by his side, eyes flickering between each of the depicted Seven Magi-cum-Gods.

"Do you think they truly understood the consequences of the scripture, Sneed? What their words would demand of the people?"

said Lord Penance, tapping his walking stick, adorned with a glowing sigil, against the stone floor as he rested his chin upon it.

"Does anybody? We have a habit of assuming our people are predictable, like sheep, following the herd. Is that not why we call our followers flocks? Because we need them to blindly accept that we know what we are doing, whether the evidence is there or not?"

"I thought *I* was the cynic. We position ourselves as shepherds, as well you know, to herd, care for and protect our followers. Each of the Seven, in their own way, adhered to scripture as interpreted by their House." Lord Penance let his eyes shift from the Magi to focus on the depiction of his own God, and the plate inscribed with the kneeling devotee, the scourge beneath their feet. "How else were we to survive the last thousand years, if not with a religion that provides for all? Those who chafe at rules, those who welcome more. Ones who ask for the whip and pain to sear the sins from their body, and those who need to weave a deep understanding within each word. The rebels, the saints, the scholars and the warriors, Sneed. For a millennium we held them in—"

"—thrall." The servant eyed his Lord, a half-smile on his face, knowing the goading would fall on already open ears.

"Yes. But what now? Without the Seven, and the prayers, we lose the veils. The Constructors will reave this world, drink our souls. And for most, being slave to a God will feel far lesser a penance than being a spirit-doll to a soul-eater. We must hold our people's faith if we are to have any chance to delay what is to come."

"Delay?"

Lord Penance stood, pushing himself upwards using the stick that remained a required affectation, his God's sigil having restored his tortured body to near its previously hale condition. Stronger now than before, the mantle of High Lord still fell heavy upon his shoulders. "Delay. Come with me, Sneed. Amid the chaos of Nathair's ascent, we may have a little hope."

He tapped his way through the torch-lit domed room, heading towards the table adorned by a thick cloth that lay over a protruding, central bulge.

"Meister Trizone," he said, rapping on the floor for attention. The clatter rose above the busy hubbub as the acolytes worked and the meister directed. "I believe it's time for a break, don't you?" He let a purple-stained grimace cross his face. The nervy meister twitched at the sight.

"Yes, Lord Penance." She pulled up her green robe, drawing out the tool belt and sliding each of her delicate, exquisitely made trowels and scrapers into the pouches.

He watched, patient despite the need to share. This woman deserved his respect, and though his position demanded he strike out at as much as lift those below him, he couldn't help but give her the time. When done, she gathered her acolytes, a stern smile and a guiding hand ushering them out. She gave a small bow before following them.

"A fine meister," said the High Lord, pulling at the chain that hung around his neck.

"I remember," said Sneed. "Does it still hurt?"

Lord Penance glanced at the ex-High Lord, not expecting the lines of sympathy written across the servant's face. "I'd be lying if I said no. But it is what I chose. Another penance for those who accept our burden, Sneed. One of the many. With what we are about to face, the Constructors and the servitude and death they herald, would I have chosen differently? Sacrificed what I bring in return for decades of selfish happiness?" He smiled, the turn of his mouth grim. "Perhaps best not answer that." Looking around, noting the inner door was closed, he tapped over to the table and lifted the cloth. Below, the dragon's heartstone softly pulsed, a blue light in its centre swirling in on itself.

Sneed raised an eyebrow and pursed his lips. "Is that Fate's glow? I thought the heart dead, like Leront."

"Fate? Yes, and more, though it remains weak." Lord Penance reached out a rough palm, keeping the blackened hand aside, and his fingers lightly caressed one facet. Fate's light swirled as he let a tendril of purple spiritfire enter the crystal. The glow rose, its beat a little steadier.

"Is that wise?"

"Ah, now that's a good question. I have not made my mind up as yet, my friend."

The swirling light formed a face, its lines pulsing in and out of focus. The features flickered between human and dragon in an uncomfortable pattern. Sneed flinched when the woman's smile fully formed. It spoke of many things, a complexity he found strange as the Ranger's cowl appeared over her hair.

"Gowan, this is Sneed. In all things, he speaks with my voice, understand?"

"Yes, Lord Penance. We do."

"We?" interjected Sneed. "Leront is in there with her?"

"I believe I have control of the dragon spirit, Sneed. But yes, we are entwined, though as my strength returns, and with Fate's will, I remain in control. Leront is cowed."

"And who are you? You wear a Ranger's garb."

"Sit," said Lord Penance. "Gowan has a tale to tell, the like of which has not been heard within this realm since the Seven and the Journey. One I, with Lady Death and Lord Hope, only experienced the end of."

The High Lord stood aside and let Sneed take up the seat. He squeezed the man's shoulder as Gowan spoke.

4
A QUEEN STANDS TALL

ERSTENBURGH, BRANDSHOLD

"**S**how me, Captain," said Queen Erin, her smile taut, eyes sharp despite the wind biting at her cheeks. She kept her eyes firmly on the stuttering Mordant while wrapping the intricately woven scarf around her neck.

I hate protocol. It won't save us from what's coming.

Captain Mordant met the queen's eyes, faltered, and dropped his gaze with deference before she gripped his arm. The entire City Guard along the walls halted, the atmosphere suddenly fraught as they awaited their queen's usual ire befalling their commander. Beside her, the queen sensed Prime Vardrin straighten, sucking in a breath as panic set in. She enjoyed the moment immensely.

This is the Weister in me, just a new place to demonstrate it. No more Court walls and manners.

She reached out and used a single finger to lift the man's chin. The ring upon her finger was the greatest symbol of her connection to the Brand lineage – however tenuous that link may be. She felt the captain shake, a tremor of anger at the potential embarrassment, and the duty to behave as his queen wished, before withdrawing her touch.

Mindful, Queen Erin relaxed her face but kept her eyes steely. "If we are to prepare for the Unbelievers and their dragon, Captain, you need to stop regarding me as your queen and start seeing me as the commander of Brandshold's army – as is my right with the traitorous consort locked away. See me not as your ruler, but as a green recruit who needs to learn quickly. Explain your defences. I will ask when I wish for more detail. Understand?" She lowered her voice so only the prime and Grand Meister Arknold could pick out the words. "But do not regard me as cosseted, stupid or soft, Mordant. For I am none of these. No more deference, Captain. Not out here. We do not have the time, nor I the patience. In Court, we play the game. Out here, I need the respect to enable me to *lead*." Letting that sink in, her smile returned.

"Yes, Your Majesty. This way."

Mordant, caught between fear and respect, showed Queen Erin and her small entourage to a mechanised lift. Prime Vardrin entered first before the rest, including its designer, Arknold, followed. A guard heaved the wheel, spinning the handle. The elevator, initially resistant before the pulley system engaged, gave them a smooth ride to the topmost level. The grand meister talked all the way up, explaining the effects of multiple pulleys and how she'd transferred what she'd learned to the trebuchets. The queen soaked in every word and, perhaps for the first time, Captain Mordant paid keen interest too.

Stepping out first at the prime's request, the captain approached the walls, hands placed on two merlons as he peered out over the exposed training ground to the north of the city. Below, raw recruits, the last of those taken on before the Unspoken's dragon struck fear into the Union, were going through their initial paces.

As the sergeant-at-arms goaded them into a set of physical exercises, Mordant turned back to his queen as she approached. "We need to clear back the forest," he stated. "It has encroached over the past decade, the periphery full of bushes and saplings." Pointing to where the Queen's Road cut through the forest edge, he continued, "And for all the trade benefits of your road, it provides an easy approach for their wheeled machines."

"And a place for ambush, Captain?" interjected Jacka Vardrin, the prime, looking at where the road disappeared into the thicker region of the wood as it bent towards Farnford.

"Which they'll be prepared for, but yes. If we can maintain the trees, keep key areas thick and tight, it would impede an army's access to the city."

"So," said Arknold, stepping forwards, "you suggest we cut sparingly?"

"I suggest we thin out at random or cut intensively from less strategic areas. Consult on where to gain the wood we need." The captain peered back at the queen. "We have high walls here. We can see the impact on the forest of any cutting and plan ahead. But Farnford and Dent have neither walls nor a defensive screen – farmland mainly. Rusholme has the river at its back, and the hill. I know you want a rundown on our capabilities, but our greatest defence is those towns. Reinforce those, and you buy time should the Unbelievers come. My true advice is to start there."

Erin nodded, turning to Jacka. "Prime Vardrin? You agree?"

"If the reports of the beast are true, will it not just fly over such walls or fortifications?" Jacka maintained the role of sceptic, one he'd allotted to himself in agreement with the queen.

"Likely," said Mordant, "but I can only surmise what an army would do. This beast, if it comes for us, is something I know not how to fight."

"If I may?" said the grand meister. "Trebuchets are of use against soldiers in known positions. These can be set up inside the castle, my Queen. Range markers placed and drilled into the ground with spotters on the walls – operators we can train. But they will be of little use when the opponent is mobile, and in the air. I would suggest we look towards ballistae, placed along the wall. It may mean extending the inner walkway and possibly setting scaffolding behind the city towers to provide protection."

"How soon?" asked Jacka.

"It will depend on who I have to help. The House of Wisdom is offering some of their acolytes, so we could be talking a month for, say, three of the sky-focused weaponry, and similar for five or six of the ones to cover the walls. Kinst is already working on providing additional Erin's Wrath, though remember, using that mounted high along the castle has an inherent danger, should it catch."

"But we can prepare? Lord Penance already knows of these weapons and the alchemical fire. They are *now* approved, and within the restrictions of scripture. Can they not be made and safely stored?" asked the queen.

"Safely? A good question. Certainly, it is within bounds to explore the possibilities."

The captain nodded along, eyes to the floor, thinking. "May I make a suggestion, Your Majesty?"

"As I've already said, Captain, I am here to learn."

"Pull in the veterans of the Crusade, pay them to advise. You want to defend the towns from an army, get them involved in training your militia and planning the battle. Raise the people's confidence by using what we already have. That will leave the meisters free to focus on these machines of theirs."

Queen Erin nodded, half an eye on her prime, who raised an eyebrow in return. "Are you suggesting, Captain Mordant, that I need someone specific? Because I fear I know which path you're leading me along, and it is lined with thorns."

"Aye, that it is. But she'd inspire others to return to the fold, my Queen. There are many who question your cons ..." It was the queen's turn to raise an eyebrow. "... ex-consort's decision to remove her from the battlefield at the Forest of Cairn."

"Tell me, Captain. Just how many bones of the consort's Honour Guard did she break?"

"Three, and knocked two unconscious, with another still hobbling. I understand that one joined the same House as her. She has presence, a capacity to instil raw courage."

"And makes mistakes, Mordant. Though rarely on the battlefield."

5
WHEN BOUNDARIES ARE PUSHED

INNEALTÓIR, REALM OF THE CONSTRUCTORS

Sura, perplexed, focused her mind upon the sigil. Honour caressed her spirit as it wove within her. Permission had been given, but the more Honour entwined herself, the more violated she felt. Trying to contain those thoughts was near impossible with Honour's touch inducing searing pain – like the sting of the hornet or a fire wasp – burning at what she perceived as her skin. Non-existent nerve endings fired off at the mere wisp of the avatar's presence.

It became too much. A silent shout of agony slipped from her ethereal lips and Honour withdrew, surging back into the metallic sigil locked in the spear across Laoch's back. With the agony instantly at an end, Sura reached out, forging fingers from her own spirit, casting thoughts to lay upon Honour's metal walls.

"I am sorry. I do not know how it was for Gowan, but for me the pain is great. Perhaps ... perhaps my Schenterenta heritage is a barrier?"

Sura sensed Honour's call – of apology, and internal strife – a message she understood. Another thought passed, one of *time*, though Sura doubted how that could be measured by something asleep for a millennium. For now, she needed to be content with being present and push away the fading memory of the physicality Honour promised.

Laoch rose from behind the strangely configured gate, an arrow nocked on Fate's bow as he peered down the street. The Ranger was still clearly unsettled by Oisin's refusal to carry the God's weapon – a continued denial of their obvious need to be as capable as possible. Sura understood that Oisin's reticence originated from Gowan inhabiting the weapon, but she had remained behind on Brandshold. Therefore, Laoch couldn't see the sense of the Handren's stance other than pure stubbornness. Sura had been party to the argument as they swept the tower floor by floor, yet remained silent, deep in her own thoughts. The relationships between the weapons and their wielders would only grow more intimate. Perhaps that's what Oisin truly feared.

They had searched for food and water as they descended the tower, hope rising when they discovered the building's maze of internal pipework. Somehow, the Constructors had built a system to transport water throughout the building, despite its height. However, the taste was bitter, metallic, and Ecne had warned of potential sickness related to it. As bitter, Sura thought, as Laoch felt right now, carrying the burden of three of the Gods' weapons.

Sura expanded her awareness into the street, experimenting with what she could and couldn't do. Her sense of smell was non-existent, the trees and plants she passed, bland. Likewise, her taste. Letting her fingers alight upon the fronds of a plant springing from the cracked road, she focused on her spirit form. With concentration, the fingertips rested on a leaf. It brought her a brief smile of relief.

She glanced over to where Oisin waited at the corner of the next stone building, shoulder against the sturdy wall, eyes on the street while Laoch covered. Ecne watched the rear entrance of the alleyway, her glowing crossbow in hand, muttering away about the floors they had rushed past in their hunt to meet basic needs.

Sura's hearing was good – though she found herself interpreting the movement of the air and objects rather than sound itself – and she heard Oisin call Laoch to move on. She watched as he ran. Bent low, he aimed for the far side of the wide street littered with the wonderful and the weird – broken, rusted contraptions with no obvious purpose. Amid this mechanical carnage, nature took back what it could. The grey material used for the roads cracking, trees and bushes taking advantage to secure their roots and sprout upwards. None held seasonal fruit or nuts, but life chittered and sang in the branches. They had eyed the creatures that gnawed at the grasses and chewed upon the bark. It all meant water and food were to hand, despite Ecne's worries over how edible they would find the meat, and the potential of poisonous plants.

Sura's thoughts wandered to the conversation with Ecne, only a few days past though it felt like an age, about how her people would have experimented to find what was edible.

Now, they will have to risk such things.

Laoch stopped, eyes searching down the street. Nothing mechanical appeared to stir in either direction.

Sura watched him. She needed to help, to be an equal to those who worked against the threat of the Constructors. Maybe not a Ranger, if she could not fight, but their first role had always been as scouts.

"I can look," she thought as she focused on the Ranger, willing Laoch to hear.

Laoch smiled back at her from across the street. "Aye? This a new trick?" he said out loud, but the words reached her, their tone a salve.

Sura let herself fade and willed her spirit across to Laoch. She reappeared next to him and crouched low, imitating him.

"You heard me?" she said.

"I did, as if you were next to me, or in my mind. I'm not sure which." He glanced ahead, watching the street.

"I need to help. I can travel at least as far as that second wheeled beast to the east, and behind, to the tree copse," Sura pointed out the places as she spoke, like the Ranger she had been.

"Aye, and maybe you proving useful will encourage our stubborn mountain man to accept Fate's bow. There's no point in all this power being in one Ranger's hands." Laoch glanced over to where the mountain man waited.

"I always knew I was too much for you," she whispered in response, her tone playful.

Sura faded, then flowed eastwards through the air. As she left, Laoch signalled Oisin to have eyes on, indicating Sura's direction. He hoped the First Ranger could see the spirit.

Sura felt the rush of wind, her spirit body sliding between the shifting currents as she focused on the tree copse. As she neared it, the richness of the foliage caught her eye. A flock of birds burst from the branches, the ruckus making her shimmer as they took flight. Sura immediately took a defensive stance before gathering herself. No threat had appeared. She edged around the first rough trunk. The deft, familiar tinkle coming from between the trees drew her closer. The cracks in the road widened, the plant life appearing more varied as she approached the sound, which grew in volume. A glance into the rift confirmed the sparkle of water flowing below. Her first thought was of an underground river, evidenced by the plant roots dropping from their tangles above to enter along its sluggish route. The more she looked, however, the less natural it felt. Though not party to the water systems in human towns, the tunnel was straight, most likely crafted by hands – or their machines.

Sura turned back. Should she return to Laoch or were there alternatives in her new form? She attempted to speak in his mind again, but to no avail. Drawing a wisp of inner spiritfire, she spoke instead, lacing the words with her spirit. She hoped to send them gently upon the wind. The first word, 'Come', boomed, bellowing as loud as Nathair's roar. The animal life immediately fell silent, and Sura ducked behind a tree as a tension erupted where her heart used to be. Half-expecting the wildlife to burst into life anew, she was surprised when they remained cowed and still. Except for Laoch, who was now on the run, approaching at a speed Sura could only assume was driven by her putting the fear of the Seven into him. Oisin followed close behind, wearing a scowl as he struggled to cover Laoch.

She scanned the nearest side streets and tall blocks, then rose, palm out, the Ranger signal for *all-clear*. He seemed oblivious until Sura realised she was ghost-like, and so focused her *self* to sharpen her spirit body. Drawing a little more from the swiftly approaching sigil, she pictured herself through Laoch's eyes and enriched the light. Increasing her opacity in this way, she achieved the first step Honour had been attempting by her own means.

Maybe I know myself better than Honour. Fate had read and dissected Gowan, examined the many directions and decisions she'd taken in her life, whereas Honour saw but one painful moment of mine.

Laoch's pace slowed as Sura's spirit solidified, relief evident as his body relaxed. Oisin, eyes flashing with frustration caused, Sura assumed, by Laoch's break from the Code, remained wary. The Handren's eyes darting along the crossroads and over buildings Laoch had barely acknowledged. The animal life remained subdued, the presence of strangers, coupled with the violent noise, deadening the atmosphere. Not ominously. More a reflection that all was not normal.

Sura signalled Laoch over to her, and disappeared behind a rough-barked tree while the Ranger indicated to Oisin he was following.

By the time Laoch stood by her, Sura had knelt next to the hole, the tinkling of water echoing from below as it flowed over fallen rocks. The Ranger's posture stiffened when Oisin joined them, realisation creeping into his face as the mountain man growled by his side.

"It's raw, I know. The loss," said the First Ranger, "but acting like that puts me, and Ecne, in unnecessary danger."

Sura knew better than to interject, despite the guilt she carried for her uncontrolled shout.

"Aye," said Laoch. Jaw tense, he kept his eyes on the stream. "I was not thinking straight. You're right. Perhaps it's all these bloody weapons I'm carrying, eh? Is there nothing in the Code about sharing the load?"

Sura waited for Oisin to bristle, the first signs of camaraderie to fade as tensions rose amid the strangeness.

"Whatever I choose, Ranger, I do so for the good of us all. And *you* are to follow *orders*."

To Sura, the glare in Oisin's eyes spoke more of personal conflict and guilt than the words did. The Handren had an inner, and outer, strength, one she thought borne from careful consideration, not knee-jerk reactions. Laoch needed to be careful; something he wasn't exactly known for.

"We have water," she said, cutting through the mood. Oisin turned her way, a nod of acknowledgement paired with a grim smile.

Raw, yes, but he knows it.

"A start. We should set snares. A watering hole will attract life. We also need to scout the immediate area – the roads and streets – make sure we are safe to camp while we gather what we need."

Laoch peered at the First Ranger. "Camp? Are we not sleeping in the first building? Secure walls and ..." Sura smiled as Laoch's mind clicked into place. A Handren, and, for that matter, a plains elf, was unused to a roof over their head and the confinement of four walls. "Okay. How about we camp at the building's entrance? So, we can fall back should anything bigger or meaner turn up, like a pissed off bloody dragon."

"That's my thinking."

———

Ecne awoke to find herself rolled up in moth-eaten blankets, just inside the building's main doors. The fire remained banked. Oisin sat on watch with the flame to his back. Her heart hammered, a crash of adrenaline from the events of the past few days pressing in. The acolyte felt suddenly extraneous to events, as if looking on from the outside. Her mind dragged back memories of the attack on Smerral Clearing, and the ensuing battle with Nathair. The fire-breathing dragon had come close to ending them all. If it hadn't been for Keran and Sura wrestling its Spirit Walker into submission. And Sura, dead, yet not. Walking and talking, but fading away to reside within Honour's Spear. And, finally, arriving in a new land, one full of broken wonders that entranced her curiosity while grating with their sense of wrongness.

She rubbed at her eyes and calmed her breathing, stepping back from the panic by giving herself time and space to think. She pieced together the Seven's scripture and the shackles it placed upon their science. Gradually, her logic overcame the adrenaline-fuelled fear and excitement. If this place, and Nathair, were where unfettered experimentation led, then, perhaps, the Gods were in the right. Yet, she still saw better ways to steer learning.

Calmer, the stirrings of hunger made her reach for the food at her side. She gnawed intently upon the bone before sucking off the last of the meat. It tasted good. Her stomach had bellowed so loud after the first taste, she'd have eaten it raw if necessary. Last night, she'd had the first half of the rabbit-like creature, falling asleep with a half-eaten piece still in hand as the warmth and sustenance took hold.

Tired, legs and arms aching, she rose and finished her cold breakfast, wandering out through the shattered glass doors just as the sun broke along the street. Oisin had also stood, allowing the first rays to warm his face as he turned, arms out, to greet the dawn. Ecne sidled in next to the man and waited for him to speak as she kicked at the ground before cinching her jerkin in tight.

"I miss the mountains," said Oisin. "Especially when the dawn came and pierced the mist, filling my valley. It was like being on top of the world. This place ... ah, I don't know. It feels like everything is trying to forget the past. That it was too horrible to contemplate. So, move on and hope it doesn't repeat itself."

"To me, it waits."

"Aye. Perhaps. But it appears to have been doing so for a long time. Tired?" Oisin enquired, noting the stiffness in Ecne's stance.

"I have to admit, yes. I felt refreshed after we travelled on Nathair, but it hits me now."

Oisin looked at the acolyte, eyebrows knitting together. "Does not Wisdom provide you with strength? From the God's sigil? It is what Laoch said."

"Amid the battle, it drew upon me when it was near done. Without it, I fear Nathair would have swallowed you both whole." Ecne let a rueful smile grace her lips, side-eyeing the First Ranger. "So, it has its advantages. But it does not do so at the moment. Nor does it sustain me. Perhaps this exertion is something I need to get used to."

Oisin nodded, eyes on the street, scanning for anything of concern as his breath billowed. "Laoch wants me to take Fate's bow. To share the weapons out. It makes sense, Ecne. But ..."

"I understand. My own crisis of knowledge and science versus faith is still playing out. Everything that has happened has them working in unison – the spirits, the artifacts, the drawing of strength – all contradictions to the Seven's scripture. Keran says it was a way to protect us, to help us hide from the Constructors. But it is all I knew growing up, and it now lies in tatters." Ecne faced Oisin, who kept his attention on the street.

"I think you know the Handren are famed for their stubbornness—how else could we have repelled the Union army? But I would put it more down to a people who consider long, then act decisively. I studied your faith afterwards, wanting to know why you opposed our ancient traditions. I found a surprising comfort there, and it helped build the alliance between old enemies. But Fate's bow challenges that faith, the foundation of my belief."

"All I know is that I have people I care about back in Erstenburgh. I am trying to focus on them, and if it means sealing my beliefs away, then so be it. I fired a God's crossbow, Oisin, that shot... I don't know what to call it ... a quarrel? Or a bolt of light? Keran terms it spiritfire, drawn from around and within us. Without it, we may have been lost."

She turned to head back inside, when Oisin glanced over. "How old are you, girl?" he asked.

"Eighteen. Why?"

"Because you have a clarity in your thoughts that I am jealous of. Perhaps, with age, we lose the courage to just *decide*."

Ecne nodded. "But when you lead, you do so with focus. Perhaps you need to command yourself. What would *you* order yourself to do?"

"Ah, girl. That was uncalled for."

Ecne smiled as the mountain man clasped her on the shoulder, meeting her eyes.

6

THE HIDDEN MAGI

CITY OF SIGHS, REPANTI

Smoke washed across the old market square, hot winds catching, billowing soot and ash across broken buildings and shattered stone. The Scorpions guarded each street, tails high, stingers bared as they awaited the Inhibitors, scouring the nearby buildings to return with their prizes. Mewling life knelt amid the flame. The Fleshmaster eyed each as he strode over bone and brick with equal disdain towards Captain Popsilin, who stood, hands on hips, sneering down from her Scorpion's hull.

"Eyes down," she bellowed.

The families and shopkeepers, soldiers and farmers, with bloodied clothes and bruised faces all complied. The dead and the dying, strewn on the ground before them, were left where they had fallen when the vanguard tore a hole in the city's defences.

Emperor Tarin reached a position he was satisfied with and swept his arms wide towards the hundreds who knelt before him. "Ahhh, the City of Sighs. I thank you for the sport, good people. You held out well, no doubt stories of your past filling your heads with dread and fear of my Inhibitors. But hear me, *citizens*. These *magi* poison your minds with lies and deceit. They led you here out of jealousy, running from a life many enjoyed, safe under my wing, never wanting for anything. When the Seven Magi ran, they did so because they wanted that control, that power. Selfish. And ever since, my scouts tell me you have bent to their weaker brethren's will, doing *their* bidding when you could have been following *mine*."

The emperor reached down, and his black-gloved hand grasped the chin of an injured soldier kneeling at the front. Tarin let a foul smile cross his ancient lips. The tang of the man's fear set his spirit racing. Blades at the tips of his fingers snicked, cutting into the flesh, forcing the soldier to rise to his feet.

"But you still fought my Inhibitors. Many of your people gave up their precious lives, unknowing that it is the magi who hide, cowering behind you, protecting themselves." Tarin's other hand grasped the back of the soldier's head, the blood pouring from his stump of an ear ignored. The Fleshmaster drew the man's spirit towards the glove, turning him to face the now-watching crowd. The man's lips turned blue, shrivelling, his sallow cheeks sucking in as the skin dried, flakes drifting to mix with the ash on the wind. Tarin, sensing the first vestige of spiritfire as it graced his fingertips, was unable to quell the pleasure that grew upon his face.

Let them quail.

As the soldier's eyes rolled, whites matching the emperor's own stared out at his fellow citizens. Tarin let out a sigh of feeding as the soul rushed through his arm. Opening gauntleted fingers, he held the twisted body in the air with his power, eyes on the people laid out before him.

"I want the magi, the ones you call The Sodality. You have little time left." Tarin reached for another. He drew the middle-aged woman, her tangled grey hair streaked with blood and grime, from the floor. Her face twisted, desperate hands grasping at the Fleshmaster's arm as his fingertips bit into her skull. Legs kicking, he spun her around to face the mewling crowd. A child rose, her face tear-streaked, and reached for her mother's legs.

Tarin drained the woman quickly, her skin husk-like in mere seconds. Tendons cracking as her bones were pulled into unnatural positions, she died under the gaze of her people. The child screamed, and an Inhibitor intercepted as a fruit knife appeared in the child's hand, the blade flashing towards the Fleshmaster. It bit into the Inhibitor's wrist instead. The soldier snapped the child's neck, leaving her to fall at the emperor's feet.

"The magi," he repeated, throwing the carcass at those shaking in the front row. "Soon."

Tarin pivoted, armour gleaming in the light from the flames, and approached Popsilin's Scorpion, one hand raised. The Mechanised Inhibitor captain ordered the artifice's tail to reach over and flatten on the ground, ready for her emperor to step onto. Rising into the air on the tail, he glowered at the people, arms spread wide, before joining his captain. Below, the Inhibitors, his infantry, moved between the rows, black helms throwing question after question.

"Well?" said the Fleshmaster. "Any sign?"

"Not as yet, Emperor. Is it worth the ornithopters scouring the forest and hills to the east?"

Tarin's aged white eyes turned to glare at the captain. "They are here, Popsilin. Inside these broken walls. I can taste them on the ash and char of their fallen city. They are a priority. Not only for the promise of their spiritfire nectar, but for their knowledge of this realm – and possibly others. Do not underestimate the power of *knowing*, child. It provides purpose over and above simply feeding. Without it, we would be like the locusts of old, simply falling upon a world in frenzied feeding. Those hordes died in their thousands because they could not see the potential of careful nurturing or understand what lay in their future."

A cry echoed below. An Inhibitor grasped and lifted one from the kneeling crowd and strode towards the Scorpion.

"Gentle," shouted Popsilin, mindful of the emperor's wishes.

The Inhibitor waited at the head of the machine, its bulbous, crystalline windows staring back like the faceted eyes they were modelled upon. Popsilin ordered the tail to lower again, and this time the sinuous, metal limb wrapped the youth and lifted him up to hover before the Fleshmaster. The boy kicked, arms fighting the strength of the Scorpion, his energy waning as the metal scales slid a little tighter. Tarin motioned down and the pilot responded, lowering the boy until he came face-to-face with the emperor.

Tarin reached out, and a single finger ran along the boy's moist, tear-stained cheek. Wild eyes, unfocused, whirled at the touch.

"Ah, you *know* something, don't you, lad? Yes." Tarin removed the finger, and his leathery tongue flicked out to lick its tip. "The taste of spiritfire. You have been in the presence of a magus. Speak."

The boy dithered, eyes darting, desperation creeping into the tremors that spread through his body. Tarin sent out a sliver of power. The whitefire, crackling through the air, swathed the youth's mind with an aura of peace and calm.

As the boy stilled, Popsilin reached across and tore away the boy's outer cloak, exposing a roughly stained blue robe beneath. "An acolyte."

The boy moaned and, lips moving, his betrayals fell upon expectant ears.

———

One of the Scorpion's razor-edged claws cut deep into the dual wooden doors, scything through their iron bindings and throwing them aside. Popsilin's Scorpion pilot whipped out a second claw and dragged the blades across the soldier who appeared, bow in hand, its crystal-tipped arrow already spiralling away to erupt against his window. Orange flame billowed briefly. As it guttered, the man's head was clasped in the claw, eyes distant, while the body twitched beneath.

'Inhibitors, subdue, not kill.' Her thoughts drilled into the minds of the support team that poured through the entranceway, ducking under the clawed limbs. "Back up, pilot. And follow orders. You kill a magus, the emperor will gut you and feed on your soul. Then he'll dine on mine." She unclasped the seatbelt, rose to grasp the ladder and clambered up top. Exiting the hatch, she was soon on the muddied ground, stepping through the detritus of war to enter the building, the raucous shouts of her Inhibitors echoing down the ascending stairways.

Drawing her soulreaver, she lifted the polished buckler shield from across her back and waited for her personal guard to walk ahead. Broad-shouldered, he filled the hallway. His halberd – far too large a weapon for house-to-house combat – was strapped across his back. Instead, he carried an Inhibitor's mace in one hand, its spiked ball-shaped head glowing white. In his other hand he held a slightly larger version of her shield, buffed and silver. He wore the old-style armour bearing thicker crystal, yet just as reflective. It was designed to maximise protection against spiritfire, as far as was possible.

Calls echoed throughout the house. The chaos was mainly centred on the higher floors, where the Inhibitors struggled against an enemy willing to fight to the death. An army so unused to sparing life was struggling with an enemy that was fighting tooth and nail to remain free.

"Wait," she said, eyes glaring down the hallway towards a feeding area. A kitchen, according to those who had hosted the now-lost menageries. "On my order only, Inhibitor Marklin."

Spiritfire erupted, tearing down the stairway, residual power soon followed by a tumbling Inhibitor. They crashed against the bottom step, neck shattered. The head lolled to one side, the helm's visor cracked. The Inhibitor's eyes stared out vacantly towards the ceiling.

Popsilin felt the spirit depart, swirling around the hallway before wrapping itself around Marklin and entering his rear gourd – a spirit container, able to hold the Inhibitor's essence for one cycle of the sun. After that, without a new host body, they would be lost.

A second bolt crashed in.

Popsilin ignored it as she sidled up to the edge of the stairway and peered up through the banister. At the top was an aged woman. Her hair stood on end, crackling with spiritfire, and her eyes were filled with blue as she pulled in whatever energy she could. Hands splayed, and a third bolt slammed into the Inhibitor's body lying at Popsilin's feet. Their plate armour fragmented and the ancient body burned, filling the air with the scent of charred meat.

The magus twitched. The blue glow in her eyes faded a little before sparking back, revitalised, as her skin dried and lips shrivelled. Popsilin recognised the weakening. The woman was draining herself dry as she watched, smiling, teeth bared.

"Now, Marklin. Shield up, but the wily bitch may well fire low," she ordered.

The soldier crouched and took the first step slowly before charging upwards. Lightning crackled, forks lashing against his buckler and bouncing back to strike the whitewashed walls, scorches marking their passing. Popsilin fell in behind him, her own shield over her head, mindful to keep her legs behind her guard's bulk. The spiritfire bolt cracked into the Inhibitor's shield, and was deflecting upwards and over his shoulder to strike her own. With its power depleted, she held tight, then pushed the buckler back up as she noted Marklin's shattered wrist. He dropped his shield. With nowhere else to go, the

Inhibitor charged, heaving the whitefire mace at the female magus's hip.

Popsilin, a few steps behind, heard the crack echo back off the stairs, only to find it was the mace that lay shattered in the Inhibitor's hand. The mage clutched the handle of a knife. The rest of the weapon was in smoking shards that peppered the wooden floor and Marklin's armour. Ignoring her guard's scream, Popsilin pushed past the writhing soldier and swung her soulreaver down towards the mage's exposed arm. The woman stepped backwards, her robe sleeves sliding away to reveal metal greaves. One arm greeted the sword with a clang, sparks flying as she parried. Popsilin allowed the blade to scrape downwards. Its edge bit into the magus's skin, sucking life briefly from her before she withdrew it.

A reminder, bitch.

The woman's other hand crackled and blue spiritfire danced across her knuckles. Popsilin recognised the spiked knuckleduster rushing towards her head just in time. It crashed into the raised buckler. The spikes penetrated the metal and spiritfire arced against her exposed forearm. The new black armour reflected it back, and Popsilin swung her sword wide and inwards. The flat of the blade slapped against the magus's ear. Stunned, she staggered, only for the Mechanised Inhibitor captain to lash out again, striking the same ear before kicking at her leg. The woman fell. Popsilin dropped onto her, both knees pinning her arms down, and struck out, punching until the magus faded into unconsciousness.

7

PULLING AT FATE'S WEAVE

House of Penance, Erstenburgh, Brandshold

The cane tapped against the stone floor, each strike echoing through the empty prayer chamber. Lord Penance took each step with feigned pain, his stiff joints and complaining muscles relieved as the God's weapon in his hand, drawing residual spiritfire from the vaulted room, eased the burdens of his office. The polished grip, which bore the sigil of his House – the penitent at prayer, the scourge below – was encased in a gloved hand that still carried the scars of the scrying, though the black, cracked skin had healed under his God's touch.

The High Lord glanced behind him, knowing two of the priests-in-waiting would be nearby, hands hovering near their weapons, ready to lay their lives down for their Lord. A necessity his scorn could not end, for if he were to fall, who would tend to the realm? Who would lead?

There is no precedent. Perhaps Sneed, if my priests could hold back their ambitions. Though it may be that the close-up view of Nathair's might has quelled such thoughts without my interference. Heh. Welcome to your future.

When he reached the end of the chamber, he turned to face his two guardians and drink in the mighty chamber. Above him, the symbol of evil – the stylised dragon – adorned the vaulted ceiling. Each scale was picked out in silver, the notched back spines rising towards the huge head, jaws wide, teeth bearing down upon Penance as he lashed out with whip and shield. The singular red eye flashed back, its crystal facets caught in the flicker of the chamber's torches. It echoed Nathair's eyes, the evil in that glare demanding their faith, talons outstretched to subjugate each of the pious flock as they knelt down to pray for its defeat.

A likeness born from conflict. Are we to see its return? Will that which we have only read about, feared in our dreams, come to pass? Our people chained and shackled, fed upon at the whim of our new masters. When you consider such things, perhaps the burden of the Houses, and of maintaining the veils, has not been so bad. Lies, deceit. But without them, would we have remained hidden for so long?

Lord Penance cracked his neck as he looked away from the depiction of the dragon, and he allowed the sigil to ease the pain a little, though he maintained his mummery as a matter of habit. Swinging the cane, he began the walk towards the meeting chamber and the waiting Gods' Council. Taking each stair with exaggerated care, he soon reached the carved door, the sound of his cane announcing the High Lord's approach. Sneed opened it on his arrival.

All of the six Lords and Ladies awaiting him stood as one, their robes of office resplendent, swirling as they pushed their chairs back. Lord Penance allowed a sliver of a smile to appear, a warmth he truly felt for those present. They were the wall against which the realm's faith may crash. He needed them strong, their self-worth high, to cement each prayer into place. Should one falter, should one waver in the face of their flock's fear, then all the Houses could come crashing down. Couching this in scripture, and bringing the Unspoken into play, was their only hope to quell rumour and disquiet. The die had been cast when the prince consort was imprisoned within his walls, accused of revealing where the dragon's heart lay. So, they had blamed Nathair's rising on a fabricated treason. It fooled most. His priests-in-waiting had spread the half-truth with agreed abandon after witnessing Nathair's might firsthand – though Lord Penance had named it the Unspoken's beast to all who would listen. It was enough, for now.

"Penance," he stated, sitting as each of the House Lords or Ladies placed their withered right hands on the gold metal glyph inlaid within the table. Waves of spiritfire merged into the glinting metal, forging a single white light as Lord Penance added his own. The room crackled with power, which then receded as the metal symbol absorbed every drop until once again its lustre dulled. "Thank you." He placed the cane on the tabletop and, his mind connecting with the sigil, willed the stick to transform into his God's scourge.

A display of my power, however distasteful.

"Before we begin, I would like to check on Lady Death and Lord Hope. How are the injuries?"

"Healed," said Lady Death, "by my God's hand."

The High Lord nodded, noting the skin on her face and hands showed little sign of the raw blisters caused by Nathair's dragon fire.

"Same, but taking a little longer than Lady Death," added Lord Hope, flexing his shoulders and body before jutting out a chiselled chin. "Though the legs ache from time to time. And you say Nathair was weak? How are we to stand against such beasts when they are fed?"

"I believe we must first do our best to delay or prevent that happening before considering the tools we will need to face it once again. Nathair is but one of the many weapons we have all read about. Seeing him in the flesh, so to speak, has perhaps brought home the might of the Constructors. A new reality. One we hoped we would never see."

"Delay?" said Lord Justice, his face reddening to match the cowl of his robes. "Is that not what we've been doing for the past thousand years?"

Lord Penance eyed the man over steepled fingers. He knew the pain and loss laced through Lord Justice's words. Bereft of his God's weapon, he had been searching for clues within the Forbidden Library since forever, only to have it snatched away by Nathair as it took the Rangers in a last act before returning to its masters.

"Yes, and successfully. Until now. Ladies Fate and Death, perhaps you can provide some insight for us?"

Lady Fate, her red hair splayed against the deep blue of her cloak, placed both hands upon the table. The blackened, withered right hand pulsed with a recent pain they all recognised. Without the sigils, such as those now carried by Death and Hope, as well as Penance, it would not heal. Only the black elixir prevented the pain from consuming them. "I have scried the House of the Seven, the place where Leront's heart remains buried, and retraced the tale told. I believe, from the writings, that the enemy that attacked our Rangers were *not* Constructors."

Lord Penance sensed the shift in the Council's mood, a balance of curiosity mixed with fear of the unknown.

"Nor were they Unbelievers. They all had the taint of spiritfire. Their bodies showed signs of being drained by its use. Their armour appears to serve a dual purpose – to contain the power they hold and reflect any that attacks them."

"Magi?" interjected Lord Wisdom, his face full of worry.

"Possibly, though weaker than we Seven."

"And dual of spirit," added Lady Death, her ice-blue eyes hardening as she spoke. To the High Lord's eye, she was holding back distaste. "I have scried the bodies. The residual spiritfire leaves the impression of paired spirits overlaid within one body. But close; siblings maybe. Perhaps twins."

"Any thoughts on this?" he asked, his eyes roaming between Death, Wisdom and Fate.

"Maybe the weft and weave of two intertwined paths relays strength, a purpose," replied Lady Fate, eyes distant.

"Or paired spirits provide fortitude, inner strength. But one must have abandoned their body to do so. Such sacrifice. And it felt … loved, if that makes sense." Lady Death reached out a hand to squeeze Fate's forearm, a smile of reassurance passed on.

"Or all of those," said Lord Wisdom, "combined with an increase in spiritfire – twice the power to draw upon. Though, if this is permanent or until the passenger spirit is spent would need further research. I do not think it is something the Seven decreed within their understanding, but I remember hearing or reading something on this. I will do some research, Overseer, if I may."

The High Lord winced at the use of the old honorific. "Something new, then."

"There's more," continued Lord Wisdom, a shake evident in his voice, ill at ease with having to engage so much with his peers. He lifted the quarrel from the bag at his side and placed it upon the table. "The crystal tip has been imbued. Like the pot bombs of the meisters, it likely explodes on impact, though I only have the two recovered from the clearing where the first battle took place."

Of all the revelations, it was this one that took Lord Penance most by surprise. Not because it was stranger than the rest, but due to its familiarity. They all used crystal plinths to retain spiritfire at prayer in their Houses, and the House Wyrding Stones were channels to the veil and beyond. It appeared blatantly obvious, perhaps an area blinded by scripture.

"Is this within the library?" he asked.

"Tangentially, yes. I spent an hour or two researching before coming here. There is mention of channelling, as we do, but also the retention of spiritfire within a vessel. This spurs off towards the use of glyphs and the sigils. Not something so small as a stone or crystal."

"Blinded by necessity and a missed opportunity. Wherever these … these people came from, they have not been so constrained." The High Lord pushed his chair back, wooden legs scraping against the grey stone. Standing, he said, "We have a conundrum, one we do not yet understand. But we must learn from it. Lord Wisdom, more books for you. Research this area, and perhaps you will need a meister's help. But if we can harness the potential of crystals for us—"

"Everyone," cut in Lady Honour, raising her hand. "Not to reveal such power to all and sundry, but in preparation, my Lord. These new warriors used such weapons against us effectively, bringing down our people, armoured or not. This is something the Waiting could do – imbue such weapons and store them, ready for when we are forced to announce the existence of spiritfire to the people. And that time *will* come. When the dragons arrive – and the monsters that ride them – have no doubt our flocks will accept the breaking of our Gods' laws in exchange for hope."

Lord Penance sensed the anger rooted within Lady Honour's words. Fury often hid something deeper, such as pain or loss.

Though her words may speak truly, we cannot rush to make decisions about the flock.

Lord Justice thumped the table. "The priests-in-waiting are a tool to use, High Lord. They have started the journey, and we have individually explored their potential. If this remains in the House, and we ensure they are unaware of the other, we could keep it quiet for a while."

"And if it gets out, we can focus it as a response to the Unspoken," said Lord Hope. "A lie within a lie. We have enough to shoulder, what is one more?"

"Agreed. Sneed will consult with each of you and set up a process regarding how far we are to stretch our acolytes, and how we will bind them to silence. And, I might add, what we may be forced to do with those that fail to adhere." Lord Penance sat back down, tapping his hand upon the table as he pondered. "And think on why these *spirit mages* came here. I suspect the Constructors have a hand in it somewhere – they sought a dragon's heart, or, possibly, Leront or Nathair. They must have a purpose in mind."

The High Lord reached for his scourge, indicating the meeting was at an end. The sigil immediately soothed his returning aches, but he glanced up at the pain he sensed within the chamber. With the leaders of the Houses rising to leave, he caught Lady Honour's eye. A brief smile and a gesture for her to wait was acknowledged.

"Shut the door, Sneed, if you don't mind," he said, before drawing the tear-filled Lady Honour into a gentle embrace. "Is this Nesca?"

"Yes and no, High Lord." She let the right-hand side of her robe drop, revealing the blackening that streaked beyond her elbow and up to the shoulder. "The Constructors' evil burned me through during the Wyrding. My spirit is raw, undone."

"You mean ..."

"My mantle needs to be passed on, but Nesca's mind is currently lost. I have to choose another. And soon, if the veil is to be healed."

"Have you asked Lady Death? She may have a way – with Nesca that is."

"No. Our Houses rarely commune on such things, unlike Death and Fate. We are more aligned with Justice in that way."

"Old thinking, my Lady. It is time we moved on, before it is too late."

8

A SPIRIT LONG ABANDONED

Oisin glanced down the side street as he edged up to the warped metal door. Ecne had stationed herself at the alleyway entrance to the rear of some bizarre mechanism that he prayed didn't distract her. Satisfied she was focused for now, he examined the door. Its handle was broken off, and the lock pummelled by something heavy.

"Either to keep us out, or to ensure something stays in," he said. He sensed Sura's presence at his side. "Can you?"

"No. There's some form of barrier here. Like the armour Keran wore, reflecting me back out. It's woven into the structure of the building."

"The old-fashioned way, then." Oisin looked upwards. The window above the door was filled with either glass or crystal. Estimating the lower sill to be twelve feet above the ground, he signalled Laoch over. The Ranger had been examining the far corner of the huge building sitting one block down. Laoch caught the hand gesture and took one last glance before making his way back to Oisin.

"Going to have to go through that," said Oisin, pointing to the window. "If we can crack it open."

Laoch nodded in agreement and reached around for Fate's bow. As he grasped it, Oisin's hand fell on his shoulder.

"Show me," the mountain man said, lips tight and eyes pained, yet sincere. Laoch let a smile slip. "How does it work?"

"If I knew that, I'd be a lot happier. Hold it so," Laoch responded, showing where to place the thumb on the bow's grip. "Unlike Justice, I don't sense a connection. More, a warmth. That's when I know it is ready and pull back the *string*. If Fate agrees, then it will shine with her blue. Mind you, this is probably the first time I've *thought* about what I do."

Oisin, following Laoch's guidance, winced at the first tingle of spiritfire upon his thumb. It rose, encasing his hand, and the developing tremor subsided as a calmness rode his nerves and up into his mind. Steadying himself, Oisin looked towards the window before pulling back on the string. Blue flame slid along it, and as he drew it back further, Fate's arrow formed. With the target chosen, he let fly, imaging, as he always did, the exact spot where he wanted the arrowhead to strike. With such a short distance, his aim was accurate. Except, the God's spiritfire splashed outwards and was reflected back into the alley.

"Ah?" he said, looking to Laoch. "Doesn't work for me." Oisin made to hand the bow over, when Sura coalesced nearby, eyes locked on the spot he'd hit.

"Try a real arrow," she said. "Focus Fate on just the tip. If the window can be fractured, then I think it'll give out."

Oisin shook his head. His world was so odd now, Sura's appearance hadn't fazed him, whereas the thought of focusing a God, or a sliver of one, did.

Laoch slapped the Ranger's shoulder, a grin on his face. "Come on, can't harm."

Oisin pulled a real arrow from his quiver, nocked it, and aimed for the same spot. As the string drew back, he focused solely on its tip, willing the warmth, or Fate, to enter it. This time the blue shimmer rode the arrow's shaft to enshroud the metal tip. He let it fly. The arrowhead struck home, and fractures spread, arcs of blue lightning whipping across the window until its entire face teetered before collapsing. The two Rangers dodged to one side as the pieces cascaded through Sura.

Oisin let a little joy warm his heart. The success and ease of using Fate's bow was a relief, though it didn't quite soothe the raw, pious worry over the sacrilege. But a glance over at Laoch brought him up short. The man looked crestfallen, close to tears, as the shards spilled through Sura. The sight brought home to him just how much another had sacrificed. Looking down at the bow, his mouth quivered as Ecne's words bit home.

Not the time for selfishness.

"Laoch," he said, gesturing to the window. "On your shoulders, yes?"

"Aye," responded the Ranger, sheathing his sword and cupping his hands.

Oisin placed one foot in the Ranger's hands and lifted himself up to place a second boot on his shoulder, before reaching and grasping the sill. Once both hands were on it, he pulled himself up. He didn't need any boost from Laoch as he scrabbled over the window ledge to fall into the space beyond. Sura arrived and increased her glow to light the room. It stank; the wooden desks and chairs were all rotten, damp and streaked with mould. In the far corner lay an old carpet, shredded and torn – an ancient nest strewn with small bones and fur, the source of the lesser of the smells.

"By the Seven, it stinks," said Oisin, holding his jerkin's sleeve against his nose.

"I can't smell, Oisin," said Sura, half floating, half walking over to the dishevelled cupboard, its doors cracked and open. Inside, a set of metal-bound boxes lay haphazardly on top of each other, the result of the shelves collapsing at some time in the distant past. "I can see and hear, though." She turned and found the First Ranger gazing upon her. It was the first time the man had truly looked at her since she died.

"He suffers, though it comes in waves," Oisin whispered.

"Laoch? Yes. When Justice withdraws, or his emotions are spurred." Sura looked to the floor, hands clasped about her shoulders. "Without his God's touch, he would be of no use to Justice. The grief too much. We are but tools of the Gods."

"And you?"

"I ... I feel a distance between what I was and what I am now. I am filled with love for him, a purity no longer riven with the doubt sown by my people – or my past grief. But it doesn't seem real, Oisin. I am dead. How can these emotions be real when I am a shadow?"

"I have no answers. Only questions. Except, perhaps, the need for us all not to ignore what is happening to each other. Look outwards more. Heh, even these words I speak come from the young acolyte waiting below." Oisin blinked, lost in thought for a second. "But he will need to grieve, of that I am certain."

"I am still here, Oisin. I still think and act. If he grieves for my passing, what am I, then?"

A thump resounded through the building's fabric, the echo of four taloned feet and a mighty tail lashing against the roof's edge, heralding Nathair's arrival.

"The dragon grows impatient. Let's find the beast what it needs before it chooses one of us as a snack." Oisin strode to the broken window and fed through one end of the rope Ecne had purloined from the workshop when they had first arrived. "I will help you both find answers, if I can. That, I promise."

"Thank you, Oisin."

Laoch grasped hold of the rope and pulled himself up while Oisin braced against the wall on the other side, below the opening. Once Laoch was inside, Oisin called to Ecne. The acolyte needed a little more help than the Ranger. Once her grin appeared over the window ledge, he pulled her in. Laoch was already at the only inner door, and edged it open at Oisin's signal.

———

The building, four storeys high, sat lower than most in the city, but its chimneys dwarfed many of those near the tower Nathair had originally landed on. When they arrived, Keran and Nathair had sensed nothing within it, though their trust of Nathair's twisted Spirit Walker was not absolute. Then, overnight, crystal eyes flared and the forked tongue flicked as it tasted spiritfire upon the ether. Whether human, or another source, was an unknown they were here to answer before Nathair made her own decision about how to find out.

Laoch pushed the door wider with his knuckles, eyes focused on the darkness of the walkway beyond that split to left and right. The ambient light seeped in through the dirtied windows set at an angle in the huge roof above, adding to the motes dancing amid the thin beams. The room's layout, to Laoch, appeared far closer to that of one of the Gods' Houses than the multi-roomed tower they'd first explored. Instead of wood and stone, metal struts criss-crossed above, underpinning the roof in a complexity of triangles that took his breath away. At times they appeared regular, patterned, but a glance away or a stare at another section disavowed that symmetry.

Shaking his head, he stepped out onto the walkway, placing his booted feet gently on the hardened wood decking, laced with the same dull grey metal as the ceiling. No dust rose, unlike in the other building. This space was clean and ordered, with little clutter except for the bound boxes stacked neatly against the brick walls. Taking another step while Sura swept gently past, he peered over the intricately woven rail and down into a strangely configured space. The four chimneys plunged down to the floor, each as wide as a battlecart at their base. Two were encased by internal brick-built structures, while the others were open with huge, charred pots placed in their centres.

"This is ... vast," he said, the hoarse whisper slipping out.

"And something sleeps here," added Sura. "A presence. More than one, perhaps."

Oisin crept up beside Laoch, one glance over the rail explaining the reason for Laoch's amazement. "What is it you sense?"

"I wish I knew. It is ... a gathering, perhaps. A layering of spirits. I can go look."

"No," replied Oisin. "We stay together, for now. Ecne, take the middle and I'll watch our rear. Do you need light, Laoch?"

"I'll be fine; my eyes are adjusting. And I have Sura."

The gasp from behind took Laoch by surprise until he realised Ecne had arrived and was taking in the scene below. An acolyte's dream, perhaps. Turning, he caught the flickers of amazement and fear that fought for supremacy in her expression. Oisin grasped her shoulder, finger to lips. Though Ecne couldn't drag her eyes away, she nodded in agreement.

Laoch selected the left-hand walkway, noting that the stepped access to the ground floor lay closer in that direction. Keeping as close to the internal wall as he could, he set off. With Fate's bow still in Oisin's hands – for which he thanked the Seven, and Fate in particular – he gripped Justice's sword, quelling its red glow. He sensed, rather than saw, Sura at his side; the spirit thinned out to near invisibility, minimising the likelihood of anything alive catching sight of her.

I'm putting no coin on whatever's down there breathing, anyway.

The walkway followed the wall around a corner, and past two shrouded windows that Laoch assumed looked down upon a street they had explored the day before. The grime, ancient and sooty, rose in layered waves, giving off a smell of old smoke and damp ash. Keran had used the word *foundry* to describe some of the buildings. Places where the Constructors did not just build their machines, but did so with fervour.

Not a place I'd like to spend my days. But then again, who worked these chimneys? Constructors or their slaves – the spirit-dolls?

He caught movement – a shifting of position, perhaps – out of the corner of one eye. Raising a fist to halt those behind, he ducked low and crept to the rail to peer down.

"I saw it too," whispered Sura, ghost lips close to his ear – or in his mind, it was becoming hard to tell. She floated off, thinning further, and slid through the metal filigree. Laoch balked, his mind still unable to disassociate the echo of her words from the reality of the elf's death. Ecne eased in next to him, her eyes alight with wonder as she stared at the intricate metalwork. Laoch shook his thoughts clear as the acolyte's presence grounded him in reality.

"There are vermin down here, Laoch. Disturbed by us. We are something new. Their hearts beat fast as they hide."

Sura's words echoed in his head, or at least reached through to him from Honour's sigil, the spear strapped across his back. He needed to understand how she communicated, and when, create some order to it so he knew how to respond. It had been easier with Gowan. Their relationship hadn't been so intertwined, nor had the loss hit him so hard. The First Ranger maintained the same demeanour, matching the image he already held of her. With Sura, her spirit had shed much of the doubt she carried and become something more. Closer.

"Wait. Watch while we come and join you," he said, whispering out loud and in his mind. The caress of Honour's sigil let him know his words had been heard.

When Oisin acknowledged his signal, he took the next few steps to the top of the stairway. Its strangely curved spiral was odd, and the first sign of the weirdness they'd experienced. Directing Ecne to cover their descent with her crossbow, and keeping low, he sidestepped his way down to the floor far below.

The shadows were longer and deeper at the base – the residual light hardly penetrated so far down. Pans and boxes suddenly shifted in response to his leather boot striking the stone floor, the scurry of tiny legs reacting to perceived danger.

Laoch assumed anything so small, short of being venomous, wasn't a concern. He ignored them. Sura floated next to the nearest chimney, and appeared more corporeal, yet her eyes were distant. He sent a thought in the hope she would hear. She returned to him, smiling faintly.

"*Yes, I am spreading my—*" Sura's face filled with fear. "Ecne!" she bellowed, the power in her voice as strong as when she had first found water.

Laoch's head swirled, and he was forced to jam his hands over his ears. He pivoted and looked up. Ecne rose from behind the balustrade. Open-mouthed, she stared down the walkway. A flash of Fate's blue light washed over her shoulder. Laoch tracked Oisin's arrow, the shaft setting the walls aglow as it spiralled to crash into something monstrous that was barrelling across the wooden planks.

All arms and mechanical limbs, its riveted body rolled low upon three metal wheels. A pair of white glowing eyes lit the walkway. Oisin's arrow smacked into one of the forelimbs, and the resultant explosion sent an arm careering over the rail to slap against a mound of cogs and pistons on the foundry floor they hadn't spotted.

Laoch had taken one step towards the spiral staircase when Sura gasped. Hearing the twang of Ecne's crossbow, glimpsing the emerald light of the quarrel, he turned back to find the Schenterenta in a defensive stance, eyes locked on the spinning wheels and complaining metal that rose from where the mechanical limb had fallen. A brass head, with four pairs of multi-faceted crystals atop protruding tubes – like paired spyglasses – spun, and each ... eye ... turned to look their way.

As Laoch moved, Justice reformed into the composite bow he'd wished to have. Drawing back the string, he let fly. The arrow's flare highlighted four human skulls, slack-jawed and screaming below their protruding spyglass eyes. It struck the head, and a fracture formed in the dome above the yellowed bones. Paired crystals swivelled to stare straight at him. A flash of white light lanced from both, striking the place where Laoch would have been if he hadn't thrown himself behind the chimney.

A clash of metal resounded from above, the echo bouncing back from the forged struts and ancient roof. Winged creatures scattered – clearly they'd been roosting up there. Ecne shouted, making his heart pound with hope. Laoch stepped out to release another arrow. The metal creature stirred in response, head turning, whitefire searing through the air. Not daring to watch his arrow land, Laoch spun away. His mind was split between worry for Ecne and Oisin, and wondering where in the Seven Hells Sura had gone.

The whirr of metal upon metal set his teeth on edge, jarring, scraping at his thoughts. Taking a risk, he edged to the other side of the cold chimney and peered around the hearth's left side, expecting the monstrous machine to have drawn closer. However, it remained in place, its four skulls spinning wildly as it searched. A heavy crash from above drew his attention. Laoch sealed any thoughts of it away as the dual glow of green and blue washed towards the ceiling and disturbed life fluttered.

"Laoch, the spear. Take Honour and pierce the centre. The head is not where its power lies."

The words touched his mind, and a weight lifted. The Ranger found himself reaching behind, as instructed, to collect the weapon. With Justice hooked over his shoulder, he held the unfamiliar spear like one would a quarterstaff, in a dual-handed defensive pose. Rows of corroded tables stood to one side of the mechanised beast, their rotten feet amid dark, viscous puddles. Cover enough, he hoped.

Keeping low, he sped towards them. A whirr and a click greeted his efforts, and a dual slash of searing light burned wood and scorched metal. Laoch dived to the floor, a sense of warning piercing his thoughts, followed by a second flash as power rushed over his back to explode against a rusted pile of discarded metal. Thanking Justice, Sura, Honour, or whoever would listen, the Ranger rose to his feet. Hot shards had peppered the table at his side.

"Seven Hells!" he swore.

He leaped over the tabletop and drove for the collection of metal-lined shelves a few yards away. A welcome green bolt powered downwards and crashed into the far set of skulls, lighting the maddened machine. Plainly riveted to the floor, its central core comprised a box-like body. Spirals of green wires were fed in, and then outwards to four, spindly limbs, each built from triangular pieces similar to the roof. Three lay shattered, twisted and bent, their joints entwined with the skeletal remains of whatever humans had assailed it – or it had attacked. The fourth limb swayed menacingly, a faux hand at its tip that pulsed in and out as the four joints twitched. Laoch didn't discount it. He suspected the core ring it was attached to spun much like the head, so it was a threat whichever direction he attacked from.

"Again, Ecne," he shouted, shivering.

Sura's touch alighted on the back of his neck, and her arms wrapped around his as he drew the weapon back, ready to throw. The embrace felt natural, almost real, her left, ethereal arm placed against his stomach. Together, they rose and threw. The spearhead glowing with Honour's orange light. The machine spun, and death's gaze fell upon them as the tip drove home, cutting through the maelstrom of wires and cogs to pierce the box at its core. Orange energy flared, bathed in a white, sparkling cloud that rushed out and upwards. The spinning head seized. One set of eyes remaining locked on them, a flare within the crystal facets rising only to be greeted by Ecne's green. Her quarrel smashed home, driving down into the already fractured dome. It erupted. Laoch dived to the floor, instinctively pulling Sura with him. But his fingers slipped through her. He sprawled awkwardly on the ground, alone, as hot metal shards flew through the spirit.

"*It ends,*" whispered Sura, and he felt her leave. Her thoughts lingered on his before she let him go.

Kneeling, he peered over the shattered shelves. Metallic shards and charred wires peppered their surface. The newly made pile of metal smoked and quivered as whatever drove the nightmare rose towards the ceiling. Windows creaked, then shattered. A sword-toothed maw crashed through the dirtied crystal, wide open, tongue lashing as it sucked in the white cloud. A low, metallic groan shook the roof, emanating from Nathair's throat. A rumble Laoch associated with pleasure; a thought he pushed away.

"Laoch," Oisin said. The Ranger, sword in hand, stood above the mass of limbs that lay motionless at his feet. "Okay?"

A man of few words. We just blew up a bloody metal monstrosity that tried to kill us. A thinking collection of cogs and bloody wires. It knew where I was, and was likely inhabited by the spirits or souls of long dead humans. Am I okay? Huh? What in the Seven Hells?

"Yeah, all good," he replied as he stepped carefully around the shelving, shaking his head. "What do we call this, Ecne? A machine?"

"An artifice. More complicated than simple machines like trebuchets," replied the acolyte, halfway down the stairs. "At least, that's my chosen word. No meister here to correct me." Her rueful smile was streaked with smoke residue, her long hair tangled, with black ash amid the braids. "Grand Meister Arknold once dabbled with these," she added as she reached the pile of twisted, scorched metal and lifted out a cog, "looking beyond the trebuchet, trying to make them smaller. But she couldn't get the metal strong enough despite Kinst's help. And of course, we couldn't experiment without the Houses' say-so."

Laoch kicked at the wires and the smoking box. "I can see why. What was that thing on the walkway?"

"I don't know. I'll need time to examine it, if Oisin allows. But it was wheeled, like a cart, so I don't think it climbed the staircase."

Another low rumble echoed through the huge room. Everyone was drawn to Nathair's gaze as the metal jaw flexed, tongue lashing out.

"It can taste more spiritfire," said Sura, appearing next to Laoch. "Can you crack the central box?" She pointed to a container beyond the shattered limbs.

"There are spirits in there? Is that what moves these things?" Oisin asked, his expression pained.

"Yes, Oisin. But long dead. And who they once were has faded to nothing. I understand your reticence." Sura turned her head his way. "But Nathair is a tool, and one Keran can wield to prevent more slavery and death."

"Yes, but one barely under his control. Should it shake the reins free, then we may be the sweet treat at the end of its meal." Oisin stood and glanced over to Laoch, who nodded his agreement. Oisin sheathed his sword and unhooked Fate's bow. "Balance, Sura. We cannot feed this beast too much."

He took Laoch by surprise, then. Drawing and loosing into the box, the arrow pierced the metal casing. A hiss of release was soon followed by a swirl of white energy. Nathair's expectant rumble echoed around the chamber. Laoch lifted his head, his gaze drawn to the creature's maw. A flicker of fire laced the forked, metallic tongue, spreading to fill its crystal gaze.

"It bides its time, Sura," continued Oisin. "If you truly fought and defeated this Spirit Walker, you may well have to do so again. Be wary."

9

WHEN ONCE WE WERE SCORNED

HOUSE OF DEATH, ERSTENBURGH, BRANDSHOLD

The queen stood before the 30-foot-high carved doors. Each was inlaid with a skeletal dragon, eyes aflame, their sinuous bodies wrapped around Death as the God lifted a scythe above the bearded heads. It sparkled in the sun's first rays. Erin brushed down her breeches and the functional coat she had settled on after spending the night fussing over her choices.

"Wait here, Jacka. You will only antagonise her." She sensed her prime stiffen. The Honour Guard paused behind at a respectful distance.

"Me? Why?"

"Because you exist. You fill the role she coveted. The one I am sure, before the consort's intervention, I would have given her despite the … the antagonism."

"That's a much more subtle word than the last one you used to describe her."

"Yes. Times change." She let her eyes meet his. "She would have driven the Houses mad and me to despair, while courting the people. And for all the effort spent denying her will, I would have caved." Erin looked back to the mighty doors, tracing over Death's robes as they plunged downwards, black against the dragons' white. "And like I said, in war she was unmatched by the other generals. But in Court, and the politics of our Union, there would have been more peace in the Seven Hells."

With lips thin and tight, she took the first step up the marbled stairs, each as slippery as she remembered. A reminder to the pious that Death took those unwary, as well as those ready to embrace her will. On reaching the top, she strode on, eyes forwards, and allowed herself a smile as Lady Death welcomed her. Jacka's whisperers had told of her bravery when the metal dragon Nathair had risen from its tomb. Few had seen her since, though the woman's battle injuries appeared fully healed.

Queen Erin greeted her with a gentle tip of the head. Both stretched their hands out to touch, to merge in a laced grip. In her House, Lady Death reigned. The queen was maybe the lesser, though none of the heads of Houses dared to make her feel so. Even High Lord Penance decried the need for her to kneel.

"Sucreta," Erin said, letting the almost silent words hang on her lips.

"That is not my name now, cousin," replied the black-robed Lady. She squeezed the interlaced fingers, letting the queen see the sympathy in her expression before she released. "But it is good to hear my name spoken again. Come. Your fate awaits you." She stepped aside,

and Erin caught sight of the scythe at her waist. The sigil pulsed once
– whether caught by dawn's light or as a reminder of Death's new
strength, she did not know. Either served the purpose.

"Does she fare well?"

"I'd say so, though she speaks little. Mander speaks for her, most-
ly." Death grimaced, twisting her head a little to catch Erin's eye. "I
think that man worships her more than Death. Normally, we would
turn him out to find his true path, but he is the only one who seems
to keep her calm. A constant reminder, perhaps."

The worship chamber was half full, a silence upon it. The wor-
shippers awaited their turn at the prayer stone. Many of Death's pious were older, expectant. Wanting to place their souls in good order
before joining their God in the veil. The House chambers always
caught the queen slightly unaware, her allegiance to Fate sealed by
the expectations of her ascendancy to the throne after the weft and
weave required to survive the Court and its machinations. Chosen
by the Council of the Gods to lead, and plucked from the sons and
daughters of the aristocracy who vied in the lower echelons of the
White Palace for the right to the Crown. There were still those who
thought that she, Erin Weister, daughter of the previous Duke of
Ridth, was the least deserving of the crown. Yet, Fate had spoken,
and with it her future was decided.

In Fate's prayer chamber, a few worshipers were at peace like in
Death's House, having accepted where their life was heading. But
many weren't, beseeching their God with prayer and song for a
different path. It made for a rowdy flock, their bleatings listened to
by the priests with their never-ending patience. And therefore, Erin
had to admit, the queen's personal prayer chamber was a blessing she
readily accepted for the peace and time to contemplate.

Lady Death touched those she could as she walked by. A squeeze
of a hand, a slip of a smile shared with the aged and the ready. Neither
cold nor unwelcoming, the House felt more alive for it. No sadness

lay upon these people, and the lady's presence brought the warmth Erin had always seen in her cousin. Maybe it was the young who perceived Death as a distant spectre to dread.

Passing the prayer stone and the frail woman being helped up from it, they walked onwards, heading for the right-hand archway and the priests' cells beneath. The steps, polished and curved by centuries of wear, were a marker for the passage of beliefs Erin now understood lay mired in the social politics and manipulation of her people. Tears welled, swiftly brushed away. Sucreta's brief but gentle touch upon her cheek was accepted before they came face-to-face with the iron-bound door.

"She awaits inside. I suspect her usual patience will have cracked after about ten seconds or so of waiting."

"Is Mander in there with her?" asked the queen, one hand ready to knock. She paused. The thought of a queen knocking brought a smile to her face as flashes of her past rolled by.

"No. I said he couldn't be present. I think that may have stoked the fire. But this is a matter of state." With a last squeeze of the hand to wish her luck, Lady Death swept her black robe away from the door and headed back the way they'd come. "I'll give you five minutes, then be along to rescue you."

Queen Erin Weister swallowed, brushed her hair back behind the simple, inlaid headband she wore as a symbol of her status, then knocked.

The sound was met with a muffled, but clear enough, reply. "Since when has a queen knocked on a peasant's door?"

Erin twisted her head to the side and stepped back three years as she entered the priest's cell. She was greeted by Zendril's low, mocking bow.

"My Queen," the former general said, her full-length priest's robe dirt-strewn at its hem.

"Arise, Zendril, Priest of Death."

The head flicked up. The mocking spread to the lined, aged face. Brown eyes sparkled bright below the woman's thick eyebrows. Under the cowl, the black hair she had once been so proud of was streaked with grey, the frizz bound back tight to her skull.

"As you wish, my Queen."

"Sit, Zendril. Please."

With a shift of the head, the priest dropped onto the bed. Erin picked out the slight pop of an aged knee and an accompanying wince.

Erin steeled herself. Subtlety was wasted on this woman. She made to speak, only to be shushed by the first hand to be raised to her since she ascended the throne. The memories came flooding back.

"Before we begin the pleading, perhaps you should understand, it will fall on deaf ears. I know that scum-sucking sonofabitch prince consort of yours resides with High Lord Penance, and that the Unbelievers are thought to be on the rise again. The answer remains the same as when I needed you. You shook your head, I shake mine. Daughter." The eyes hardened, hands squeezed tight before the ex-general.

"You speak as if I had a choice, Mother. The prince consort holds sway over the army, as stated in scripture, to prevent too much power in one set of hands. And I—"

"—did not choose the bastard. Yes, I know. But since when did I bring you up to do as you're bloody told?"

"You brought me up to be queen, and you got your wish. There are consequences to every act." Erin let steel enter her eyes, the gruff jousting a family trait. But she'd had plenty of practice growing up, and knew backing down would only provoke the matriarch of the Weister lineage. Her mother would eat her for breakfast if she allowed herself to break.

"And it took you three years to say that? Eh? You abandoned me! Cut me down in front of the bloody Court, took away the only two things that meant anything to me. You, and saving what remained of the army."

"You know what was happening to him, how he was acting. He was wayward. It took all I had as queen-in-waiting to keep him from ordering another assault, to save what was left of the Union. Once he was in charge … he understood."

"Of course he bloody did. Like a child always wanting a new toy, until they realise it was never what they really wanted. And look what he did with it. How many more died than necessary during the retreat from Handren's Pass, eh? More than the Unspoken could have dreamed of." Zendril crossed her arms, hands squeezing at her robes.

A regret Queen Erin had to live with – alongside causing her parent's fall from grace – one that had driven a wedge between the Crown and the Gods' Houses.

After they forced me to marry him.

"You hid yourself away, skulking in the dark. Is that what you taught me? To run from my problems?" Erin said, straightening her back and making the decision to sit. Maintaining the higher repose was for when dealing with those of lesser will, not those who jousted with the best.

"Fuck me, daughter."

Erin winced. The Court was barely a place for the language of the battlefield, and she'd heard little since her mother had been removed from her role. On that night, every swear word had drilled into her mind.

"You got any backbone left under those fancy robes?"

"And you under the garb of Death? You hid away, not me. Leaving the glare of the people on my shoulders when we returned, tails between our legs. And they elevated me to queenhood."

"Not our war to win, Erin. Never was." Zendril Weister's stiff shoulders relaxed a little and her arms slipped apart. "Just an exercise in futility. They were holed up in those mountains with no desire to venture out. And for all this shit about dragons bouncing off Death's walls, I find it hard to believe they intend to come here."

Erin blinked.

Her mother looked up from her hands to stare straight into her daughter's eyes. "And fucking useless Adama is no more a fucking traitor than me. So, what in the Seven Hells are you here for, eh? Not a family reunion. House politics? Not interested."

"Perhaps I am, Mother. Whether by choice or not, the decision I ... allowed ... weighs heavy. But I have something you need to read."

"Read, girl? Not more scripture, please. These priests ... ahh."

"Then perhaps you should not sit here and await Death's scythe like a sulking old woman and listen to your ... your fucking queen."

"Ahh. There's the girl I brought up." Zendril rose from the bed, the knee pop less prevalent this time, and shuffled the robe off to reveal her faded general's uniform beneath. "Mander, you useless pile of horse dung. In here! Now!" she bellowed.

"I didn't say I was giving you your old role back."

"Not yet, my Queen. Not yet."

Mander ran through the door, the 40-something's weather-beaten face crashing as he took in the queen. He dropped to one knee, head low, the other leg stiff. Erin noted the pain lacing his brow.

"Stand, Mander," she said.

The consort's ex-Honour Guard, the only one who still stood after General Zendril Weister had beat the rest, did so, eyes darting from daughter to mother.

"We're going for a walk. Guard my stuff, understand? Nothing out of place or you'll be back in your own bed tonight, yes?"

"Mother!"

"Get to my age, girl, and you take what you can when Death's scythe is against your neck."

10
THE HUNT BEGINS

The *Kraken* lifted, ascending the shattered city walls. The Fleshmaster pressed his hands against the balustrade, his shoulders set wide and strong. Leathered lungs breathed in the last of the smoke and ash of their victory, and he felt his empowered spirit whirl with the magus's essence, which he'd drunk a little too much of. The warrior magus was a follower of Fate, his most favoured of the Seven Magi. Their blue spirit had the sweetest of flavours.

The clink of chains and moans lifted his mood further, and Tarin turned, spreading one arm wide towards the trussed magi. "This is my gift to you. No more worrying about when we will come, no more concerns over your flocks of pathetic people. I have taken your cares away. The only worries you have now," he said, and reached one hand out to lift the warrior magus's head, "are to grow strong and hale. Well, enough to keep me fed. Don't taint that spiritfire with ego and selfishness, for I will taste it upon your essence.

"And—" The Fleshmaster drew the chain out from beneath the magus's chin. The grey-haired woman's spite and hate sweated through every pore. "—you have your ancestors to thank for your predicament. Before their betrayal, you drank and ate your fill. Enjoyed freedoms within our menageries. Even endured some of those disgusting human *relationships* you all so *need*. But those times are gone. Your spiritfire is too precious for us to lose again, and your resistance has condemned your people to a worse fate."

The Fleshmaster rattled the restraining chain, its links aglow with the sliver of an ancient Spirit Walker – one driven insane by age, and woven amid the restructured links that drained the magus should she gather her power, replacing it with agonies Tarin so enjoyed watching.

Releasing the chain, he waved to the waiting guards. The first one led the four bound magi towards the awaiting cells within the *Kraken*. The emperor turned away, eyes scanning the horizon. He allowed anticipation of what was to come to wash over him before reining it back.

Work to do. Too soon.

"Captain Popsilin," he whispered low, allowing his power to float the words through the wind and weather to the Inhibitor's ears. "Come here and bring Adjutant Renat."

Tarin tapped a finger against the brass rail, pondering the needs of the Inhibitors who feasted below. They needed their moment to savour the victory, and he to use those held in reserve to act as his hand in what came next.

"Emperor," said Popsilin, waiting behind him.

"Yes," he said, lifting a hand. A single finger indicated he wanted them both by his side. "Adjutant, the ornithopters, yes. I want them in the air." He let a wisp of dust-filled power float from his blue lips while lifting a messenger tube. The spiritfire wafted in, and he handed it to the second-in-command of the Ornithopter Core.

"They are to seek the Schenterenta. They have a week, understand? No more. If they fail, my captain here will feed upon them ... and you, yes?"

Wide-eyed, the adjutant nodded vigorously. The message tube wavered above the emperor's shoulders, black, gauntleted fingers holding it in place as Renat grasped the end. "Yes, my Emperor. I will send the command now."

"Good. Let them all have a taste of what I offer, should they succeed." The Fleshmaster turned his white eyes upon the adjutant. "Don't fail me."

"W-What if they are not here?"

"Then hope you have enough proof, Renat. Leave your other duties to your captain. Make this your priority." A wave of the hand dismissed the man.

The Fleshmaster glanced over to Popsilin, who waited on her own directives. "Captain, were you in this body when we left Innealtóir?"

"No, my liege. This is my third incarnation."

"As I thought. It was a place of great wonders, and so ... creative. Yes. There was little order when the Seven Magi revolted, our people decadent in their riches and ease of life. I too, had come under the spell of plenty, Popsilin. Grown lazy and unwary. Dependent on the veil dragons to stock our food while we whiled our time away in ... fancies."

The Fleshmaster didn't look over his shoulder, sensing the discomfort Popsilin encapsulated in her body and mind. An emperor's whimsy was not something she was used to.

Ah. The new ones don't know what we had in our grasp and let slip, unmindful of what our servants had become.

"That loss is important. It has brought us back to our true nature, Popsilin." He turned, eye-to-eye with her, a grim smile twisted upon dry lips. "And I see in you what we could become once again. No mercy, for whomever we face – including our own. Your example serves my purpose. But do not overstretch, understand? You have risen fast, and there will be more to come if you do not let that ambition cloud your judgement."

The Inhibitor captain shifted her feet, unease seeping into her shoulders as the Fleshmaster's words wandered around the point he was trying to make. It felt like a trap.

"No, sir. I am loyal."

"Oh, I know that." He reached out, a single finger resting upon her forehead. "I can read your spirit like one of the artificer's beloved books. It remains true, and unsullied at this point. When the time comes, though, remember this conversation." Tarin turned back, arms wide as he embraced the oncoming wind. The *Kraken* was finally escaping the city's last vestiges of ash-bearing smoke. "I have a task, Popsilin. I need you to choose Mechanised Inhibitors to scout this new realm for the Seven. We lack information other than the hints of the great magi they worship and the dragons they revile, brought to us by the last vestige of our ancient compatriot's spirit. The Seven were powerful when acting as one, maybe even my equal. Understand? I need to *know* if they are there, and what we may face. If they have found a way to live on or preserve their knowledge, the Inhibitor's bludgeoning will flail against their might."

"But how? We used the last of the Wyrm's strength to break Repanti's veil. If we find more Spirit Walkers, I understand the process ..."

"Leave that with me. For now, prepare a team of two Scorpions and make sure they are prepared for a passenger. They will be carrying an *Infected* with them."

"Emp—"

"Like I said, Popsilin. Know your place."

"Yes, Fleshmaster." She fell to her knee.

"I will ensure it is shielded, Captain, the madness locked away until needed. Or not. Prepare, while I arrange a way to enter their veil. Now go."

Tarin waited while Popsilin made her exit, reading her spirit. The captain's mood was halfway between the pleasure of being chosen for such a role, and the dread he'd just placed inside her mind. An Infected, one of the insane Constructor spirits that became deviant after inhabiting a new, but too-long-dead, body. They had to be contained, for slivers of their essence shed like skin, insinuating their way into others and blackening their spirits in turn. Most were crushed, bodies burned, leaving their *selves* to dissipate upon the wind. But, as with everything, the Fleshmaster saw opportunity when others failed to, and had kept a few alive.

A weapon.

"Pilot!" he bellowed towards the *Kraken*'s bridge. "Take us up!"

The Wyrm has waited so long to complete her bargain, I wonder if she is ready for the sacrifice I ask?

II

A RESIDENCE DISCOVERED

Innealtóir, Realm of the Constructors

"It is enough, for now."

Laoch eyed the dragon's heart with Keran inside. The spirit's hands were braced against the inner facets. "For what?"

"To function. Perhaps walk and fly a short way. But she'll need more if we are to move realms. Much more. And in a fight …"

Laoch nodded. Keran's assessment hung between them, understood. "There's likely more of these *artifices* in the rest of the foundry buildings. Will they suffice? Is Nathair capable of collecting her own now, while we look for whatever you think is here? This weapon you hoped for?"

"I believe so, though her reluctance will be interesting should we meet a live Constructor. But I think I can handle that should it be an issue."

"As for a weapon, what did you expect us to find?" said Ecne, her hands flitting amid the bag of cogs and metal rods she'd gathered from the foundry boxes. "I can't imagine them leaving any weapon here, especially one powerful enough that it threatens them."

"Not so much a weapon, Ecne. More a way to defeat them. My people expected me to return to our own realm, to defend it. Possibly pull Nathair's mechanics apart, research what the veil dragons truly are. This is something I feel compelled to do, yet it pains me, as they will simply move on to feed on another people. With Nathair's Spirit Walker so difficult, coming here became my only option. Perhaps, to gain a modicum of trust and the chance to achieve more control as she weakened. But I didn't expect Innealtóir to be so empty. I thought we would be hiding away or fighting for our lives, not wandering a city that appears abandoned."

Sura walked over, Oisin beside her. The two of them had been exploring the foundry roof where Nathair had crashed through to feed. Looking out through the mechanical dragon's chest as the scales faded like a window on their approach, Laoch waved a greeting. Just another thing to get used to.

"Keran says he doesn't know what we're looking for. In fact, that we should feed the dragon, and go to *his* realm and defend that." Laoch let his cynicism drip. He was annoyed, so twisted the meaning of Keran's words a little. He hoped to feed it into Sura, who appeared to trust the spirit too much for his liking.

"He says many things, but without sustenance, Nathair is trapped here. As we are. The Spirit Walker within is weak and will not be passing through veils anytime soon. Keran needs us as much as we need him – don't you, Captain?"

Sura only got silence in response.

"But you need to be more open, less bloody-minded, Laoch. Keran chose to save us. While we are in this city, we should look together for anything we can use against them."

"Agreed," said Oisin, rubbing at his scalp, where a few fine hairs were beginning to sprout. "At least, if we understand more of their nature. Compare Keran's words against what we find and experience. Not that I question what you say. More, they have had a thousand years to change. Know your enemy."

Laoch spat on the floor and peered back over his shoulder at Keran, who had emerged from the heartstone to give a shrug in response.

"I do not wish you ill, Laoch. You worry about your people; I worry for mine. Somewhere in that, we can find common ground." Keran let a smile slip. Laoch caught a glimpse of elongated canine teeth with a start.

"Aye, well. Perhaps. But you piss off without us, and I warned you what would happen."

"I witnessed Sura fight within the dragon's heart, Laoch. I assure you, I know exactly what you mean." The smile widened, and the Ranger couldn't decide whether it improved his mood or not.

"You know how you look, don't you, Keran?" said Sura. "Every time your mood shifts, more of the Spirit Walker appears. You need to be careful it does not sneak up on you. It may consume you as you seek to control it."

Keran swivelled his head, apparently peering into something. Laoch assumed it was reflective, as his scaled hands explored his own features with curiosity. He noted the worried frown, and unexpected sympathy bubbled to the surface.

He's made sacrifices I can only imagine, but that doesn't make him any less dangerous should he choose the dragon and his people over ours.

Laoch caught Oisin's eye. The First Ranger was watching Keran with the same mix of curiosity and concern as himself. The slight, barely perceptible nod of the chin affirmed they were on the same wavelength.

"I hear you," said Sura, this time definitely in his head and not aloud. *"I trust Keran to do the right thing by us. But I will keep a guard as best I can, in case my judgement is lacking. Remember, he saved us."*

Aye, as tools. And maybe as a snack for later.

"Laoch," said Oisin, hand ushering the Ranger towards him. "Bring your spyglass, see if you agree with Sura and I."

He led Laoch up to the western edge of the tower roof, and pointed with his own spyglass past the newly concave foundry roof. "There. See those two buildings? What's the difference?"

Laoch followed the Handren's line of sight and picked out a dip in the roofline where a twisted chimney poked upwards. Following it down, the angled brick-upon-brick design was reminiscent of the spiral staircase he'd charged down when facing the static artifice. Underneath, the sides of a distinctly odd building bulged, its surrounding wall curving out onto the street below.

The scrape of metal claws upon the roof accompanied Laoch's observations. Both Rangers turning in unison to find Nathair's neck stretching above them, its hot metallic breath steaming into the sky. Keran emerged from within the metal chest, his ghostly body shimmering to the beat of the dragon's heart inside. A new connection, and one to be wary of.

"Nathair picks up the scent of humans down there, brought up on the wind. A few. She says it is a master's building, their home. Probably belonging to whomever operated the new foundry you entered."

"How new?" asked Laoch, dropping the spyglass after watching for any signs of movement or life.

"For an old Spirit Walker, who knows? I get the sense she means there is more order to it. The difference between a lone ship wandering the local waterways in search of our seaweed, and one that works with others to scour the sea. She finds it odd."

"And then they left," said Oisin, eyes looking to the sky. "Ecne," he called, "any thoughts on Keran's words?" He recounted them as the acolyte approached.

"Well, it sounds like an argument Grand Meister Arknold and my meister had all the time. Kinst thought big, wanting to mine and produce Erin's Wrath and the flash powders in much larger quantities. And the Prime agreed. They wanted to go beyond just a meister working on their own to training others how to do it, whereas Arknold wanted to tinker. Her rooms were a mass of projects, many half-finished, but each amazing in its own way. I saw at least eight different versions of the ballistae for Erin's Wrath. The mechanisms each an adaptation on the last ..." Ecne's voice trailed off as she remembered. "I was young when we prepared for the Crusades, but I remember Erstenburgh being full, the tented city outside the walls full of heat, smoke and the pounding of hammers."

"Preparing for war," said Oisin, "on a much bigger scale. Where we have individuals at work, perhaps they work as a team, like a Spear, each with a role. That seems possible with what Keran has told us about the building. We have no proof, though. Except they are no longer here."

"Nathair spoke of other cities that could still be functioning, but I suspect that may be a memory rather than any real truth," Keran said. "A hope rooted in its twisted nature. On Mondrein, we knew the Constructors would hunt us down, and that eventually time would run out for us. When they realised the Seven had been separated from us, my people panicked, for they were the strongest among us. They feared more dragons and a return to slavery, and despite our magi's best efforts, they failed to match the heights of the Seven. It was why I was sent, after they felt something disturb our veil."

Oisin waited, ensuring Keran had finished. "We head over there and take a look in one of these master's houses; more, if we have to. And if they were arming themselves, somewhere in this city there should be a headquarters of some form, or a palace for us to search. Did they have a regent?"

"An emperor, so the stories say. A Fleshmaster, by title. At the time of the Journey, he was named Tarin. I suspect it is he who Nathair would seek out if she becomes strong enough."

"Then that is our secondary plan. We search a few houses and look for any clue as to what happened, and possibly a weapon to use. You and Nathair, hunt the artifices, feed and prepare. But Keran ... keep her on a leash." Oisin's glare was met with a nod. Both Rangers noted the spirit's shift in body language. Maybe they were getting through.

—

"What in the Seven Hells?" said Laoch, his first close view of the building unsettling him further. Its surrounding stone wall was cut with achingly accurate precision that would take an Erstenburgh stonemason decades to perfect. Each piece was carved with a set of letters that, according to the fascinated Ecne, formed a poem with a jarring rhythm that hurt her head. Between the wall's columns, railings overlaid each other in copper cut to resemble flames, though a green tinge dulled their burnished appearance. It was finished with gates that stood tall, the spars covered in a filigree that matched the foundry they had raided. The lock was long broken.

Behind all this lay a bulbous building that was way beyond Laoch's experience. Erstenburgh's White Palace was stark in comparison, its opulence and grandeur shamed by the Constructor's house. The waves of sculpted stone rose outwards and upwards, smoothly rising in a gentle curve before bending back to reach a point some twenty yards above its centre. In Laoch's mind, now he was closer, it resembled a closed flower head, like a lily, the petals ready to spring open at the first touch of sunshine. The windows, made of faceted pieces of coloured glass or crystal, were inlaid into the stonework, and set at different angles to reflect light in patterns that dappled the street. At the building's base, a bed of rusted metal thorns sprang from the ground, barbs upon barbs – a threat that belied the building's strange beauty.

Between the building and the gate, weeds and small bushes had woven their way into cracks, unkempt, wild. Decades, perhaps centuries, of growth. And as Laoch brought his spyglass to bear, he began to pick out the flaws of age, the roughness to the building's intricate façade. Time awaits no one, not even a Constructor.

Sura emerged from the wild garden, her spirit form sending a shudder down his spine as she walked through the plants, only to be foiled by the wall and the metal rails. At the foundry, she'd mentioned something being used to block, or contain, spiritfire. It appeared to be inbuilt into this abode too. A safety feature, perhaps. Clearly frustrated, she slid between the bent gates, signalling all-clear as her form fully coalesced.

Better than a shout that could wake the Seven.

Laoch checked on Oisin. The First Ranger was signalling he wanted Laoch to head in, with Ecne and himself following. Laoch swiftly crossed the road and stepped over the shattered, multi-legged remains of the artifice that lay on the ground outside the gates. Acknowledging Sura with a nod, they weaved between the open gates, keeping low.

"The grounds are small, overgrown, and there are signs of occupation. An old firepit, gnawed bones. But nothing recent," Sura reported.

"Keran talked of people. Is there a back door?" he asked.

Sura's spirit fingers touched the back of his head. The picture of a metal-bound door at the rear slid into his mind. A ramp sloped towards it from another, much wider, set of gates that were still closed.

"Can you see that?" Sura said.

"Yes. That wide enough for a horse and cart?"

"Likely, though I suspect something more mechanical. I thought Nathair was an abomination of spirit, but these artifices are disturbing. How they are powered is sickening."

"And," said Laoch, bypassing the ivy spread amid the iron thorns, "their creators feed on us. It seems as if we are their cattle, to milk and cull as they see fit. Is it clear?"

"I believe so."

Laoch scanned around both edges of the building that curved away from them for thirty yards in either direction, its scale enormous for one self-contained house. He trusted Sura, but a Spear worked together, always checking for danger. Sura would expect continued caution. Satisfied, he shouldered the simple bow and drew Justice as he approached the inlaid doors heralding the building's entrance, their outline only exposed due to the dirt accumulated there. He walked up the precision-cut steps to the inlaid stone floor before the entranceway. An intricate set of letters, white marble against sheer black stone, were cut into it. With a shake of his head, he took a step. His feet splashed in water, glassy smooth despite the gentle wind.

"Deliberate?" he asked. "Perhaps washing your boots before entry, like when entering Hope's House where you are supposed to clean away doubts before facing your God?"

"I do not know your Houses, Laoch. But I didn't notice the moon pool. It's so perfectly made and clean."

"Moon pool?"

"My people found natural pools, bowls that constantly held water, scattered across the plains. The herds often gathered nearby. And when the night was clear, they could reflect back the sky. The shamans named each, and our tribal gatherings are always beside one."

"Aye. Though when this city was belching smoke and ash, I think the beauty may have been lost."

He reached the doorway. It held no handle or lock. He recalled Leront's hidden resting place, and the doors inside. Reaching out, he placed a hand upon the streak of mottled green metal. It was cold to the touch. No tingle or response.

Dead.

Oisin and Ecne soon joined them. They both examined the door, Ecne musing over their lack of pot bombs to force their way in. Laoch had his doubts even Erin's Wrath could crack it open. Having examined a window via his spyglass, the lack of a long rope and handholds led him to discount those as ways in too. Half-tempted to try and break one open with Fate's bow, Sura had floated up to declare them truly solid. She doubted much would damage the surface of the opaque crystals.

After walking warily around the back to examine the firepit Sura had spotted, and the old bones on the way, they found themselves before the far less ornate, but no less stout, rear entrance. Beneath the doors lay another old fire surrounded by stones. The remnants of cloth covers were pitched over dried branches at the side.

"A good spot. Out of the weather," stated Laoch. "So, we have people roaming free here, somewhere. Or at least, we did. Have they attacked the door, Ecne?"

"Yes." The acolyte stepped back from the bound dual doors, her fingers still resting on the locking mechanism that bore no keyhole. "But to no avail. I think this is a sliding lock, like a bolt you push to set a bar on an outhouse or an acolyte's cell." Laoch caught the brief smile, and found himself warming to the girl who appeared to have overcome her brush with crushed piety. At least, for now. "They chipped away at the floor here," she said, pointing to a spot along the base. "There's a gap as wide as a hand, though I've not risked mine. There'll be vermin."

"You weren't so fussed when you were eating them," Oisin said as he dropped to his haunches. He slid his dagger from its sheath and waggled it beneath the doors. He couldn't resist a smile at Ecne's wrinkled nose. "A sliding lock, you say?"

"Likely, but I can't know for certain."

"If the gap is clear of the material that rejects me, I could go in and look around," mused Sura. "Describe what I see."

Oisin rose and stepped back to follow the line of the doorway. "Yes, I can think of no other option other than moving on. Laoch?"

"I don't need his permission," bit Sura, eyes flaring orange before she caught herself. Her expression, however, remained unapologetic.

"No, nor was I asking." Oisin raised both hands, indicating calm. "More for him to bring Honour's spear closer – and my next thought was to expose the sigil next to the door."

"Heh, I've missed that fiery temper." Laoch drew Honour's spear from the sheath across his back and placed it near the hole. He turned with raised eyebrows towards Sura. "Can't do this one side-by-side."

12
A SPIRIT'S SONG

INNEALTÓIR, REALM OF THE CONSTRUCTORS

Sura sensed the pull of the crystal shards embedded in the walls and doorway. She attempted to place the remembered sensation in her mind, hold the experience, but found it far harder than when she'd had a physical brain. It was no longer a natural act, but one she had to focus upon. After considerable effort, the recollection formed. The crystal-clad Sealgair hunters Keran had brought in search of Nathair. They had worn a copy of the Constructor's armour Keran had later been forced to inhabit – the set that currently lay inside the mechanical dragon.

Must remember that. A tool. Perhaps we can search for more in this forgotten city.

Her spirit form thinned out and she stretched towards the hole dug beneath the door. The rejection from its base flattened her. If the Constructors had had the foresight to place more in the stone and tile floor, she'd have been expunged. Feeling disparate, empty, she struggled to keep her thoughts coherent. That which was her *self* stretched, pulling apart. Dread crept through her being. True death lay that way. A loss of who she was. And she realised that, once the *will* to remain together wavered, she'd be lost, just another wisp of spiritfire, her essence washed away by the wind.

The first vestige of her awareness reached through the hole, and Sura anchored each part that followed around a kernel of her being, reforging herself in her own image. The warrior, the Schenterenta, the Patterning. Love, and the fire at her core. Amid those elements seeped the dishonour to her people, the depths of loss and depression, and a keen sense of detachment from home. Each facet forged an entwined strand of Sura, what she was. Without one, the others would not bind. No longer Sura but a lesser being.

She knelt out of habit and scanned the room. The ambient light from the hole was enough for her elven eyes and spirit senses to garner a picture of a delivery space. A ramp, ropes. Metal and hardened wood storage boxes lay carefully stacked or pinned to the walls. Behind the ramp, two doorways led inwards, their construction simple. She sensed no rejection from their makeup. However unremarkable all this was, the artifice in the centre was something else. Bulging eyes peered her way, over two legs held high. Two more legs, behind the first, were set against the floor with what she took to be metal wheels. Sura noted that she did not fear it, only sensed the wrongness that accompanied each artifice she came across. Inside, something squirmed in slumber – a spirit, once alive, but ancient, its mind absent. Now, with time to think and compare with those others they discovered back in the foundry, she recognised the void within it. It remained an energy, but soulless, devoid of personality. This would be her fate if she forgot who she was. Unable to reform, she would become nothing more than a source of food for a Constructor or their machines. A swirling mass of ... nothing.

Not me. I can't let this happen. I am needed by Honour, and I have Laoch. His thoughts and memories can keep me bound. His ... his love.

Sura drew herself away from the soul void, the shudder of a potential future ignored as she studied the dual doors. A mechanism was bolted to its back. Sura began running through the mechanics of pulleys and wheels she had experienced, fighting the fog to draw on memories of the crossbow, ballistae and finally the trebuchets she had either used or seen in operation. They were never a natural draw for her. The Schenterenta always refined what they *knew* rather than sought to invent. Their creativity lay in song and music, crafts used to retain their ancestors' stories and tales, so important to their culture. Every child had the first verse of their lifesong woven at birth, a lullaby to soothe and calm. Their parents – and later the child themselves – adding to it as they grew. Of course, each of their great heroes and the most revered shamans' lifesongs became tribal retellings, often widened and added to by the people in celebration together. A song of binding.

Sura let a hint of a smile cross her ghostly face at memories of the duality, the interweaving of her and her twin's songs. Until one came to an end, the last verse bitter.

And now mine has ... not ended. I am here. Perhaps Nura's spirit resides somewhere, his song to be finished without bitterness. Though I scoffed at the shaman and their talk of Spirit Walkers. And look at me now. The lifesong ...

She reached out, letting her hand caress the metal mechanism. A lever jutting upwards reminded her of the trebuchet ratchet, a lock for the cogs. It had a purpose. She soon worked out it could not move towards her, its retaining bracket and central bolt indicating a sideways movement. Unable to visualise how it worked, she memorised as much as she could. A memory of the lifesongs sung around a hearth slid in, and Sura hummed a mental pattern, imagining each piece as part of the song. The picture strengthened in her mind's eye.

At least she should be able to describe it – if the song remained after stretching herself thin to slide through the hole.

"Sura," called Laoch.

Sura sensed his tension release and body relax as she reformed.

"All good?"

"Yes," came the drawn-out reply, her tone dreamy. Sura mentally blinked, recognising she remained *thin*. She concentrated on her *self*. "Yes. Though it taxes me a little. Ecne, there was a lever on the far side of the door. It moves sideways, I believe. It stands tall above a longer bar and a few smaller metal bars are bolted to it."

Ecne scrunched her face. "Can you tell me any more? Hang on." She spun her pack around, drawing out a bound book and a leather pouch. Inside were broken charcoal sticks, Ecne found one just about large enough to draw with. Her first strokes defining the doors, the acolyte described each line and what it represented. As they conversed, Sura's frustration grew.

"No. Not like that. It had ... erm ... cogs here." She tried to outline with her finger. She closed her eyes and hummed the song, trying to visualise the difference between Ecne's version and what she'd seen.

"Sura," Ecne said. "Is that it? The mechanism?"

Sura opened her eyes. The picture of the door hung in the air before her. Ecne's shocked expression indicated the acolyte saw it too. "You can see it?"

"Yes," Ecne replied. She quickly sketched what hovered between them. Laoch and Oisin stood behind, both caught up in the spectacle.

"How – how did you do that?" asked Laoch. He reached out a hand and lightly caressed one corner. He sensed a presence. Sura. Part of her.

"I used a song," she smiled, side-eyeing Laoch. "Are you laughing?"

Laoch squeezed the chortle away, a smile replacing it. "No. My mother used to do that when we went to market – she made me memorise the list by singing it. We – I can't read and write and … well. That's amazing."

"Yes, it is, isn't it? Song and story. Something our people share." Unthinking, Sura reached out and touched the back of Laoch's hand. And she sensed the contact, the roughness of his skin. A spark of orange lit her eyes, her lips parting. "Did you?"

He nodded. He tried to put his other hand on top of hers, but it slid through. Yet, there was a resistance, and a warmth to her spirit. "I felt something."

"There," said Ecne. She turned the charcoal picture around and showed it to Sura, who agreed the likeness. "So, I think it's a catch and release. The lever is a lock or a brake. Pull it back, and the bar can be slid back and forth on the cog wheels, let go and it's locked into place."

"So how do we do that from this side?" asked Oisin.

—

"Higher," said Sura, repeating it louder as Laoch's arm remained static. "Push it up further."

Laoch held Honour's spearhead. A rope was tied about it in a loose slip knot. The tip wavered fifteen inches below the top of the handle.

Laoch's arm slid further under the door. The thin cloth of his vest scraped across the stone floor as his bicep was squeezed in the gap.

"No. You are a forearm's length away. Make the spear grow. Think of it as longer. Tell Honour what you need – a Ranger's quarterstaff length."

The glow let her know he'd listened. Her own connection with Honour's sigil enabled her to sense the change. As the spearhead grew, she found herself directing Honour as much as Laoch was. Between the three of them, they got the height and position just right.

"Knock it back towards the door," she shouted. Laoch's wrist twisted back in response. The rope now above the lever, she let Honour know to reduce the spear's size back to that of an elven spear. As it shrank, and to her amazement, the loop settled upon the lever, just as Ecne had requested.

"It's on!" And with that, Ecne yanked the rope, pulling back just enough to release the cogs.

"Ecne's tied it off, Sura. Are we good?" asked Laoch. Sura picked up pain in the man's voice, likely from his wrist. She urged Honour to ease it and enjoyed the warmth of the response.

Working as a three. Connecting.

"Yes."

Laoch flattened the spear and drew it back under the door before returning it with a second rope attached. This time, Sura directed the tip towards the end of the heavy bar that lay across the doors. Using the same process, though much slower with the metal bands holding it in place, they eased the bar along until its rounded end reached the final band.

Frustration kicked in. "There's no way to loop the rope over now," said Sura. "The band blocks the way to the locking bar."

"Can you show me?" asked Ecne.

After a minute or so of frustration, Sura eased under the door and visualised her new memory song for Ecne to scribble down.

"Here," Ecne said. "If we had a tool like a hoe, you could direct the point inwards, and we could pull it back to push the bar through."

Laoch peered over Ecne's shoulder. Then, letting his contact with Honour flow, he imagined a hoe from his mother's vegetable garden. Though he was rewarded with a God's combination of sulking and admonishment, a hoe formed.

"Like this?" he said, then refined it as Sura and Ecne worked on adjusting its length and size.

Within a few minutes, the bar was released. Oisin pulled one door open using the hole to grasp the door's edge, his mountain-honed muscles setting it on its path outwards.

Drawn swords greeted Sura. Her eyes grew wide and fire-lit until she realised they were staring over her shoulder at the artifice.

"It's not going to harm you," she said, raising her hands for the all-clear. She turned towards it. "The spirit has been dormant a long time and has forgotten what it was."

Oisin and Laoch strode forwards to stand on either side of the elf spirit, wary as they sidled between the artifice and the room's walls. The ancient machine didn't react; no white light or tremor of movement. The only sound was Ecne's barely constrained squeal.

"It's in one piece!" she said. Keeping Wisdom's crossbow ready, she watched the eye-like windows carefully as she approached. "Those front limbs are weapons. Look at the edges on those claws."

"Keep away," growled Laoch. "Until we know for certain it is dead. Don't want to be picking up your pieces and sewing you back together. You should see how crap my stitches are."

Ecne smiled and stepped away, but kept half an eye on the burnished metal hull as she walked up the ramp. Her eyes wandered over a set of wooden boxes, the stamps and words still readable in the ultra-hard wood, though what they contained was mere dust.

"These are foodstuffs – or were. Dried fruits and unleavened bread."

Oisin joined her and pulled out a few of the trays. "So, there were humans, or animals, here. Yes?"

"Seems likely. And everything is so—"

"—neat and ordered. There was no rush to leave. Fits with the idea they prepared before going to war – except, why leave food?"

———

Oisin lifted the ribcage with his sword tip. The bone crumbled, turning to dust that floated down to join the rotting cloth and debris upon the floor. Only tangled chains and bangles remained. The metal on the shackles still gleamed.

"How many?" asked Ecne, stepping around the pile. She tried to ignore the acid rising in her throat. They'd been dead a long time, but each had died wrapped around another. Some of the bodies were clearly children.

"Twenty or so," replied Oisin. "These died of hunger and thirst, left to rot."

Ecne caught the pain in the Ranger's voice and walked over, hoping her proximity might help. If the big Ranger was willing to accept it.

"Seven Hells, Ecne. Who are these Constructors? Why would they do this? People wouldn't treat animals this way! I heard tales of what the Unspoken and the Unbelievers were capable of – some terrible things I struggle to repeat aloud. But children?" He bent down, his eyes roaming the corpses. "You know, I don't know what I'd do. Would I let my child die, or smother them to keep them from the pain?"

Ecne choked back a sob, unable to relate to minds that could build such wonders and have so little humanity. "I cannot answer that, Oisin. This is too much."

"And deliberate, perhaps, to let them suffer."

"Or inconsequential, unimportant. Baggage," spat Laoch as he came through the wooden door. The window in the door was barred and the feeding slot below splintered, torn by desperate hands. "It's the same next door. Three cells empty, just one the same as this. Except someone tried to force it open from the outside. Sura has asked us to come and see another room beyond the corridor's end." Laoch scanned the dust-filled room. Four cells long, three of which were open, and the last forced by Ecne and Oisin. On one side lay shelves and tables, the wood rotting down. The floor was cold stone.

"Yes," said Oisin. "Is it any worse than here?"

"She won't say," replied Laoch. He pressed his fingers to his eyeballs, whether because of the irritating dust or hot tears, Ecne couldn't say. "But she says we need to look."

Oisin rose from his haunches and, with a grim look back at the cell floor, gripped and squeezed Ecne's shoulder before turning away. "Come on, let's get this over with. But remember, when we face this enemy, Ecne, on this floor you see what they truly are. Yes? This is what the evil of their souls allows them to do. Anyone who chooses such a path, this way of life, cannot be allowed to continue." As he turned to leave, Ecne caught the flash of blue from his bow's grip as the sigil flared. A responding warmth spread through her hand. Looking down, she found her thumb glowing green where it sat against Wisdom's sigil. She couldn't help but agree.

They followed Laoch down the stone corridor to reach an open, metal-bound door; an entry to the main house. The section they stood in lay directly below the goods entrance. Next to the entrance was a lift pulley system like those on Erstenburgh's wall. Everyone but Ecne, despite her enthusiasm, had refused to access it. Inside lay three aged, dust-filled broken crates alongside a pitcher of some long-dried-up liquid.

Having taken one flight of steps down, they had found a kitchen area – rough-hewn and filth-ridden, the vermin from above having nested there for some while. At the first light of Laoch's sword, the rooms had emptied, the scurrying and scratching of clawed feet announcing their retreat. They had found the cells two doorways further on, each with a metal lock. The keys on the outside had made entry easy enough despite the age of the mechanisms. This door, however, was of far more intricate and superior quality, the metalwork inlaid with images of strange animals and what Laoch took to be birds.

Striding through, they found themselves in a space that stretched away twenty yards in every direction; circular, like the building above. The floor was laid with small, hand-sized tiles, forming a large mosaic depicting armour-clad Constructors, their husked faces writhing in ecstasy as they laid hands upon supplicant humans at their feet. Each individual scene was posed so that pain and joy overlapped, the viewer absorbing both in unison. Above hung chandeliers of greater intricacy than those that adorned the White Palace. They reflected the light from Laoch's and Ecne's weapons as they increased their glow to fill the room.

"Over here," whispered Sura, her words riding the acoustics of the impressive hall. Laoch and Ecne approached, still taking in the images on the floor. The spirit waited by an ornate wall. "Look."

She pointed towards the wall, at a picture that almost hid the faint outline of a door. Ecne's breath vanished. Upon it, Sura, or an elf so similar the resemblance was startling, knelt. A silver-armoured Constructor loomed, each hand on either side of the Schenterenta's head. Above the pair, a spirit, its expression one of twisted joy, writhed upwards along a white pathway. Looking along the curve of the wall, Ecne noted further paintings with variations of the same scene. Each spirit followed a pathway that merged into a heavy cloud. Ecne leaned back, jaw dropping as she picked out Nathair and, if she remembered rightly, Leront, entwined on the ceiling above them. Yet, at their edge lay another two tails, the scales shimmering in Justice's glow. Ignoring Sura, she walked, head up, tracking the tails as they thickened into two more sinuous dragons, wrapped around each other, faces bearded, eyes aglow.

"Oh," said Ecne, trembling.

"Yes," came Sura's whispered response. Her spirit floated between Laoch and Ecne, one hand absent-mindedly upon the Ranger's fore-arm.

"Oisin," Ecne said, though the First Ranger already stood staring, with Fate's bow raised. The blue light enhanced the two new drag-ons.

"I see. But I do not wish to believe."

"There is more," said Sura.

Ecne sensed the pain in the words. Her heart pounded as she wondered what could possibly be worse than a fourth dragon.

13
THE BURDEN OF GUILT

HOUSE OF PENANCE, ERSTENBURGH, BRANDSHOLD

Lord Penance placed his chin on top of his hands, which rested on his cane's grip, eyes seeing but mind wandering. The prince consort sat upright at his writing desk, beavering away with a fervour rarely seen since the Crusade. Penance hadn't yet made his mind up whether Adama truly understood he was detained, and that in so doing, the queen and the Houses had committed treason by wrongly imprisoning an innocent man. In many ways, the consort was happier, the pressures of running the Union's army now a burden shed – despite, if truth were to be told, General Mandrich being the true custodian of the role in recent times.

"Prince Adama," he said, purple rotting teeth exposed as he spoke. "How goes the memoir?"

"Memoir?" replied Adama. "Ah yes, Lord Penance. It is over there somewhere ..." The prince waved towards the corner of the room where his new bed stood, the linen imported from the Court. "Taking a hiatus. Reached my teens, don't you know? Terrible time. So, I'm having a break before returning. This writing retreat of yours really gets the blood flowing." The scratch of quill upon parchment returned as Adama bent over the beautifully neat writing, straight and fluid, tongue playing along his teeth as he wrote.

"And so, what do you write between, my Prince? You seem so ... focused."

"Mmmm? This? Suggested troop movements for the defence of Ridth. Been meaning to put my thoughts down for a while. Yes – do you know the place?" The prince consort glanced over his shoulder, quill paused in midair above a pot of ink.

"The queen was born there – an interesting city port for those that have the will to dally. Why Ridth?" Lord Penance pushed; he was not sure why.

"Because that damnable woman was from there – General Weister. Argued day and night, we did. Would call everything I said on the opposite, and so I read her treatise on the subject. Thought I'd give it a bloody good critique, now I have the time." The glimmer in the prince's eye was enough. Lord Penance nodded. In that moment, he understood the prince consort was far more aware of his predicament than first suspected.

But losing himself in something – to push it away, perhaps? Hide? Or does he know of his failings and accepts his fate? I'm such a bastard.

He rose, arched his back, and lifted the cane to place it ready to leave. "Let the priests know if you need anything, my Prince."

When he reached the cell door, he heard the scratching stop. He sensed the prince consort's piercing eyes of old upon him. Turning the handle, he awaited the weight of the words to come.

"I would like to see Erin. If she will come."

Pausing, Lord Penance let out a sigh. "I will ask."

He left as quill tip met parchment.

The tap of cane upon stone echoed along the corridor. His God's sigil eased the aches and pains that were his burden to carry, but not the guilt that lay in his heart.

A few well-worn steps later, he found Sneed waiting outside his office chamber. Older than he, yet healed and hale after relinquishing the mantle Lord Penance now carried. A whiff of jealousy entered his thoughts, swiftly quashed.

"Go in, Sneed." He waved the cane towards the wooden door. Upon it, Penance's plate bore the scourge and the prayer. Sneed nodded, pulled the door wide, and preceded his Lord into the wide room that contained a simple, but comfortable, bed and a writing desk. In the centre, a table bore the Wyrding Stone. "Sit, man. I am."

Sneed took his usual seat and leaned back into the chair, dark bags under his eyes a sign of the strain of recent events. "Are you sure about this?"

"What? Saving the realm? No. I thought I would let us all be enslaved." Lord Penance eased himself onto a second chair and eyed the bottle of warm Khundish Ale – watered, but a treat he favoured when times were rough. Decision made, he reached across and offered a glass to Sneed, who nodded.

"I'm sorry, Sneed. I shouldn't have snapped. The prince consort … It doesn't sit easy with me. Some decisions weigh heavier than others, especially when they add yet another level of deceit. Carry on."

"Gowan," continued Sneed, "and what she proposes. It's a diversion of resources. It will be a mockery of … of what we stand for and cannot surely compare."

"Even if it acts as a lure? A temptation on our terms? I think that has potential. Maybe not what Gowan and Leront envisage, but a tool we could use, nevertheless."

"What if ..." Sneed took a sip, savouring the warmth sliding down his throat as he stared up at the dragon painted upon the High Lord's ceiling. It reflected a stylised version, a symbol of evil. The epitome of the Unspoken. Though it appeared very different from the art plates in the Forbidden Books.

"You agree with me and do not really think the grand meister can build a working version. In my opinion it would take decades, and constant access to the library, perhaps."

"No, I do not. Except we do not truly know if these Constructor creations really *work*. You have read Wisdom's analysis, the descriptions of the artifices and machines, yes?" Lord Penance nodded. "She theorised the machines were simply jointed collections of metal and bolts. The word *construct* indicates they were built, but not *functional*. That is how the first soul experiments started – seeking a more powerful form of spiritfire to make them work."

"A synthesis of science and spiritfire, yes – splitting the human soul from the body. And why the Seven's scripture laid down rules about both. We have lived that lie for a millennium, Sneed. what's your point?"

"What if it is Leront in charge of Gowan, or feeding her spirit with these thoughts? What if, with enough food, Leront could empower even a poor mockery of what he once was?"

"Yes. I have considered this. With Gowan in control, we would have a weapon. With Leront as puppet master, a revitalised enemy." Lord Penance took a long sip of the ale, letting it wash across his teeth. The relief was palpable. "We are making decisions from books and ancient fears. All of it pissing in the dark until we know what we truly face. The Constructors may have fallen, the loss of their spirit-dolls and menageries bringing them low. Or it may have pulled them together, ended their malaise, and we face an organised foe. We already know those that found Leront are human, and are users of spiritfire."

"So, possibly, escapees like us, on their own path."

"At our cost, but yes. I believe that they were users of mage root too. The junip brought with them by the Seven when they escaped. It is too much of a coincidence. Why would they want the dragons? To attack us? It seems unlikely, but I won't discount it. For greed and conquest? Again, possible. But for them to get here smacks of power we no longer have."

"Or knowledge hidden within the Forbidden Library." Sneed reached for the bottle, pouring the Lord's measure before his own.

"True. You feel this is too much of a risk? That we may hand our enemy another weapon? But I have a hunch Leront has a part to play, even if it's as an empty piece of mummery."

"You are the High Lord." Sneed threw the last of the warming brew down an old throat. "And I see the logic. I will, as always, do as you ask." He made to stand, both hands on the chair, when Lord Penance grimaced.

"Then, before your meeting with the meisters, I require your help with the Wyrding Stone."

"Now?"

A heavy sigh slipped through his moistened lips. "Yes. Then you are free for a time. And remember, Penance healed much of the previous damage. I have to admit, I was enjoying the sensation of touch once again." The High Lord peered at the cloth over the stone, memories of pain rushing back.

How odd that when you live with pain, you can accept more. Yet in its absence, you fear a mere touch.

—

Blood spurted. Teeth clamped down upon the mountain goat, crystalline eyes briefly ablaze as the small creature's essence imbued the dragon with a wisp of power. Metal-skinned wings beat, talons reached out to grasp the creature's mate and progeny, pulling them in tight to its body as the sinuous scarlet beast rose from the cliff edge.

The Unspoken sighed. The pleasure coursing from the animal's spirit, running through the dragon's heart, laced her own soul with its brief caress. An Chéad roared in response, the boom echoing back as a third wingbeat took him above the ledge.

A nagging thought pressed in on the Unspoken's mind, porcelain white fingers sparkling in response as Penance's blunt power knocked on her mind for acceptance.

"Humans. So little time to perfect their manipulations. Using a hammer where a caress would do. Land, An Chéad. Rest a while."

The dragon's metallic body responded, the twist and curl of its spiked tail adding power to the wings as forelegs reached out to grasp the rock strata, talons biting deep. The rear legs tucked under, taking hold of the rocky ledge while the scarlet wings added one more settling beat before the jointed tail wrapped itself around. The mechanical beast calmed cogs and wire, and rested his bearded head to peer into the river valley below.

The Unspoken lifted her hands away from the heartstone, mindful that she wanted the High Lord to know as little about her, and An Chéad, as possible. She had seen many a Lord of Penance's House come and go, and few had the presence of mind to keep contact. Some, she feared, truly believed she was the evil their religion required; others, that she was a hero.

And all wrong. For I am simply me.

This High Lord, however, was weak in his spiritfire, but not in his guile. A balance, one he used wisely, in her judgement. Even more reason not to trust the man, for the pious and the fervent were much easier to understand and control.

She mentally checked her glamour, a habit forged from necessity. When satisfied, red hair and metallic powdered cheeks sparkling in the light of the dragon's heart, she spoke. "I am here, Lord Penance. Apologies, but I was otherwise engaged."

The human Lord appeared in the air before her, projected from a spirit's mind. After a thousand years of growing her herd, she found she needed to visualise when interacting with humans, their emotions as much within their body language as their words – unlike her kind.

"Thank you for listening out for my scrying," replied the High Lord, the wince not for show; she recognised the pain. "I suppose I'm checking in, letting you know where my plans lie."

"Go ahead. I can feel your pain, Lord Penance. Your haste, I understand."

"I appreciate that. We are preparing as if you, the Unspoken, are planning an attack. The rumours of a dragon after Nathair's emergence are too strong. We have used these reports to persuade the people that we are ready for your imminent assault on our lands."

"As expected." She felt her dragon stir as she answered, a response to something in the distant hills.

"Yes. Perhaps you could build on that rumour for us?"

"An attack? I thought ..."

"The northern and southern parts of the Union are slower in their responses, believing the Crown and the Houses care only for Erstenburgh. I can deal with the north, but the southern cities could do with a reminder of the need."

"Are you proposing my Unbelievers leave their valley? They are as tired of war as your people, Lord Penance. I seek ways to raise their ire and rush to my banner, but not to send them into a fruitless battle."

"Ah. Perhaps I was wrong in my assumption. I thought An Chéad?"

Red lips broke into a rueful smile, the Unspoken's spirit shaking its head within the glamour, eyes alight with this Lord's astuteness.

Maybe they can survive what comes with such a man leading them. And I.

"Have you spies in my valley, Lord Penance? Anyone, perhaps, that my dragon can feed on? If you have, I will root them out. You know this. I can smell treachery."

She noted the Lord's wince, felt the leeching of pain through their connection. A little admiration crept into her thoughts.

"A simple guess. I have no spies within your people, but a belief you wish to live as you have. A thousand years is a long time to remain hidden from your own kind, especially when you have the means to return."

The glamour hid the sudden pang of absence that swirled across her face. A sense of loss, a memory that had dried into a mere husk, resembling the body she hid. Not an emptiness she grieved, more a hole in her past self, which the Unspoken busied themselves filling with the beauty of her existence.

"I can help, but ..."

Now the pain he showed was beyond the scrying, and it filled her mind, the wall between them weakened by agony-filled resolve.

"I ask that you keep the ... casualties low. That is all."

"Mind that Spirit Walkers have needs, but I will try. Anything else?"

"No. I assume you've had no sign?"

She shook her head, an affectation borne from her time amid her herd. "No. I would inform you. But I have, as you call it, *scried* the veil disruptions. I cannot envisage the emperor missing the beacon set by the ancient Construct spirit, and Nathair headed home, as is her will. We do not know what they have been doing since your people's Journey, but I cannot imagine it will be long before they arrive. The Fleshmaster was never someone you would classify as *patient*."

"Thank you, Unspoken. I must go."

Noting his pain and cutting the connection, she hid her thoughts in a place An Chéad could not read. The dragon let out a rumbling purr when she placed her hands upon the crystal heart, and his forked tongue lashed outwards, tasting the wind.

"A scent? Mmmm. And a human one, An Chéad. Forbidden fruit, until now."

Metal struts widened and wings unfurled, joints splayed as the artifice beat at the air, the dragon rising into the frigid sky. With orange eyes aglow, the head whipped around, focused on a forbidden prey as they scampered along the far ridge.

"Handren. Not my people, but ones loosely allied with the Union," said the Unspoken, her mind linked and awash with the dragon's senses. "Just the three. Probably the herders of the goats you took." A fourth, then a fifth beat of the wings took them upwards. The sinuous body framed against the sparkling blue above the valley's inversion, plumped white cloud sitting lightly within the rocky walls. "Do you remember the hunt? To use the sun?"

Of course you do.

Muting its roar, the mechanical beat of metalled wings propelled the beast upwards, and it arced to form a silhouette against the sun's blinding light. Then, arrowing downwards, talons extended, ready for the kill, maw closed until the last second before releasing a roar that shook stone and rock. The remaining goats screamed, and the three herders turned to see death on the wing. Talons ripped through rib and chest, crushed hips and broke legs. A beat of metal-sheened skin took the dragon back skywards, blood upon its legs, clasping the agonised humans and draining their very souls. The Unspoken writhed at the ecstasy, the kills swirling through her mind, spirits that overpowered and scourged with their taste of pained death. Nothing could compare, and she fought the *need*, the *desire* An Chéad poured into her before it overwhelmed her control, desperate to prevent the call upon the bestial within her.

Panting, she forged a box of iron *will* around the portion of spirit-fire the dragon sent her way, only letting a sliver touch her mind lest she lose herself again. For a millennium, she had been a leech. Too much at once, and the predator would soon return.

14
A HOUSE OF PAIN AND RETRIBUTION

INNEALTÓIR, REALM OF THE CONSTRUCTORS

Laoch's gaze, pain- and fear-filled, fell upon Sura after they had pried the smoothly inlaid door open. Beyond it sat a bizarre prison, one composed of windows instead of bars, each cell aligned to meet the needs of whatever creature lay inside. The first bore two skeletons, likely feline, with long tails, and four incisors set in a large, cat-like skull. They had fallen upon each other. One creature's skeletal remains were broken, the bones scraped by tooth and claw, the marrow drained. Their cage included a nesting area of hardened wood to mimic trees, and a faded background picture of a far-off jungle.

As they moved between each enclosure, the remains varied as much as the environment did. Lizards, large and small, snakes, birds … before moving onto the weird and strange. Creatures from nightmares they could not make sense of. Each lay dead, some near turned to dust, others mummified, their empty eye sockets pressed against the perfectly clean glass.

It was not these that had caused the burden in Laoch's gaze, but the final, larger dual enclosure. Made up of multiple rooms, each with functional, though now broken, furniture. The glass here was covered with fractures that emanated from circular strikes made by something hard. One section had collapsed inwards, the glass shards black-edged, with similar dust underneath where the pieces had been wielded as weapons. Human remains lay face down within the carnage, looking inwards towards the four dismembered skeletons inside.

"Schenterenta," repeated Sura. "A family."

"But. I—" Laoch stared at her, knowing the fire in her eyes was for the enclosure, the violence.

Oisin stood among the remains. His movements mirrored what he thought had happened, playing the scene through his mind. When he finished, he looked back over his shoulder to Laoch. "Thoughts?"

Laoch shook himself. He could sense the oppression of Sura's anger and pain through the link they shared with Honour across his back. "These two, and probably a few more, attacked the glass and broke through. This one," Laoch pointed to the skeleton at the back, "fought until the end. Forced back while their family died using the glass shards."

He knelt and reached out, before remembering the elves and their death rites. He looked to Sura, who nodded. Laoch touched the wrist, turning the hand to show the deep cuts within the hand bones.

"I agree," said Oisin. "You say these remains are elven?"

Sura's gaze lashed Oisin, who flinched. "Yes."

"I don't understand," said Ecne, drawn in after her study of the other enclosures. "Why?"

"I do not know," replied Sura, her fury dripping from every word. "This was a long time ago, Oisin?"

"Hundreds of years," cut in Ecne, kneeling to examine the humans. "The decomposition of a body, the breaking down of muscle and skin, takes an extended time, I believe. The bones even longer. And nothing's been moved."

"In the wild, such a thing is hastened by animals and bugs feeding on the corpses," added Oisin. "Not like here. What about the animals, Ecne? How long do you think?"

"Again, my best guess is hundreds of years. If, as we have been surmising, the Constructors left together for war, then I would suggest these were left here to die."

"Except the elves," added Laoch. "And they were targeted. Though we are guessing, I think Oisin and I have it right."

"There was a forced cell, back there," said Sura, finally looking away from her people to lock eyes with Laoch. "I know this happened a long time ago, but from what you say, they came for my people – targeted them. Not the animals that could be food. My people. They even risked dying to do so."

"So, were they a threat, perhaps?" Laoch flinched as Sura's gaze hardened.

"Or a grudge," said Oisin. "Something worth dying over."

"And it indicates there are elves within this land, somewhere." Ecne backed away from the enclosure and looked back down the corridor, her hand rubbing at her chin.

"No," said Sura, brushing away non-existent tears. "It means the Constructors took these people from wherever they were and locked them away here on ... on show for others. My people do not have legends of such things, or at least ones they have shared. But we know

Nathair and Leront were bonded with Spirit Walkers – Schenterenta shamans – from elsewhere."

"If Keran speaks true. Yes?" Oisin faced Sura. "And that may mean these were Spirit Walkers, or one among them was. Likely killed because of their potential."

"No. Surely they would take such a one with them?" said Ecne. "You don't leave something that useful behind. The animals in the cells are likely unimportant and troublesome to feed, so I can understand that. Maybe these humans thought they were shamans, or grew fearful of them because of that potential."

"Sorry, Sura," Laoch said, breaking their gaze. "But we need to move on."

Finally, she turned away from him and headed down the corridor, the light from the sigils streaming through her. Shaking his head, Oisin clapped Laoch on the back, an understanding of his predicament shared as they followed.

Sura waited for them in the huge chamber, her eyes on the dragons above. Oisin and Ecne searched the rest of the chamber for any more doors.

"You need me to go with them? Leave you to think?" Laoch asked as he stood by her side.

"Honour speaks to me, I must … yes. I must perform my people's death rites as best as I can remember, Laoch. You understand? I can't leave them like that." Sura's gaze locked onto Laoch's. The fire and guilt within were enough to hold him back. "Come back when the search is done." She spun around and headed back through the still-open door.

"I will ask Ecne to stay here with Honour's spear. Outside the door."

"Thank you. Perhaps bring the spear inside, if you would. Honour may help. But Ecne must not come in."

———

Laoch kept low as he reached the top of the first flight of steps and scanned the hallway. Only vermin responded to the soft glow of Justice's light. The walls here were straight, not curved like in the strange room below, and their layout reminded him of the White Palace, but on a grander scale. Laoch assumed this was the entrance space, with a sweeping staircase and corridors off to the side. He signalled for Oisin, who passed him and, using Fate's glow, climbed the staircase. The light from the two sources glinted off the tiled floor, forming a dazzling pattern of shapes that threatened a headache until Laoch looked away, squeezing his eyelids. The scrape of tiny feet increased as the First Ranger passed the balustrade. Then Laoch headed out and took a position to cover. With the entrance doors in view, Laoch spotted a stack of human skeletons nearby, huddled cross-legged next to a pile of broken and burnt furniture near a cold fire. It seemed so out of place, yet not. The juxtaposition of riches and opulence claimed by the discarded, only to be rejected as its riches failed to feed them.

Oisin raised his fingers, showing three, pointing towards the cold hearth before turning away, hand on bow and stock still.

Laoch, sensing the tension, moved slowly to peer into the murk, to where his leader gazed. Amid the dancing shadows cast by Fate, tiny legs pattered against the tiles and blue eyes reflected the light back. But none were in sets of two, and there were far too many to count as they weaved and bobbed, almost bouncing a few inches off the floor. Laoch swore under his breath. If only he hadn't left Honour's spear with Ecne to guard Sura's doorway. Then he admonished himself. Spirit or not, Sura deserved the same respect, and her usual role within the group.

Expecting Oisin to back away, Laoch grumbled as the Handren took another half-step forwards, followed by another. Fate's glow sank into the darkness, the flickering shadows coalescing into multiple horrors.

Oh crap.

The creatures were metallic, their eyes crystalline. Again, multi-legged, though many sported shattered joints and splintered shells. Somewhere between crab and spider at four inches long, they bobbed at the rear, climbing over each other. And all peered their way. The corner was a mass of woven metal strands, akin to the wire Laoch had seen bound around some of Arknold's larger ballistae. If he hadn't known better, he would have used the term nest. Spotting the litter of small animal bones around it, he feared he was more right than he wanted to be. Oisin froze, uncertainty in his body language. Something Laoch could relate to.

And realisation hit – the first hint garnered from a raised leg; a bone bound by wire to replace a missing lower half. The second was the slightly larger artifice emerging from within the bundle of metal strands, its body pulsing. A white light, familiar yet sickening. Two raised forelegs, a weave of its lower body, and the horrors spread out, metallic feet scraping against the ceramic tiled floor.

"Oisin, step back," he found himself whispering. The sound carried above the taps and screeches emanating from the corner.

"They are small, Laoch."

"But many, and they mimic spiders. These are things we don't understand yet."

Laoch sensed the change of mood as the mountain man took a step backwards. That movement triggered the swarm. The spider-like artifices rushed, legs in a flurry, bodies flat along the smooth tiles as they pushed themselves at speed towards Oisin. Before he'd managed a second step, clawed legs dug into his boot. More clambered over and onto his laces. For every one that latched on, another used them as purchase to clamber over. Oisin vainly shook his leg in response. His panic rose. Laoch called Justice to brighten. Red spiritfire flared and flooded the room, sending a rippling wave of skittering through the tiny beasts. The sword suddenly lit with a fire he'd not called for, but, taking its lead, Laoch brought the blade low and swished it from side to side as he stepped between the swarm and the panicked Oisin, who now kicked his boots against anything he could find.

A deeper rumble swept over the creatures as they lashed limbs towards the sword's flame, and Laoch saw the much larger artifice take its first step forwards. Justice flared again; an arrow nocked as it forged a bow at his command. Sighting what he took to be the matriarch, she froze in response. Laoch blinked, amazed that she understood the threat. And loosed the arrow. The red arrow seared across the room. The artifice almost managed to leap away, but the burning tip slammed into her exposed underbelly. Her legs curled around the flame as a crack resounded through the chamber, followed swiftly by a nerve-shredding screech. Legs twitching, the burning carcass slapped against the tiles. Everything froze, except for Oisin, who was now dancing about the room on one leg.

Laoch waited with a second arrow drawn, before moving backwards, one slow step at a time. No quiver ran through the small machines. No legs trembled. They remained stock still, though their eyes continued to reflect Justice's eerie glow.

"Oisin, stop," he said, his whisper hoarse, throat dry.

Another step and he risked a glance behind him. Oisin now lay on the steps, panting, sweat beading as he gripped his thigh. Checking on the swarm again, Laoch turned and headed for the Ranger. Dropping to his knees, he reached out gloved fingers and searched the man's trouser leg. He cut the material away with his boot knife to expose the single mechanised creature whose fangs were digging into the meat of Oisin's calf. Whether paralysed or dead, he didn't know, but it fell away and onto his hand. Laoch flicked the monstrosity towards its brothers.

"Stay still," he said to Oisin, and sliced the rest of the cloth away. Redness spread from the bite towards the knee joint. Nothing he knew of could help. He reckoned any attempt to do so was more likely to harm than be of benefit.

"Laoch, please. I need to be outside, in the open – see the sky. It's stifling in here, oppressive." The mountain man gripped his shoulder, squeezing. "Please."

With a grim smile, Laoch nodded. He sheathed the knife, gripped the man's arm, and lifted the First Ranger onto his back. A pained grunt greeted the shift in weight. He bent low to collect Fate's bow when a thought occurred to him.

"Oisin, the bow. Take it."

The Handren's fingers reached out, and Laoch laced them onto the grip. Blue spiritfire greeted Oisin's hand as it wrapped around the bow. Laoch descended the stairs, mind focused on joining the others, and taking care to keep Oisin's hand on Fate's sigil.

His legs protested at the weight as he began the journey downwards. He faltered once, only for Justice to gently strengthen his legs to help regain his balance.

As if it knows my body inside and out.

"Ecne," he shouted, ignoring the echoes and the unnatural fear they caused. "Oisin has been bit on the leg."

By the time he reached the bottom step, the acolyte stood waiting, hands out to help as he dropped Oisin to the floor.

The look she gave Oisin was full of concern. She put her hands on the wounded man's sweat-beaded forehead. "Prop him up with his heart above the wound," she said.

"Aye," he replied. "He's bloody hot, Ecne. By the Seven, he wants out of here. Thinks he's dying and wants to see the sky." Laoch took

Fate's bow from Oisin's hand, placed the grip near to the wound, then pressed the sigil against it. "I thought Fate may help."

"Fate? What in the Seven's name has bitten him?"

Laoch pointed at the two dormant mechanised spiders, still attached with legs and fangs, to Oisin's leather boot. "These not-so-little bastards."

Reaching for his knife, he prised one off while, with his other hand, he pressed Fate's warm glow against the bite. He handed the knife to the acolyte. She prodded at the now-curling legs that wrapped beneath the artifice's underbelly.

"How ...? They're so small. How can cogs and wheels move such things? The metal required ... the precision."

She dug the blade's tip into one. Splitting the outer shell, she warily placed a gloved hand on one side to pull it apart. Tiny, interlaced cogs lay alongside pulleys and thin wires, and at the centre, a small crystal shaped like a dragon's heart. Ecne dug it out, noting the copper-coloured wire that laced the stone. An eyebrow lifted as memories of loosing just such a crystal at a writhing dragon's head popped into her mind. Wisdom glowed, followed by a pulse, and the connection became a kernel of thought in her mind. It took root and, spinning her belt pouch, she levered the whole artifice into an attached leather bag, placing the crystal in another.

"Is Sura finished?" Laoch asked. His hand was now upon their leader's brow, a look of worry rolling over his features as Oisin's eyes flickered. "I think we need to get him out soon."

"I'll check."

Ecne rose to her feet and padded over to the doorway, where green light shrouded her hand. Listening, she caught the last vestiges of Sura's song, the tone mournful but steady as it ended. Risking the elf's wrath, she peered around the door. Sura's form was framed by the glow from Honour's spear. Swallowing, then breathing out, she was about to take a step when the mood shifted. Sura stood and turned towards her, beckoning. The acolyte ran over and reached down for the spear.

"Oisin is hurt. He's been bitten and is in a bad way," she said. "Laoch wants us out of here." Ecne glanced at the remains. The bones were now ash, heat rising from within the piles.

"Bitten?" replied Sura. The spirit floated down the passageway. Ecne rushing to keep up. "By a snake?"

"No. Artifice spiders, I think. I have one. Oisin's a little delirious, his skin sickly."

Sura shimmered, and a wave of worry from Sura washed over Ecne in a way she'd never experienced before. Emotions normally borne by posture and expression were now conveyed through the touch of her spirit. The ethereal Ranger sped through the door to alight at Laoch's side. The brush of her presence and concern causing him to shiver.

"Fate is helping. That's good," she whispered as she placed a hand lightly on the mountain man's brow. She eased her spirit fingers inwards. Laoch biting back a tang of fear as they disappeared into Oisin's skull. Sura quivered, her spirit form pulsing. Then a lacing of the Constructor's whitefire, drawn from Oisin, crackled up her forearm. "It is poisoning his soul ..."

"Sura ..."

"I need Honour," she stated.

Ecne appeared at her side and swiftly placed the sigil-bound spear at the spirit's feet. Its engraved symbol, Honour's scroll, flared. The orange spiritfire coursed into Sura's spirit body, spiralling into her shoulder and down along the arm towards the whitefire, enveloping, smothering. Sura let a gasp slip between her lips, and a ghostly white cloud billowed into the air. A second and third followed, until Honour finally withdrew, the God's light dissipating from within Sura. The white veins were now absent from her arm.

Sura bowed her head and withdrew her hand from Oisin's head. She placed it gently upon Laoch's arm, where it held Fate's bow. The squeeze was real. A light caress, the tips full of energy. "I have helped draw out most of the venom, but it has left scars upon his spirit, Laoch. It will probably cause a malaise, a darkness, until it heals."

"And you?"

"My first taste of how they twisted my kin, my love. This was the cause of their downfall. A distilled blackness of their own souls, used against them. A pure evil. A sliver of which they laid upon Leront and Nathair's Spirit Walkers. But they, I fear, are too far gone. I can feel that now. Gowan and Keran ride their blackened souls. It lies deep and binds like a chain. I cannot see them curing it." Sura floated backwards to place her feet upon the ground. Honour's spear now lay dormant.

"Are we still to take him outside?" asked Ecne.

"We really need to finish the search, or else it has all been for nothing. Sura?"

"I can help Oisin. Sense the tremors and ease his mind. I am best suited here. Take Ecne, but leave Honour so I can draw upon the sigil. The doors are locked behind, yes?"

"Aye, but should something happen, promise to come and find us."

—

Ecne drew the knife across the cracked shell. The still-soft metal parted, causing the legs to twitch. The acolyte jumped back with a start. Laoch's boots thumped down beside her, but she held her finger up. The request for patience was met with silent, grudging approval.

She knelt back down and pried the hull open, separating cogs and linked chains until she found the centre. There was no crystal here.

Rather, a small box radiating a soft white glow. A growl at her side was greeted with another demand for patience, and Ecne fished a set of tweezers from her belt to grasp the inch-square cube whilst prying it loose. She dropped it into the waiting pouch that not so long ago had swaddled pot bombs.

"Why?"

"I told you; we need to learn. Perhaps the greatest weapon we have is *knowledge*, Ranger. And of that, we are bereft. But the more I can learn, the more hope we have."

"If it doesn't come back and bite you. How many of the little ones have you collected?"

"Six more. They are dormant, though I want this box well away from them. Would you?"

Laoch grimaced while twisting his neck. The crook of a single finger pulled the jerkin back to allow some air onto his sweaty skin. He then took the pouch by the gut string and tied it to his belt. "Fine. Now, can we search the bloody place so we can get out of here?"

Laoch led the way upstairs. The ground floor had proved sparse of anything useful; even a room Ecne described as a personal library was absent of a large section of books. The remainder was described by the acolyte as chaotic flights of fiction rather than informative. Like the tales Rangers told around the campfire. Yet one look at the drawings were enough to disparage those thoughts. The weird and the less-than-wonderful did not appeal.

"I wonder if they sleep," mused Ecne as they reached the summit of the steps. "If they are spirits that inhabit a body, would it be needed?"

The first few rooms seemed to indicate some form of rest, rotting or dust-laden mattresses set upon strangely carved, or forged, fancies they took for beds. Some sported jointed legs, others filigreed wheels and levers. Few, as they moved from room to room, were plain.

"No wonder the survivors slept in the hallway," Laoch said, the light from Justice's bow lighting the corridor walls, "though I think those spiders may have ended their time here."

"It's as though Grand Meister Arknold designed the decoration," replied Ecne, head turned up to view a bedroom ceiling adorned with interlaced wires in the shape of screaming lips. "While Meister Suerese made the furniture."

"Suerese?"

"Our Meister of the Arts. A painter and sculptor."

"And this is but one home. There will be more. Each with its own collection on show like those below. Can you imagine being one of the slaved? Fed upon and chained with no hope?"

"Or a spirit-doll, as Keran said, giving of yourself for a little freedom. Is this our future, Laoch? For the Union, for everyone we know or love."

Laoch scraped his chin, the rough stubble a trigger for memories of home, the smells of the forest rising in his nostrils. "It's why we're here. And, for all the distrust I have for him, it's why Keran brought us. He no more wants wherever he calls home to fall than we do Brandshold."

Laoch started to head for the stairs when Ecne stopped, eyes wide as she gazed up at something on the hallway landing. She touched Wisdom's sigil, and the green light spread to flicker over a huge painting. The acolyte moved a step backwards, stopping beside Laoch as they took in the ten-foot-high monstrosity. The cracked paint depicted a Constructor, resplendent in crystalline armour, with curved lines that ended with a hook driven through a screaming human head. The figure's vambrace leant against a huge sword, the pommel an open-mouthed skull, the cross-guard shaped like bone with the grip bound in a leather that sickened them both. White eyes, shrouded by grey eyebrows that matched the hair swept back from bone-white skin, seemed to sear into theirs. A battlefield raged in the background. Bolts of spiritfire lit the air, crashing into shattered stone walls, while one huge, mechanised creature hung above. Its bulbous hull was brass coloured, and from it, tendrils descended towards the ground, with people wrapped in their hooked barbs.

All of this they soaked in as they stood, mesmerised by the ferocious, unforgiving white eyes that hung heavy upon their souls, demanding their supplication.

Laoch reached across and covered Ecne's tear-filled eyes with his hand before pulling the young woman close. "We leave now," he whispered, his duty to the acolyte helping him to wrest his soul away from the picture's glamour.

The first step was difficult, but the rest were easier as the tendrils of the Constructor's power weakened. Justice pressed reassuringly back in on his mind.

And that was just a hell-spawned picture!

15
WHEN THE HUNTER FALLS PREY

INNEALTÓIR, REALM OF THE CONSTRUCTORS

The tremor rippled beneath every scale, from Nathair's snout to the very tip of her spiked tail. The sharp intake of air, the tang of spiritfire rife upon it, thrilled the artifice's senses. The Spirit Walker whirled within the heartstone. Salivating? Perhaps. Awaiting – no, Keran decided – *needing* the kill. The separation of spirit from flesh.

The talons ripped downwards to pierce the tiger's fur, tearing into the ribcage and crushing the heart and lungs beneath. The gush of warm blood splashed upon the beast's feet, absorbing into the dragon where the scales overlapped, sucked into the mechanism beneath.

Lubricating? Is the spiritfire within the lifeblood enough to keep Nathair moving?

Razor-edged teeth scythed through muscle and bone, tearing away the striped pelt from the creature's back, crunching on the bone as the dragon reared. A choked roar broke through the trees. The predator, now prey, realised its own death. Nathair lashed her tail, an instinctive swipe, crashing it into the prowling mate behind her. With the tail spikes missing their target, the cogs and wires merely sent the tiger flying into the nearest branches. The tiger spun to land on her feet and a yowl slipped between her jaws. The animal cast a backwards glance as Nathair crashed a foreleg down onto her single cub. A crack echoed amid the trunks, and the tiger ran, hope lost.

Keran rode the surge of pleasure running through the heartstone, but a dread formed within him. He quickly wrapped it within a shroud of feigned indifference. The animal's spirit washed over the Spirit Walker, immersing it, briefly empowering the shaman to attempt a separation from Keran's grip. Keran balked, suddenly aware of the bestial power Nathair encapsulated when truly feeding. The foundries' trapped spirits, ancient and almost spent, had sustained the dragon/spirit hybrid but not roused it. A predator's feeding had the complete opposite effect, the empowerment short and intoxicating. Keran could visualise the balance required between compulsion and need, but not what it would take to prevent Nathair's addiction arising if she was set loose upon stronger prey.

More to learn.

The artifice bared blood-spattered teeth to the air as the veil dragon silently trumpeted its kill. The roar was suppressed as Nathair's primal thoughts entwined with Keran's.

"Announcing a kill works on a battlefield to cow the herd. But we are hunters now, and do not want our prey to go to ground."

Nathair responded by dropping her neck, her tongue sliding along the tiger's ragged corpse, seeking every last wisp of spiritfire before sitting back on her haunches. She lifted a foot to reveal the cub splayed between its talons. With barely formed incisors bared, the cub emitted a tiny roar of defiance and fear. The dragon paused. Keran experienced a shared flicker of recognition within the Spirit Walker – a memory of a hearth, fat-stained meat roasted over a fire. A withered hand, though the knife was firmly gripped, reached out and sliced the cooked skin and flesh before raising the morsel to elven lips. The taste thrilled Keran, moist, tender, sparking his senses until mewling interrupted the reverie. A head turned and elven eyes were drawn to the tethered cub that intently watched the meat, its tongue dripping. Keran felt a sigh slip out, followed by unrecognised words until the head dipped, and a second hand threw a slimy bone across to the young tiger.

Keran, sucked back into the now, sensed a shift in Nathair – an awareness of loss and, finally, a shape to what it once was. There, amid the rising pain, whitefire took hold. It gripped the shaman in an evil embrace, and moved to insinuate its way into Keran where their spirits touched. Predatory, hungry, and completely amoral. The snap of the tiger-child's body reverberated through the dragon's leg. Front and back half, gore-stained, dropped to the ground. Nathair lapped at the corpse to savour the tiny sliver of energy coursing along her tongue before she leant back and leapt into the air with a single flap of her huge wings. The white lacing pulsed once, easing away from Keran as the heartstone empowered the beast's flight.

Perhaps Laoch is right. Am I enough?

The dragon pitched sideways. A confusion emerged within Keran until a scent pervaded the crystal – a taste of human spiritfire upon the wind. Within this heady sensory mix, Keran could feel his own people. Ones that Nathair, when able to think, separated into the *not food* category of its mind at Keran's insistence. Eyes roaming the gaps between tower blocks, chimneys and the ancient foundries, Nathair's vision narrowed upon one area. A section of the road colonised by bushes and low trees, grass flowing from every crack. Humans waited hidden between the foliage, their attention on the strange house. Clothed in skins with spears and bows in hands, Nathair visualised their spirits. They appeared tinged with excitement, a mix of fear and curiosity the dragon regarded as normal for such creatures. Keran immersed himself amid the Spirit Walker as they flew, attempting to strengthen their connection after the kill while easing the predator's mind with thoughts of patience. He felt Nathair's agreement, and as her barriers dropped, the mighty dragon wheeled and, catching the air on the far side of a foundry roof, alighted far more gently than Keran thought possible.

"They don't look up. Their focus is on the ground, Nathair. Maybe that is something we can use."

Nathair lifted each leg carefully, at Keran's insistence, before settling down upon the roof's edge with her eyes just above the ledge, body flat with wings furled. Waiting.

'Sssssssomething is wrongggg, Captain.'

—

Laoch eased the lever to unlock the rear outer doors to the service entrance, and was sliding the bar back when a prickle rose along the nape of his neck, instinct tickling at his sense of danger.

"Don't feel right," he growled over his shoulder, leaving the metal lock in place just inside the last metal strap. "Something's out there."

Ecne leant Oisin against the bulbous front of the dormant artifice, hand still across his shoulder. The mountain man's eyes swirled in their sockets. "Need me to cover you?" she said.

"Wait." Sura floated towards Laoch. "I can look."

"Aye. For the best, I reckon. Unless my mind's playing tricks after the weirdness back there, in which case I apologise now."

Sura's finger graced his cheek, a wan smile sent his way before she stretched herself beneath the door and out through the hole.

It was dusk. The cloud-shrouded sun dipped behind the taller buildings, but her spirit retained her elven sight. Keeping herself near invisible, her form shedding little light of its own, she wafted along the paved entrance. Few sounds broke the silence, with no bird calls as they settled for the night. Just the swish of leaves as the trees swayed gently on a cool breeze. However, eyes stared her way from the foliage, oblivious to the spirit that looked back. She counted eight, each armed with a spear, a bow and a dagger. Their countenances were curiosity mixed with dread of the unknown. She sensed they would spring an ambush if panicked.

Turning around, Sura tracked back along their line of sight. Their position, just outside the house gates, was well-conceived. If Laoch chose to go through the gardens, would they follow? Or were there more waiting around the back? Sura urged herself onwards, the pull at her spirit making her aware that salving Oisin had taken more from her than she had first thought. She needed to know how far she could push this spirit form, what happened when her reserves emptied. But this was not the time. So far, recovery had come from a natural leeching of the life around her. When she spent spiritfire, it was absorbed somewhere, be it by other life, such as the plants, insects or animals, even the air or some rocks. When she focused and spent spiritfire quickly, she weakened faster, and it returned slower than it had been used.

Caught up by a breeze as she floated, she was forced to spend a little of that spiritfire to resist the air's movements as it threatened to stretch her thin. A hidden cost to the growing bond with Honour, perhaps? And her growing ability to touch?

She made her way along the curved outer wall to the front, where she sensed four more waiting in ambush. All human, and similarly armed. Their mood was different, however, though she couldn't quite grasp why. More fearful, perhaps?

Using a little more of her *self*, she returned, and let Laoch and Ecne know what she'd encountered before sliding her mind over Oisin and the rawness of his spirit.

"We can't stay." Laoch padded across the small space in front of the artifice. "We need food and water. Oisin needs the sky, and rest." He stroked the beginnings of a new beard. "But Oisin needs to be carried, so we can't run, or I would have gone for the front. Damn this bloody place."

"The Gods' weapons would take them down," Ecne said. "Wisdom's bolts, Fate's arrows, and whatever you choose."

"Survival, yes. I understand, Acolyte. But we're here to find a weapon, and for that, we need information. You said it yourself. These people will know this city's ins and outs. Especially useful if they continue to speak our tongue. Sura?" Laoch glanced towards the elf, her hands set on Oisin's cheeks. "Are you able to find Nathair?"

"It depends. I am tired from administering to Oisin. If Honour has spiritfire to share, possibly, but I weaken the further I am from her." Her voice quavered, a softness to it that spoke of her tiredness more than the words themselves. Laoch brought Honour's spear over and placed it next to the spirit. Sura faded, her eyes locking with his, before being absorbed into the sigil.

—

'Therrreeee.'

Keran felt the dragon's sight pull his spirit outwards, dragging his thoughts and visions into a maelstrom of colours before coalescing into a large, segmented creature. At least ten yards across, head to tail, its sinuous hull was adorned with rust-coloured spikes, each sporting a cracked bone, a skull, even skin. Fading in and out of view, the body gently writhed as its many legs rippled along the tower wall.

"An animal?" As soon as he said it, Keran knew he was wrong. Nathair guffawed, and sharing incredulity at him for not knowing.

'No. A Feeder. A tender of battlefields, sweeping up the remains after spirit ssstripping. But it huntsss. See how it positions itself on high, above the prey, creeping from behind. It hasss learnt a new way to replenish its energy source.'

"We must s—"

Keran caught himself, aware that controlling Nathair was hard enough when she accepted his role as master. Giving her reason to suspect he was not the spirit of a Constructor, one who had abandoned their Inhibitor armour to join her in the heartstone, would raise her suspicions further. Their goals needed to align for as long as possible while he learned.

'Yesss?'

"Repurpose it. Let this Feeder know the might of the Constructors is returning. And that we need those humans alive for now, to find where our brethren have gone."

'Ahhh, yesss. Thinking.'

Nathair rose onto four legs and spread her glistening wings in the failing light before pushing herself off the foundry's ledge. Arrowing downwards, she twisted the angle of each metal-skinned limb to catch the air thirty feet above the bush- and tree-covered road. Her scaled underbelly rushed over the humans, causing shock and awe, mixed with more than a little fear, to enrich the taste of their spirits. The mechanised dragon twisted, spiritfire surging, pushing the beast's tremendous weight into a turn augmented by angled wings. Almost on her back, her talons extended and sliced through the air.

The Feeder reared, antennae clattering together in panic, mandibles scything. Nathair beat her wings once to surge away from the tower wall in a curve, bringing her rear talons to bear. Keran understood instantly. These legs were thicker, more powerful, the metal tendons and wheeled cogs stronger. The Spirit Walker had thought ahead.

Nathair lashed outwards and, catching the Feeder's head, attempted to pull the centipede-like creature from the wall. The artifice's many feet gripped and hooked into the stone and the window apertures. Keran sensed Nathair's frustration as her talons slid off the metal segments protecting the mechanised creature. A flash of spiritfire then pulsed into her hind legs and, feet twitching, her talons grasped metal, and she tore the battlefield scavenger from the wall. Unable to maintain her grip, Keran felt Nathair choose to let the artifice fall, instead spinning herself about to catch the air and swoop around the chimneys that lay ahead.

The dragon's head twisted, enabling crystal eyes to peer downwards as it finished its turn. The segmented monstrosity writhed on the road amid tethered beasts that reminded Keran of eight-legged bison. Saddles and reins tore, necks and legs shattering as the animals screamed. Blood flew, and the Feeder righted itself. Keran spied the humans, their attention and fear now directed towards the Constructors' beasts instead of the house.

Nathair dropped, slowing herself with outstretched wings, and brought all four sets of talons to bear as she landed upon the segmented artifice. Her crushing weight pinned much of the sinuous, writhing body to the ground. Mandibles lashed, squirting a black liquid across the dragon's neck scales. A shiver of pain ran through Nathair, a moment of anger rising in response. Her head reared back before crashing down to bite deep with her razor-edged teeth.

'It's insane, lossst.'

Keran immediately knew Nathair had chosen to kill and feed over taming the mad spirits inside. His mind touched upon those squirming souls, which burned with hate. Their perpetual cycle of feeding on life had distanced the artifice from its purpose, with survival its only goal. He sensed Nathair's frustration, a desire to burn the Feeder in response to the perceived pain in her neck. With her resources low, she chose instead to rip and tear.

———

Laoch shoved the dual doors open and dropped to the sloped ground, Justice in the form of a bow in hand, as Nathair bit down upon whatever in the Seven Hells she had found. Shouts rose. Human tribespeople stood, pointing, the shock redefining their focus. Laoch and his people were forgotten.

He released, choosing to strike more fear, hoping to spook the ambush into running.

Seven Hells, I feel like running.

The searing arrow struck a tree trunk within the eyeline of the tribespeople, who backed away from Nathair. The dragon had reared up, the artifice's head between her jaws, and torn it clear of the writhing, yet pinned, body. White light exploded and bathed the trees, smothering Laoch's first arrow and its attempt to gain the people's attention. With fear overriding thought, they turned and ran directly towards Laoch and the open doorway behind.

He rose, arrow flaring.

"Ecne! Move towards me," he bellowed, backing away sideways towards the entrance. Ecne complied, dragging Oisin along while her other hand gripped a shaking crossbow – an action that would have been far too difficult without Wisdom's glow shining through her arm.

Sura formed beside her. The acolyte watched, wide-eyed, as Sura seemed to enter the mountain man, only for Fate's blue to pulse through his body as she emerged. Life returned to Oisin's eyes, and his weight lifted away from Ecne. Sura guided them both as the tribespeople hurtled into the garden.

"Peace!" Laoch bellowed. "We mean no harm!" He backed away, giving the fur- and skin-clothed warriors distance. The Ranger caught their fear and indecision. Just then, the scream of an animal sparked their legs into action. They scattered away from the house, fleeing the glowing bow and the roaring metallic dragon. Legs pounded; shouts echoed in all directions as they pelted for the far side of the building.

"Keep wary," Laoch said. "Watch the other side of the house in case they come back." A dreadful ripping sound from behind set Laoch's teeth on edge. "Not that I think they will."

16
A General Makes Her Mark

The University, Erstenburgh, Brandshold

"General." Captain Mordant saluted, keeping his feet tight together and back straight.

"Not fucking yet," replied Zendril. Prime Vardrin, at her side, winced, bringing a sneer of a smile to her face. "But soon, once the queen and the prime see sense." She held out a hand. The captain gripped her forearm in return.

"Then why am I here?" he said, glancing about the meister's room. In the centre, a cloth lay draped over what he assumed was a sculpture of some form, matching the countless smaller ones clustered and half-finished about the workspace.

Meister Suerese stepped forwards, wringing his clay-streaked hands; more clay hardened within the man's grey beard and wispy hair. "The ... the prime has asked whether you would find my work of use," he said, his high-pitched voice indicative of the stress caused by their presence in his private sanctum. The meister's face flushed in response to the disbelief in Mordant's eyes, and he grabbed the edge of the cloth to lift it clear of the wide but low table. Laid out in clay before them was the city, set out in great detail, from the outer walls to its inner streets. The White Palace sat behind a lower ring of stone, near the centre.

"I ..." Mordant peered down upon his beautifully rendered home. "Yes, Meister. Yes."

"Widen your thinking, Captain," Zendril said, eyes dancing. "I have spent the last day with my daughter, and we are fucked. Understand me? If the Unspoken turns up here with that dragon, she'll roast your balls and eat them with a shot of green-leaf rum on the side."

"I thought I was the one doing you a favour by putting a word in."

"Yep. They need someone talking with their brain, not out of their arse. And the queen listened. But that doesn't make this an easy ride, Captain. You need to plan the outer defence, and an inner, street-by-street, retreat. This city and the outliers were never designed to defend against an attack inside the walls. Stupid and shortsighted, yes, and you get the pleasure of rectifying it for Erstenburgh as my thank you."

Jacka eyed them both while listening to the banter, holding back his objections lest he raise Zendril's ire more. "What about the other towns and cities?" he asked, turning to Meister Suerese.

"Each of the northern cities has a university outlier. Though we do not have such a model as mine, there are drawn plans. Ones I have already requested to be copied and sent here."

"I will need to see these places in person, Jacka. Erin wants me to raise the veterans, call them to arms, and set them into a defence alongside the main army. I cannot do that from here – they need to see this old, scarred face." Zendril, hands on the edge of the model, twisted her head to look at the prime. "There is no time to worry about position and status, Jacka. You have a responsibility to fulfil. I have a different role. And we both know what's at stake."

Jacka nodded, lips curled in thought. "Yes. We can send you with an Honour Guard. I assume you want to travel swiftly."

"You said it. But I could do with those plans, so a queen's messenger or two would be useful. Mordant will have Erstenburgh to secure, I, the north." Zendril raised a grey eyebrow, creasing her forehead in query.

"I hear you. The south."

"But the Unspoken rears her Unbelievers in the Handren mountains," cut in Mordant, lifting his eyes from the model of Erstenburgh for the first time. "She wouldn't leave us at her hell-spawned back."

"It's a fucking dragon. It goes where it wants. Someone needs to get the message across to Ridth, and beyond. If we require more soldiers to defend our Union, then the queen will need them readied. A thoughtful enemy prepares for that; even destroys those reserves before an attack. And we're not dealing with *people*, Mordant, until the Unbelievers leave their valleys."

"It's just one beast," said Mordant. "One. It can't be everywhere."

Zendril side-eyed the prime. A heavy sigh left the administrator's lips while his eyes rose to the ceiling.

In his mind, Jacka ticked off the list of what he'd advised would happen should the queen unleash Zendril with such knowledge. Being right was going to play Seven Hells with his nerves.

"In the Houses, Mordant, do you ever trace the dragon's form?" asked Jacka.

"We all do. Your point?"

"Why, in every House, do you think the dragon looks different?"

"I get to go south?" said Jacka, dropping into the chair set at the new table Queen Erin had commissioned for her meeting chamber.

Erin nodded in reply, eyes flickering to meet her prime's. "Yes. But it's not what you think."

Jacka tapped the table, fingers drumming briefly, before looking to his queen. "Zendril—"

"Not my doing, Prime Vardrin. I spoke true, balls-out language or not. If these Constructors arrive before we are remotely ready, we're going to be squealing like suckling pigs over the fire. It was Erin's idea and, as per usual with my daughter, a step ahead of our conversation at the meister's." Zendril, hand raised in supplication, eased back into her chair. "I just happen to agree."

"Politically, it would be seen as a slight by your uncle."

"Perhaps. But we are talking of a war footing, and this queen has preparations to make. I asked Su ... Lady Death, but she feels it is not her role."

"He has the Weister mean streak in spades."

The queen smiled at that. "True, Jacka. But he also has the second strongest army within the Union and our southern fleet in his port. It is vital we garner his understanding of the threat. Lord Penance will be sending Sneed with you, and the strange armour from the Unbelievers our Rangers apparently killed – evidence enough that they struck here."

"Sneed? Doesn't ..."

"Yes, the duke blames him for my father's death, when he served as my master. I think our High Lord hopes it is a sign of the Houses' concern that he would send someone so unwilling. Each House will provide a priest-in-waiting to accompany you with messages for Ridth's churches, Jacka. As there will be with you, Mother."

"Hah. Little rays of sunshine in my life. Hope they can fucking ride at my pace, or they'll be eating dust. We done? I need to prep the Honour Guard. I hope they're as tough as they used to be. And Mander is coming with me."

"Mander? Is that the right role model for a general's army? To have your … companion with you?" asked Queen Erin.

Zendril broke out in a huge smile and pulsed her hands. "See, Jacka? It's not your job I'm after. And yes, daughter. The bastard feigns the limp for sympathy, but it'll keep my legend in the forefront of every officer's mind. Especially the new ones. You asked for me to draw the veterans back into the field. Well, Mander is a fucking good reminder that if they don't turn up, I'll personally kick their arses until they change their mind." She rose from the chair. "By your leave, my Queen."

Erin acknowledged Zendril, watching as her mother bowed slightly, then pushed the chair inwards before heading for the door.

"Is there another reason I'm going?" asked Jacka, unable to help himself as his eyes wandered over the queen. "Sending me away? Perhaps out of sight, and therefore out of mind?"

Erin squeezed her fingers tight in front of her and stared at the table's centre, refusing to look Jacka's way. "Adama has asked to see me, Jacka. Lord Penance says he has more lucid moments than he expected. He suspects the writing is a way of acting out the pain. We condemned an innocent man with the taint of treason for the sake of the Union. And me."

"You know how we—"

"It cannot happen, Jacka. Will not. We have a people to defend. People we've lied to for over a thousand years, and whose future may be as bleak as my heart feels now."

"You hated him." Jacka made to stand and move towards Erin.

A fierce glare from the queen stopped him in his tracks. "You are wrong. I never hated him. More what he represented, and that I was forced to marry him in the Union's name. The crown sits heavy, and Adama was just a puppet for the Houses to play me with. I know that now, and he sits in a cell, with everything he stood and fought for blackened, because of House politics."

"A necessity."

Jacka's pleading tone turned Erin's stomach. This was not what she needed now. She rose from her chair, a fire raging in her heart. Which, for once, she allowed to bleed through into her posture.

"As is this. I am not sending you because of your feelings for me, Jacka, but because the Union and Brandshold need us to stand in their defence. This is but one piece in the protection of the realm. Without it, the rest may fall. When they come, we do not know where they'll start. What if it's Ridth? Or the Isle of Khund?" Queen Erin rose from her chair, fists balled, eyes finally on Jacka. "We are unimportant. *We serve*. When it is over, maybe that will change. But right now, you *will* carry out your duty as you have sworn."

She turned to leave, her heart heavy, unused to the emotions coursing through her, all reinforced by a pressing guilt.

"Yes, my Queen," replied Jacka. "As you say. Duty and service."

17

A SECRET EXPOSED

ERSTEN FOREST, BRANDSHOLD

Lord Penance urged his horse through the blackened trees and churned mud, eyes on the ground, wary of the reluctant horse's potential for turning a fetlock. Despite its nervousness, he reached a clear spot near the newly made rock pile. Letting the reins relax, his horse dropped its head to nuzzle at the ground for anything edible.

"How ...?" started Meister Kinst at his side, her own sturdy, barrel-chested horse having ploughed through the mud with more abandon.

"Grand Meister Arknold's knowledge of the block and tackle has amazed even me, and the city's builders were all tasked, until yesterday, to lend a hand – in return for a little less tax investigation from the prime and the Treasury."

"Yesterday? But is it finished?"

"No, Meister Kinst. Far from it. But we couldn't let anyone else see what we are about to do. All the remaining workers are my acolytes and priests, until we decide what to do next. Come."

Lord Penance dismounted, careful to maintain his mummery as a priest-in-waiting, Senza, appeared to help him down. The woman's grip was firm and assured, though he noted her eyes were alight with fervour. Apparently, she had a tale to tell.

"Lord Penance, we have ..." She briefly glanced over to Kinst. There was a question in her eyes when they turned back to him. "... the artifacts you tasked us to find."

"Good, Senza. Stay with us. Once the meister has seen what we have, we can stop talking in code. Or she'll be in one of the cells of the repentant." Lord Penance smiled to himself, sensing the tension that entered Kinst's posture – a friend to the newly converted Yanpet.

"One of the two, eh, Meister Kinst?"

I do so hate this game.

He clapped a hand on the meister's back. The woman lifted her green robes above the ground, letting only the sturdy riding boots she'd been warned to wear to grace the mud beneath. The meister sighed and took a step before stopping, an awe-filled look directed towards the hill, and what appeared to be metal teeth set above an intricately carved doorway of an unknown House.

"Come. Sneed and the grand meister are waiting."

Lord Penance drew his walking stick from the sheath beside the saddle, the sigil-embedded tip sharing its energy and relieving the aches from the ride. Taking careful steps, he crossed the intervening space to the completely exposed doorway and its metal dragon snout – the inlaid Seven motif on the door was dulled by the heavy cloud. He knew Kinst was unable to take her eyes off the dragon's head, despite the fact he'd warned her of the ancient House exposed by the Unbelievers' attack. A lie, in kind, but it wouldn't do for her to discover everything at once. Not like the grand meister, whose mind had already taken in the joints and mechanisms from the head itself, never mind what Senza hinted at.

Surrounding the now-half-absent hill and its remaining exposed rock were several towers with overhanging block and tackle, roughly cut struts holding them in place. A team worked one tower's ropes as others pushed the human-sized rock they were shifting to one side. Sneed and Arknold were in deep conversation, the latter hopping from foot to foot as she watched the teams work. Kinst sped up, her eagerness, Lord Penance assumed, in response to her friend's excitement. A tingle rose in his own mind at the thought of what they were digging out.

Sneed, sensing his presence, turned to greet him. "Just in time, my Lord. We believe we have found the first ... err."

"Wing," added the grand meister. "Kinst, come and see." She grabbed her friend, yanking her over to see past the workers to the metal struts sticking upwards, where another roped tower held it clear.

"What am I seeing?"

"Exactly what your brain is telling you and your heart is denying. A dragon. A metal dragon. One the Houses have warned us of for the past ten centuries."

"I don't understand. The Unspoken, yes? This is hers? So, what are the rumours flying around the university, the call to arms?"

Arknold spun her friend around and pointed to the dragon's snout as Lord Penance and Sneed waited, one eye on them as they chatted. "Here. The High Lord is only telling me so much. There are more secrets. Ones I think we'll be drip-fed as we go. But there was more than one dragon, and this lost House was built by the Seven around its body, and then buried. More of their ..." Arknold turned back into the wind, spinning Kinst around again. "... their half-truths. There is something much deeper going on, my friend.

Much, much, deeper. And the reason why we are suddenly being given this scientific freedom. I do think there is a threat coming, that much is true, and the word of a flying dragon too strong amid the masses to quell and deny."

"Are you sure you're not caught up in the excitement, Arknold? You know you lose yourself in things, and the temptations here are right up your alleyway."

Kinst's worried frown caught the grand meister's breath, and she blinked back intrusive thoughts and her personal fears. "That sounds like me, but no. The queen is adamant she wants us to help – you have already inspected the widening of the mines, and I understand the potters have met with the metal casters about improving the process? Yes?"

Kinst nodded. "And I have Lord Wisdom's priests in training now. After your meeting with the queen, it appears we are making a slightly more storable, less volatile elixir. I feel less like a meister and more like a merchant every day." She gestured towards the bent wing tip resting on a large boulder, three quarters of the way towards the pile they'd passed on the way in. "Can we get closer?"

"Of course." Arknold checked the floor, tucking her robe into the breeches she wore underneath. A few muddy strides and they stood beside the exposed wing, a metallic skin that stretched between metal rods splayed like the bones in a bat's wing. "I think it'll be at least twenty yards long, larger, perhaps, once we dig it all out. See there?" The grand meister pointed towards the central dome cleared of rock and soil, its rough curve formed by cut-stone pieces. "That is the main body, and there the tail curls in on itself. I've been inside the first door and seen the corridor beyond. I think it's built around the dragon's neck – or maybe it *is* its neck."

"It is huge. This would suggest the Houses' dragons—"

"—are to scale, yes? All this time we talked of the Seven Houses' demands, their rules, the restrictions of our scripture. But if this is a measure of what they were built for, then perhaps we should do what we can."

"And what is that, Arknold? Why are we here?"

"To rebuild it. To make it work." Excitement trilled through the words. Kinst caught the sparkle in her friend's eyes and knew, whether for ill or good, that was exactly what Arknold would do.

—

"It's an impossible task," said Sneed, facing the meisters as they approached the dragon's wing.

"Which? Rebuilding Leront or meeting the duke?"

"Both. Why me, High Lord? What good will come of it?"

"Because I cannot. I need to be here to keep the Seven Houses working together. You know they gnash and grumble without my leash – more so now four of the Gods' weapons are known to be lost. They feel lesser, betrayed. I fear they will fracture, and this is not the time for the veils to be under threat. They will give us much-needed time."

The servant sighed, rubbing the back of his head. "The duke is … difficult. Our relationship strained."

"And you have been under penance for close to twenty-five years, Sneed. Enough for anyone to see you have paid for the pain caused."

"In your eyes, maybe. But Simeon Weister has a way of firing himself up, and when I became the High Lord, he was vocal in court. The regent sent a deposition in response after he whipped them up." Sneed's eyes flickered over to the High Lord, who gave him a rueful smile.

"Water under the bridge. Erin's father was your advocate to join the House before his death. And the queen herself has a warmth for you despite the horrors of our role. If you stood where I do now, she would be the happier for it. The first crusades were a necessary travesty, one of the crosses we have to bear. The Union was on the edge of falling apart with all the petty squabbles, the Houses divided between the countries. I know my history."

"You didn't live it, though. Still wet nursing at your mother's teat. I am old, and I don't know if I have the patience of my middle years. I cannot promise I won't react." Sneed dabbed his boot into the mud, his face betraying painful memories.

"You were a High Lord, and in this task, my blackened right hand. If you were to be passive, you would be dismissed as a nobody. Enough of this."

"And the dragon? Surely, they have not the skill to resurrect the beast?"

"Let me worry about that. Perhaps resurrection is not what I had in mind."

The High Lord gazed over at the animated meisters and the ancient metal wing they were examining.

18
THE HUNT CONTINUES

ABOVE THE CITY OF SIGHS, REPANTI

Tarin could taste the future, his tongue clicking at the roof of his mouth where the tang in the false atmosphere of the *Kraken* bridge enthralled his senses. The palpable tension that permeated the Inhibitor bridge crew was nothing compared to what they could soon experience if his machinations came to fruition. Plans within plans, each part a step closer to redemption and the subjugation of the Seven, or their progeny.

"Souls that I will savour for centuries, no doubt."

Within the shine of the polished wood-and-brass bridge, his people moved swiftly from panel to panel. Bulbs flashed as patterns formed in the multi-coloured control panels the crew button-pressed and twiddled with. A plethora of information each of the *Kraken* Inhibitors understood in their individual roles, pulled together like a puppet master by the admiral incarnate – she who was as old as himself. One of the originators whom he had pulled from her reverie in a dusty, far-flung workshop to build the *Kraken* in all its glory. And as difficult to manipulate as the brass she favoured, or the crystals laid deep within the magnificent machinery.

"This is a waste, Tarin. All that spiritfire spent, just for you."

"May I remind you, Lelion, that I am your emperor. If I want my soulship to take me on a jaunt, it shall happen. We will await my battle barge at the balance point to reduce your worries." The admiral's grimace annoyed the Fleshmaster, a half-agreement that signalled she perceived it as a victory in her own head.

Too long without a fresh body, that one. Long in the soul, for she has forgotten her place; not that she ever cared for it.

"Get those tendrils stowed, Inhibitor Ranket. Now. The drag is a waste. Henar, where, in this forsaken *Kraken*, did you learn to monitor the spirit engine output?" The admiral, resplendent in her brass armour, shouldered the Inhibitor aside. "Here," she pointed, spinning the metal handle. "The needle should be at the fourth mark to match the port side, understand? You'll be tipping the emperor off the side, Inhibitor Ranket – probably with your skin ripped off along with him and used as a windsail." The admiral incarnate strained her neck and cast a white eye towards the Fleshmaster. "They need a fight, Tarin. A battle to hone their lackadaisical attitudes. If you wanted a bloody ornament, I could have built you one out of wood and bronze paint. Stuck a flower on it."

"That is why we ascend, Admiral. To find that very thing. Something to get your ancient teeth into and challenge your beloved *Kraken*. But everything takes time when you are beholden to others, and that we must put paid to as well."

Lelion shoved the Inhibitor back into his spot, teeth exposed as she tasted his spirit to add a little fear into his thoughts. Walking back to her post, one arm placed behind her back, the other reposing on her telescope, which jutted from the holster at her armoured hip, she took a dusty breath. "Words. Repanti was supposed to be a test, and they fall at our feet like quivering dogs. Pathetic. I need to bloody my chains, Fleshmaster, feel the thrill of tearing spirits free again. Otherwise, I would have preferred a slow soul death back at my workshop."

"We followed the signs to this realm and found it wanting. However, we have a goal now, Lelion. The Seven are within our grasp. But I suspect we do not have what is required to get your mighty ship there. The Wyrm fades. You know this. The journey here was fraught. Therefore we require Spirit Walkers if we are to split the veils of any world in the future, never mind one as strong as that our ancient kin gave up their last vestige of spirit life to show us."

The Fleshmaster sensed an Inhibitor arrive at his side, the body young, fresh, the skin only now drying as the Constructor spirit took hold. He held out his hand with head bowed, and the emperor took the messenger tube. A snarl crossed his lips as he popped the top, allowing the whiff of spiritfire to enter his nose and mouth.

"Popsilin reports little success. One last rumour to follow for Renat." He leant back, eyes focused on the domed metal ceiling, the embedded crystals casting a golden light upon the brass and wood of the bridge. A sliver of power exuded from the corner of his mouth, the message sliding into the tube before he sealed it again.

He handed it back to the waiting youngling. "Send this back with the pilot."

Sensing the crew's gazes on him, he dropped his chin with a snarl. The accompanying glare caused all the Inhibitors' focus to instantly return to their posts.

"How long, Lelion?"

"Four hours."

"Ahhh. Don't tax me. Faster, Lelion. We are close."

Popsilin slid the looped wire over the man's bloodied wrist and pulled tight. The metal bit into the skin and squeezed around the joint. She handed the end of the wire to her assigned pilot. The woman pulled it tight before attaching a second loop up and around the townsfolk's elbow. Buildings burned behind them. Ash-strewn bodies, many lying in their doorways, a testament to the waste created by the Fleshmaster's haste.

Checking his legs were tied tight, Popsilin slapped the man's forehead and forced it against the metal of the ornithopter's nose. "Here's how it works, you piece of soul-filled shit. We fly up in the air and you tell us which way to go. Then we fly there. We find the elves your children spoke of, and I let them live while you get a nice pat on the head. Understand? If not, I'll give them to my crew – they like nothing more than draining a squirming child to the last drop of their soul. You know what it's like to be alone in a void, all hope lost, watching yourself fade? Can you imagine that as a child? The emotional pain – it tastes divine. A delicacy so intoxicating that the emperor has banned it." She leant in closer, blue lips to his ear. "But he's not here."

With a last pat on the cheek, she flicked her head towards the pilot, who opened the artifice's canopy, dropped into the fore seat and strapped in. Popsilin clambered in behind, wishing the artifice was her beloved ground-hogging Scorpion, not the ungainly flying machines she so despised.

But you keep weakness hidden.

Once buckled in, she slapped the pilot on the shoulder. A thumbs-up preceded the first flap of the four wings that mimicked a dragonfly's. The wider, longer rear wings began their beat, soon followed by the front pair, and Popsilin felt the machine rise from the ground before lurching downwards. For all its similarities with the insect hunter, the artificer's mimicry could not match its grace – each beat signalled the rise, then minor fall, of the whole machine as it fought to stay aloft. She unconsciously gripped her seat before forcing herself to let go and focus on the task in hand.

The Mechanised Inhibitor captain let her spirit flow, giving the pilot a gentle caress on her way to touching upon the man's fearful mind. She had chosen his position – on the nose – and the method of garnering his cooperation as a purposeful distraction from their transportation method. Savouring the townsfolk's fear, her whispers in his head were soon rewarded by a finger flickering out, pointing towards the foothills he'd described under torture. Barren, covered in thick grass between jutting rock strata, they stretched forty miles into the distance. It would take their squadron of ornithopters weeks of searching before they found the Schenterenta, even if they were waving from the hilltops. Months if, as rumoured, they had taken refuge in the myriad caves that supposedly wended their way underneath.

If they exist. It would have been better to have hunted them first, before the magi of the cities.

The man's dread rose, responding to the onrushing air numbing his limbs. The strong taste threatened to erase her self-control and she withdrew a little, maintaining enough of her *self* to urge him to comply. The pilot, satisfied with their height, adjusted the wing angle, and they began a steady forwards motion much more in line with Popsilin's needs. Finally, she allowed herself to relax.

'*Show me,*' she thought.

The man conjured a picture of a smooth-sided valley. At its head, a gentle waterfall splashed over a limestone ledge, while beneath lay a dark-mouthed cave. A plateau of flat stone lay on one side, a stream bed on the other.

Within the hour, the pilot adjusted the levers to set the ornithopter into a gentle, wide bank, the remembered image coming into view as they flew upstream.

Likely just in time. This male is near useless as the cold infects his mind and body.

"Bank right. Bring us down out of sight," Popsilin ordered, turning her head to check on the six machines that followed. A small force. Each co-pilot seat was taken by an infantry Inhibitor. Should they fail, more would follow.

The dragonfly lurched, the artifice dropping in ungainly steps until it reached the relatively flat ground. Forcing herself to remain calm and in control of herself in front of the pilot, and those flying behind, Popsilin awaited the moment the wheeled legs hit dirt. As soon as the pilot indicated it was safe, she had the buckles undone and was helping to raise the canopy, freeing herself from the hateful confines of the cockpit.

While her team gathered and readied themselves, she placed her hand behind the captured man's head. "Thank you," she whispered. "To make sure they don't suffer, I will drain your children myself."

She trapped the words in his spirit mind, then drained his dread-laced soul dry. Each sliver washed through her body, an ecstasy her team duly ignored. The privilege of an officer, and an aspiration to clamber over your peers for – not a right. Leaving the pilot to cut the corpse free, she signalled to her team. Sending them down-slope in pairs, she followed behind, one hand on her whip and the other on the soulreaver, while lingering traces of the man's pained soul danced across her dried lips.

The grassy slope proved little obstacle until they reached the lowest ten yards, where the stream had cut through the limestone. The drop to the plateau near the small waterfall, with the cave mouth at its side, promised to be a dangerous spot for her team to be picked off. Popsilin set two Inhibitors, with their crystal slingers, into position with eyes on it. She had never liked the weapon, which utilised a chemical elixir to hurl the metal-cased crystal towards their target. These were infused with writhing spiritfire, drained from their menageries, and required the bonds to be perfectly formed for it to explode on impact. One in ten would crack, however, proving ineffective against even the simplest of armour. The alternative – to throw spiritfire like it wasn't a necessary food – was anathema. Often, the first enemy bolt triggered the Inhibitors ire, the waste unconscionable. They had to have specific control training before they were allowed to tackle the lesser mages and the magi themselves. The combination of madness and hunger rarely meant ordered ranks, nor success. Something savvy humans played upon.

Leaving them with their spyglasses upon the dark void, she signalled the first Inhibitor pair down the slope. Their fibrous, bonded ropes and pulleys allowed them to drop at speed over the small valley's side. Just before the first armoured boots hit rock, a slinger fired. The explosion of gunpowder echoed across the rocks. A white flare lit the inner edge of the cave, accompanied by a scream of pain.

"Someone's here! Get yourselves down there!" she shouted to the second pair as another report crashed into her ears.

This time the crystal flash struck the limestone floor inside the cave, lighting up a pair of Schenterenta with recurved bows. They loosed their arrows, tips spiralling as the helical fletched shafts flew towards the slingers. Both arrows struck the same Inhibitor. The first caught her beneath a knee joint, driving inwards, and the other struck her hand. Spasms took hold and she dropped the slinger to the floor. With the second Inhibitor team halfway down the drop, the first pair released their metal quarrels from handheld bows and charged the cave, drawing their curved short swords. The blade edges sparkled in the sunlight.

The leader took an arrow to the neck, between the guard and helm, and she crumpled onto the stone plateau. The archer screamed in return as his hand splattered against the cave wall. The cry cut off when a shield bit deep into his jaw. A slinger crystal struck the other Schenterenta, smashing into their hip. The shieldless Inhibitor ignored the explosion as his spiritfire-infused eyes adjusted to the flash. His sword slashed across the elf's neck, cracking through bone and meat, and the last archer slid to the cave floor.

Popsilin checked on the slinger pair. The snapping of arrows and subsequent glow signified the damage was being healed. Satisfied, she clipped herself to a rope and dropped down, to be greeted by the other injured Constructor. The woman had grasped both sides of the arrow protruding from her neck and was drawing it out slowly. Casting it aside, the whitefire glimmering from the hole showed she would survive.

"Feed," Popsilin said, pointing to the elf with blood pumping from their neck. Normally her right, but they had a nest to flush out. She needed them all healthy. Elven spirits were tasteless, and most Constructors chose to avoid such opportunities. This, however, was an order, and the Inhibitor complied.

Stepping into the darkness of the cave mouth, eyes adjusting, Popsilin grasped the still-whimpering archer's stump and pressed a gauntleted thumb into the nub of bone. The resultant scream echoed along the tunnel behind. The two Inhibitors on guard listened for any movement in response.

"Where are your shaman? The Spirit Walkers?"

She pressed harder, digging the thumb-tip into the flesh surrounding the wound. The elf spat. Popsilin, ready for it, dodged. A sizzle greeted her ears, and she turned. A green glob burned its way into the rock face. When she looked back at the archer, green foam spilled from his mouth. She pushed the dying elf away. His twisted tongue slipped between loose teeth, and his eyes rolled.

No!

Popsilin glanced back to the feeding Inhibitor. The woman's silent scream was written upon her rigid, shaking body, and her fears wrapped in the greenfire that tore through her soul. Like an acid, it ate away at the Inhibitor, consuming the Constructor spirit – a denial of life and rebirth. Her body jolted, and then a single puff of green, acrid smoke rose from her mouth. A mere cloud of what she had once been.

"Shit!"

The Inhibitor's partner looked to Popsilin for orders.

She blew out, dust-filled air expelling into the cave, leaving behind an unusual sliver of fear that insinuated itself into her mind. "We collect her on the way back for the Fleshmaster and the thaumaturge."

With those words, Popsilin shoved the soldier into action, signalling back to the slingers to be on guard, ready for any retreat. Reaching down, she gathered the dead Inhibitor's handbow and crystal-tipped quarrels, a newfound wariness impinging on her mind.

"Team two, take the lead," Popsilin ordered.

The three remaining team members waited for her as she passed the one-handed archer, its head now sunken, eye sockets boiling green. The elf's spirit had slipped away, though a whiff of its passing convinced Popsilin the soul had not been corrupted as the Inhibitor's had.

"And no one feeds, understand? Kill everyone except the shaman. You will know them by their twisted bodies, covered in ritual tattoos. Their eyes are often coloured, though never white, understand?"

—

Tarin shifted the helm between his gauntleted hands and snapped together two of his left fingers, the physical call for the emperor's whitefire. He'd trained himself for over a century to master such techniques in secret. The disconnect of body and soul enabled his people to switch from corpse to corpse should one fail them; the fresher, the better, for it was the brain they could not heal. Once imbued, however, keeping the corpse animated drained their souls, each action to maintain the body drawing resources from the Constructor's spirit form. The older and more evolved the connection, the less energy it took. Hence the most powerful among the Constructors were those who'd inhabited the fewest of the newly dead. The Fleshmaster kept his only reanimation a closely guarded secret, a blemish he refused to share. But, in that time, he had become a master of the flesh, and one of the few who could wield the whitefire external to his body if need be – something gleaned from the cursed Seven, and abhorrent to his people.

Tarin swept his eyes around Repanti's seeping outer veil, wisps of its spiritfire floating between the stars where it had risen through the cracks. The damage was a sign of a unique skill that had kept his people alive during the first decades after the Sundering, when the Constructors fell upon each other in a frenzy of survival feeding. Bereft of their human menageries and spirit-dolls, panic had set in. Doors were closed, colleagues and friends parted as the city streets became a battlefield for those young and inefficient in their bodies – or those ancient and gluttonous. Decadence brought them low and kept them there; the irony of their cannibalistic behaviour was not lost upon their emperor. Yet, a simple trick, a hundred years in the making, coupled with the deft control of the heat within his body, had saved his people.

And here I stand, animated, in the coldest of places, waiting above the clouds and the veils.

"Wyrm," Tarin bellowed, eyes flaring with the calling sent across the near-empty atmosphere above Repanti. "Come now."

The spiritfire message crackled across the vastness, sparking along errant particles until it wrapped itself around the once-mighty creature that slowly sipped from the shattered veil. The calling spurred its way into her collar, the crystal band shimmering as it simultaneously echoed the words while sparking a gentle pain into the Wyrm Ship's mind. With a soft sigh, she unfurled her topmost skin sails, the cartilage bending upwards, spines springing to sheath each and hold them straight. Catching the realm's pathway, energy slowly nudged the beast into action.

"Hurry, Wyrm. I have not the patience. Remember your children."

The second calling raced across the void, insistent. The demand forced the creature's fin sails to extend. Smaller, but rigid, they turned the Wyrm, and she let the compulsion drag her towards her fate. With fin sails flapping, she crossed the divide towards its betrayer, a Constructor who bore promises he never kept, and shackled her into servitude in return.

The Fleshmaster watched the animal's approach, its snout long and angled beneath, giving the appearance of a sail-ship's bow. Along its back, three skin sails glistened in the sunlight, twisting, gathering energy to push the ribbed main body towards the Fleshmaster's barge. The bulges to either side of the bony nasal protrusion were not eyes, but sensory organs, attuned to the food upon which it grazed – the energy that, in ancient times, had seeped from within a realm's atmosphere, a heady mix of a sun's energy and the elixir of natural spiritfire. The human-formed veils and their curtains had cut the beasts off from their natural feeding grounds, and the veil dragons' taste for their spirit-imbued flesh had accelerated a rapid decline.

With a warmed hand held high, the emperor awaited the Wyrm Ship's mental touch of greeting. A crooked smile wavered on his blue lips as the creature defied him to the last second.

Then the connecting pulse wove its way into his mind. *'I am here.'*

"Yes, though oh so slowly. A continued reluctance to complete our agreement."

'*You have made no attempt to keep your word. None.*'

"*You were to find me a realm of the Schenterenta.*"

'*This I have done. Your failures are not mine.*'

The Fleshmaster squeezed his fingers deep into ancient palms, requiring the control, aware that the alien thing was not a minion to abase itself at his feet. A slave bound by its collar, and the children he held in thrall.

"*We have not found them, yet. But soon.*"

A thrum vibrated across Tarin's wrist. Spreading his boots a little wider, and with whitefire crackling to reset them on the brass deck, he looked back over his shoulder towards the small bridge of the barge. The captain waved towards the curved tube protruding from below the strengthened, crystalline windows.

"*Wait,*" he murmured, and strode towards the tube and the promise of a much-needed message. Popsilin, perhaps. Something that could change the course of this conversation. Fumbling briefly with the tube cap, he extracted the message tube, sliding the top next to his helm and briefly unbuckling it to allow the sliver within to wash over his face and drive into his mind.

Images filled his thoughts, pictures of dead Schenterenta, their heads empty, skulls melted. A wrongness filled his nostrils with dread. The link to the Schenterenta spirit had been shrived, stripped clean, unfollowable. But, also, it spoke to him of soul death, a weapon he had never encountered before. One that could wither the spirit of the weaker, younger-bodied Constructors. His army. Popsilin turned and his view changed, encompassing a large cavern, stalagmites strewn with the dead. All of whom were devoid of souls. No Spirit Walkers were in sight. The captain's thoughts agreed with his assessment, until she brought one Schenterenta into view. Popsilin had splayed the woman upon the floor, each ankle and wrist staked out with a leather strap, a fifth around the throat. Whitefire writhed along each limb as Popsilin's soulreaver drew the elf's soul, the sparks causing nerves to fry, the agony shouted to the rooftops through a mouth devoid of tongue and teeth after the captain's intervention. A single, gauntleted hand landed upon the agonised woman's forehead, and one word rode the pain.

"Mondrein." The Fleshmaster said the word on blue lips, spinning, boots sparkling, to face the looming Wyrm.

"Mondrein," he bellowed. The creature flinched as the force of the words crashed through to rouse the crystal collar. *"MONDREIN."*

The Wyrm Ship fought, pushing down, wrapping its urges in personal pain and tragedy. But to no avail. The thought slipped, an image from its travels, the trail laid bare. Of course, they had been there before and tested the veil, before moving on to Repanti. The pathway was unreadable to the Fleshmaster, but he knew. And that was enough.

"Yes. You will take us."

'I am weak. I have not fed enough.'

"How long?"

'A year.'

"You lie, beast. But to exaggerate. Yes. A third of that I sense, but we do not have that much time. One week."

'I will be scarred, Constructor. I will not survive the veil.'

"But your progeny will. I will keep them safe elsewhere, with one duty to perform. Find me the Spirit Walkers, and you and your children will be free, Wyrm. Free when my dragon rises, and falls upon the seven traitors. This was our bargain."

'My children?'

"Yes. One task, one instruction to follow. Once complete, they will be released to the ether as you wish. Instruct them, then prepare yourself for your last journey." The Fleshmaster spun, an unbid cackle slipping from his throat as he felt the Wyrm draw upon her reserves, a strike upon him in the offing. *"Strike me and they will die, Wyrm. I am the holder of their collars, the key upon which they are bound.*

You know this. Should I die, their death will be unimaginable. A slow, agonising passing as they outgrow their restraining collars. So much pain. I believe they will go mad long before they bite their own ..."

'Stop.'

19
A PICTURE IN SONG

INNEALTÓIR, REALM OF THE CONSTRUCTORS

Oisin lay slumped on the ground, glaring at Laoch, who watched Nathair's rending of the eight-legged beasts through his spyglass. Laoch had sensed the anger running through the Handren. A soreness of spirit the mountain man couldn't hold back, urging raw words from his mouth; ones so different from his normal speech, as if there were two men trapped in the same body. Laoch had chosen to walk away, leaving Sura's spirit hands to tend him. One alighted upon Oisin's forehead and more unbidden anger rose, causing him to lash out. Only, his arm flailed through Sura's spirit body to hit his own shoulder.

"Calm, Oisin," she said, the words almost lost within Nathair's rending of bone and flesh. "I can feel your rage, but it is not real. Nor is it imagined. The Constructor poison has frayed your emotions. It will take time."

"Time?" he spat, pointing to the dragon's bloodied mouth. "Do we have that?"

"Who knows the answer, Oisin? But pulling at that nagging doubt and taking it out on us – especially Laoch – will end in nothing but despair." Sura knelt back over him and, replacing the hand, let a faint tendril touch the First Ranger's mind.

"No suggestions, Sura. Do not press your thoughts into me. That is something I cannot burden amidst all else. Whatever befalls me, my words and deeds must be my own." A snarl laced his words.

"Outwardly, I say what I will," she bit back.

"I can rag your arse, as Laoch would say," Ecne said from where she watched the far side of the building, "because I am not a Ranger. Here on sufferance and bad luck."

Oisin glanced over. The young woman's smile appeared to smooth his ragged thoughts. He lay back down and accepted Sura's touch. "You people will be the death of me."

Laoch walked back, spyglass stowed and an urgency to his stride. "You up to active duty?" he asked.

"Honestly, I don't think I could trust myself to make the right decisions. And whether I can trust myself in a fight is yet another matter."

"Like that answer. Aye, I know the feeling but was never so honest to voice it. There's one of the locals trapped under a broken tree out there. Thinking I should go get him before Nathair notices and has dessert. If you are able to watch the rear with Fate's bow, then I'll take Ecne."

With a heavy weight upon his legs, the First Ranger pushed himself up from the floor and limped over to Ecne and squeezed her on the shoulder. "Get going, *not* Ranger. Work to do."

Ecne slid backwards and eased herself up before glancing back towards the waiting Laoch. "I'm on it, First Ranger Oisin, sir."

Once on her feet, she checked the sigil on the crossbow out of habit, her thumb aglow, before crouching behind Laoch as he stepped out of the rear gate.

They moved low from tree to tree, the air rife with smoke and ash. The smell of cooked meat wafted on a warm breeze. Wrinkling her nose, Ecne took her place as directed by Laoch, watching the wide-eyed tribesman, his legs trapped under a half-snapped tree trunk, blood seeping from torn flesh.

Nathair's snout was buried deep into the final eight-legged beast. Already dead, the haze of its spirit shrouded the dragon's mouth, sucked inwards as its tongue graced the flesh before the jaws bit down. The two halves tumbled to the floor, and a triumphant roar emanated from between the sword-like teeth to reverberate into the sky.

Laoch moved ever-so slowly, each step measured, eyes switching between the ground and Nathair. A breath of wind sailed past, setting his senses tingling, as Sura swept by. The faded elven spirit approached the dragon's belly and flowed inside, her bootheel the last of her that he saw.

Calming the beastie, I hope.

He checked Ecne was focused and watching him before approaching the wounded man, weapons stowed, palms out. "Peace on you," he said slowly.

The wide-eyed response was an indicator of the distinct lack of it within the man.

A huge, feeding mechanical dragon kind of does that.

"Calm. I mean no harm."

Bloodshot eyes briefly held his before refocusing back on the metal dragon. Its taloned feet were now firmly planted, its jaws shut, but the flaring eyes peered their way. The man wailed, fear taking hold as he pulled at his legs in desperation.

Nathair chuffed, the cough of pleasure soon followed by the huge neck pulling away, lifting her head, full of bloodied teeth, to look elsewhere. Laoch breathed a little easier as the dragon began to nuzzle the metallic aftermath of its battle with the artifice.

"It will leave you be, yes? Let me help." Laoch edged closer. It was now apparent the man's leg was broken, and likely pierced by a splinter from the trunk. He dropped to his haunches by the man's side and stretched a hand out towards the tree, making it obvious he was waiting for permission. An agonised nod ensued, and he heaved at the trunk. A three-inch piece of wood slid out from the man's lower thigh and over the top of the protruding bone.

"Seven Hells," said Laoch. The wound was far beyond his basic skills. He threw the trunk aside, the clunk accompanied by Nathair's crunching of metal segments. Sura coalesced at his side while he wondered what to do next. The already delusional tribesman screamed; his screams even stopped Nathair's feeding for a second.

"Sorry," she said. "I wasn't thinking." Laoch felt her touch on the back of his neck as she faded away, the vestige of her spirit sliding into the spear. In that moment, Sura had felt stronger to him, her vitality fully recovered.

Where did she regain that? From Nathair?

A weight suddenly sat heavy in his stomach, and the Ranger pushed intrusive thoughts away.

"Are we clear, Ecne?" he said, looking over to where he'd left the acolyte. He received an all-clear in response. "Over here. I need to save this man before he shits himself to death."

"Fine." Ecne rose, scanning.

Laoch smiled at that. The young woman had worried him after they discovered the Gods' weapons, yet she remained resilient.

Maybe questioning was her way, just the answers not always forthcoming how she expected.

Laoch's hopes were crushed by Ecne's grim expression as she approached, but the acolyte dropped to her haunches, ignoring the mumblings from the tribesman as she laid hands around the injury. After a minute, she stood and pulled Laoch away as the man's ravings stilled and his eyes rolled back, lids shutting.

"He won't live. I think the blood loss is far too high. The bone nicked an artery. Beyond a meister's skill, never mind a sawbones like me."

Laoch grasped Honour's spear, nodded to Ecne, and called to Sura in his mind. Hopefully it worked both ways.

"I do not like to ask, but can you enter the wounded man's mind like you do mine? We need to know whether we are wasting our time."

Sura slid into his thoughts. *"I can try, though I do not feel it is right. Wait."*

Laoch felt another strange weight fall upon him, a power comparable to Justice at his side – Honour's presence. Remaining quiet, he waited.

"On balance, and with the man's impending death being such a waste if any knowledge is lost, Honour feels it is for the best. But it is not something I feel good with, Laoch."

"I understand – and agree. If you went too willingly, you would be stepping away from the Sura I ...."

"Love? Death brings a clarity of the spirit, of mind. Uncluttered. If only I could have seen that before."

Sura slid out of his mind, a final lingering wisp of spirit caressing his thoughts before she flowed, low and nearly invisible, along the ground to slide into the man's head.

Again, he was enthralled, yet concerned, by her strength.

—

The pain overrode all his thoughts. Nsint, as he named himself, rode a storm of raw nerves pulsing to the beat of a dying heart. Sensing the man's spirit, Sura let her *being* touch upon his. Their *self* connected, and soothing words spilled from her imagined lips. Nsint, well aware of what the injury meant, had accepted his fate. The memories of a past hunt and subsequent death of a friend to the crack of a beast's horn sat high in his thoughts.

She formed an image, allowing Nsint to paint upon it a memory of his family, and a goodbye. Pushing back the tears, Sura let him work. The common language of family soon spilled into a deeper trust as she forged his thoughts into the picture – one not written, but spoken, as it would have been heard by those he loved.

An innocent man just trying to survive and care for his loved ones.

Sura wrapped the scene in her mind, understanding the heaviness of the burden, but also the honour of carrying it. Sending a warning first, she formed a second image. Nsint's mind railed until soothed by her touch as she removed the immediacy. Keran, his appearance for once more in the form of the spirit Captain rather than the dragon-scaled Spirit Walker he wrestled with, stood, his armour shining white, the longsword, tip down, pointing forwards. Palpable fear bled from the wounded man, recognition entwined with dread. Sura sent a tendril of her *self* to wrap the image and shrink it down, inviting Nsint to lay his own imprint upon it with the promise of sharing his goodbye – the price to be paid.

For a bribe it is, though honour declares I will share it whatever.

The man's heartbeat slowed. The blood flow nourishing the man's spirit faded, but his mind reached out. A picture formed of a great hall and a mighty winged throne. Upon it sat a Constructor, and about it, more of their kind, though their armour was *different*, a sense of wrongness difficult to place as the man faded. On his last breath, the scene pulled out, spiralling through the hall. A glimpse of an artifice, lost as she rushed backwards out through a doorway. Grass and trees flittered through her peripheral vision, mixed with fleeting twisted figures and forms Sura could not hold. But the building, yes. That she could see. She grabbed and held its solid lines, etched into her spirit image, as Nsint died.

Sura sensed the spirit, the soul, detach. Expecting something akin to her, she felt a surprise and joy as Nsint spread wide, stretching out. That which was *him* merged with the air to drift amid the trees and foliage. She felt Nathair stir, and Keran soothe the beast.

His spirit was not like mine. Is that Honour's doing? Or my will?

"Both," came the smooth, whispered reply from Honour's sigil. *"In unison. And there is more to come."*

Sura reformed next to Laoch, her eyes on the last twitch of Nsint's body.

"I have a burden, Laoch – a request – to share something with his people. Honour has directed me how. In return, Nsint showed me Constructors in this city. There is a palace—" Sura stood to one side, eyes closed as she focused, pointing the way. "—in that direction. I saw many Constructors, though it did not feel the same as when we were around the Captain's armour. It is hard to put in words."

"How far?"

"The city is vast compared to Erstenburgh. Perhaps half a day on foot?"

"And by dragon?" asked Ecne.

"We will see."

—

Oisin sat upon the roof's edge, spyglass locked on the tribesman's body. To the north, a patch of ground, smashed and trampled by a metallic dragon whose head now hovered behind him, peering over his shoulder.

"She is learning," croaked Keran, his scaled hand upon Nathair's nostril, which protruded from the solid metal snout. "Without her, your spirit would be tainted, twisted, like my passenger."

Oisin let the spyglass drop to his knee. "It is still raw. I feel the joins where Sura and Fate worked upon them. My soul has been violated."

"Has it changed your path?"

"Path?"

"Are you Fate's now? Or do you remain unbonded?"

"I would turn that back on you, Keran. Are you Nathair's? The destruction below seemed unbound."

"You can see I battle the spirit, Oisin. She remains bridled, but wild at times. Without me, your soul would be powering her wings, Ecne the legs, and no doubt Laoch's, the rear."

Oisin snickered as he looked back to Keran. "In another time, I would have looked to you as a kindred soul. One to share a campfire and a drink with."

"If you live through this, I am sure I can train Nathair to sit. They come."

Nathair's snout released a gassy cloud. The smell of phosphor and dragon's fire caused Oisin to cough as he lifted the spyglass. Far below, a ragtag group approached the new clearing. It didn't take them long to locate their compatriot's body. A wail shattered the silence, brief, cut short as an orange glow rose about the body. Whomever had cried out sat gazing upon the light, hand raised, their fingers spread within the light. Sura had wanted to be there, and he touched Honour's spear at his side, Laoch having left it there while resting with Ecne behind the dragon's tail. Emerging, Sura gazed down upon the scene, a smile playing upon her lips.

"She sees," was all she said, and wrapped her arms around herself.

Oisin let the silence hang. The balm of an act of decency soothed his frayed nerves a little as his mind wandered back to the Constructor's house and the spider-like creatures inside. The venom burned still, yet remained calm, contained by his own will, strengthened by Fate and Sura. Yet it sat there, watching and waiting, ready to strike again. He held so much faith in those he travelled this path with, but the venom already seeped doubt and failure into his mind whenever it could.

He turned, ready for sleep, when Keran caught his gaze. The spirit watched him intently, his head on the half-turn, scaled eyelids blinking. Oisin shook his head, a rueful smile in place as he left the two spirits to watch the events below.

20
WHERE AN ENEMY HIDES

INNEALTÓIR, REALM OF THE
CONSTRUCTORS

"There."

"I can't ... yes. Got it. It moved?"

"Yes, though it appears different to the artifice we found in the house," replied Ecne, one hand on her hip, the other holding Laoch's spyglass. She pointed to the cracked roadway entering the gardens and handed the instrument back to the Ranger.

Once Ecne described the spot, he caught the twitching brass leg. "Got it. How big do you reckon?"

"I'd judge around twelve feet wide, ten feet tall," replied Ecne, her hands automatically shaping the artifice's breadth and height.

"There has to be more," added Oisin. "But if Nathair flies overhead to search the area, surely the Constructors will pick her out and either panic or celebrate. Either way, they'll be prepared. And we do not yet know how she'll react if there's a fight."

"We need to be subtle. Rangers, not the soldiers we've been," mused Laoch. "And leave Ecne behind, within crossbow range of the bloody mechanical beast thing."

"You can't leave me." Ecne had both hands on her hips, lips twisted in thought as her tongue played along the inside of her teeth. "Sorry, but what if this information or weapon you're searching for is written down? Can you decipher anything complex, Oisin? Like a meister's instructions, or a set of plans? You need me there, or at least a way for me to get hands-on with whatever you find."

"We work this both ways." Oisin winced, scraping nails against his neck as his internal anger rose with his frustration. "But you'll need to lead, Laoch. My mind is unable to hold on to anything ... challenging. We search for a way in, scout the grounds, and signal Ecne over if it's the right thing to do."

"Agreed." Laoch ignored the peeved glare from Ecne. "Besides, if your arse gets an arrow up it, Sura won't forgive me."

"Damn right," cut in Sura, striding out from below the dragon's chin beard.

"Stay here, watch that bloody machine. If it moves our way, you have my permission to bring Wisdom's wrath down upon it as a warning for us to get out. Got it?"

"What if you don't come back? If they find you?"

"Then you ride with Keran, keep going until you succeed or fall. I don't want our people behind a glass wall on display, nor yours fed upon by these soul-eaters."

Sura's eyes flared with Honour's orange, and she sought eye-contact with Ecne. "This will end with blood on the battlefield. We need Nathair."

"Aye, what she said," added Laoch, and a grin cracked as he lifted Justice from its scabbard. He pictured his favoured composite bow and sensed the change as the sigil responded. "Except I probably would have told you that later rather than have left you shitting yourself."

———

The palace loomed, its twisting main turret of brass and stone jutting skywards. It hurt Laoch's neck as he gazed up, trying to find the top. Three others rose, though none matched its height. One was bathed in a glinting gold and silver circle as the moon shone from behind, another a contortion of disjointed stone the Ranger could not look upon. The final tower, rising on the right-hand side to sixty feet, was wrapped in a sinuous silver dragon body, culminating in a head from whose jaws a balcony jutted. He couldn't see the main structure, its purple and brass façade lost behind the cracked white walls that surrounded the entire building. Segments of the render had turned to dust upon the ground, exposing regular brick beneath. Close up, they were in as much disrepair as the city itself. Yet, somewhere inside, the enemy waited.

"Just hope they're not expecting company," whispered Laoch to himself.

"Sura?" he thought, feeling out for the spirit as she scouted the palace gardens. The wall was inlaid with the same restraining crystal as the foundry and house, and no response was forthcoming.

"Laoch."

He looked over his shoulder. Oisin waited in what was once a fountain of some kind, the central spout so bent out of shape he couldn't tell its original design. The First Ranger stood, leather boots planted where once water would have shimmered. Despite the slightly pained expression the man had worn since the venom bite, his eyes shone bright in the moonlight. He was signalling towards the eastern side of the wall. Laoch peered over into the wall's shadow, and spied Sura. The spirit elf shifted, aiming now for where he stood and casting the faintest of moon shadows as she walked.

Best not to dwell on it. She's here. What else could I ask for?

On her arrival she crouched next to him, her eyes distant until Laoch felt the connection and an image flowed from her touch into his mind. It moved, as if he was seeing through her eyes, as she flitted from cover to cover within the grounds. Unseen, barely a passing flicker of her presence, yet still she behaved as if she was alive – a Ranger, and an elf.

"No guards at all. Nothing responded to my presence. I felt spiritfire within the palace, tainted, like the venom that affected Oisin, but not individually as powerful ... watered down," she whispered.

"Were there many?" Laoch asked.

"I could not say. The flow was strange, intertwined. This building is old. Much older than what we have seen before, and bereft of the crushed crystal that rejects me."

"And the artifice, the gate guard?"

"Dormant, but there is some spirit akin to the other artifices within it. There is another on the inside," she replied.

Sura then touched him with a second memory. A curved hull, much like a crab, squashed against the floor, four legs on either side with one huge claw out front. Two crystalline eyes caught the moonlight, both on immobile stalks that rose from the front of its shell.

"Then we go over the wall," Laoch replied, and signalled Oisin. He turned back to his chosen spot along the six-yard-high wall, where there was enough exposed brick to find footholds and handholds. The smooth top of the wall denied any chance of getting a rope secured, and Sura's *mind's-eye view* had portrayed no trees close by.

Laoch relayed what Sura had seen when the mountain man arrived. "We climb," he added, pointing.

Oisin grinned, his first easy smile since the bite. "Not there," he replied, and crumbled away a piece of the brick beneath the render. He tapped around to find a better spot. "This I can do."

Laoch let a breath free, pleased to be going second.

Oisin stowed Fate's bow and wrapped the stolen rope around himself. Digging his fingers into the handhold, he placed a toe next, then swiftly scuttled up the wall-face. Laoch stared, marvelling at the man's speed and skill.

When the rope dropped, Laoch tied it around his waist and waited for Oisin's tug. With the extra support, he was soon at the top. The rope remained taut, however, as Oisin waited on the far side of the wall, where he'd clambered down to brace himself. Laoch grimaced. They'd have to repeat the process on the way out or face the artifice.

A sudden tingle ran along his lower back. Laoch rubbed at the strangeness, and warmth spread along his glove. When he brought it around to look at it, whitefire danced along his fingertips, low and dull. He glanced down at the waiting Oisin. The same glow ran along his inner thighs and forearms. His sense of foreboding was heightened by a creak, metal upon metal, and a soft whirr. Then a pulsing light searched over the wall's eastern curve.

"Woken up," Sura whispered into his ear. Laoch almost lost his balance. "The guard, the whitefire, must be a kind of warning. Sorry."

"Aye, well, no need for that. Watch the palace, see if they respond," he replied before waving down to Oisin. The First Ranger frowned. "The guard – it's moving. Look at your legs."

Oisin glanced down, then batted at the dregs of white spiritfire running along the trouser seams. His fingers were soon similarly covered, though the energy remained weak. The volume of the clanks rose, leg tips driving into the manicured lawn as the monstrosity came into view. The foreclaw snapped, more a twitch than with menace, while seven of the eight legs moved in jerk-filled unison, the eighth held high, whirring in frustration. Despite its staccato movements, the mechanical beast made unerringly for Oisin's newly acquired position behind a thick, clipped bush, cut to resemble a woman's crowned head.

Oisin ran, keeping the foliage between himself and the multi-legged guard, weaving to slide behind a working fountain. The crab-like beast altered course, sidestepping around the shaped bush, only for Justice's flaming red arrow to crash into its rear legs. Laoch drew another that flared in the night before he dulled the red glow with a thought, then loosed it, aiming for the same joint. The spiritfire tip drove in, slicing the leg clean off and leaving the creature yawing towards its left, where only two legs now operated.

Up high, Laoch had just drawn another arrow when a flash of green caught his eye. He spotted a bolt flying down from Ecne's rooftop position to smash into something against the outside wall. He looked down and found a brass artifice leaning against the bricks beneath him. Its hooked leg tips had dragged the mechanical guard within striking range of his back, but Wisdom's spiritfire coursed over its upper shell, causing its legs to twitch. Still, its claw snapped out, slapping Laoch's back and sending him tumbling off the wall and into the garden.

Hands lashed out, orange-laced and solid. Grabbing hold, they pulled his forearms back. Laoch's desperate fingers grabbed the wall's curved edge as Justice fell to the ground. A whisper of Sura's breath graced his cheek, and Honour's spear warmed his back. As a huge, rusty-edged claw rose above the wall, Laoch fumbled, one-handed, for the weapon. Wisdom's arrow snapped into the rear of the artifice's raised eyes. Crystals shattered and the metal casing melted as spiritfire burned. Under the shower of hot metal and stone, Laoch's grip on the wall broke. As he fell backwards, his fingers wrapped around the spear's tip. With no spirit hands to catch him this time, he whipped the God's weapon from over his shoulder and called for the weapon to reform. To his relief, the curved blade of a war axe hooked over the wall's edge, catching his fall.

"Bloody hell!"

As he clung on, he heard the mechanical beast's legs scrape at the wall's top before it lost its purchase and toppled down to the ground on the other side. Something pressed against his boots' soles, and Laoch glanced down to find Oisin's concerned, pained face halfway up the wall. The First Ranger was balancing on the severed leg of the guard artifice, which lay smoking behind him, legs shuddering.

"I think we may have woken up the neighbours," he said, sliding down the axe's haft before hooking it off. Working together, they reached the ground. Behind them, the palace lit up as whitefire erupted in the lanterns stationed around the multiple windows and the main entrance doors.

"You could say that," replied Oisin.

21
A QUEEN'S WILL

THE WHITE PALACE, ERSTENBURGH, BRANDSHOLD

Queen Erin gripped the throne's arms tight as the weight of the Union bore down upon her. More so since the smaller throne at her side loomed large in her mind. Its emptiness spoke of sadness and loss, an absence, long wished for, now soured by guilt.

Pushing herself up from the gilded seat of power – a symbol she had already used to its maximum today – she walked down the steps, eyes locked on the large meeting table she'd had built. Its wood and varnish still shimmered with newness. A fresh beginning for *her* vision of the Union, not the Gods' Houses'.

If only.

She eased the chair out herself, shooing away the servant, who raised an eyebrow. Its high back matched those of the seven others, now inhabited by the Lords and Ladies of the Houses, as she took her position in the Gods' Council for the first time. Expecting animosity, she received only the whiff of fear – and dread. She was, after all, the first outside of the Council to *know* some of what they knew.

But not all. You still hide much under those damned ceremonial robes. It lies somewhere in the Forbidden Library, alongside the stolen glances and withheld thoughts.

"Queen Erin," Lord Penance intoned, his cane on the table beside the cup of water he sipped from. "Thank you for your patience with us. We are still reeling from events, the ripples of which still cause issues within our Houses. And the new table – well, it's impressive."

Lord Penance let his semi-blackened hand fall upon his House's sigil, inlaid into the wood; each of the places bore each House's mark. Jacka had provided the usual positions about their own tables, relayed from the House of Penance, and Erin had done her best to ensure it wasn't adhered to. A first step.

"No matter, High Lord. We are here now." She waved the servant away, and waited for the young man to leave the room and close the door. "I am sure you all believe the prime has eyes and ears everywhere, and that this room is being spied upon. Jacka assured me, before he left, that this was not the truth."

"Ah," said Lady Fate, catching the queen's eye with a raised hand. "A promise made to ensure we are aware of your candid view of the Council. To put us at ease, though we meet within the Crown's household instead of ours. A choice made to put us in our place, I assume."

Erin blinked, unused to having her motives questioned, or being spoken to as a near equal within her palace – by anyone other than Lord Penance. She steeled herself. It was good Jacka was not present. He would have butted in, riding to her defence when she needed to stand her own ground.

"Absolutely," she said, and placed her hands upon the table. "Correct. Have I lowered your status, Lady Fate? Or raised mine?"

"Hah, still feisty," came the reply. "Good. We're going to need that. Neither, my Queen. I foresee a new beginning."

Lord Penance raised his withered hand, the hint of a smile playing at the edge of his lips. Lady Fate squirmed into her seat as she settled in for what came next. "Queen Erin has stated that the queen, as Crown of the Union of Brandshold, should hold a place on this Council. Insisted would be a better description ..." He let a little laugh escape, eyes alight with mirth. "I have had my say on this. We need to secure the Houses to ensure our flocks do not deny us, as that would be disastrous. And for that, we need solidarity across state and religion."

The queen let the tip of her tongue slide across her bottom lip. "I understand that you may be reticent. But know this: should you remain divorced from the Crown, and my laws and matters of state, conflict will arise. I have had little time to absorb all you have hidden from my people, and I'm sure you have more to reveal. But I am no fool. You continue as you are, then I will speak up for my subjects based on what I *assume* rather than on what I *know*. It would be better for the truth to be laid bare, for us to face the Constructors unified."

Erin made sure each was aware she was speaking to them as she met the eyes of each Lord and Lady, judging, and being judged. Penance held sway over the Council, but they were powerful people. Naysayers would cause rifts they could ill afford.

"Threats?" said Lord Hope, face and hands sending very different signals. Erin struggled to read where he was heading. "We faced down one of the dragons of the veil, my Queen. Threats mean little—"

"Do they? I speak of my disquiet with the Houses amid rumours of disbelief about the Unspoken's dragon. Doubts about the Houses' word on the Unbelievers. What then, Lord Hope?" As Erin's cheeks flared, she reined in the rest of her anger, just in case.

"You wouldn't—" he replied.

"Hah, yes, the queen would." Lord Penance shifted his chair backwards, his hips hurting without his touch upon the cane. "And we'd deserve it. I have hated this mummery for far too long, but the façade must continue. Lady Honour, if you would."

Honour bowed her head and raised her hands to reveal a piece of Wyrding crystal. Justice, Hope and Wisdom gasped.

"You cannot …" started Lord Hope, but any more words were cut off by Lord Penance's glare.

"What is going on?" asked the queen. The masks had fallen, three of the Houses clearly shocked by Honour's action. Only Fate and Death remained impassive, expectant, even. Erin filed that away, recognising the true order of the hierarchy within the Seven. "Please explain."

"This is a Wyrding Stone," Lady Honour placed the crystal upon the table. "Or a piece of one. Mine. Shattered by the evil spilled from a Constructor spirit when calling their own down upon us. If you believe dragons truly exist, and the Magi brought us here, then ask yourself by what means, my Queen. They did not fly, walk or ride. They fled from another realm, a place beyond the veils that separate our worlds. These stones are what the Magi used to form a breach between our two worlds, to pull back the curtain."

"Lady Honour." Lord Justice stood, hands pressed to the table as he leaned forwards. "Please, no more."

She dismissed his words with a glance, disdain borne from an inner pain that flickered in pulses across her cheeks. She let an orange glow flow from her fingertips to swirl in ribbons in the air, mingling the lines into a braid she then placed upon her hair. Mesmerised, Queen Erin gasped, hand halfway to her mouth before she caught herself.

"Spiritfire," stated Lord Penance. "Others would call it magic, I suppose. Leeched from our own souls. An energy the Magi manipulated and used to cross the realms, to forge the Seven Veils and protect us."

"I don't understand. Have you always been able to do this? Why aren't you fighting the Constructors? I – I …"

Lord Penance reached out with his hale left hand, leaving it to hover above the queen's forearm, before withdrawing it as Erin gathered herself in. A smile reached his aged lips as she swallowed and sat up straight, smoothing her royal garb.

"Why show me this now? After a thousand years of hiding?"

"Because," said Lord Justice, "now you know, we *have* to let you join our little Council, eh, Lord Penance? You sneaky bastard." The tone was affectionate, and Justice added a guffaw. "We'd have done it anyway, but now we've cut through the crap. Sorry, Your Majesty. Cut to the chase."

"Forgiven. I assume you've never heard General Zendril hold a conversation in my presence. Is this true, High Lord?"

"Of course it is." Erin caught the silent tut at the end of Lord Hope's words. "No choice in the matter. Did you foresee this, Lady Fate – a way to forestay those who disagree? Don't answer. I for one, do not want to know where you weft and weave. I vote yes, and as we know Lord Wisdom does what he's told, I assume we are unanimous?"

Lord Wisdom's cough and nod, soon followed by the rest of the Council, left Lord Penance with the final approval. "And I say yes. So done."

"That it? The great Council of the Gods is more like the palace Court than I thought."

"This is a good day," added Lady Death. "Now, Lady Honour. You have more to share."

Erin looked across to Lady Honour, her hair still aglow with the spiritfire garland, but whose eyes filled with tears she swiftly blinked back.

"My Queen, the Seven Veils are a barrier. I believe you've read enough to know this, yes?" Erin nodded, casting her thoughts back to the Seven's sacrifice. "But they weaken over time. The spiritfire drifts and loses its potency. The Seven tasked us, the Leaders of our Houses, to maintain the veils. Without this, we would soon be exposed to the Constructors' hunters. Even if they know where we are, they must still force their way through the veils. Vital time for us to delay and prepare."

"Yes, like water dripping from a tub?"

"A good analogy, my Queen. Seven Veils, seven drips. We feed the veils, top them up via the Wyrding Stones. It is why the flocks are essential."

Queen Erin rocked back in her chair, pieces slotting home amid recognition of another great deceit.

Not just a lie, but one built to steal from those who worship.

The tears rolled down Lady Honour's cheeks, and as the shock rolled over her, Erin witnessed as all seven of the Houses' Leaders bowed their heads, shoulders sagging. The pain was palpable. With that insight, Erin's role was laid bare to her: she had to shoulder the burden these people carried, lift it from them, allow the Seven Houses the freedom to act.

Unify my banner.

Let us pray.

—

Lady Honour stepped in beside Lord Penance as they awaited the carriages, her eyes red-rimmed, her body held stiff.

"Yes," he said, the lightest of finger-touches upon her sleeve, decorum allowing little more before the royal servants. "I know."

"Will you join us, Lord Penance? I think I need you there, if things go wrong." Green eyes flitted his way, bloodshot and needy.

The High Lord shifted his hip, allowing his sigil to ease the pain in the other with a sliver of spiritfire. But it could not touch the pain that wracked the Lady next to him. Word of Nesca had reached his ears, and standing by Lady Honour now, he sensed the loss ran deeper than her protégé's soul death. Closeness to another within your House was not denied, but the Lady held a burden of knowledge she could not fully share until her future replacement had been chosen from the priests-in-waiting. Keep your secrets close, closer than your lovers, or all else could wither. Such a weight. One that had driven him to choose chastity after leaving his wife. Though he doubted a body such as his was worthy of love anymore.

"No, Lady Honour. I think it would be best for you to be alone. Nor Lord Justice. I feel his empathy would be lacking. No one to smite to make it better, so to speak. You must face this first step by yourself, but I will do all I can to help you heal." The finger touching her sleeve again, the High Lord turned to offer a mummery of hope when his heart felt nothing but concern. Honour's veil was their last defence, and the glyph would not reform without Honour's shaping. Her wound from the Constructor's poison wept. Should she fall, her mind and body unable to heal, then the House would be of little use until he trained another. She was dangerously on the edge, and he saw Lady Death as her last real hope.

And damn this conscience. Do I ask too much?

"Take this carriage, my Lady. I will await the next."

Lady Honour, her body language monotone, lifeless, stepped up to take her place. Orange robes spread across the bench seat, and she stared ahead. Lord Penance knew it wasn't anger; more, dejection. A refusal to look back and accept her fate for fear she would crack before her flock.

"She's close, Penance," Fate said from over his right shoulder, before appearing at his left. "What game do you play with this one? She is undeserving of the Overseer's machinations. That poison would have brought us all low." Fate picked at a seam in her robes, eyes flashing with unreadable thoughts.

"Are you casting a line to see what you hook? I thought more of you, my Lady, than that."

"I thought I was more poking the hornets' nest, to see which way they fly into the weave. She is pained, Lord Penance. Be kind."

"To whom? To the people under our shepherding, or to one of their servants?" He let out a heavy sigh and cast his eyes towards the fiery woman in the green robes. The closest, apart from Sneed, to someone he could trust. Almost. "Our opportunity for honesty has passed, Lady Fate. That stitch has been severed. I will be as gentle as I can be, but she must find the strength to heal the veil and the glyph. Before ..."

"Yes? Go on."

"No. You prod with your needles into the past. What's done is done."

"A thousand years of agony borne by a people now soulless, bereft of their past. There will be a reckoning, High Lord. Yes, we need to prevent it before the Constructors arrive. And we require the Schenterenta on our side in such a battle, their Spirit Walkers a near forgotten memory of their past, their ancient ones trapped within Honour's veil. But the cost ..."

"Is another burden we must bear."

"Lady Honour more than most. Remember that. A fallacy of a title when you consider such lack of it in what the Magi chose." Fate grasped his wrist, urging the High Lord to look her way despite the footman holding the door ready for him. "And you? You hold it all up, the miner taking the weight of the collapsing roof as his colleagues work a repair. Who is there for you?"

Lord Penance took the door from the footman, ushering the woman away with a well-practised glare. "Is this the time and place for such talk?"

"In your mind, unless you pull the strings, nowhere ever will be." Lady Fate, now ignoring the High Lord, strode into the carriage, usurping the carriage meant for him. The second Lady to stare ahead, refusing to engage as the horse gently pulled them away.

Lord Penance leant upon his stick as the Lady left in a fit of mummery and deception.

And what was that all about? An attempt at sharing the weight upon my shoulders? Or a request to do so?

22

EVEN DEATH MAY DIE

"They are in trouble," stated Ecne, sighting down Wisdom's crossbow, accepting the closeness of what she saw as Wisdom's work. Unlike the raw power resident within Laoch's maul, and the subtlety of Honour's sigil, Wisdom appeared to use guile and – dare she say it – *science* in its workings. Direction, accuracy and adjustments to enable rather than overpower. Without looking over her shoulder, she knew Nathair's snout hovered above her, the air hotter, likely a cloud forming as the dragon artifice vented gases from within.

"Apparently," replied Keran, his voice floating near Ecne's ear, divorced from the beast behind. "They seem to have a talent for it."

"Says the spirit that broke our veils to find his own."

"Ah. I never said they weren't kindred ... spirits. Heh." The gases streamed, almost obscuring Ecne's view as Nathair and Keran laughed as one. "They come, Acolyte. I can feel the *soldiers* leave the palace. Tell me, what do you see?"

Ecne, noting Keran's choice of words, peered down Wisdom's sighting rail. The image drew close – or was she going to meet it? Either way, four Constructors, going by their armour, emerged from the palace with mini-bows and buckler shields to hand. The armour, though, was not quite like those she'd seen back on Brandshold. It lacked the shine. The craftsmanship, clearly efficient and functional, possibly meant it remained light upon the body as they ran towards the burning artifice.

"I see guards. Four. Their armour does not match your people's. I thought that your ..."

"We called them Sealgairs – hunters. And yes, they wore copies of the one I *inhabited*. But it was a thousand years old. They shine to reflect spiritfire out, and inwards to contain their detached twin spirits. These do neither."

Nathair's neck stretched upwards while her crystalline eyes glinted with spiritfire. The glow gave the mechanised beast an even more disconcerting level of implied threat.

"Nathair and I concur. They are not Constructors."

"Human?"

"No. Or, at least, not fully. We need to be closer. Remain vigilant, Acolyte."

With the smell of hot oil, Nathair's great wings opened and flecked skin stretched across metallic bones to catch the air as she leapt upwards. A second rush of wind beat against Ecne's back, carrying with it the heat and spiritfire of the artifice's efforts. Doing her best to ignore the great dragon rising above her, she peered again along the weapon's rail. Wisdom's touch upon her mind drew her sight towards the approaching guards' elbow and knee joints as they ran.

"Is that? No ... no."

—

The first bolt crashed into the dead artifice's outer hull. The crystal tip exploded with whitefire, and a metal shard flew over Oisin's head as Laoch pulled the man down. A second bolt flew over. It sailed straight through Sura as she stood above them, fully formed and making herself an obvious target. As a second quarrel spiralled towards her, Sura chose that moment to throw herself to the ground. It exploded against the wall behind.

"Won't fool them forever," she said. Her fierce grin reminded Laoch of when she fought in the barracks' yard with Topsun. Full of pent-up frustration with a need to release it, but by what means when you are but a spirit?

With no time to think, Laoch tapped Oisin's shoulder and indicated to go right. His first thought was to split the guards' attention. Not always the best tactic when you don't know your enemy, but they had Ecne and her crossbow. Separating gave her a greater chance of sighting a target without them in the way.

Laoch crouched, waiting for the Constructors to round the burning brass legs, still twitching in the heat. He expected them to move wide and approach slowly. But no. They tore past the legs with no mind to the heat. Nor, it appeared, to the sword in Laoch's hand. The guard had dropped the handbow, and the thick, heavy-bladed broadsword now in its hand crashed down towards Laoch's head. Laoch burst upwards, Justice – now in the form of a short sword – riding the attacking weapon's blade edge as he parried and slid inside to slash downwards at the soldier's breastplate. As the sword bit into the armour, the clang of metal against metal took Laoch by surprise. The Construct staggered backwards. Instead of pressing the advantage, Laoch rose to take a defensive stance as his eyes struggled to factor out the flames against the night. He paused, searching for the likely second assailant.

"On your right!" Sura shouted, appearing beside him, spear raised in one hand as if to parry as a second guard barrelled in. The sword sliced through the spirit spear and onwards, into her hip. Sura, feigning being hit, threw herself down while the guard toppled forwards, his heavy blade having struck nothing but air and spirit. Laoch drove his short sword into its neck, biting deep between helm and shoulder, and the armoured figure stumbled and fell. The blade, though, had crunched into something far more solid than flesh. Black liquid spurted out over the blade, and Justice glowed in response to the white light that leaked from the wound. Laoch spun, sensing the other guard had recovered.

It drove onwards without any fear of Laoch's weapon, the notched sword sweeping towards his head. Laoch rocked back as Justice infused his arm. His muscles screamed as they moved faster than they ought to catch the blade before it ended him. His other hand grasped the guard's buckler shield as the momentum of the soldier's blow sent him backwards onto the ground. He shoved a foot into the armour's crotch, and the soldier flew over his head. Green light seared the air, crashing into something to his left. Laoch prayed Ecne's aim was true when Oisin's grunts rose in volume.

Laoch spun onto his front and rose to find the stricken guard on all fours. He chopped his blade down onto its rear leg, urging Justice to empower the edge. Metal shattered as he severed the limb. The soldier collapsed, its silence eerie.

"Down, Laoch!"

Laoch dropped, swinging his sword. Air whistled over his head, and his blade bit deep into the legless soldier's hip. Laoch rolled away, his body sliding through Sura's legs as she stood above him, and rose to his feet. Sura's spear was again whole, and held ready.

The night lit up with the flare of a second green quarrel ramming home, accompanied by the clash of metal upon metal that indicated Oisin still fought.

Laoch's guard, distracted, attempted a defensive stance as Sura's spear and body swirled towards him. Justice roared in Laoch's mind and fury drove the sword blade through the armour's metal to sever the other foot. Liquid black again spurted, covering the blade. Justice's fire boiled the concoction, and the air filled with a familiar acrid smoke.

Like Nathair's breath.

The soldier collapsed, no sound other than the clatter of armour. No scream; just silence. Laoch's skin crawled.

As he rose from the ground, blue light announced that Fate's weapon was joining Oisin's defence. Laoch spun and raced towards the rapidly tiring mountain man, who frantically parried and dodged. Hoping Ecne was watching carefully, Laoch aimed a strike to the guard's left upper thigh, slicing downwards. Red spiritfire raged as it parted armour, flesh and bone. The guard toppled his way. Oisin, punching forwards with Fate's hilt and a gauntleted fist, sent the Construct flying backwards.

"Laoch!" bellowed Sura.

The two wounded guards were crawling his way, hot black blood pouring from their severed limbs. Yet their eyeless helms were focused on him as they dragged themselves across the ground.

"Oisin!" he shouted, adrenaline pounding in his ears as Justice whipped up his desire to rend and tear. "They live on!"

Heavy of breath and mind, Laoch strode to one side. But both guards adjusted their courses, gauntlets digging into the ground to drag their wrecked bodies onwards. One began to stand, its stubbed leg grinding into the grass and soil, sword raised. Ecne's quarrel drove into its helm. Wisdom's spiritfire cracked the metal open, splitting the visor in two. Dead eyes stared back. Below them, a chin braced in metal links, stinking skin exposed upon cheek and forehead. A sickness squirmed in Laoch's stomach, matched by the anger and pain in Sura's scream. She drove the spirit spear into the thing's forehead, its tip burning with orange fire. The head exploded into a mire of rot and spiritfire-infused wire.

Shit.

Sura stood stock still, the spear's tip smoking. Fierce cat-like eyes turned to lock with his, and a grin split the elf's face.

Laoch shook himself, not allowing himself to be hooked into the moment with danger still present. He brought the short sword's blade down to finish the second crawling armour, severing the head. A twitch in his mind echoed as he exposed wire and vertebrae. The body finally coming to a silent stop.

"Laoch," said Oisin, the man's breath heavy with effort. "The palace."

He spun. The mountain man, his blue blade driven deep into the back of a guard's helm, was twisting, and grunting with the effort.

"Eyes on."

Laoch nodded. Justice's sigil seeped a little more of its energy into tired muscles, and he moved past the twisted artifice to watch the entrance.

"They must know. So why wait?"

"In fear, maybe?" Sura touched his mind, the caress belying the fury with which she'd defended him. "Laoch, did you see me? I could fight."

"How could I not?" Shifting his feet, he stole a glance at the warrior spirit who stood next to him, one hand resting on his. Heat rose in his cheeks, a sense of wonder and warmth milling through his body and mind. "And I felt your hands upon me when I was knocked from the wall. You are changing."

An inner heat flourished. His heart ached as the last few days crashed back into his mind's eye. Followed by a vertigo that overcame his senses as his thoughts roiled in a maelstrom of pain. Justice had chosen that moment to withdraw, exposing his grief. He staggered to the ground. Soft hands gripped his forearms as he began to fall.

"Laoch? I—" Sura's words swept over his mind, each touch gentle, a balm, recognising the agony and its cause. *"I should…"*

"No," he said, pushing himself up from one knee, one hand on top of hers, fingers wrapping in a way he'd never imagined possible. "I need this. Justice is letting me know the reality."

"Laoch, are you okay? Seen anything?" called Oisin, concern lacing his tone.

"No. Strangely, nothing," replied Laoch, blinking before recognising there was a change, but not where he should be watching. "Except Nathair has landed on the roof."

'Tainted.'

"The guards?"

'Yesss, they are … lesser.'

Nathair peered at the body upon the floor, her dragon sight drawing out numerous intertwined lines within the armour, each alight with whitefire, but rapidly fading. *'Stretched. Too thin and too long inside the dead to be food.'*

Keran tried to piece together the words and the sight, but little made sense until Nathair focused on a single point. An exposed neck, a milieu of wire and bone leaking whitefire.

"Was that once human?"

'Yes. A body reformed, mechanical. Riding the spiritfire.'

"Like you?"

'NOT like me. Flesh made unalive. Mere cogs, flesh and wire, imbued with a disconnected spirit long dead. Mind gone, lost amid the dead meat. A mere follower.'

Keran, taking the words to mean this new creature did not think, but acted as told, felt the Spirit Walker's indignance at his words, and a creeping sense of disquiet at his presence. Soon, she would make another attempt to wrest control. Perhaps Laoch had been right about the need to balance her feeding to prevent the spirit's strength rising too fast.

Or I need to consume her, become one. No longer ride the beast but become it. Am I ready?

Needing to move Nathair's thoughts onwards, he contemplated the palace and those within.

"Our kind, are they inside? If we are to rescue them, inform them of the Seven, then we need to know whether there are more of these abominations."

'And strange that we are doing so by attacking the City Palace. But yes, I can sense their presence, though I do not know them. There are more of the unalive in the entranceway. Too many. Dormant, waiting. Wrong.'

"Then this is our work to be done."

'Work? Yes, though enjoyable. These are not ... right. The Fleshmaster would not allow such thingsss. He would see them as your favoured word – abominations.'

And for all the pain in the words, the vision drilling into Keran's mind was of a dry cave, bodies bound in stained cloth, each marked with runes he could not read. A part of Nathair, long buried, brought forth by the unalive monstrosities that finally faded below them. Where the Spirit Walker-cum-dragon had said 'abomination', it had thought of a past. The song rites and a life laid out for all to honour. Except Nathair would never sing that song, the verses ending the moment she was wrenched from her Schenterenta body. Yet, he did not envision her death; more a separation of spirit and soul. As if another rode her body at that moment; one she craved, needed. A twisted belief that the dragon they rode, and the souls they consumed, would compensate for the grief and loss of another. An emotional poison sown by her maker, perhaps.

But I can ill afford sympathy. For all the painful memories, she is too far gone. I must push that aside.

With his urging, Nathair lifted her wings. Mighty, spiritfire-driven pistons thrust her upwards, only to twist, curling in on herself, and drop to land upon the ground before the entrance doors. A roar tore from deep within her ribbed throat. Gel and heat splashed against ornate double doors that rose to equal her height between columns carved into twisted visions of damned, imploring faces. Nathair's tail lashed, crashing through manicured trees, splitting bushes and scything a fountain's spout as she drove it into the brass-embossed stone. The metal spikes bit deep. The dragon pulled back, then swiped against the join. The boom echoed across the gardens. With a second thrum of her mighty throat, she screamed at the doors' defiance and thrashed again, drilling the tip between the doors, then heaving backwards. Stone split, brass scratched, and a shattered lock flew as the doors gave. Nathair opened her maw, exposing glinting teeth, and a rumble rose from deep inside. Dragon fire poured forth, sticky, angry, roiling into the hallway beyond. Engulfing the armoured guards as they twitched, helms rising, recognising and marking the threat.

Nathair pulled her head back, faceted eyes reflecting the orange flame engulfing the unalive as they raised swords and charged as fire raged along their armour. As she clamoured for a second fiery breath, Keran noted the energy each breath took, whittling the dragon's stores.

The first sword clanged against her scales. A raised paw slapped the guard aside, talons splitting the chest plate. Cooking meat and wire spilled to the marbled floor. A second attacked from the left, only to be greeted by a blue arrow crashing into its helm. Metal and bone exploded. The broadsword clattered to the floor. Nathair gathered her breath again and released a focused flame, using the thinner stream like a blade to slash across the charging guards. It bit deep, severing arms, cutting through neck guards. Heads and limbs slapped against the floor as she closed her jaws, cutting the fire off.

Keran eyed the carnage, mind reeling, thankful he and the Sealgair had not faced the mechanised creature at her full power. The doubts were strong, not helped by Nathair squeezing into the doorway, slamming her body into the architrave, desperate to get in and seek her masters.

"Calm, Nathair. Even you cannot enter. Your wings are too big. You will bring it all down, and endanger those you seek."

The dragon gave the doorway one last, mighty bash. The stone strained, but resisted, the weight of the building holding it fast.

"Settle down. My people will enter."

A snort. Derision, perhaps. A flame spout seared the ceiling, then the rear legs pulled the dragon clear of the entrance. Crumbling stone added dust to the smoke and flame pouring from the palace.

'Agreed.'

23
FIRST STEPS

HOUSE OF DEATH, ERSTENBURGH, BRANDSHOLD

"I fear there is no recovery."

Piercing grey eyes flickered towards Lady Honour, lips tight, a blackened hand falling upon her forearm with the gentlest of touches before withdrawing.

Lady Honour stared down at Nesca. The woman's brown hair was damp with sweat, the eyes beneath in constant movement under dried lids. Impulse took over, and her left hand cupped the woman's cheek. A thumb played along the smooth skin beside her upturned, freckled nose.

Lady Death turned away, letting the moment be hers, and eased down into the cushioned chair beside the bed while brushing away whatever lint threatened the uniformity of her black robes. Parting her lips, she let her mind wander. A tendril of power touched upon the priest-in-waiting's addled mind. Almost a ritual now, an act she performed twice a day. The balm of her caress soothed the whitefire lacing the woman's brain, calming the lightning arcs that fired off beneath her skull. Nesca's eye movements slowed, then came to a stop.

Lady Honour released a breath, pulling away her hand as she drew back her lips to fight the encroaching tears. A single drop ran across her sallow cheek, stark as the rivulet hydrated the dry skin beneath.

"Thank you," she whispered.

"Sit." Lady Death indicated the other chair next to the cell bed.

Nodding, Lady Honour sat, her public face gone, the private one betraying her pain.

"I could lie to you, but the words would be but salt in an already painful wound. I fear she was *Becoming* when the Constructor's taint took you, the backwash from the spiritfire lashing an evolving mind. Had you ...?" Death let the words hang, hoping to pull her away from the guilt. Eventually.

"Yes," Lady Honour blurted. "My decision had been made. Unbeknown to her, I had started the *Becoming*, quickened her mind. I had instructed Nesca to give a little less upon the prayer stone."

"Did she know?"

"No. As with all the Houses, we in Honour are careful. If she has not the propensity for the Wyrding, then we would be exposing someone only to have to silence them. Slow. As it should be. She had taken on the duties of transference with greater regularity, and the connections were forming." Lady Honour blinked back another tear, casting a finger to stroke away the moisture beneath her eye.

"Yet ... closer than just that." Lady Death didn't couch the words as a question, leaving Lady Honour an exit from the conversation, if she so wished.

The tide broke. Choked sobs stuttered into the bare room, echoing from the whitewashed walls. Lady Death reached out, pulled the woman close and settled her head against her shoulder. No words passed. Only raw breaths until the emotions exhausted themselves.

Lady Honour pulled a cloth from within her sleeve, wiping herself dry. She pulled away from Death's shoulder to lay a thankful hand upon a black-robed arm. "We …"

"Were lovers?"

Honour shook her wild hair, the grey streaks shimmering in the candlelight. "We sought comfort in each other. Nesca was never one for attachments, but she had an earthiness that kept me grounded. Lovers, perhaps, but on occasion." She looked directly at her counterpart. "It is difficult when we have so many secrets to hold in our hearts, is it not? How do we let go enough to love when we expose such deceit? Everything we do is a lie. Even the mummery with the queen. Lord Penance asked me to demonstrate the Wyrding crystal because of my pain, to drill home to Queen Erin the cost *we* pay. A sleight of mind, if you will, while hiding the price to our people." Anger flashed underneath the unkempt hair. Honour brushed her hair back, highlighting the slowly healing burns upon her right hand. "You know this."

Twisting her lips, Lady Death reached out, clasped both their hands together, and squeezed. "You twist and turn amid your emotions, Honour, as if avoiding the true problem. You grieve for Nesca, and the flock. Blame Lord Penance if you wish, though it was the Seven that laid down the scripture. But these are not what ails you the most. I feel it trapped inside you, but you must air it before it poisons your thoughts."

Honour pulled her hands away, pressing them tightly against herself, and gazed back towards Nesca. "I already voiced them to Lord Penance. I am raw, burned out. I do not know if …" The words fell away.

"A beginning, then. I may be able to help, but you will have to let me in." Lady Death let her hands fall to her knees, drawing back, her countenance serious, yet holding the warmth her flock needed. "It is the only way I can help."

Lady Honour's body tightened under the orange robe, emotions overflowing the dam she had set. "Has Lord Penance spoken to you, put you up to this? Are these his words spilling from your lips?"

With tongue pressed against her teeth, Lady Death sighed, and eased back her white hair to wrap behind her ears. What use would a lie be? "You knew he would intervene. But these are not his words, nor his thoughts. He wants you to heal, just as much as I do."

"To seal the veil, empower the glyph, save the realm."

"Of course. Though he also sees a need to heal your soul. As do I." Lady Death reached out and, curling her hand, with a gentle touch caught the tear rolling down Honour's pale cheek. "And you must trust that and let me in."

—

Meister Kinst stepped back; eyes cast along the line of metal pipes extruding from the long-jointed metal bone that ran the length of the huge wing. A thin, metallic material between each element shimmered in the sunlight finally peeping out from the thin clouds over the forest. She grasped one edge, running it between her fingers. The coarse, almost cloth-like material tore at her skin; it gripped in one direction, yet the nap was smooth in the other. It was all so far beyond what she knew that grasping at smoke was likely more achievable. It hurt to consider what Lord Penance was asking of her friend, the likely failure it would bring.

"Impossible," she whispered, teeth nipping at her tongue tip. "Impossible."

The repeat caught the grand meister's attention, whose hands dropped the mechanised joint she flexed between her cracked fingers – winter's wet, cold weather taking its toll. "Agreed. There is so much

I can learn from this, but to recreate it? Rebuild? It's not just a giant puzzle, but the mechanics, the way everything interacts, is so difficult to perceive." She pressed knuckles into her spine, easing her back.

"I'm wasting valuable time. I should be overseeing the mining and Erin's Wrath, not … fishing in the mud for impossibilities." Kinst kicked at the ground, a splash of mud soiling the last part of her green robe still free of dirt. "Bother."

A whinny caught their attention, and they turned as Lord Penance's priests hailed the approaching High Lord. The old man slipped from the saddle, landing with a wince upon the rock placed for his convenience, before sliding out his walking stick to press against the wooden batten leading towards the dragon skull entrance. Kinst pulled up her robes and strode over.

Arknold recognised the set to her shoulders and the determined walk: a meister's version of being on the warpath. "Damn. This isn't going to go well." Sighing, she pulled her own dirtied robe up from the floor, tucked it into her breeches, and headed off to intercept, knowing it was far too late.

"Lord Penance!" bellowed Kinst, boots splashing muddy prints as she strode after the High Lord. Give the man his due, he must have known what was coming. He stopped mid-step and, standing straight, rolled a shoulder as Arknold joined her university compatriot.

Expecting the Lord's wrath, the grand meister pulled her friend back by the shoulder, the eye-lashing she received, calmed by raised eyebrows and a finger to her lips. Scrunching her mouth, the meister nodded agreement, though her eyes still boiled, wrinkles pulsing, "Calm," mouthed Arknold.

"Grand Meister," said Lord Penance, bowing his head. "Meister Kinst. How can I be of help?" Though he chose to ignore Kinst's outburst, the man's slight smile plucked at Arknold's patience. Did it hold anything other than contempt for them, despite his supposed change of heart about their science?

"We need to discuss this ..." She waved a hand towards the metallic pieces laid out about the House, Leront's body. "And the impossibility of what you ask, Lord Penance."

"I didn't think science had any boundaries, Grand Meister."

The smirk riled her, and now Kinst squeezed her arm, recognising where this was going. "It does. Time is the true factor, High Lord. We have been shackled for a thousand years, yet you ask us to catch up in days."

That smile again, this time, sadder. The Lord's shoulders dropped. "True." He glanced over to the busy priests, his thoughts clearly mulling over something painful. "Hah. Follow me, both of you. But I warn you ..." The stick rose, jabbing towards them both. "Yanpet's fate, yes? This is between us. Any hint of a shared word out of place and ..." The High Lord didn't finish. The smile dropped to a grimace, and he slowly turned back towards the dragon's maw.

The tap of the cane tip upon the metalled floor echoed within Leront's neck as both meisters finally entered past the stone door inscribed with the Seven Gods layered upon each other.

On reaching another stone door at the end, Lord Penance stopped and rested the cane against his thigh. "Not. A. Word," he said sternly, and waited for their confirmation. On receiving it, he splayed his fingers upon the door. A purple glow rose between them, spreading across the inlaid carving. The grind of stone upon stone reverberated through the corridor, and the heavy door slid back.

Kinst and Arknold stood frozen, mouths wordlessly repeating silent nonsense.

"Are you coming in, or do you wish to remain ignorant forever?"

Kinst, glancing at her friend, took the lead and headed inwards. With Arknold's feet finally responding, she followed, stepping through the inner entrance to be met by the huge metal rib cage that held back the scaled covering of the dragon. Purple light flowed from the High Lord's hand and, once shaped into a globe, he tossed it into the air. Light washed over the length of the domed interior.

"Follow me," he said. "There's someone you need to meet."

By the time they reached the heartstone, the meisters were walking hand-in-hand, shaking, minds reeling with a thousand thoughts as the High Lord proffered two seats. "Sit. It looks like you need these more than I. Gowan?"

The heartstone pulsed. Gowan, cheeks scaled green, eyes balls of blue-tinged fire, coalesced within the crystal. "Here, Lord Penance. Where else would I be?"

"Is this enough proof, meisters, that science has not the answer to everything?"

"I ..."

"We ..."

"Quiet, and listen. You want to learn, then you ask only of the dragon, nothing else. I cannot accept any more than that. Hear me, Gowan? Keep to what we need to rebuild Leront, and only that."

"Rebuild?" said Gowan. "You mean, like fly?"

"That I can accept is a dream too far, spirit. But I need it whole enough to fool the Constructors."

"Ah," replied Gowan, her forked tongue running along her canine teeth. "A lure. Now that I can relate to. I like your thinking. So, we need wings to flap, a tail to swish and a head to rise. Leront retains much knowledge. I can gain that."

"Good. Then let's begin." Lord Penance let both hands fall upon the meisters' shoulders, a gentle tap. "Yanpet, yes?"

24
ARISING FROM THE ASHES

Sura swept past the dragon's taloned feet, sensing the anger it directed at the smoking bodies in the polished stone hallway. The pull of Honour's sigil tugged at her senses. Tendrils of their interconnected spirit, a dual energy, shared the same dread as the foul palace noted her presence and tried to draw upon her. She forged ahead, aware that Laoch and Oisin waited for a report on what lay inside, their Gods' weapons drawn ready, their patience thin.

No wonder the walls are not filled with the barrier stone, for it is, in itself, a feeder.

Sura glided amid the charred armour and the bodies they contained. Sickened, but accepting her role, she let her spirit mind touch upon some of the remains, only for Honour to quail and attempt to pull her away. Dismissing the sigil's misgivings, she slid a wisp of her *self* inside. It didn't take long for her to sense the emptiness of a stretched soul as it disentangled from the meat and mechanical mechanism within.

Old, thin. Not like the artifices' spirits – they no longer had a lifesong, their memories gone. These are even lesser, nothing but a partial soul contained within a façade of metal and flesh.

Withdrawing, she sensed Laoch's concerned gaze and turned to wave she was fine. She added a whispered, feathery touch upon his mind before proceeding. Two corridors spun out either side of a wide, grand staircase, empty except for dragon smoke and the dance of ash upon the warm breeze. She chose the right side, the closest to Laoch. As her connection to Honour stretched, the palace's regard pressed on her spirit.

Then it attacked. The atmosphere crackled with a *hunger*. Sura sensed Honour's shift. The tendrils spread, hardening to form a thin shell to ward off the assault. Honour then called her back, and Sura responded. She'd been at the edge of her limits. Perhaps Laoch could follow, bring Honour's spear to keep the connection close.

A pulse rode the connection to Honour and orange light streamed back, wrapping about Laoch before sliding into his skull. Schenterenta and human connected, sealed by the merest caress of power.

"I need you to bring Honour closer. The palace … it feeds like a Construct. It's trying to consume what I am. I need Honour's shield."

"Aye," he replied.

Sura knew the concern in his thoughts but revelled in the contact. She forced herself to withdraw, a thank you left in her wake as Laoch signalled to Oisin, who waited at the entrance. A low, sombre rumble from the floor grew in volume as he approached, the noise merging into a mournful wind. Whitefire seeped from the ashes, rising to swirl amid the gusts.

Sura locked her gaze on him and, forging a connection, insisted Laoch focus on her as he walked through the haze. The haze began to shift, roiling slowly before being drawn to the palace walls and absorbed into the marble.

When he reached her, Laoch raised an eyebrow, a slight smile across his face.

"Not afraid of a soul-eating palace?" she asked.

"Hardly anything to be concerned about, considering we may have a traitorous mechanical dragon at our backs," he replied, and broke contact to look behind him.

With Honour's sigil pulsing, and its glow encompassing her, the barrier between Sura and the palace was reinforced. Laoch followed behind the warrior spirit as she made her way along the ornately decorated corridor. Every stride was met by yet another statue or bust set into an alcove. Every one appeared to be a strained version of humanity – beauty and familiarity marred by the weird and wonderful. A smile with lips drawn back by hooked chains, one eye a swirl of metal, or a head ensconced in razor-sharp wire. Aberrations to a simple Ranger's eyes, and a marker of whatever the Constructors had become. The smell of charred flesh and metal from the entrance began to fade as the corridor curved back on itself, but the pungent mist returned as they arrived back in the main hallway.

Oisin sent a querying look their way.

"Madness," Laoch said as he pulled his cloak about himself, a chill rising despite the dragon's heat. "I do not understand this place."

"No, nor I. The stairs, perhaps?" added Sura aloud.

"Only within sight of Oisin, no further," he replied, letting her feel his concern.

Honour's glow lit the way as Sura took the first marbled step up the open stairway. A second rumble reverberated through the room – this one from Nathair's maw, the sound laced with Keran's touch. She understood the warning and warily climbed the stairs.

A balustrade came into view, as ornate as the corridor, each spindle a carved human. No. A spirit, writhing in agony or ecstasy – it was difficult to tell which – mouth wide and howling. Behind it was a shadow, a white glow amid the darkness. Sura now understood the rail marked the edge of a circular viewing gallery. Wary, with the palace's sickening hunger weighing her down despite Honour's shield, she ascended the last step, and echoed Laoch's gasp as a grand hall came into view.

"Oh." She gaped, struggling to tear her gaze from what lay before them. Her spirit hand reached for Laoch's. "Oh no."

Below them, a magnificent dragon lay stretched around the entire hall. Its silver-blue head glistened, teeth glinting as it rested upon the foot-long talons of its forefeet. The sheen of metal scales along its length caught their eyes. A sinuous neck stretched behind a huge dais, spikes rising, lengthening as they pierced the air above its back, then shortening along the tail to end with a bulbous, metal-shod tip.

"Bigger than Nathair," was all Laoch could manage before his eyes were drawn to the dais and the metal-boned throne that rested upon it. Wings erupted from both sides of the brass back, their metallic skin reflecting a rainbow sheen, framing the sheer-black armoured figure that sat there. By its side, a longsword pulsed, whitefire running along its edge, lighting the dragon and the room, yet leaving the occupant in ominous shadow.

Sura moved closer to the balustrade and, laying her hands upon the cold white stone, stared into the hall below. Lit by the sword stood more of the unalive, unmoving. An army of silent statues, waiting for orders.

25
WHEN GUILT IS EARNED

HOUSE OF PENANCE, ERSTENBURGH, BRANDSHOLD

"Are you sure this is the best way, Lord Penance? I feel as if I am intruding on your House." Queen Erin gazed at the empty pews within the prayer chamber, eyes running along the many worn cushions placed below the benches. Her back itched as thoughts intruded, of the scourge and other implements many of the penitents chose. She knew well enough the taste of such a whip; her uncle, now Duke of Ridth since her father's death, was an advocate of such pain. To free the soul, as he put it, though his need seemed bound by more self-loathing and spite than most.

"You are as welcome here as in all the Houses, my Queen. I understand you have recently visited Death's cells, so why not mine?" Lord Penance waited by the prayer stone, the raised dais at its side empty with morning supplications not due for another hour. "And he has repeated his request to see you."

"Do you feel it too, Lord Penance? The guilt?"

Queen Erin searched the High Lord's face for some form of answer, not trusting whatever words he chose to use. For all his support in recent days, the Overseer had an agenda of his own, which put the Houses' needs front and centre. If she was to cut the strings of this puppet master, she needed to read him better. In her eyes, the real truth would never be between them. There was much pain, though she doubted he had anything but the belief he was acting for the sake of his flock. She glanced up at the Overseer's version of the Unspoken's dragon. The scarlet beast was sinuous, its wings smaller than most, but the tongue that spoke of its evil, long and forked, was wrapped around the God's body.

But who tells the most lies, I wonder?

"Come, my Queen. The priests will be preparing this chamber soon. Not the ideal experience for one of Fate's children. This way." The High Lord waited for the queen to move, to overcome reluctance he well understood. "And as for guilt? My burdens are heavy, the weight of my flock hard to bear. This is but another day amid a thousand years, and I am simply one piece of the scaffold holding up our people." His cane tapped against the stone floor, and he led the queen to the dreaded stairs. He took the opportunity to cheat a little and allowed the sigil to imbue his hips and knees.

The queen smiled to herself, reading the test that sat before her. "For all my distrust of you, Lord Penance, I see past such falsehoods. The word you seek is keystone, and without your machinations, I fear the defence of my people would fail before it has started."

The tap of the cane stopped before he took the first step, and the High Lord turned to deliver a purple-toothed grin to his queen. "Sneed tells me you are the greatest of all the Regents. That we could not ask for anyone more astute to lead our people, strengthen our resolve. Even be the crutch the Seven Lords and Ladies need to prop their Houses. I thought him prone to exaggeration, though I have always admired your resolve. But I fear – no, I hope – that I misjudged you in the past. You are right to not trust me, nor anyone else, for that matter. But belief can heal cracks, forge the strength we are going to need to face the storm that approaches. We broke your faith in the Gods, my Queen, but not in the power of working together. We will only survive this through belief. The Houses must remain strong, to maintain the veils, to feed whatever spiritfire we can glean into ways to defend ourselves. And after, if the Constructors are defeated, then let the people choose what happens to the Houses." Lord Penance turned back and took the first step down the stairs. "I expect they will dwindle and eventually fall, the lies, perhaps, too much to bear. But people, my Queen, *need* to believe in something."

She watched the High Lord descend, each step taken carefully. Within the murk, though, she spotted the soft glow from the cane top that leaked between his fingers.

Belief? Sacrifices too. Who else will be given over to this cause, their names trodden into the mud, before this is over?

On reaching the next level, Lord Penance stepped aside and, resting his hands upon the cane, directing those about their business to continue and pay no mind. The corridor swiftly cleared as the queen emerged from the stairwell.

"I assumed you would prefer not to face all that bowing and scraping. It must prove tiresome. This way."

They walked side by side along the poorly lit murk of the corridor, the smells of must and damp assailing the queen's nose, bringing back memories of her time in Ridth and the cellars beneath the stronghold. Hide and seek, muck and dirt. A far cry from the political games she now played – and sometimes lost without realising it.

"In here," Lord Penance said, tapping the door. "It is unlocked, and we informed him at prayers you were coming."

"Prayers? He has joined your House?"

"Yes, though he spares the scourge for now. I think the distance from the Court has perhaps cleared his mind. Lady Death believes his head injury may cause a *clutter* within him, where thoughts are unclear and tumbling on top of each other. Here, he seems to have more clarity."

"Do you think ...?"

The Lord grimaced, his head twisting to one side. "That I cannot answer for sure, my Queen. But I would not be surprised if he suspects some of what we have done." He turned to leave. "I will return in a few minutes, unless you prefer for me to wait?"

"No, Lord Penance. I should be fine."

"Good."

The queen effected a small bow laced with a little gratitude, and lifted the latch to step inside, while the Overseer tapped his way down the corridor. She steeled herself, then opened the door to walk inside.

Adama sat on his bed, back stiff, hands upon his lap. He wore parade uniform, medals resplendent, and his eyes were focused solely on her as she walked in. He was everything she remembered from before the retreat and the Unbeliever attack upon his Honour Guard. His thick, grey hair was combed back and greased, a serious smile upon his lips. But his eyes were the betrayer; the haughtiness was absent. For all her old memories of a man so caught up in their own importance, there was an absence.

No. This is different. A sadness.

"Erin," he said, "I am pleased you could visit." He rose, holding his hands out low. She approached and let him take hers. As was his way, he kissed the back of each in turn. Then he stopped to stare into her eyes. Erin used all her resolve not to crumble there and then. Such a proud man, brought low by a wound. One she had built up in her own mind as the reason for her unhappiness. But it had never been deliberate. He'd never hurt her, other than by being so far from the prince she'd dreamed of as she grew up.

"Take a seat. I'm sorry my room is not to our usual standard, but I believe it has helped me think, have clarity." Erin sat at his behest, taking the chair next to the ink-stained writing desk that lay covered in parchment and notebooks.

"It is fine, Adama. Pay no mind. You seem ... busy."

"Yes, yes ..." He had made to sit, but a sudden light hit his eyes, and he reached past her to grasp a pile of papers. "I have been ... I have been analysing the defence of Ridth. Here. Take a look." The prince consort shoved the pile of papers towards her, tutting as a few slipped out of place before slotting them back in.

Queen Erin glanced at the first sheet, expecting the hand to be illegible, as it had always been, only to be caught by its precision. She mouthed the first words to show she was reading, before sliding the top sheet aside to examine the one below.

"This is very detailed, Adama."

He nodded vigorously. "Yes. Being here, I can focus. At least, that's the word the priests use. Clear thinking. I have more – though none are yet finished. I ..." The tumble of words suddenly stopped, the prince consort no longer looking at his collection of writings but at Erin herself. "I have been writing my memoirs. Hoping, erm, to recall why I am here. The blow ... my worries ..."

Erin rose from the chair to kneel at his feet and clasp her husband's hands in her own. "I am sorry. It was—"

"—necessary? That I can understand. I know I am not what I was, Erin. I am sure I disappoint you in many ways. But ..."

"You want to leave?" She squeezed his hands, as much to force her own tears back as to reassure.

"Leave? No. I hope to become the man I was … a leader, again … a husband you can be proud of, as I am of you. I worry that you sent me away, that I may have hurt you. The absences … did I? Have you sent me here because I did something to you?"

"No, Adama." She squeezed harder. "You have never harmed me."

It is I who have harmed you and, in turn, myself. A burden of guilt Lord Penance would be proud of.

Another flicker of life sparked in his eyes, and her husband and consort relaxed, relieved. "I feared I had. Is this for my benefit, then? To help me heal."

And now a lie, to compound it all.

"Yes. For your benefit. And I can already see it working. Stay here until we all agree you are ready. I believe you can return to yourself. And in the meantime—" She released his hand to retrieve the treatise from the floor. "—you can help me to oversee our defences."

"Yes. I would like that very much." Adama smiled and reached out a hand to cup Erin's cheek. "I believe in you. You know that, don't you? You are a light amid the void of the palace and its Court. If I were to help you in one way, it would be to advise you to let it shine brighter. Be seen."

Erin blinked and, standing up, placed her consort's hand back into his lap as he gazed up at her. "Seen? Yes. I think, once again, you are right."

A tap came upon the iron-bound door. Metal upon wood, followed by a gentle cough. The prince consort's eyebrow rose at the sound and his smile shifted to one side in resignation.

"You will come again soon, Erin? It will help me."

"Of course." She reached out and rested the back of a hand briefly against his cheek. "Take care."

Bracing herself, once again becoming Queen Erin, she opened the door to find Lord Penance staring at the floor, waiting. She closed it behind her, not dismissing the man inside, but building a higher, thicker emotional wall around him. He was, at least, finding some solace in being in Penance's House.

"Thank you, Lord Penance."

"I have done little except ensure he does not reside in Mordant's jail. That, he does not deserve. He has shared his writings?"

"Yes." Queen Erin waved the papers. "Have you read them? The hand is unrecognisable from his past attempts."

"No, though I would like to be there if you share them with your mother. That would give some relief on a difficult day. I believe she has a list of swear words the like of which would turn Honour's ears red."

"That she has. Most she chooses to share with me. I have, however, had a first thought on how I may support the Gods' Council."

26
WHERE SCIENCE AND MAGIC MEET

THE UNIVERSITY, ERSTENBURGH, BRANDSHOLD

"I'm coming, yes. Have some patience." The rapping at the door increased in loudness and regularity, gnawing at Meister Kinst's patience. Her lack of sleep since her conversation with the spirit Gowan was likely down to the sheer impossibility of the world she'd suddenly entered. Slipping on a robe and tying it off, she slid open the bolt of her chamber door. Standing there, red-faced against his embossed emerald collar, was Lord Wisdom, a very impatient-looking priest-in-waiting at his back.

"Kinst," he rasped, partially out of breath.

"Meister Kinst, Lord Wisdom, if you please." She stood there, her stout frame barring the entrance. She had no intention of letting the Lord anywhere near her chambers. "Yes? Can I help?"

"Sorry, Meister Kinst."

Kinst immediately had her hackles raised. Lord Wisdom, for all his meek and mild affectations outside of the House of Wisdom and the university, rarely let himself be cowed by the meisters. Thinking back, this was the first apology she'd ever heard from his lips.

"I have something that needs your attention. I understand you have been tasked with a special role by Lord Penance. What I have to share may well help with that and ... other things."

"But," said Meister Kinst, bursting with curiosity despite her tiredness, and unable to let such an opportunity pass, "is it so important you wake me at this hour?"

"The Overseer said you would want to know straight away. I assume, as would you, Meister, that means *now* in Lord Penance's vernacular."

Kinst harrumphed. Lord Wisdom had recovered some of his decorum; his usual attitude was bound to follow.

"Give me half an hour, Lord Wisdom. If this is work, would my workroom be a more acceptable place?"

"Agreed." He indicated the priest behind him, and Kinst realised the woman carried a large set of books. At a quick glance, she recognised absolutely none of them. An impossibility to her mind. "My seneschal, Greeth, will be there. I suggest you read this passage—" Lord Wisdom indicated the topmost book, a green silk marker hanging from between the pages. "—by the time I arrive."

The Lord spun, far more gracefully than the meister could ever have expected, and stormed down the corridor, the quills and scrolls adorning his robes shimmering in the early sunlight that streamed through the vaulted window above her room.

Meister Kinst closed the door, shaking her head. "It appears all is not well in the House of Wisdom either," she mused to herself. "That was almost ... civil."

———

Seneschal Greeth skimmed the parchment title and checked it off against the list written in Lord Wisdom's cribbed hand before passing it over to Meister Kinst.

"This describes the differences in quality. How the purity of the stone affects the length of time it will retain the ..."

"Spiritfire, girl. Spit it out and say it."

"The spiritfire. Here—" She pointed to the bottom of the first roll, before flicking the parchment over to reveal its continuance. "—the Magi talks of recreating a facsimile via elixirs. For when the crystal is not readily available."

"And how long have you had this knowledge, Seneschal? This would have allowed such wonders to be created."

"I have known of its existence approximately half a day before you, Meister Kinst. And I believe Lord Wisdom only a few hours before that. This was knowledge buried deep within the library. We found hints to its existence, but it had not been catalogued in any way. My task is now to search for any references that may help with, well, combat. And ... dragons."

Now Kinst got a better look at the priest, it was clear she was older than Kinst had first thought. She doubted that skin had seen the sun in a decade, or the hair a brush, for that matter. In fact, the seneschal reminded her very much of herself.

There was another, familiar, rap at the door and Lord Wisdom let himself in. Kinst, deciding against an argument, shoved a third chair aside, proffering it to the sweating Lord.

"Thank you," he said, taking up the offer and placing his bulk next to Greeth. "Ah, I assume you have read the passage, yes? You have the Magi's instructions, I see."

"Yes, but ..."

Lord Wisdom held up his hand. Kinst noted the mix of old and new ink staining, as well as remnants of sweat from his brow. "No, Meister. Do not. You are astute enough to work much out, and have a remarkable curiosity that will lead you into trouble. What I present here is enough for now, and as much as the Overseer regards as prudent. The Unspoken and her dragon present a threat the Magi foresaw. I am now tasked with providing you with ways to help. No more than that. You and Grand Meister Arknold are as far outside the Houses as this goes."

"I have already agreed to that, Lord Wisdom. But these books are of a like I have never seen before. The writing, its structure, is old, like ..."

"Please, Meister Kinst. Enough. Let me parcel this out for you so you understand. You have knowledge Greeth is not privy to. I have knowledge that neither of you are privy to. It is how it will be until the Gods' Council sees otherwise, or we burn under the Unspoken's dragon breath, or at their stakes over an open fire."

"So, I am to remain silent. To what end? What do you envisage using this knowledge for?"

"Mainly, weapons. Ones we can use. Here." Lord Wisdom dropped a wrapped oil cloth onto the table and untied the string. It unfurled with an arrow and quarrel inside, each with a crystal at its tip, and copper binding around it. "These were in use before the Gods brought us here. The crystals described in the book hold spiritfire, and retain it for later use. These," he tapped the scroll, "Greeth has discovered can be grown from water, like salt, and hardened."

"Not from water, but from liquids, Lord Wisdom. Yes, I read the treatise briefly. And I have studied how salts form upon the Stenning Flats. You want me to do this?"

"With Greeth's help, yes. You have lost your acolyte. My seneschal can help in their stead. And," Lord Wisdom held up his hand, cutting off Kinst before she could protest, "you can assume she will speak to me about everything to do with the crystals, but your other work is solely for you and Grand Meister Arknold. She understands. Nor will she repeat your usual slights and moans about me. Agreed?"

"I am knowledgeable, Meister Kinst. I will be of help," Greeth said, giving the meister a look of such serious intent, Kinst nearly choked. Yet it all felt just a little too late.

"Yes, dear girl. But can you get your hands dirty, because elixirs and powders are *not* for the reticent?"

27
THE STRANGEST OF PARTNERS

THE ROAD TO RIDTH, BRANDSHOLD

The carriage jolted, sending Prime Vardrin towards the footwell. Sneed grabbed him with a firm, slightly blackened hand, and dragged the prime back onto the cushioned seat. He pointed to the grip Jacka had released only a few moments earlier.

"We are no longer on the Queen's Road, Prime Vardrin. You will need your wits about you. The ruts lead you into a false sense of security, and then attack your dignity with relish." Sneed adjusted his own position, pressing his feet into the base of the opposite bench and releasing his left hand, squeezing away the numbness.

"This is not quite how I envisaged turning up in Ridth. We'll be battered and bruised, a fine sight for a duke. I doubt he'll believe a word, looking at the pair of us." Another jolt pulled at his arm. Jacka winced.

"Then perhaps we should ride? I know it is not your favoured method, Prime Vardrin, but I promise it will be less arduous after a few days. Saddle-sore perhaps, but I can request some stops to take my age into consideration." Sneed stared ahead, avoiding any eye contact. The frustrated prime needed some thinking space. After a while, he felt the man relax beside him, likely giving up on his own insistence on the carriage.

"If that would be amenable, perhaps it would be for the best. And we could return to the carriage on our approach to Ridth. I understand the duke keeps his roads smooth in the surrounding areas." Vardrin let a rueful smile play across his face.

"Oh, I'm sure he still loves his comforts, for all the bluster and show he puts on. Have you had many dealings with the duke, err ..."

"For the purposes of this journey, call me Jacka when we are alone, Sneed. In private. You understand, I find all of this a little uncomfortable – beyond the ruts and the travel. We ... well, your status ..."

"Is in the past. Where I hope it remains, Jacka. I am a servant tasked to speak with my High Lord's words and blessing. That is all." Sneed placed his blackened hand upon his right knee, exposing the wrist for the prime's eyes. The skin continued to heal, yet the veins were still prominent. "And you would do well to remember that before Duke Weister. He will enjoy playing on my status, as he always has since I left. Do not rise to my defence, Jacka, when he fences with words. They will not hurt me. I have tended my flock and served the Union as the High Lord, and I am at peace with that. It will be a joy for him to see me low."

"What happened? The queen said little."

"That is between the duke and me. Queen Erin knows of the cause of the antagonism, and thankfully disagrees with the duke, but that is all I will share. You would not divulge your most private thoughts with me, would you, Prime Vardrin? Expose yourself to others when they could either gain advantage or leave you to be ridiculed? We all have our penance to bear. Even you."

"Humph," replied Jacka, and braced himself against the cushion on the carriage wall. "Are you sure you are just a servant, Sneed? I believe you have lost nothing of your abilities."

"You will find that as the pressure builds, your thoughts tumble in on each other. When things overload, and the pull of each element of your net or web yanks you in a different direction, that clarity can only be maintained for so long. You can feel ... ah ... *invincible*, and that is when the Gods play their meanest of tricks." Sneed once again took his left hand from the carriage's handles. He hoped the prime would soon end the conversation and allow them to take up the horses.

"The Crusade, you mean? And the prince consort?"

"You fish, Jacka. But the river is empty. It is well known in Court that my last act, and my best, was to raise Erin to queen, whatever the people assume." Sneed caught Jacka's twitch of nose and eye, and stopped the smile of victory from appearing on his lips, his suspicion confirmed. "And nor will I answer your next question, about King Panset. His name deserves a little peace. Suffice to say, none of the rumours are true."

"It is going to be a boring journey if we are to maintain our walls, Sneed. But I suppose that is the way of things, and I should respect that. So perhaps a little more about the duke – I would be interested to know how you think I should approach the issue of the Unspoken."

"Hah. That'll be interesting. Let us say, the only God that man believes in is himself – for good or evil. Don't get me wrong, he has no ambitions towards the throne, though his nephews and nieces attend Court as they should. Bullish with intent, powerful with words, and frustrated if you do not rise to his challenges. Patience will be key; stick to your path."

"You know, I believe Lord Penance sent you as a distraction. Let the storm fall upon the companion, so I can be heard and not played with for his own enjoyment. Would I be wrong?" Vardrin watched Sneed for a reaction; his eyes lit up when he got one.

"No. Though I think you are astute in your assumption," Sneed replied, glancing outside before meeting the prime's eyes. "But you will need to be quick of mind whatever happens."

The carriage tipped slightly, and both men clung on tight until it righted itself. Vardrin opened the window and shouted a request for their horses to the sergeant-at-arms. When the carriage finally came to a halt, they both stepped out to a little spring sunshine and eased their backs.

"Thank you," Sneed said to the soldier who handed over the reins. "Another five minutes in there and you would be putting my aged pieces back together."

Despite his age, he couldn't help but sweep up easily into the saddle, mounting with a style practised on many a hunt. He turned the horse, readying himself while the prime eventually mounted his own, the soldier pointedly looking away as he did so. Vardrin ignored the woman, though whether from embarrassment or expectations was hard to discern.

Jacka Vardrin, slowly and carefully, approached the sergeant-at-arms who headed the small detachment around the carriage, the rest of the company spread wide in a circle, tracking the muddy and rutted road. A few words passed, Lord Penance's servant allowing his meagre spiritfire to draw each to his ears, the puff of wind unnoticed. The prime explained they needed a little air and would return to the carriage when ready, preferably with a different soldier at the reins – not thanking the sergeant for his counsel or stating that he had been right about choosing horseback over the carriage.

Sneed raised a saddened eyebrow. It was how he had expected it to be, and likely the attitude that would be helpful within Court dealings, especially with those such as the duke. However, he had hoped for more; the promise of his suggestions around the prince consort were tainted amid suspicions over his intentions towards the queen. And now, likely, sealed if he was the type to use obvious lies to save face, especially ones that fell upon deaf ears. The sergeant would care nothing for their decision, but would for some simple recognition.

They started up once again, Jacka waiting to bring his horse next to Sneed's.

"All okay?" Sneed asked.

"Upon a horse? I doubt it very much."

28
THE SHAME OF SHARING A TRUTH

THE UNIVERSITY, ERSTENBURGH,
BRANDSHOLD

Lord Penance sniffed, eyes watering, nose complaining at the incense burning within the university study room. He sighed and reached inside his robe sleeve to retrieve a cloth, with which he cleared his eyes before replacing it. His vision a little less blurry, he scanned the books and rolled-up parchments scattered about the room and its various shelves. There seemed little rhyme or reason to their organisation, but that was the Schenterenta for you. They appeared to have a way of seeing the world that was at odds with humanity, an organic eye that understood far more than it admitted – and hated to share.

And who can blame them? A people whose land we invaded almost by accident. Not with aggression, but just by arrival and acquisition. A people so alien to their way of life, they stood back in shock rather than intervene or go to war. And then their ancestor spirits left, their whole religion bereft of its foundation overnight. What would humanity have done? Wailed and thrashed, then started again. The elves? Fade and deny.

The inner door creaked and a dappled elven cheek, and a single, cat-like eye, peered through the crack before it shut once again. Lord Penance let out a second sigh, clearing the tears, before tapping the cane down on the floor with less than feigned impatience.

"Please, Terana Fiotir Na Partera, we need to speak." He knew he'd mangled the name, his tongue thick with the junip he'd been overusing to keep focused, and the spiritfire on hand. "Please come out with your partner. I am not here to examine what books you have borrowed, nor scrolls you have read. I am not here to bring the House of Penance down upon you for reading something we did not agree on. Nor am I here to try to convert you to our faith. We must talk, and let it be known that I will not leave until we do so, face to face."

May Penance check my burden, but these Schenterenta are more frustrating than Lord Wisdom.

"It's about the Soul Tears, is it not?" said the old academic, finally emerging from the room. Her hair was braided back against her skull, ears prominent, her ageing eyes a little wider than normal. "They were not our doing. I spoke to Grand Meister Arknold on this, and she assured me it was enough."

"Please sit with me, Terana. I am too tired, and my neck too aged, to be peering up at you."

The elf twitched a nose, eyelids flickering as her gaze met his, and likely accepted that he told at least a sliver of truth amid his weave of words.

"It is Tixar who waits. In the other room, that is." Nervous hands played with the frayed green robe she wore.

"I do not know this Tixar."

"My son, Lord Penance." She locked onto his eyes, as the High Lord let his own settle upon her as expected.

"He is welcome, Terana. We laid no rules about who could visit, nor when. Only about what you could share with the meisters. I assume he was versed in what lore he is allowed to share?"

"I think he is far from wanting to share anything with … with the meisters. He finds being among humans uncomfortable. His reasons for being here, however, may coincide with yours. We shall see." The aged elven Learned stopped her fiddling, resting her palms upon both knees. Her focus remained upon the High Lord. "Shall we discuss your matters?"

Lord Penance coughed, blinking away the smoky incense. "Yes, if I may. You are right about the Soul Tears; they are of concern. Anything we discuss must remain, as usual, between us." Terana nodded her agreement. "Good. I know of your lore on this matter insofar as your predecessor shared. But you do not know ours – at least, fully."

"Ah. You intend to share more? And for whose ears is this? Mine alone?"

"I was hoping you would arrange for me to meet with your shaman, the Spirit Walkers," he said, holding up his hand as the academic made to interrupt. "Hear me out, please. There is a darkness coming. One you have been shielded from in the past. It is time some of you knew the truth. But it is for the ears of your Spirit Walkers, and not these four walls. Nor your son."

"A bit much, wouldn't you say, Lord Penance? The Soul Tears are in our myths, the mightiest of which the shaman speak of occurring when your people arrived here. It has many names, but marks a time of pain in their eyes and the slow soul death of my people."

He noted the hands, now tightly held, though her gaze never wavered. There was, however, a firmness around her eyes and mouth. She had just exposed exactly why they were here in the university, though it came as no surprise to him.

"I will not disagree with you, nor ask for consideration of our acts as nothing but desperation. But you should question *why* we are here, why we came to *your* lands. I think you may well know the answer, though only a shallow version with little depth. What has your research found, mmm?" He let his own inner emotions invade his face – a little sternness coupled with some false indignation. It was just more mummery. He needed to find a connection with this elf.

The Schenterenta sat back, dropping her eyes, knowing the act was readable even by humans, but unable to do ought else. "I am not at liberty to share anything, *High* Lord Penance."

"No? Then how are we to continue your presence here? Of what benefit is it for us? You mark us as a selfish people, and you are right to do so. But it comes from a need for survival. We know ... *I* know what's coming. And the only Schenterenta I can share it with has a closed mind."

The study door rammed open, a sudden wrench, followed by the appearance of a slight elven adult. Lord Penance put him somewhere in human terms as late teens, so expected to double that. There was a shake to his hand, though he could see no weapon other than the curl to his lip.

"Tixar, no," his mother said, rising, arms wide, to prevent whatever her son intended. He didn't move, though his eyes betrayed anger, mirroring the story his body language also told.

A flow of words passed between them, the language a mix of fluidity and harshness no human had ever got their mind around. With a last retort, he slammed the door shut. Terana leaned against it as she looked back at him.

"I am sorry you had to see that," she stated, pushing herself off the door and walking across to her seat. "Emotions are running high."

"Because of the Soul Tears? It is what we need to discuss."

"If more of your people are arriving, Lord Penance, there will be little to talk about." She read his startled expression, the look of incredulity usually reserved for words humans could not understand. "Is this not what they signify? A new invasion of humans to take our land?"

"No, Terana. Not at all. How did I not see this? You think the Soul Tears are heralding arrivals? No. You could not be further from the truth. This is not about that. It's ... no, I can't say. At least, not all of it. Not here. There is something coming – the darkness I spoke of, and you need to be aware. I would trade something of importance to your people in return for the opportunity to share what is happening with your Spirit Walkers." Lord Penance pushed himself forwards as he spoke, hands on his cane, locking eyes with the aged elf.

"I struggle to see what you can offer when I do not believe you either, High Lord. You have a reputation for manipulation and control. The Overseer, they call you, and my people see you full of deceit and contrivance, as all your Lords and Ladies have been before you." She sat back, keeping the contact, though he sensed a nervous twitch allied with the presence in the other room. "First, give me something for free, and then I will *listen*. Without promise."

"If I can."

"Where is the Oheneba? What has happened to Sura-nista?"

"Oheneba? I don't know that word, nor this Sura-nista ... Oh. You mean Sura. The Ranger in Gowan's Spear. Yes?"

The academic nodded, eyes steely.

Lord Penance looked to the palms of his hands, one black, one wrinkled, examining the lines. "We believe she may have died, though we have no body to show for it. Killed by the darkness I speak of, in Ersten Forest. After the Soul Tear."

"By your incomers." Her face was set firm, except for the tremble below her lips.

"No, Terana. They were not our people."

"But human. You have spread a rumour of the Unspoken and her dragon, yet you do not say that to me. Are you so caught up in your webs that even *you* do not know the truth?"

"I think I may have met my match in you, Terana. I am sorry for the loss of your Oheneba, but the dragon was real. You know of our Houses, of the Unspoken and her evil. What killed Sura-nista breathed fire and broke bones – flew, like our scriptures say. But it did not arrive here with the recent Soul Tear – it came soon after the very first. A thousand years ago. And now it returns to call its masters – the darkness of which I speak."

"And it took Sura-nista."

"She died."

Though Gowan says her spirit survived, I have no proof other than another spirit's word.

"Maybe. But her spirit did not. I know this; it is why Tixar is here. The Spirit Walkers felt her death, but no more. At least your lies reflect what we know; that is something in your favour, at least." The aged Schenterenta had resolved the tremble and set her features firm. "What do you offer the tribes, High Lord, in return for a meet?"

Lord Penance leant back into the high-backed chair, his initial thoughts askew with the woman's change in countenance from the meek and mild to the ferocity this Sura-nista had a reputation for.

And so more of our dreadful past must be shared.

He leaned forwards, keeping his eyes upon hers, his voice barely a whisper. "I know what happened to your ancestors, to their spirits. I know of their fate, and what may happen to all Schenterenta spirits in the future. This I am not only willing to share, but seek the Spirit Walkers' help in bringing to an end."

"I struggle to believe you."

"Then it is an opportunity lost. I have no more. Again, I am sorry for your loss." He pressed both hands into the cane top, knees cracking as he made to get up.

Terana held out her hand, placing it on top of his, making the High Lord's heart flutter. Schenterenta only touched upon their own terms, or when something was of import. And never a human.

"Wait," she said. "Sit. It does not mean I should not share it with the Elders and the Spirit Walkers themselves. Tixar." The young elf opened the door a little more calmly, walking to stand beside the academic. "Tell him why you came to see me. Go on, child."

A nervousness took over the elf's countenance. Lord Penance took it as a sign the elf rarely conversed with humans. Especially those in the Union's main city. His voice was vaguely high-pitched. "I am here to request Terana Fiotir Na Partera attend a meeting of the tribes."

"Tribes? You do not—"

"It is difficult to deal with things out of your control, is it not? Yes, we do meet, though not under your prying eyes. And only if something is of great importance."

"Like the arrival of more humans ..."

"That would do it, yes."

29
DIVIDE AND RULE

"You are to manage the ravaging of Repanti, then return to Innealtóir and prepare the Inhibitors for the invasion."

"Me? Tarin, you are asking an artist to prepare a rough sketch. What am I to this?" The admiral incarnate strode across the brass and wooden bridge deck, stopping beside Inhibitor Henar. Disdain filled her glare, and she adjusted the second of her brass wheels with a mere touch to one side. "Focus, Inhibitor, or I will be the one sipping on your spirit."

"Lelion, you asked for a chance to show what the *Kraken* can do, and to prepare your crew appropriately. Stop and look at me, as *your* emperor." The last words were mixed with a puff of dry dust, the sound echoing off the solid walls and bringing the bridge crew to a sudden halt. Only the creak of the mighty soulship, the deep thrum of its engines, could be heard.

Tarin felt the mood shift. Eyes fell upon the admiral incarnate, expectant.

Lelion paused, waiting just long enough to display a level of malice in her movements as she finally turned to give the faintest of bows to the Fleshmaster.

"As you *command*."

Tarin sealed his anger away. This was not the time to rise to Lelion's bait, if that was what it was. It could just as easily be a heightened version of her usual attitude, given the stress he'd just put the *Kraken* under.

Will she challenge me? I think not. But others may, in her stead and with the admiral incarnate's backing.

"I said ravage, Lelion. You have free rein to wreak havoc upon these people. Test your machine, drain the people dry. Feed my army. We will be going to war; they need a taste of what is on offer. You have a week, then return to Innealtóir and ready your machine for *battle*. If the Magi or their ilk are on this Brandshold, then it, and you, will be tested to your very limits."

The admiral incarnate placed brass-clad hands against her armoured hips, eyes now fully upon Tarin, perhaps the slightest of smiles gracing her blue lips. "Agreed. And may I ask what *you* will be doing?"

"Hunting."

—

The twisted mouth released an agonised scream, and the body shook, its skeleton reverberating as once-dead nerves flayed at the new soul driving through it. Muscles rippled with whitefire, connected tendons stretching to their limits as the spine arched off the brass slab. With their stomach distended and purple teeth exposed, the agonised rictus continued.

"You really need to get over this quickly, Inhibitor Marklin, if you are to be whole for what is to come." Popsilin slid her hand over the soldier's brow and down to the watering eyes and nose, enjoying the pain. "You need to remember who you are and what you do, and soon. Otherwise, I will need a new guard when we bring the Magi to their knees. And you are such a good one. Strong, protective, and above all else, big."

The captain stepped back from the freshly imbued corpse – a muscled warrior she had chosen and bled herself, a real find. Rare were those this tall, yet lithe and quick. One who would protect their captain with skill. She had drained the body slowly, feasted upon the spirit, and allowed its dead blood to return to the earth.

"What better gift for the one who will fight before me?" she whispered.

"Captain Popsilin." Popsilin forced her reluctant eyes to look away from the pain emanating from the slab, masking her pleasure as the assistant thaumaturge spoke from across the infusion chamber. "I believe you wanted a reminder of the time?" His withered, black-gloved hands pointed towards the cogged clock upon the wall. She nodded in reply, and took one last look at Marklin. A pang of jealousy crept in, aimed towards those who would get to watch the final throes of his imbuement.

With a sigh, she headed for the door, picking up her pack and weapons along the way. Out of military habit, she checked each pocket with a touch of her fingers and mind, ensuring the spiritfire crystals of her handbow were whole and still bonded. Satisfied, her first step rang out along the *Kraken's* corridor towards the external dock, where the Fleshmaster's barge awaited. A ridiculous name, one affected from their past, when gaudy parades and decadent parties were in vogue. Her incarnations had wiped most of those memories away; just wisps remained. Fleeting glimpses of a time when she, or he, or whatever she had chosen to be at the time, was lost in the hedonism before the Sundering, and the horror that came after.

Popsilin reached the gangway, eyeing the ten-yard gap with little trepidation. Heights held no fear, though being in the hands of others in an ornithopter certainly did. She strode across the wind-swept plank, hands eschewing the brass rail as she walked with head held high onto the emperor's barge. A fleeting memory of its past embellishments surfaced – the brass-boned chair with its dragon wings splayed wide, placed at its front, while crowds pretended to wave as it passed. No. This version was sleek, arrow-sharp, and the brass shone with a powerful energy. Rumours were that at its centre lay a dragon's heartstone, that of Tabharthoir. A final gift from the Great Artificer, Viseri. The last of the dragons of the veil, but never infused with the Schenterenta spirit after the Magi had them murdered before they left.

An Inhibitor waited on the other side. The leader of the team she had taken into the caves on Repanti. "Inhibitor Tenith," she said in greeting. "Is your unit aboard?"

"Yes, Captain. Crammed in with the ornithopter pilots in the lower decks."

"It will not be for long, Tenith. The Fleshmaster predicts only a few days, if all goes well."

"Captain, if I may ask?"

Popsilin nodded; she'd been expecting questions.

"Why us? We are an obscure unit, hardly the vanguard of an attack."

"No. But we are not attacking this realm. We are on a seek-and-capture mission, exactly like the caves, and with the same targets. A snatch team. You proved yourselves on Repanti, and you've seen firsthand their use of this new alchemical concoction to force soul death. You will save me time. And besides, you are as used to the ornithopters as any."

"Ornithopters?"

"Yes, Tenith. We are to be unseen. They may prove to be the fastest method in such circumstances."

Popsilin strode onwards, keeping her demeanour confident and stern as she approached the outer door of the bridge. Behind her, the gangplank was unhitched. She felt the moment when the barge dropped away from the *Kraken* soulship. She pushed the handle, the smooth mechanism enabling the door to open towards her. After entering the small hallway beyond, she opened the next door and shut the weather out.

Now on the bridge, she saluted the barge captain and waited, hands bunched before her, while the Fleshmaster peered out through the bridge windows.

"I mean to land," said the Fleshmaster, his words meant for the whole bridge. "Understand? We will go in at night to the edge of whatever small town we find, and question until we find what we want. If that fails, we wait and repeat until we have a target for Popsilin. That means we are to act as if we are keeping a secret, not the hammer and anvil we usually use. Understand? We are to be *unseen*."

A silence followed, broken by the barge captain and Popsilin, "Yes, Emperor."

"Good." He turned to face Popsilin, his white eyes almost dancing in their sockets. The captain recognised the signs of recent feeding. "Adjutant Renat and his ornithopters are packed in tight, Captain. They will need a few hours to prepare once we find a place to land. My Honour Guard will see to their safety. You will scout the area, ensure we are undisturbed while we ready them. Once they are rebuilt, we will begin the hunt."

Popsilin held her counsel, her mind already whirling as she realised the emperor was talking about being with them on the mission.

"You disagree, Captain. I can taste it."

"What if …?"

"If I should fall? We cannot risk losing out on the Spirit Walkers. You simply will not fail. Think more of what happens if *you* do. I am not in the habit of explaining myself, Captain, but there is a reason I sent the admiral back to Innealtóir and I remain here. Find me the Spirit Walkers, and we will not have to worry about what she'll do. Yes?"

"Yes, Emperor." Popsilin bowed her head.

"Go see to your Inhibitors, make sure they understand what we are doing here and its importance. And that we are to be *subtle*."

"Emperor, if I may, before I go?" She took the twitch of blue lips as agreement to continue. "My Mechanised Vanguard. I did as you asked and chose the best. May I ask—"

"No, Popsilin. You may not. Focus on this task. Whatever happens, without the Spirit Walkers, I doubt it will make any difference."

Popsilin, her mouth tight, bowed and left, keeping the sudden burst of frustration in her spirit from her body movements. She knew the Fleshmaster would read her anyway but, needing to show she understood her place, she suppressed her thoughts until she had exited the bridge. On reaching the wooden stairway down to the lower decks, she hit her hand in frustration against the metal rail.

Has he really sent them as scouts? Or are they meant to fail, to release the Infected as a warning of what is to come? To sow fear. I could have sent some less capable to achieve that. Has he lessened the Mechanised Vanguard on purpose?

Swearing, she banged each booted foot into the steps as she pummelled her way down the stairs.

30

A SPIRIT BOUND IN LOVE AND HONOUR

INNEALTÓIR, REALM OF THE CONSTRUCTORS

Laoch signalled for Oisin's attention. The Handren mounted the stairs with tired, heavy feet, wary. When he reached the top of the stairs, the First Ranger's eyes widened, his jaw dropping a little. Laoch reckoned he didn't look much different. Nothing had moved below. The figure upon the dragon-wing throne sat stock still, the army at his feet, unmoving. But he could taste the danger in the air, the atmosphere dead and cold, and his instincts screamed.

"There's death down there," whispered the First Ranger, a twitch at the corner of his eye causing Laoch to assess the man. Sura was already watching him. "They look the same as the ones we fought, that Nathair incinerated below. What is happening here?"

"Maybe the corruption Nathair expected?" said Laoch. "It has been a very long time. Have they slept? Like animals do over winter?"

Sura cocked her head to the side, eyes flashing with Honour's orange. Then an absence slid in, and she gazed into the distance. Laoch waited, knowing she communed with the spear he carried. Or, possibly, with Keran and the Spirit Walker. It put him on edge, this *otherness*. It reminded him she was dead, lost to him. Yet not. Unaware, Laoch squeezed the grip of his weapon out of habit. A God's touch at the back of his mind quashed the concern.

"Nathair describes them as *unalive*. Mechanised humans with a mindless spirit infusing the body. Perhaps the residue from the palace." Sura's eyes flickered, the light receding as she blinked and locked eyes with Laoch. "Abominations. The work of a necromancer, she says. Using flesh like an artificer uses metal. She wishes to enter and burn them to ash."

"On that, we can agree, but the dragon will only bring the palace down, and we need to find what we came for before that. If it does not lie down there, amid all that death, then we should leave them be." Oisin stepped forwards and placed a hand upon the balustrade. A tremor ran through his body.

Sura clasped Laoch, her fingers' touch solid, her face betraying a sudden fear. Before Laoch could respond, the spirit elf had stepped towards Oisin, wrapped her arms around him, and melded herself to his body.

"The poison re-emerges," she said.

The words bounced inside his head, and Honour's sigil warmed the spear. He raised it and pressed the sigil against Oisin's back, where Sura's spirit wavered.

"Too late," Sura whispered in his mind.

The mountain man scrambled onto the marble rail, then fell to crash amid the dead.

"No," mouthed Laoch, staring over the balcony. Oisin's body lay, spreadeagled, over one of the dead guards upon the stone floor, his eye movements jerky and wild. Fate glowed. The bow's light washed over the Ranger, highlighting the sweat glistening upon his red scalp. Laoch made to climb over when Sura's touch upon his thoughts drew him back.

"Let me," she said.

She climbed over the marble to avoid merging with the stone, and was floating downwards when a creak emanated from the metal-boned throne. Laoch watched as the dark figure's helm turned, dust puffing from the joint between it and the neck brace. Whitefire glowed between the slits, and a gauntleted hand flexed.

"Nathair," bellowed Laoch, "fetch Ecne."

He climbed to the top of the balustrade, turned, and clambered down to its base. "Seven Hells."

On Justice's insistence, he dropped the last two yards. A red glow infused his legs as he hit the floor, Justice's spiritfire flowing through muscle and bone. He spun around, drawing the God's weapon while holding Honour's spear. Sura was nowhere to be seen. Oisin rose from the floor, Fate reforging into a blue-edged short sword in his hand.

"What in the Gods' names, Oisin?"

Laoch stood by the Handren's side as the sword bit into the prone guard's neck, severing the head. The bone and the metal that protruded from the gap sparked with a sliver of whitefire.

The First Ranger turned to Laoch, gaze locking on his. An orange fire flared within.

Sura is in there. How?

The Handren took a familiar stance by Laoch's side, one honed by the Patterning, not that of the Ranger's training.

"He's going to love this if we survive," said Laoch.

The first sweep of a longsword woke Laoch up to their danger. Its slow descent fostered a little hope until thirty helms turned their way. Oisin's blade cut through the forearms holding it, slicing back up to bite deep into the monstrosity's waist. Blue fire flared and the plate armour parted. The stink of dry rot washed out as the jumble of cogged innards and dust clattered to the floor.

Bodies swivelled, and all the dead drew their swords as one. Sword tips pointed their way, glinting in the light of their weapons. A flash lit the whole chamber, green and bright, as a bolt splashed into the figure upon the throne. A roar reverberated around the room, anger-laden, and the giant figure rose from its seat. Green light laced across his armour, dissipating into the surrounding air before the sword rose and pointed upwards, towards where Laoch assumed Ecne stood. A second green bolt lashed across the space, wreathing the angered armour. All the guards moved, piling towards a seamless doorway that opened to allow them through.

"Run, Ecne!" Laoch shouted, handing off the animated bodies that drove past him for the doorway. "Head for Nathair!"

Oisin stepped in closer, and between them they parried and hacked at those that came too close. The hall emptied, leaving naught but dry dust and the stink of old death. That, and the huge, armoured figure still stepping down from its dais. Each joint creaked as it moved, the noise of aged leather and metal upon metal filling the circular room.

Laoch stepped away from Oisin, sidestepping quickly, spreading the attack wide as he would against a human opponent. Memories of the Sealgair, as Keran called them, flickered through his mind. The combat he would have lost without Sura's aid. And here she was, again.

He took the chance to stow Honour's spear, needing to be balanced and fighting in an accustomed style. The longsword could be unwieldy, though this monstrous figure likely had the strength to overcome that. However, it suited the open space, and not the corridors he knew lay beyond the doors.

"*Laoch, keep wide,*" said Sura, her touch upon his mind strained, as if she battled something.

Probably an angered and poisoned Handren soul, as wild as the horses they stole.

"No. Go for the circular hallway. That sword will be hampered in there." He felt the agreement, and Oisin turned and ran, Sura trusting Laoch as she sprinted for the doorway, which immediately started to close. He swore, but then caught their feint to the right – past the hulking armour now hurtling towards him. An image appeared in his head, and he immediately knelt. Oisin's boot hit Laoch's shoulder, his bent leg straightening as Laoch exploded upwards, sending the mountain man and his Sura-imbued body up towards the balcony. He heard the clunk of a landing and had to assume they'd made it, just as the longsword cut through the air towards him. The arc was long, slower than he expected, until a spurt of whitefire emanated from the shoulder and elbow. The swing accelerated to cleave his shoulder. Laoch threw himself to one side, hit the floor and rolled to his feet, immediately on the run towards the throne and its dais.

A roar of flame burst over the balustrade as dragon's breath filled the ceiling of the chamber. Dust and seared ash billowed in its wake.

Oh shit.

———

Ecne panicked. She tried to think of an alternative but, considering the horde of rampaging unalive guards running up the marble steps, it was perhaps her only choice. The crossbow would take out one, maybe they'd crash into a few others, but little more. What she needed was a very big bloody dragon, and enough fire to reave the dead and leave the alive pretty much standing.

Wisdom pulsed as a roar shook the palace doors. She was about to get *half* her wish. Then something slammed into her from behind, sending her tumbling down the balcony steps. Green light blazed in her eyeline, a warmth that spread across her cheeks and hair, then onto her exposed hands. It erupted into an emerald flare, cold as ice, and the world turned into a battle of colours surging for supremacy – orange layered upon the green and red – flash fires that rose and fell with the extreme hot and cold washing over her. Ecne hit the bottom step, rolled to a stop at the base, and lay, coughing and spluttering, amid ash and black smoke. Rubbing her eyes, she felt the ice-cold touch of Wisdom fade.

She rose from the floor, cheeks grey with ash, to stare at a dragon whose forked tongue licked at metallic teeth with more than a little glee. Nathair coughed and slid her gleaming head out of the entranceway while Ecne's memory dragged back to the moment when she'd been hit. Spinning, the entrance full of fluttering ash and melted cogs and bones, she found Oisin at her feet, Sura on her knees by his side, shimmering with an orange hue.

Her head jerked, eyes locking on Ecne. "Laoch," she said, then rose and flew back up the steps towards the balcony.

Ecne knelt and felt for Oisin's pulse at neck and wrist. She was relieved at its strength. The mountain man appeared unharmed. Fate lay at his feet, the bow's grip glowing. She reached for it and placed the sigil in the man's hand.

A cry from Sura brought her up short and, puffing out her cheeks, she followed her back in.

By the time Ecne reached the balustrade, Sura had dropped down to land behind Laoch. The Ranger was bloodied along his left arm and limping slightly. His eyes were solely on the huge set of armour that filled the chamber with whitefire, each plate throbbing with barely contained power.

Ecne placed the crossbow on the marbled rail. Wisdom's sigil pulsed a sickly green. Knowing what came next, she gave the weapon permission to draw from her. She felt her skin dry as a surge of spirit-fire rushed through her nerves to fill Wisdom's sigil. Ecne released as Laoch fell, the longsword sweeping away his good leg from beneath him with the flat of its blade. The bolt, with Wisdom choosing the shot, struck the giant armour's knee. The momentum of the spiritfire was rewarded with a crack, and whatever filled the armour staggered backwards. The sword was still held high for the killing blow.

Ecne let a pained growl slip from her lips, her wrists pulsing as Wisdom drew more from her. She knew it would be her last, and waited. Wisdom's touch calmed her mind, easing the panicked breathing. But she had given them time, a chance.

Sura was scrabbling at the Ranger's back when the clunk of metallic feet resounded through the chamber – the armour recovering. It charged with a deathly scream towards her.

Now.

The bolt fired, emerald sizzling through the smoke-filled chamber, burning ash in its wake, to slam into the creature's helm. The armour jerked sideways and crashed to the floor. The clang and scrape of metal and crystal was the last thing Ecne heard as she slipped into unconsciousness.

✦

Sura grasped the spear strapped to Laoch's back, urging her fingers to grab hold, feeling Honour's touch spread through the tips. And time stood watching, the sand's inexorable slide through the aperture that measured Sura's presence, her spirit life, pausing.

'A choice.'

Sura stared down upon Laoch. Her spirit heart hurt, aching for the man she had died beside. An ethereal hand reached out, fingers touched the Ranger's cheek. She ran the back of her hand along the skin.

Honour offered, but the cost was high.

Will I still be me?

'Somewhat'

But not?

'With what I offer, you will be part of me. Not lesser, but different.'

I don't want to let this love go, to fade. I have waited so long.

'A thousand years? A lifetime? Forever, and a day. What is time when the veil calls?'

I can't lose him.

'We will be Honour, Sura. You choose what you give up. But I make no promises; once we are bonded, you may well make such a choice yourself.'

'It is time.'

'Choose.'

I choose Laoch.

'There is only one way for that to happen.'

Sura grasped the spear. The orange glow shattered into a maelstrom of light. Shards filled her spirit, ricocheting amid her ghost-like form. Each reflection bonded to another, linking, forging her *will* to Honour's call. Sura rose and stepped before Laoch, the Patterning surging through her body as she swirled the spear once to take her stance.

"Come on, you big bastard. He's mine."

Her feet sensed the *otherness* in the floor, the whitefire being drawn upwards from the stone, feeding the monstrous armour as it rose once again. The last of Wisdom's spirit fire danced along its hip before fading into the air. Reaching upwards, an infused gauntlet punched the helm. Crystalline pieces parted to bounce onto the floor. The face staring back shone with whitefire, eyes aglow, skin stretched over brass cogs and wires, the tongue thick and alive amid steel teeth. Dust flared about its head, lit white; a halo to herald death's arrival. When the mouth stretched wide, the void within raged with whitefire, and the scream spoke of insanity and need, hunger and age.

But what is death to one who already swims in its veil?

The armour charged, sword raised above one shoulder, hips flexing in a way that caught Sura's eye far more than the show of strength and power it used to disguise its intent. It had marked her now, and the sword swirled, the half-mechanised creature bringing the blade down way before convention to use its length as an advantage.

Sura waited, eyes aflame, watching shoulder and hip, the Patterning working in unison with Honour's bonds. She dropped to a low stance as the armour's tremor indicated intent. A second change of tactic brought the sword lower, the aim to rip upwards, expecting Sura to use her agility and remain close to the floor.

She leapt left, tucked in the spear and rolled, then rose to her feet to see the swing of the sword reach its apex. She stepped in. A second stride, and she powered the thrust of her spear between the shoulders. The tip scraped against the crystal plates, and orange and whitefire clashed for supremacy. The armour shattered, exposing blackened skin interspersed with rope-like wires and the whirr of linked cogs. Sura withdrew, the Patterning urging her to step back and assess, as her opponent staggered away before turning to raise its sword in defence.

Yet Sura couldn't stop. She knew little of how long she could retain her new form, nor the level of spiritfire Honour could draw upon. The palace was feeding this creature, yet everything felt old, tainted. It lacked the strength of recent life Honour's gift spoke of, but the building was immense.

How much does it have to draw upon?

In answer, the armour's crystal-shod boots glowed. And Sura attacked. Feinting towards the armour's left, she stepped right and spun low to sweep the heavy boots away while keeping the spear mid-height to parry. The armour, in her eyes, chose wrongly, accepting the kick to thrust the sword down in a backslash after missing the first time. Her spiritfire-imbued shin slammed into the armoured boots – again, orange and white flashed bright – but this time the armour held fast. Sura felt herself topple, only just managing to raise the spear in time to deflect a bludgeoning attack. Overbalanced, she rolled backwards and up over her shoulders, bringing the spear round to parry a second blow chopping at her hips. A third reined in, and only Sura's years of training prevented the strike as she whiplashed the spear to knock the sword from its trajectory.

A fourth blow never came. A blue arrow smashed into the back of the monstrous head, and searing light exploded from the once-white eyes. The mouth opened to release a scream, and Sura drove the spear point inwards and upwards, plunging towards whatever the thing had for a brain. Orange swirled amid the blue and the skull exploded, bone, metal and something wet splattering against the wall and the solidified spirit. The armour collapsed, whitefire playing amid the plates before being absorbed into the stone floor.

Sura fell to her knees, one hand landing upon Laoch as the Ranger stirred.

31
MUMMERY FOR THE MASSES

The White Palace, Erstenburgh, Brandshold

Queen Erin Weister strode through the White Palace doors and looked up to the veils, to where the sun broke through shower clouds to set the stone gleaming. Swords and quills clattered in equal measure, echoing off the ground and the vast, white walls as the palace staff fell to a knee as one.

Resplendent in a royal yellow and green dress, laced with Fate's Blue, she took each stride down the marbled steps with considered care, not rushing, keeping her heart calm and steady.

On reaching the final step, she waited a moment before raising both hands. The servants of the Crown rose as one, their eyes shining and bright as they reflected love for their queen.

Erin looked upon the waiting carriage, its white and gold brocade tied with royal ribbons, the velvet-cushioned interior waiting for the queen to visit her people in comfort.

"Thank you, Captain Mordant. However, I shall take the city air by foot, if you please." She gave him a look of expectation, and mild sympathy, for a man suddenly thrust into organising the safety of a monarch amid her people. The captain bowed in response, grimaced, then ordered the Royal Guard to take up their position. They had already been briefed, Mordant's response all part of the mummery of a queen's desire to be among her people, and to follow her God's scripture.

The huge, iron-bound palace doors opened wide, the hinges oiled and silent. The roar of the people beyond was not. With Prime Vardrin on his way south, he had left his deputy to report back to her on certain aspects of the comings and goings of the city. The woman had clearly got the word out of the queen's private intention to pray at Fate's House.

The Royal Guard set four soldiers before her, their uniforms beautifully pressed, plumed helms fluttering in the wind. On the captain's call, they stepped out of the entranceway. The queen made to follow on Mordant's hand signal, the city's defender checking first with his soldiers upon the wall that the roofs were manned with archers.

With her handmaid following behind, holding the train of the sequined dress above the muddied road, she followed her guards stride for stride, keeping to the agreed pace as she walked before her people for the first time since the coronation. For all her life, she had been taught to keep the titled away from the masses – a distance necessary when ruling. Set yourself on high for others to see how you glow, how much *better* than them you are. Provide a reason to both fear and follow, like the flocks that attended the Gods' Houses.

Where they bring scripture, a way of living, I bring a light into their world. An aspiration and admiration, to rise from the ashes of the Crusades. And now I must join the two, because what was hidden from our eyes is coming, with blood upon its metal tongue. These are my people, and to protect them, I must fool them.

Am I to be another Lord Penance?

The queen reached the crossroads marking the end of the Royal Quarter. The next mile was festooned with the unwashed and pious, awaiting the Houses to open their doors for morning Mass. The smell of sweat and dirt rolled her way upon the wind, mingling with the murmurs of expectation that turned into a rising cheer as Erin continued her promenade. The city militia eased the hordes back, though gently, as had been drummed into them at the queen's wish, and she proceeded the half mile towards Fate's House, whose seven marbled steps were laced with hues of azure.

The cries of the crowd grew the closer she came, and those with flashes of blue upon their clothes, the loudest among them. She made a point of looking to those, not making eye contact, but enough to ensure they knew they had been noticed. She stifled her sigh of relief as she finally reached Fate's doors.

The Queen's Guards spread out before the entrance, their presence solidifying the militia and bringing the nearest of the crowds to a standstill. With the merest nod of approval, Queen Erin waited at the base of the steps, eyes on the first azure-streaked stone slab.

"You are welcome," said the firm, half-amused voice from the House doorway, where Lady Fate appeared, her red hair vibrant against the blue of her robe. "Please enter, Queen Weister. Your presence is an honour upon my House."

She again took careful, measured steps, her guards following before taking station at the doorway, along with the handmaid, as the queen entered. Only one, her sergeant-at-arms, followed to wait inside the doorway – the result of careful negotiation between

Mordant and Lady Fate herself, one that enhanced the red-haired woman's reputation for bluntness.

"Thank you, Lady Fate. I may have brought a little *attention* with me." Erin let a smile pass over her lips. As they walked into the prayer chamber, her eyes flickered briefly up to the dragon painted upon the ceiling. Fate's version was thick-bodied and bearded, with a long tongue. The queen didn't associate it with any of the art plates she had seen in the Forbidden Library.

"Something tells me that was your intent. And much appreciated, if I read your reasons correctly." They walked slowly towards the prayer stone, the echo of their steps compounded by the empty chamber.

"I promise I will use a carriage in the future, but I hope this will galvanise your flocks somewhat, as they are my people too. We all face the threat of the *Unspoken*."

"That would be prudent. We have—" Lady Fate glanced behind to eye the sergeant-at-arms before speaking further, keeping her voice low. "—a need, do we not? Are you sure you wish to give?"

"Yes, Lady Fate. I always prayed within the palace chamber, though I suspect this may be a little more tiring. I need to experience what my own people do, to understand it once again. Back in Ridth, I prayed in the House with regularity, but I was younger then, with greater vitality."

Lady Fate reached out a hand. The queen briefly flinched, as the fingers were lit with sapphire, before allowing the touch. The faint glow, hidden from the sergeant, felt warm upon her exposed forearm. Erin pursed her lips, unsure what the moment meant, until she felt a connection blossom between her and Lady Fate. A single image slid into her mind – a mechanised dragon, beating orange-metal wings against the spiritfire of Fate's veil. She experienced the abhorrence at its passing, and the hapless glyph sensing, but unable to act upon, its presence.

"I am close to resetting my marker, the glyph that resides in Fate's veil. Your gift today – not the sliver of spiritfire you provide, but that waiting outside – may well gain us time. Each second is precious." The hand lifted away, gathered in front to rest upon the blackened scrying hand all the House Lords and Ladies bore.

Erin swallowed, and glanced back up towards the waiting dragon, its eye keen. She felt its weight upon her shoulders.

Each day they reveal a little more, as if I am unready to take it all at once. What can be so horrendous that they feel I must be drip-fed like an orphaned pup?

They stopped at the prayer stone, and Queen Erin pulled her dress clear to press her stockinged knees upon the stone. Lady Fate took both her hands, gently murmuring scripture. She locked eyes with Erin as she recognised the draw of the stone. Another gift bestowed by the Lady, an awareness of what was happening. For the first time, she gave of herself freely to her God and their veil. The spiritfire spiralled along her nerves, swirling gently to rest upon her skin before the crystal drew it inwards, absorbing the power. As soon as the tingle of its passing left, the connection was cut, and Erin was awash with a sudden tiredness. Lady Fate kept hold of her hands, waiting for the wave to pass, as she knew it would, before helping her queen to her feet.

"Yes. This is how much the people give. We would have had to draw more, but perhaps your work today will negate that if our flocks increase. It is Honour that is in most need, however."

"So I understand. I will act upon that next." The queen glanced over to her Royal Guard. "I believe I have the means to help there, too." She looked back to find the cube of Fate's Gift in her hand. "This is the suppressant? The people believe it is to overcome the tiredness."

"It does help revitalise the body, that much is true, yet also another tool we use to hide from the Constructors. It slows the renewal somewhat, ensures the flocks do not draw from what surrounds us too quickly. That is what magi would do, and a sign the Constructors would look for even hidden behind our veils. Another lie, as you would put it." The woman grimaced, her red lips twisting. Queen Erin recognised the distaste she felt.

"And what happens if they break through the veils? Would all this be for nothing? A thousand years of lies and deceit that still ends in death or slavery?" Erin felt her eyes flash, emotions overriding the tiredness as she took the block.

"A thousand years of life our ancestors would never have had. Like all things, someone must pay the price in the end. It has fallen in our time, but, my Queen, the fault does not lie at our feet. We all see in you more hope than we thought possible once Nathair rose and the signal was sent. But beating us with our past will not solve what comes."

Erin let the block dissolve upon her tongue, felt the paste slide down her throat. Swallowing fully, she turned to leave. "You speak well, Lady Fate. But the Gods' Council drip-feeds these truths to me as if I am a petulant child and will strike out once I learn it all, or crumble under the weight."

"Perhaps some do. And yes. There is always more, and the obligation is heavy. See it another way. There are some burdens that increase when they are shared. Should they be exposed, the Houses would fall. I would be the first to break. It will come to you in time, and it will be the greatest test of your faith in what we do. But do not pick at it like a scab of unknowing. Please, my Queen, accept where we are. You need our strength as much as we need your belief that we hold the world's fate in our hearts."

"For now, Lady Fate, I will listen to your counsel. But not forever." Queen Erin gave a curt nod, and turned to walk along the aisle before stopping and looking back. "I do not mean to be petulant, nor deride what you do, Lady Fate. Your hand bears witness to the physical pain, and your bearing to the strain on your heart. But I am left alone in this sea, a choice I, perhaps, made to cope in my own way. I feel ..." The queen paused, as if searching for the correct word.

"Guilt, my Queen. Of decisions made that affect the innocent. Yes. And you have borne that for but a few weeks."

32
A NECROMANCER AWAKES

INNEALTÓIR, REALM OF THE CONSTRUCTORS

Ecne failed to cough, throat tight, lungs constricted. Fear hit as she realised her mouth was forced open, fingers wrapped about her tongue. She beat a hand at a shoulder until she felt the pressure release, and a breath rasped down her airway to fill pained lungs. She hacked again, splattering the fingers with phlegm, and grasped Oisin's arm as she rolled over to spew mucus in a second fit of coughing.

"Lovely. Thanks for that!" Oisin reeled back, wiping his arm upon an ancient drape that fell apart at his touch. "Save a girl's life and she rewards you with phlegm."

Ecne gasped a second breath and looked towards the Handren with rueful thanks. "Wouldn't have had to do that if you hadn't gone on some glory charge."

"Yeah. Sorry. The anger came over me. Like a venom in my brain. I ... I don't think I can be trusted, Ecne."

The acolyte held out her hand and Oisin pulled her up, then handed over the crossbow he'd collected from the floor. Ecne took it. Then, catching his glance towards her face, raised a finger to touch the dry, tight skin across her cheeks and nose.

"Wisdom took what was required," she said, and grabbed his arm as a moment of dizziness swept over her. "Did we win?"

"We walk and talk, so I take that as success." Oisin pointed back towards the ash-filled entranceway. "And Nathair's intervention saved us both, I believe."

Ecne stared at the devastation, the steaming bodies sparking with the vestiges of spiritfire that slid off to soak into the stone floor. Somehow, that sickened her more than the unalive it abandoned. Where was it going? A shout from behind made her turn. Oisin was already at the balcony's edge, looking over, when Ecne joined him. Sura waved to them from below, her form opaque. Honour's spear lay at her feet, its shaft touching Laoch, who leant upon his elbows, shaking his head groggily.

"We are fine," replied Oisin. "Though I owe an apology."

"Time for that later," said Sura. "Without Fate's arrow, we would all have fallen. And Ecne's bolts. Laoch needs some wounds dressing."

"I'm fine. Just make sure there are none of those bastard things left. And then, someone needs to explain what in the Seven Hells is going on." Laoch clambered to his feet a little unsteadily, favouring one leg as he walked over to the mountain of armour that fizzed, thanks to Fate's and Wisdom's intervention. Using his sword, he prodded at the remnants attached to the neck, his face twisted in disgust. "And what happens next."

"I will check on Nathair and Keran," said Sura, letting a hand grace Laoch's arm. "Could you bring Honour outside? This place drains us and prevents renewal. Wisdom and Fate too, Justice perhaps. I fear there will be more of your Gods' work to do before we can leave this foul place."

They met up at the blasted entrance doors. Nathair lay curled around herself, her crystalline eyes upon the building, spiked tail twitching. Palpable relief spread over them all as they exited, an unrealised miasma lifting as they alighted on the ground outside. Sura approached Nathair's chest, the pocket of elsewhere shimmering as she stepped through. The others followed, accepting, but not yet used to, whatever magic this was. Inside, Keran had prepared the heartstone room with metal chairs and tables, enabling Laoch to sit while a tired Ecne tended his cuts and the bruised thigh.

"Nathair will keep watch. She is already wary, with so many of these *unalive* around," said Keran, his spirit form standing by the heartstone itself. "This place is a shadow of what it once was. The High Palace of the emperor, according to her, and not one of such abhorrence."

"There's another dragon inside," said Laoch, looking to Sura. "Bigger than Nathair. Silver-blue and wrapped inside that chamber. There was also a huge one of these *unalive* in there. It attacked with intelligence, unlike the others, and white spiritfire."

"Does Nathair remember any other dragons, Keran?" asked a hoarse Ecne.

"Others? I have never asked." Keran's spirit faded, pulsing, and his face blended with that of a twisted, scaled figure they assumed was the Spirit Walker. Lips moved, though no sound could be heard. "She speaks of Leront, whom we know of – and An Chéad, with much reticence. Her thoughts are full of betrayal and mistrust with that one, though she cannot say why."

"Cannot, or will not?" Oisin mused. "Is this beast An Chéad?"

"No. That dragon is red. Scarlet-scaled and lithe – elongated. What you speak of is something new. Sura, may I?" Keran reached out a spectral arm, and Sura let her hand merge with his. A gentle whisper of spiritfire passed between them. "No. What Sura shows me is beyond Nathair's knowledge. Something new. Though not tainted, like the unalive. At least, not yet. What is this of the building, though, Sura? Can you show Nathair and me more?"

Sura nodded, and allowed another wisp to pass between them. "It is more a feeling of wrongness. It acts like a Constructor, and feeds off any spiritfire within its walls. It tried to draw upon me and Honour."

"During the combat, the big bastard's feet were covered in white lightning," added Laoch. "Saw it when I was laid on the floor, being saved by some spirit or other. Again." He smiled at Sura, and received a hint of one in return.

"And whatever spiritfire was within the unalive soaked into the entranceway floor. I thought it was just leaving, but now you mention it, there could well have been more to it."

"This is madness." Oisin stood, hands pulsing. "I know I was in the wrong—"

"Not your fault," cut in Ecne.

"But are you saying the building is ... I don't know, like one of these Constructors? Alive, somehow? Did I say that out loud?"

"No madder than a talking dragon made of metal and fire, Oisin." Ecne tied off Laoch's small bandage and rose to face Keran. "But if that's true, is it intelligent? Can it speak, like Nathair? It may have knowledge we need."

"And power we can't comprehend," added Oisin. "And there's a dragon in there for a purpose. Perhaps another like Nathair, one the

Constructors aim to use to hunt our people down, as Keran says. Do we need to stop that now?"

"It has likely been there for near a thousand years." Keran's spirit flashed, the hair again covered in scales, the teeth protruding from metalled lips. "But Nathair and I agree, it appears whole, and possibly has a heartstone ready for another Spirit Walker to possess. She is more concerned about the palace itself, and what inhabits the walls. I fear she may be right. She wants in. Nathair may appear calm to you, but inside that crystal, she rages at the abomination within the palace."

—

"There," said Ecne, pointing towards the chamber's ceiling. "They built this dragon in the palace with the intention of getting it out at some point. It is far too big to get through the main doors, Nathair proved that. So, my best guess would be out through the ceiling. But why construct it *inside*?"

"If they knew they would be gone a long time, perhaps they wanted it somewhere safe to prevent others from damaging it," said Laoch, staring down at the silver-blue mechanical beast. "If they need a Spirit Walker, then maybe they knew it would take some time?"

"Those were my people back at the house, in those cages. It could be as you suggested – that they were Spirit Walkers, and intended for the dragon," added Sura, her eyes distant as her hands wavered above the marble rail. "And that's why they were killed. What if such a thing happened in every house?"

"How would you know if they were? How is a Spirit Walker chosen?" asked Ecne. "Is it training, like myself? You learn to become a shaman the same way I seek to be a meister?"

Sura stared at her hands, their ethereal form ghostly against the white stone. "They are born. The Elders always know who ..."

"How? Sorry, Sura. But the more we know, the better chance we have to find a way to help."

Sura turned her head, a glint of a tear in one eye as her gaze flicked between Ecne and Laoch.

"Twins," said Oisin from behind, the Handren treading lightly between the still-smoking bodies of the unalive in the hallway. "Have you not worked that out yet? Twin souls, born from the same seed. And Sura's brother died in the stampede from Handren."

"Sura?" interjected Laoch, stepping closer and finding her eyes. "Why did you not say?"

"It is a moot point. Naru died, we were not there to recover his spirit before it was lost." Sura's eyes hardened. Laoch refused to take a step back despite the pain she emanated. "And I am too young. The twins are left to experience the world until they reach later life, then they are taught within the tribe until one is chosen for sacrifice."

"What?" Laoch tried to hide his surprise, and failed. Sura flinched.

"It is not your place to judge us. *It is our way.* And there is no one who wishes it wasn't more than me. But that is what a Spirit Walker is – they walk with the spirit of their twin until they pass. Or, at least, the shamans tell us that was how it used to be before you came. But we have not had a true Spirit Walker for a thousand years. Each sacrifice has failed, the spirit lost, drawn away. Our shamans are just that, shadows of our past with lore and knowledge many of the young no longer believe. Including me, until Nathair and Leront."

Sura let her gaze drop. Her shoulders were tight, even in spirit form. Laoch noted the creep of Honour's orange that wove deep within her.

"I do not know how they do it, but Nathair is a single spirit torn from her twin. Driven by the pain of that loss ..."

Ecne quieted, watching the emotions dance between Laoch and Sura as he sought a way to help. It had struck her how much closer they had become since Sura's death. With that ridiculous thought in her head, she peered down at the chamber and the mighty dragon that lay waiting within. Looking back upwards, the only possible conclusion was that the artifice had been built inside to keep others away, to wait for a return. That the unalive were its guards ... But it didn't feel right. And they had visited just the one house. Had there been Schenterenta in them all? Could there still be some of Sura's kind out there, hiding because of what lay inside? Yet no Constructors resided here; only their machines, to keep others out.

"Oisin?"

"Yes, Ecne?" The First Ranger peered up the stairs, wary of going anywhere near the chamber.

"Could you ask Keran and Nathair to survey the roof, see if they can ascertain whether this dragon could break through there?"

"Yes. I was thinking the same. I will remain outside on watch. I do not feel right, here." Oisin left, sparing no further glance for the death and ashes, his movements hurried.

Ecne nodded, eyeing Laoch as Sura shut down in her grief. Then she found herself by his side, sliding an arm inside his. It felt awkward, but somehow necessary. "Come, Laoch. We need to seek out books, or some place of learning here. I will not feel safe without another."

Laoch glanced at Ecne, then back to Sura, who stared down into the chamber pit below. Torn.

"Sura? Will you be okay?" Ecne asked.

The flash of orange eyes boring into her in response was swiftly calmed by the elf. "Yes. Go. Take Laoch. I will explore the dragon." She reached out, hand solidifying before the Ranger's eyes. Instinct drove him to slide out Honour's spear and place it in the elven hand. "I can sustain this form for a short while now, but I will come to find you should the palace make an attempt on me. And likewise, call me in return." She rose above the balustrade, the spear shimmering as she dropped down to the floor, her whole form laced with Honour's touch.

"She's changing," whispered Laoch. "Every day, something new."

"All except one thing," added Ecne. "You. Come on. I do not want to stay in this place any longer than I have to."

33
MEISTERS FOREVER LEARN

ERSTEN FOREST, BRANDSHOLD

Meister Arknold marvelled at the drawing formed by blue light that floated within the heartstone chamber. Her eyes roamed over the intricacies and impossibilities it detailed for her. "So, the main body remains intact. This chamber we stand in, is as it was?"

"You got it. Not the neck, though. That has been emptied of all the cogs and wires. Leront says he felt every rip and rend. Peeved to say the least; not that he didn't deserve it." Gowan floated at the edge of the crystal, her form switching between one with dragonesque features and her own each time she conversed with the Spirit Walker. "But the memory remains of what was there, though he moans like a drunken Ranger every time I ask him a question."

"It would take years to remake just the merest part of that which is lost. The refinement of each piece is beyond my skills and our understanding of the metals. This is an impossible task." Arknold dropped into one of the mouldy chairs, its frame's repair one of her few achievements. "These Constructors had knowledge way beyond mine, and a control of the improbable. Even if we put these parts together, the impossibility of the dragon still rages in my mind. It is too heavy to lift and move, never mind fly."

"I know this sounds distinctly strange, Grand Meister, but not to me. I don't understand the – what's the word you used? Ah. Mechanics. But being dead, and still achieving what I did to help my Spear, well, I can understand those *impossibilities*. And I feel Leront's hunger. That is real. He seeks to leech from you at every opportunity."

"So, he knows I'm here?"

Gowan nodded. "Now he has marked you, he always knows where you are in the immediate area. Like a Ranger who learns a guard's way of moving, you can *feel* them in the dark. As soon as you return from the camp or the city, Leront lusts for your spirit. Same with the priests, though more as shadows, as he has not met them."

"Lord Penance wants a trap, Ranger Gowan. One to draw in whatever these creatures are."

"Or a distraction. Like when my Spears raided the supply lines. They'd cause a hoo-hah one side, then attack from the other." Gowan feigned a lean against the table, making Arknold's mind lurch a little.

"I cannot rebuild Leront, but we could expose him. Put the pieces as close together as we can. I can see that attracting someone from above – even from afar, if we can raise the wings with pulleys. But if what you say is true, they will need to *feel* Leront is here. Like the Rangers you describe."

Gowan paused, looking towards the torch set in the wall. "There is a better way to put it. See Leront like a flame. Currently, he is like a torch: if you expose it to the night, you can see it a ways further. Bank it up and—"

"You see him from much further away. But how do we bank a … a spirit?"

"Feed it spiritfire," said Gowan. "When you are ready. Then run like you've set Erin's Wrath to explode. Once he has that, I do not know what would happen next. But he would be a spirit beacon."

"Then, at least we have an achievable task. I will set to that, something I can leave to be done while checking on the new weapons. And what of you, Gowan? How do you fit into this plan?"

"I think I may need to learn how to ride a dragon."

———

Greeth spun the three threads soaked in the cloying elixir, the small crystals binding well to her original seeding. Every time she returned to the new test, the more hopeful Meister Kinst became. On the scorched table nearby lay the swept remains of the last three attempts to imbue even a modicum of spiritfire within the grown crystals.

"Well, Greeth?"

"They are forming well, and faster than before, Meister."

Meister Kinst smiled, her patience belying the fiery exterior she was well known for – each failure was an indication they were a step closer. She had come to consider Greeth as having a calm and measured approach – and one probably as calculating and careful as any of Wisdom's priests. Someone she liked, but did not trust. At least, not yet.

"The last batch has bonded less well, unfortunately."

The knock at the door caused the meister to raise an eyebrow. Sighing as she noted Greeth's engagement with her task, Kinst rose from her stool and approached the door.

At least it isn't Lord Wisdom. There was a man I thought to have a modicum of patience until Lord Penance scared it out of him.

A royal servant waited on the other side of the door, the collar at his neck curling a little as the hallway fluttered with the constant breeze Kinst insisted upon – one that reduced lingering vapours and annoyed the Seven Hells out of Meister Brendt.

"Yes?" she said, raising her eyebrows inquiringly as the lad held out a smooth wooden box.

"For you, from the queen," he replied, and lifted the lid to expose a set of natural crystals ranging from common quartz to uncut diamond. "From her collection as a child. She says there are more, and if any prove of use, she will have her soldiers scour the city and beyond."

Kinst blinked once, then took the clearly precious box, the smooth surface a result of frequent handling and polishing. She had put in a request for someone to seek such a collection out, though the source was the true surprise. Kinst nodded to the lad, even smiled a little, then shut the door.

"Greeth. I think we have some new test subjects. I hope you have reserves aplenty."

The seneschal wandered over and placed her hands in the box, letting a little of her spiritfire glow inside. The facets reflected the green light onto her face and the ceiling. It was the first time she'd had a real chance to attempt this with impunity.

"These are so different! It is difficult to explain, but some leak, while others retain some, if not all, of the spiritfire I released."

"They won't explode, then?" Kinst stepped in closer, letting the light play against her face, enjoying the warmth and, in truth, the sense of wonder.

"I think not. The Houses each use a special Wyrding Stone to contain spiritfire, but those came from the Seven themselves. These are more like those, or at least, some of them are. The ones we grow are like the quarrel tips, though they are not yet strong enough to retain the spiritfire. They want to release it as soon as they can, whereas these are ... calmer." She lifted a small diamond. "For instance, this takes more energy to imbue than the others. It resists, but once inside, I feel it would last longer, not leak like an old bucket. I think we need to speak to Lord Wisdom."

"Not yet, girl." Kinst enjoyed Greeth's wince. "We give him nothing without a little experimentation. We explore the queen's gift, isolate which stones act in what way, then we take those results and *negotiate*."

Greeth couldn't help but smile. The meister's obvious joy in the verbal sparring was something she had begun to understand. It was on par with her discoveries, invigorating the Learned and giving her relief from the tedium of research.

34
THE HUNT CONTINUES

OUTSIDE THE VEIL OF MONDREIN

Popsilin's jaw dropped, her skin stretching like aged elastic. Puffs of dried skin rose to swirl about her on the barge's bridge. She knew the Wyrm had guided them through Repanti's veils, and those of another realm she hardly remembered after dying there, but not how. Buried deep within the vast *Kraken*, her Mechanised Vanguard had simply entered hibernation until called upon from their dreamless sleep to assault wherever the emperor demanded. Now, as the barge wavered at the edge of a spiritfire curtain, she could see the monstrous thing that led their way. Its bony exterior was cracked, mottled skin drawn back, and the sail-like fins juddered as the creature held its position before the veil.

Almost as if it is one of us.

The emperor stood impassive, hands locked behind his back, black crystalline armour reflecting the shined brass and glowing lights as his crew kept the ship steady. A deep blackness surrounded the glowing curtain, one populated by the odd swirl of colour, yet sucking in the light, framing the realm that curved across the horizon of the barge's windows.

"Hold her steady. How long have we been here?"

"Three times around the clock, Emperor," replied the ship's captain, though unmoving from his position in front of the table full of dials and switches next to his seat.

"Then we must be near done. Look." He pointed. Popsilin was already staring as the Wyrm released a surge of spiritfire to part the curtain as if two giant hands scooped it aside. She sensed a passing wash through the bridge, and noted the flicker of the emperor's eyes, the stiffening of his posture. "The Wyrm enters, Captain. Follow her in."

The engine fluttered, the steady thrum increasing, and Popsilin's mind registered the motion as the barge followed the swish of the Wyrm's tail. Light poured around them, white like theirs, shards hitting the windows in an outpouring of rage as it battered at the Wyrm-forged gates.

"Blinds," ordered the captain, and with a twirl of a small wheel, an Inhibitor lowered the stretched black cloth across the windows, easing the light's impact while allowing them to see. "Steady. Do not get too close to the tail's tip. It causes a wake that will disrupt the spirit engines."

They eased through the gap. Popsilin's thoughts lingered on what might happen if the pillars gave out and the gate slammed shut. These soon ended as she eyed the ferocious storm beyond. White energy swirled, arcs of forked lightning slamming into the barge, assaulting the hull with its anger. The *Kraken* crew had talked of such moments, about how each veil was different. Some claimed to see the faces of spirits within, releasing their frustration upon the invaders. Yet others were calmer, their power diminished by time or neglect.

The ship lurched, a thick, searing strike, ramming into the bow.

"Glyph," said Emperor Tarin, calm amidst the crew, who ran from station to station. "A big one—"

A second strike enveloped the Wyrm, this one a wave that wrapped itself around. Whitefire squeezed tight. Popsilin imagined the sound, the crack and pop of bone, as the Wyrm's ribs collapsed inwards, the creature's body driven together into a ball of flesh, dust and bone fragments.

"No!" The Fleshmaster staggered.

Popsilin was halfway to his side before a hand lashed out, shoving her away, the other gripping his skull. A passing hit, a weight that pressed against Popsilin's spirit mind. Her eyes fluttered as the immense, unfocused power roiled into the bridge.

She heard the cries, found herself upon the floor with little idea how she arrived there, and slapped her hands against the polished wood to seek out the emperor. He stood once again in the same position, hands behind his back, eyes set ahead, though his twisted lips betrayed apprehension.

Popsilin rose, staggered slightly, then helped the captain check on the crew. Most were fine. Only one had hit the floor hard enough to expose their skull beneath a flap of skin. The female Inhibitor shook any concerns away and returned to her post.

"The curtain remains." Emperor Tarin turned to face Popsilin. "The Wyrm's death wave caused an internal fracture. The realm leaks, but that is all. Good fortune, Popsilin. One we should not pass up. Check on your Inhibitors and the ornithopters, Captain. Once we have a place to land, you will be our eyes and ears."

"And be wary. They will be expecting us," added Popsilin.

"I think not. Only their magi. Maybe their shamans. But not their people, and that is where we start."

—

Popsilin leant below the crate, eyes on the sole guard who sat, smoking a pipe and sipping from a bottle at the side of his bare feet. The man's legs were lithe, his body clearly honed from time spent at sea, while his face had been ravaged by wind and spray. Deeply lined, tanned and weathered, she struggled to guess at his age. Though, the passing of a human's years was something no longer within her experience. It was a moot point. The ship was their secondary target should the first not produce what they required, despite her keening to take the sailor's spirit and feed.

She signalled her Inhibitors out to the left. The six soldiers kept low, maximising the dock's available cover as they skittered from shadow to shadow. Ahead of them, the wharf slowly changed from ancient, but cared for, stone and wood, to ramshackle huts mingled with the stone façades of more permanent shops and inns. Whatever human habitation this was, it smelt of shit and piss, on top of which was a rot she could not name that overrode everything.

A foul place. No wonder they are not wary. Who would want to raid such a shithole?

Ignoring the line of shops and huts, the Inhibitors descended upon the long building that dominated one side of the wharf, light spewing from its single window. Below it sat an ill-fitting door framed by the same light. Four of her Inhibitors split off to check for a rear entrance.

'It stinks here,' came the thought from her second-in-command, Tenith, which she duly ignored. *'We have a second door and a yard full of rotting plant husks.'*

'Hold there until I enter. Remember, we are trying not to draw any attention,' she replied, keeping the sigh from her thoughts.

Normally, Popsilin would send two Inhibitors in first, weapons raised to crash and burn, before she followed to oversee. However, she knew they needed a model, an example of what the Fleshmaster demanded. The complete change of tactic was something alien to their very nature. They had already made a huge cultural shift over the last five hundred years, from a society purely focused on the individual towards a collective approach to their long-term survival. Something the emperor and his necromancer had drilled into them after their first true failure when attacking a realm. That had been her last reincarnation, and the message had been driven home despite the hunger demands of her spirit body. Nevertheless, how they carried out war, collective or not, remained a bludgeon rather than the cut of a razor-edged blade.

And I am tasked with changing that.

Keeping her handbow ready, she darted into the shadow cast by a pile of rope that sat close by the doorway. Ensuring the two onlooking Inhibitors knew her intent with a single thought, she lifted the latch on the door and let it swing open. A strong waft of plant sap, seawater and salt washed outwards, stinging her eyes and requiring a wisp of whitefire where once, long ago, her body would have used tears to clear it away. With a second lacing of power, her eyes adjusted to the yellow light, and she took two steps inside. Expecting it to be busy, she was taken aback by the vast warehouse apparently devoid of people. The light was caused by rows of glass spheres, each full of a luminescent moss that sat, glowing, above table after table of a plant she took to be seaweed. Ducking lower, the eerie silence was only broken by the sound of waves spilling through the open door. Feeling exposed thanks to the lack of cover, she crept in. But there was nobody in sight. Her hope of taking a few quiet hostages that would be barely missed was dashed.

"You," a tired voice echoed through the quiet warmth. "What are you doing in here, eh? Get out! No place to sleep here. See your grog off somewhere else."

Popsilin, despite herself, spun, her patched cloak of grey swirling. Feeling naked without her armour, the vulnerability set an edge to her need for self-preservation. She eased a finger against the handbow trigger. Forcing herself to keep it below the tabletops, she peered into the murk. The old man's beard reached down to his rope belt, the tunic stained with green and yellow, and his face was as weather-beaten as the boat guard's outside. In his hand lay a sharp, heavy blade. One weighted for chopping.

"I said, get the fuck out of my drying house or you'll be nursing more than a 'angover." The man, broad and barrel-chested, took a step out of a small area of bed and wares she'd missed, the drying globes' light casting them in deep shadow. "Fuck off. You not understand?"

Popsilin had to admit, she was struggling to. The man's drawl was heavily accented, and the occasional word unfamiliar, though his intent was clear. Her Inhibitors breached the door, and she swore. Despite the request for discipline, they had clearly panicked, entering without mentally checking on her first. Or perhaps they *had* tried.

She side-eyed the glowing moss thoughtfully.

Spiritfire.

The guard, if that's what he was, stopped advancing. Popsilin raised the handbow, releasing a single quarrel to slap into the man's shoulder. Whitefire crackled from the tip, low-powered, but focused, and streaked along the man's nerves to slam into his spine. He hit the floor with a pained whimper.

Popsilin shook her head. *"Muffle his mouth,"* she sent.

Glancing outside, her eyes adjusting with a thought, she mulled over options and came to a decision quickly. "Then tie him up. We take the crew while they sleep, cut the ship adrift, then leave."

Move on to another town if we don't get what we need. One by one will be too slow.

She pulled her scarf down to uncover her nose, her ancient senses balking at the foul stink. With her tongue licking the inside of her blue, dry lips, she traced her fingers over the trussed man's cheek, drawing a little of the man's spirit into her own. She threw back her hood, savouring the fear in his eyes when he finally realised what stared back at him.

"Shhh, old man, or your death will be a painful one."

Delicious.

35
A Vicious Mummery

APPROACHING THE FOOTHILLS OF
RIDTH, BRANDSHOLD

T he whisper of metallic skin upon the updraft thrilled the Unspoken, her white eyes dancing as she watched the undulating ground pass below with each powerful beat of An Chéad's wings.

"Gentle, my dragon of the veil. We do not need to hurry. I have not been this far south for a thousand years. So green these fields, and the sheep plump."

The dragon's thoughts and desires invaded hers, and she felt the Spirit Walker's hunger. She had subjugated the shaman so long ago, tearing out his personality, suppressing the spirit so it would not blink to attack her own. It had been necessary and, in truth, a relief from the constant hunger An Chéad had driven into those that rode him.

"Soon," she soothed, placing a shrivelled finger upon the heart-stone. "Lord Penance wishes us to instil some fear, and I am sure we can have some ... fun."

The Unspoken felt the beast's agreement, and together they rode the winds until the foothills near Ridth arose to silhouette against the waxing moon. The metal limbs wavered, adjusting as the huge, mechanised dragon turned northwards to sweep over the stone-built manor house that nestled on the valley side. Noting the well-maintained track heading towards the arterial roads surrounding Ridth, the Unspoken felt a memory stir – of home, Innealtóir, and the smog and cloying ash of the city. A place filled with the twisted minds of her kind, unlike the peace of her mountain valleys. She had built her personal paradise with a beauty her people would never comprehend. And here, on the outer edges of Ridth's fiefdom, she saw similarities in its simplicity.

"But this is not *my* home. Here, An Chéad, is the place to begin."

The artifice adjusted its tail, the overlapping scales rippling as the dragon swooped down towards the cluster of stone buildings that formed a yard to one side of a large manor house. Within twenty yards, the dragon's chest extended, maw widening, its beard catching the last of the moonlight. A flame flickered, orange amid the scarlet metal, and An Chéad let his breath loose. With wings spread, he swooped over the smallest single-storey building. Flame enveloped the roof, turning thatch to cinder and spilling onto the farmyard beyond. Animals screamed, their voices pitched with fear. Music to the Unspoken's spirit. The thrill of their death invigorated, though she forced herself to push it away, locked in a box made of her past enmities.

Her dragon beat at the air twice, passing before the moon. Human cries rose from below as fire and fear took hold. With a thought, An Chéad banked and veered downwards once again, this time a lick of flame heralding his intent as he arrowed towards the other buildings that had flickered faintly with human spirits on their first pass.

"The Seven's draining, and the suppressants, make the hunt so much harder, do they not?"

Again, the dragon's thoughts impinged on her own, a hunger seeking satiation. Sensing the humans had departed the dwelling, the Unspoken let the beast pour dragon's breath upon it. It erupted, ash and burning wood flying into the air to rain down on the six humans fleeing into the fields. An Chéad beat his wings once, rushing over the family, the heavy pressure sending them tumbling to the ground. Bracing his wings wide, he swung around to land, talons extended, as the older humans gathered their children close. The last of the embers and charred wood fell unheeded about them as the scarlet-scaled beast drew itself inwards. Emerging like a ghost from its heaving chest, a flame-haired apparition strode out. Allowing the glamour to fully form, skin porcelain white, her lips ruby and eyes dancing with life, the Unspoken stood before the family like the terror their Houses claimed her to be.

A swathe of hunger washed over the Unspoken's mind – An Chéad, the Spirit Walker, trying to impose its will as the need rose. It thrilled her, running along her spine, alighting emotions dark and dangerous that could lead to her ruin. The sheer pleasure of *taking*, one she had to be wary of. Yet it needed a release, for if she locked it away too tight, the overwhelming desire to feed could leave her exposed to the dragon's needs in her own valley.

She surveyed the fresh meat, eyeing the parents and the four younglings she had selected despite herself. There was a need to be seen, for the word to be passed on that the Unspoken had risen – that she was real, and to be feared.

The taller, elder teenaged girl fell under her gaze. She whipped out the soulreaver, letting the tip balance beneath the girl's chin. Blonde hair wafted in the heat of the fire, gracing the green eyes and tear-stained cheeks. She let the sword draw just a little. The girl's emerald eyes widened as she felt the tug at her spirit. The Unspoken let the pleasure show, her body undulating slightly as the sliver of spiritfire slid along the blade. She shared the moment, letting the girl experience true fear. Yet, letting her pleasure flow for too long would distract from why they were here. She dropped the sword, snapping it sideways to chop into the mother's neck. It bit deep, blood spurting as the woman's spirit drained into the weapon. The excitement came close to shattering her thoughts as the children screamed, but cold reason played out and the Unspoken flicked the sword again, to clatter against the man's head. He collapsed, breathing shallow, and she felt An Chéad murmur behind her. With barely a nod from her, the dragon reacted, tongue lashing around the prone man, drawing the human in for the sharpened teeth to bite down, then flicking the body upwards before swallowing it whole.

The Unspoken turned back to the now-eldest of the family, porcelain fingers gracing the girl's blood-flecked face. "I'm hungry, child," she whispered, "and no one will be safe." She glanced towards the blubbering younglings, their arms wrapped around the girl she held. "Unless you know the location of the Starfire, yes? The jewel your lord boasts of so often."

The tear-filled girl barely nodded, mouth wide. The Unspoken could taste her fear.

"You know?" The Unspoken let her fingers spark with whitefire. "Then show me. There will be blood, girl. More than you have just witnessed. Stay by my side and your younglings may yet live."

She took a grip of the girl's shoulder, guiding her towards the manor house, where guards had spilled out, crossbows cocked.

"An Chéad, if you would?"

The mighty dragon, roaring, powered with two beats of its mighty wings towards the line of soldiers. Quarrels flew, harmlessly pinging off the metallic skin or shattering against the scales. Dragon's fire wreathed ahead. The screams of soldiers could be heard above the burning of armour and flesh. The great dragon wheeled about, its sinuous form shimmering in the fire's glow before another gout of flame shot along the mansion's front entrance to be greeted by cries of pain.

"We go now, child. An Chéad will guard your younglings until we return." The Unspoken strode on, the soulreaver aglow in her hand. She led the girl around the burning guards, unmindful of her worried glances back to her siblings. They reached the front entrance with no resistance.

The door had blown inwards, her dragon having burnt much of it to ash. Leaving a trail of boot prints as she stepped through, the snap of a quarrel string greeted her. The Unspoken stepped aside and, with a flicker of her sword, snapped the shaft. She swirled on into the room, her glamour shifting, twirling with whitefire shadows as she lashed out with sword and fist. The soulreaver drank the spirits of the three inner guards who had lain waiting for her, filling her. The soul-lust impinged on her thoughts.

Reaching the stairs, the heavy thud of metal-booted feet announced more resistance, and the Unspoken felt the thrill of battle. The vitality of her sword began to overwhelm her. She had suspected it would happen after so long, and pushed the girl into a corner.

"Stay there," she whispered through tight lips. "Until I return."

And she danced to the beat of her soul-lust for the first time in a thousand years.

36
WHISPERS OF AN OLD ARMY

Zendril shifted in the saddle, her body sore after so long away from the beasts that her old bones had decided she deserved to be punished. "Fucking saddle. Could you not have found me a more comfortable one, Mander? Where the hell did you get this one? The Duke of Ridth?"

Mander smiled. Zendril was well aware he was hiding his own discomfort as the saddle soreness rode up his cleft. If he spoke of it, she had the ridicule primed and ready, though as she suffered, it had already begun to spill out.

"And why in the Seven Hells do we have to travel at such a slow pace? This is urgent, Mander." Zendril peered back over her shoulder, taking in the carriage and the priests sat in the bench seat. "Sod this. We need to get moving. How far?"

"Ten more miles by the marker posts," replied Mander, waiting for an expletive-laden reaction that never came. "If you intend to go ahead, you need to take a guard. Queen's orders. You are now a *precious* resource the Union cannot lose."

Zendril turned her glare upon him. He winced, feeling the pain in his leg spurred by never-forgotten memories of a sound beating. "I'm sure she agreed you could come just to make my life worse."

Mander nodded, eyes to the sky. They both knew full well he was there at Zendril's insistence.

"Stay here, lest the guard feel I've gone missing."

Zendril pulled at the right rein, and the horse turned to trot down the line. She passed the priests' carriage, sparing little of her valuable attention on those inside except for Death's priest, who sent her a hand sign she recognised.

Unfortunately, I can't help. We all must bear a burden, and none of them can bloody ride. Think their arses might be sorer than mine.

When they'd set off from the Halfway Inn, there had been twenty veterans in their wake, carrying a mixture of age and weaponry Zendril admired. She recognised none, but they knew her; some by sight, all by reputation. Most were horsed, though clearly the beasts were broad of chest and shoulder. Plough horses, working animals, and as tough as they come as long as things were quiet. But of little use while untrained, and perhaps too old to learn new tricks.

She brought her horse in next to an ex-sergeant-at-arms, one Mander had heard rumour of becoming their unofficial leader by default. Zendril rechecked the name, thinking on the pronunciation with care. She had forged loyalty in the past by endearing herself to the soldiers. *If they believe in you, they'll follow you even into the mouth of hell.*

"Sergeant Sternath, how fare the veterans?"

The man smiled, two gaps within a white-toothed grin that matched the scar that ran from his cheek to the corner of his mouth. Despite everything, there was something vaguely familiar about the man, though his accent hinted at being born somewhere near Makalena. She had never commanded their forces.

"Better than the soft-arsed priests in that carriage. Thought the pious were s'pposed to 'old with their Gods in every endeavour?" Sternath replied, the grin wide.

Zendril let a laugh slip, the conspiratorial smile of a soldier reaching her lips. "Aye. Well, we're the ones usually on our knees."

"Ain't that the truth." The man hawked, then leant over his saddle to spit on the ground. "Can I speak plainly, General?"

"Not a general yet, Sergeant. But aye, you may." Zendril eased her back a little, catching the man's brief flash of sympathy. She suspected none of them had ridden for this long in a while.

"Well, is this another fucking sham reason for a crusade?"

Zendril feigned surprise, amazed it had taken this long for the initial enthusiasm to break out into rumours of falsehoods and lies. Put soldiers together, people who are willing to give their lives for their country or their faith, and they want to know if the cause is truly what they believe it to be. Part of Zendril hated what she was about to say, but it was a fact of war that you could not tell everyone everything. Besides, the cause was true, just the assailant was different to what she could admit to. Some leaders would have qualms about what needed to be said.

Fuck that. It only leads to more deaths than are necessary.

"No crusade, by my word, Sergeant. I'm not going to deny the Unspoken was seen, nor deny Ersten Forest did not have sight of a fucking dragon." She touched the side of her nose. The ex-sergeant nodded, a little wide-eyed. "But you have it true from me: this is a threat to our homes, and the towns will be the first to be targeted. We need to make them as safe as possible."

"Places people can retreat to," added Sternath, nodding.

"And places where we can hold out as long as possible. They're coming, and we won't be enough without fortifying the towns. We've been soft for too long."

"You've got a good forty behind me, General. But if you want more, then one of those firebrand speeches of yours in a town market won't cut it. The Crusade left scars. Most of us, well, we avoid people."

Zendril blinked, thinking over where the sergeant was leading her to. Being cloistered in Death's House had hidden her from the people, though not the machinations of the Houses and the Royal Court. And it struck her that, for all of Lord Penance's intentions, and those of her daughter, they would live and die by the people they tended. And they were not as blinkered, perhaps, as those on high truly thought.

"Then what, Sergeant, do you suggest?"

"Oh, I'm no sergeant, yet." The man smiled, hawking and spitting again. "But you need those riding be'ind us to truly believe in the cause. Only then will they be yours through and through. No one knows a vet—"

"—like a vet."

"Aye. See, no pretty speeches. But words around a campfire, sharing a glug or two? That will get you 'eard. They're 'ere because they *want* to believe. As do I."

"And then?"

"We scatter to the four winds and spread the word. But you'll need to let them know where you want them to go."

"And each will have their own set of skills." Zendril sat heavily back into her saddle, instantly regretting the movement as her spine reintroduced itself into the conversation.

"That they will – and a view on where's best to use them. But you and I both know they'll not 'ave a bloody clue. They'll need your guidance, or at least someone who speaks with your voice."

"You mean you?" Zendril raised an eyebrow when the veteran shook his head.

"Not my place. Mander is as much known as you."

"And will do as I instruct. You surprise me, Sergeant."

The smile was grim, pulling the cheek in close with its misshapen scar tugging at the eyebrow. "That's what the Unbeliever said when he gave me this—" He pointed to the scar, "—while I gutted 'im. Just a soldier with thoughts, General. Happy to be ignored."

—

Zendril spat into the campfire, Mander at her elbow, as they watched the flames in silence.

"Doubts? You?" Mander sneered a little, though it was all a sham. Worry for Zendril gnawed at his thoughts.

"Don't sound so bloody surprised. I wasn't cloistered in Death's House in the dingiest shithole she could find because I was feeling good about things." She nudged into his elbow, eager to have his arms around her, though she knew full well the pretence of her status dictated it couldn't happen. "But it's been years."

"You have the same mouth, the same thoughts, and the same level of swear words. Can't see 'ow you should be concerned. Get out there, like this sergeant said. Have a glug. But whatever in the Seven Hells you do, don't plan your words. Remember the last time you did that?" Mander rubbed at his calf, where the scar still pulled whenever he thought of the day Zendril had been stood down by Prince Consort Adama. A wry grin passed, not unnoticed by Zendril, who shoved him off the log.

"Fucker."

She rose, striding over his laughing form, and headed out towards the campfires at the rear of the procession their party had become.

Mander followed, collecting the green-leaf rum and limping in her wake, still guffawing. "Do you remember when you questioned his parentage? Adama's face."

"And look where it got me."

She passed the priests' fires, nodding to them as she went, but lingered by Death's priest long enough to check the man was okay. Moving onwards, Mander scampered up to walk beside her, grin still in place.

"Right where you are needed," said Mander. A sideways glance let him know she was listening.

Zendril stopped in a gap between fires. The cold bit a little, but she needed the shadows as she reached out and squeezed Mander's arm. "We would have still withdrawn, Mander. They were dug in, the mountain valleys their home."

"But you would have kept trying, and more would have died. You're brilliant, General, but bloody stubborn. Adama failed faster, and the withdrawal was a shambles after his injury. These vets remember your discipline and passion. Harness that, but—"

"Take counsel." She let a hand wander up to his face, squeezed out a smile accompanied by a brief nod. "Fucking hate it when you're right." She tapped him lightly on the cheek, then strode off towards the rear. "Bloody hurry up with that rum."

Zendril strode into the fire's light, swagger in place, face grim, but she allowed a flicker of a soldier's greeting to pass with each of those sitting around the cooking pot. From the bag wrapped around her jerkin, she pulled out the two skinned rabbits and slapped them on the butcher stone they were using.

"Thought you might be in the mood for some extra meat for the pot. I like mine cooked through, but none of that boil it until it's fucking tasteless like Mander does." She winked as Mander entered, trailing behind, mummery at play as his limp increased and a sneer played across his face. "Did you remember the bloody rum, at least?"

Mander dropped the heavy jug onto a stone next to the smaller glass bottles the soldiers had already placed there. Whistles and grunts emanated from behind, and soon the campfire had an audience huddling in close. To one side, an ex-sergeant with a grin pulled by a wicked facial scar.

Zendril gave him a short nod, then looked around the gathering. "You'd better get yourselves a shot of the green stuff before I talk, 'cos you're either gonna shit your pants or run for the hills. Those that stay are the ones I know I can count on to defend the Union. This is no fucking story. Hear me."

Mander lifted the jug, walking between the group, looking each one in the eye as he poured them a slug, Zendril talking all the while. He stopped when he faced Sternath and looked the scarred man eye-to-eye. Blinked away tears as a hand reached out and squeezed his arm. A single finger rose, requesting silence, and Mander – ever faithful – nodded in return.

By the time he'd walked back to the fire, with Zendril in full flow and the rum half gone, the sergeant had left. Only, in Mander's mind, he hadn't. A tug of duty unfulfilled strangled his thoughts until a hand slapped at his thigh.

"More rum, Mander. There's greater bravery in these fuckers than I thought. I only expected five or six of the more unbalanced ones to say."

Mander rose, eyeing the crowding veterans. Few, if any, had left. He limped around to distribute the remaining green-leaf spirit.

37
THE DESIRE

Innealtóir, Realm of the
Constructors

"Well?"

"There are hundreds of books here. Thousands, maybe. It would take years to read all this." Ecne swirled in the centre of the immaculate room. Clear of vermin, insects or even dust. It was eerie. "The only chance we have is to try to find out how they've been catalogued ..." Ecne paused, eyes locked on the doorway, head cocked.

"What is it?" asked Laoch, spinning, hand upon Justice's pommel as he eyed the entrance to the library. "You see something?"

"I ... I am not sure." She blinked. Laoch picking out the haze of green that weaved its way around her pupils. "No. I just need some time to think and browse. Look for patterns."

"I'll check on Sura, leave you to think awhile." Laoch headed for the door, hand still braced on the sword. "And yell ... loudly ..."

Ecne waved him away and reached down to place one hand on the heavy crossbow. The sigil glowed at her touch. She glanced back up at the doorway, a creeping sense of being watched growing in her mind.

"Just all this talk of the building. Nothing more. There's no un-alive. We swept every room."

Deciding she needed Wisdom's comfort, she lifted the crossbow's strap over her shoulder, letting the God's weapon rest against her back as she approached the right-hand wall of brass-edged wooden shelves. In any normal library, they would be dust-covered; even the specialist sections within the university gathered detritus as time passed. Yet here, the cleanliness was striking. When she withdrew a tome on architecture and leafed through it, she found the pages crisp with a metallic sheen to them. Near perfect.

The treatise focused upon the material combinations for small towers like those they had spied from Nathair's original landing place. Much made sense; different alchemical combinations to form elixirs that would make Meister Kinst jealous. Yet amid the familiarity, the use of spiritfire appeared common. What had been a shock to her world – and, to a degree, an attack on a faith she never realised she held – was in constant use here. She expected it to be so, but seeing it written about in such a mundane way, brought it home. The Constructors lived their lives with spiritfire, white against Wisdom's green, as a tool and an ingredient. It was special only in that the source was *taken*, not mined.

We are simply an expendable ... a resource.

"We do not matter." Ecne felt a breath of air flutter against her neck and her hair rose. A pulse of green warmed her back in response. She spun, hand reaching for the crossbow's stock, to find no one there. Except Wisdom's touch on her mind disagreed as much as her sense of danger did. "Is Laoch beginning to affect my judgement? Is everything really out to get me?"

She turned back to the shelves, running her finger along the line of books ...

Wisdom lashed out, a spike of green spiritfire that singed the very air Ecne breathed. The Learned threw herself to the ground, expecting fire and flame, and the books to cook. As she rolled over, a battle ensued in the centre of the room – spirit upon spirit. Whitefire spat, writhing in near-human form as Wisdom, appearing much as Ecne's God had in the ancient mosaic on Brandshold, held it back. Hands formed where green fought white, pressing backwards. The blurred face of Wisdom strained as the whitefire crackled wildly.

"Laoch," squealed Ecne, her voice high-pitched and raw from the heat. She swallowed, sucking in a breath before bellowing, "Laoch!"

The squeak of leather upon marble came as a relief as footfalls approached, the sound welcome but highlighting the silence of the battle that raged. Whitefire arced, lightning filling the room, and the acolyte stared as her mind struggled to process what she was seeing. These were not streaks of power lashing out, but inwards – the palace walls *feeding* the spirit creature, helping it to overwhelm Wisdom.

"Sura was correct," she whispered as she scrabbled up against the bookcase, pressing back as her legs pushed her up to gain her feet. A flash of scarlet speared through the room – Justice's arrow rammed into the white apparition. Red light writhed over the creature. Ecne saw it then, the travesty of a *human* form. Bent, twisted, wired with metal and cogs that whirred and locked in the struggle with Wisdom. A second arrow struck the creature's cowled head, the redfire highlighting what lay inside, and the first sound erupted in the room. It spoke of *hate* and *pain*, *anger* and *dismissal*. Raging, it broke off from Wisdom and tore across the space towards Laoch with terrifying speed.

Ecne moved, she didn't know how, and found herself in the doorway, blocking the attack on Laoch. The seething, roiling ball of hatred rammed into her chest. Smoke spewed from the leather jerkin as fear encased her thoughts, but Wisdom swathed her body, wrapping the white in a second battle of wills. With her mind fighting the reality of what she'd just done, the Learned spread her arms wide. Throwing her head back, with pain wracking her entire body, she fainted.

—

Water dripped, its cooling splash tickling at Ecne's nose, rolling down to grace her lips and tongue. Her eyes fluttered as a second trickle alighted on her eyebrow, flicked away as the acolyte forced the eye open. She found herself in darkness, the smell strange – a dry heat, perhaps, that left a taint of burned meat upon the air. Groaning, Ecne pushed herself up from the stone floor, hands pressed against a marble she fully expected to be cold, only to be rewarded with heat and warmth. She felt it flex beneath her palm, and a nausea rose in her stomach as whitefire licked at her fingertips.

"No."

A similar glow lit the nearby walls, each lined with far more books than the library she remembered. Ecne gained her feet to gaze along long rows, engulfed by shadow in both directions. She raised her hand, turning it this way and that, fearing the whitefire that danced there.

"Embrace it, child. This is my world. Such power I have to bring you to my spirit abode."

The voice was soothing, like honey, gentle upon her mind. Ecne could not decide whether it was truly out loud. A cackle broke her thoughts and Ecne spun, recognising the figure that sat upon a wooden throne. This one was hale, though beneath its cowl the skin remained dry and cracked, lips blue. Ecne held no doubt that it was the same creature. It seemed so real, yet had spoken of a spirit home.

"Embrace the gift I offer. Let me show you the wonders the Flesh-master and I achieved."

Ecne felt her senses swarm and recoil, forming a barrier as the Constructor closed in on her, but remained unable to reason what to do. The aged hand touched her cheek, cracked, withered skin setting a fear in her bowels. Dust flaked, and the sickness reached her throat as they fluttered up her nose when her lungs demanded air.

"Yes. You can feel the gift, child. Let me sever your spirit, free you from the flesh that imprisons it. Join with me and live the true life we were ... created for."

The white eyes flared, boring into her mind. A purple tongue licked at stained, cracked teeth as the aged hand ran down her cheek to cup the acolyte's chin.

"I can feel your *need* to know. What I offer gives you time. Know what I know, become more." The honeyed voice soothed Ecne's mind, insinuating its reason into her thoughts. She knew in her soul the evil playing out before and within her, but could not muster the will to fight it. Giving in would be so much easier. Simpler. And perhaps an end to the sickness that boiled along her veins. She felt her spirit stretch, its roots deep within her head and heart, thin and vulnerable as the voice took hold. "Let yourself be free. Your body is young, virile. Sweet to the taste."

Realisation cut through her addled thoughts. It spoke of *severing* the spirit, setting her soul free to roam the palace. The price? Her body forfeit, inhabited.

The spirit formed a blade in its hand, a scalpel, such as Meister Kinst would use to cut soft rocks or examine bodies. It glinted, whitefire dancing along the blade, and she felt the edge slice through her skin, slide into her body, cut towards the root of her *self*.

My soul.

"Yessssss."

Orange light flashed, the spear searing the air to drive deep into the Constructor spirit's back. Sura withdrew it and backed up a step before powering it into the spirit's neck and up towards the head. The tip pierced the skull and Honour screamed her will. Whitefire battled orange as the Constructor recoiled from the pain.

Ecne collapsed to the floor, heart beating, mind reeling while she searched her body for the wound and expected blood. There was none, her body whole as far as she could find. The Constructor's honeyed voice was now lost in the agony Sura inflicted. The acolyte glared upwards, Wisdom's fire, released from the internal prison the Constructor had encased around it, flashing in her eyes. The sliver of her God fought Ecne's fear for precedence, using reason to overcome the Learned's need to *destroy*.

Knowledge.

Ecne pushed herself to her feet as Sura twisted the spear tip, the elf solely focused on killing what assailed her charge. The acolyte stepped in, hands out, grasping the Constructor's flayed head, and drove her own Wisdom-enhanced thoughts deep into the evil spirit mind, which flailed at her assault.

"I need to know." Ecne's words slipped from gritted teeth. Nausea roiled as the defiler of spirit and mind poured its hate back at her. Sickened, but strengthened by knowing she was following her God's will, she pierced the veiled mind. Refuting the scalpel's subtlety, she bludgeoned inwards, flailing about the creature's thoughts with untrained abandon. All the while, Wisdom picked at the remnants she left, the fear and loathing, the true reasons the Constructor had fled to the walls of the palace. And it knew. And when Wisdom understood, it pulled Ecne clear.

"Kill it," the embittered words rasped from her throat. The acolyte stepped back as Sura drove the spear deep, a pulse of orange writing along its shaft, shattering the spirit form into a myriad shards of bitterness and ancient dread.

Ecne stood aside, hands pulsing with greenfire, mind wide, filling the space with thoughts and memories that were far from her own. Sickened, a voyeur watching bloodied hands and a hateful mind at work, she collapsed to her knees and welcomed the void.

38
LOST SOULS ENTWINED

Sucreta slipped from the bed, her white hair brushed back around her ears, smooth skin creased from the press of the pillow. She let a hand glide over the sleeping form that lay half under the covers, chest gently rising as Lady Honour slept on.

Her thoughts flickered through the memories of the night before. It had been *delicious*, the drawing of a suppurating wound healed by the touch of hand and mind. The faintest of smiles brushed her red lips and she rose, slipping on the thin black dressing robe left draped at the side of her bed. In the centre of the room lay her Wyrding Stone, inert, lifeless. But last night they had merged, wrapped their spirits about themselves and ridden the pathways to Death's veil. A moment of shared joy. Looking down upon her splayed fingers,

Lady Death sought the cracks and dying skin that accompanied such journeys. But there were none, her hand and arm no worse than the day before. A glance to the table revealed the waiting needle and black elixir that she had, for the first time, refuted. The sharing of power had been a ... a surprise and delight, heightening the joy of what followed.

Something to share with the Gods' Council.

Though not all of it.

Barefoot, the stone floor cold and unyielding beneath, she padded across to her door. Lifting the latch with practised care, she headed along the corridor to press her ear to the final cell door. Silence ensued, and she again unlatched and entered with barely a whisper of her gown.

Nesca lay upon the pallet, the mattress sweat-stained. Lady Death gently rolled the priest-in-waiting away from its cloying cloth. The smell hit her nostrils with impunity, the sores flaring with a poisonous white and purple haze. Lady Death placed her fingertips upon the largest, the heat scorching, and swore softly under her breath. Letting Nesca settle back into place, she cleaned her hand using the cloth and water beside the bed before raising Nesca's eyelid. A white orb stared back, veins pulsing with the junip she had used as a last resort.

Sucreta flinched, the *woman* encumbered by the mantle of being Lady Death moved by the horror of Nesca's plight. A gentle sliver of her power caressed Nesca's mind, only to be met by a fetid wrongness that set her senses whirling. Tears welled unbidden when the gentlest of hands reached out, fingers collecting a single tear before entwining with hers.

"You are not the only silent one," whispered Lady Honour, the thin sheet wrapped around her body. "She suffers."

Death squeezed gently, looking to her new lover, before placing a blackened hand upon Nesca's brow. "I must welcome her to Death's embrace, though not the veil itself. I cannot watch her suffer any longer. The soul has withered, Honour."

With her own tears spilling upon the hem of the sheet, Lady Honour placed her hand upon Death's. And, with unspoken agreement, spiritfire flowed. Gentle at first, but as the evil twisted and fought, clinging to its unlife and the consumption of what had once been Nesca, they both seared their *will* deep into her skull, demanding her release. Black and orange spiritfire enveloped the white, squeezing, negating. And, ultimately, killing.

A sigh left pursed lips, the single breath touching both Death and Honour, and Nesca's body sagged deeply into the soaking bed. Arms wrapped about each other, they watched a while before Lady Death touched Nesca's brow and then raised an eyelid.

"She has passed."

"If this is what the Constructors bring, we may find our time short," breathed Lady Honour, sparing a last glance, tears spilling unchecked as she rose to her feet. She squeezed her lips tight, and turned to Lady Death. "And we should act soon on what we learned last night. I – we need to repair my glyph and enhance the healing of my veil."

"Then we should break the night's fast and do so. Lord Penance has left the city, and Fate upholds the Council until his return. On her agreement, then?"

Lady Honour nodded, then buried her head into Lady Death's shoulder.

—

"What is that?"

Terana Fiotir Na Partera stared at the crystal set deep within the table. A glyph inlaid in gold surrounded it, with seven seats set around the wooden top, each with one strand of the metal pointing their way. It reminded the aged Schenterenta of a compass, though one misaligned.

"A Wyrding Stone, one linked to the Gods' Council and not an individual House. See, you have already learned something you did not know." Lord Penance dropped the backpack on the floor, weary. With one eye on the elf, he allowed a wisp of purple spiritfire to seep up his arm and into his body.

"Pffff. Your people have as many secrets as mine. The only difference is that you hide them away in buildings of stone, and we in rock and wood."

Lord Penance tried not to smile at the elf's constant need to fight her corner. An admiration he had no idea if Terana shared, but at least she was here.

How long will that modicum of trust last after what comes next? Sneed will not forgive me.

He pulled a purple crystal from the pack, placed it on the table, and allowed a gentle glow from his fingers to trigger the stone. Terana Fiotir Na Partera pulled back, eyes wide, a hand raised unbidden to cover her mouth.

"Sorry. But explaining it would take far too long. You have your myths around the spir—"

"Myths? Truths. You approach the Elders with such words and your tongue may well end up the same colour as your teeth, old man."

The folding of arms and hardening of stance brought Penance up short, a wariness he realised would be needed with these prickly people. Each time he thought he had Terana's measure, she would bite back. Likely a result of an embittered people. Which his people had caused in their desperate need to look after their own.

He raised both hands, one withered, one hale. "My apologies. And yes, I think you tend to throw me off balance, Terana."

"Be wary. We Schenterenta value our words and song. They do not spill from lips, only to be easily retracted. Each should be considered, cultivated. You need to approach this moot as a Lord and keep to our expected formalities. Outside of my university rooms, I am Terana Fiotir Na Partera, just as you are *High* Lord Penance."

"Then," he said, rising to his feet and grasping his cane from beside his chair, "perhaps a little honesty would be beneficial to us both. By our measure of time, I am 46 years young." Ignoring the apparent shock upon her face, he carried on. "The burden of my office cripples my body, yet sharpens the mind. Under this sufferance, I protect my people, all of them, in unison with the Houses and the Crown. What I am about to do has not been attempted since before High Lord Sneed gained office, that Overseer dying soon after. Drained of life. A husk. You still wish to partake?"

"If a human faces the danger, then why would a Schenterenta turn away? What do I do?"

"Place your hands upon the Wyrding Stone, focus your mind on a vision of yourself – every detail – then fill that vessel with whom you are. Your *self*. Similar to those rituals you have deigned to share with our meisters. My apologies, but I will then need to place my hands upon yours. Do I have your permission?"

With a tight smile, the elf followed the instructions, eyes closed and junip-purple lips still. The faintest of nods, and the High Lord, placing his hands on top of hers, allowed himself to be drawn inwards, though riding an unfamiliar surge of power as the Gods' Council sigil fired. With his spirit torn from its roots in mind and heart, he flooded his own body, surging through arms and fingers to the very edge of entering Terana. He sent a sliver of thought to grace her skin, an acknowledgement and permission sought. Goosebumps rose on the elf's skin, a quiver of exhilaration parting the barrier and allowing him entry. Purple-shrouded, Lord Penance's spirit entered the elven body, tugging at the roots of her spirit buried deep – far deeper than in a human – only to sense their release. Not ripped nor torn, like his, more unearthed with practised ease, a gentleness coupled with reverence that brought his spirit close to tears. With a gentleness inspired by this act, he guided her down and through her palms to alight against the harsh stone. Here, Lord Penance felt the elf's reluctance. Fear, even. The stone, a symbol of containment and reverence, where they laid their dead until the day their spirits could truly be freed again.

And this is why I am here.

More than a little pleased to match her grace, he entered the pathway between the bonds of the stone, purple spiritfire wreathing him and wrapping the Schenterenta in the softest of blankets to pull her through and ease her dread. Human and elf entered the flow surging between the paired crystals. Lord Penance embraced the current, seeking the lodestone Tixar carried – a trust between Schenterenta and human that had rarely been experienced before.

A moment to cherish.

'Speak for yourself.'

The beacon flashed in the purple void, not so much a light as a pull to steer and guide. Penance sensed Terana's reluctance to leave their freedom, but the necessity was just as strong a tug as the beacon itself. They swirled downwards, spirits embraced, as they slammed into the Wyrding Stone Tixar had carried in haste to the tribal meeting. He felt Terana squirm at the confinement, and in turn rail at him for the walls that surrounded her.

And a song rose. Woven rhythms built from voices, its pattern compelling and full of vitality. He felt a shift as if the bonds of the crystal widened, allowing space and time for him and Terana to fill. The Schenterenta words coalesced in his spirit mind, catching, hooking him closer to his companion within the stone. The path leader became the follower as he emerged from the crystal within Tixar's hand to witness the dance of Terana Fiotir Na Partera's spirit amid her people. Words solidified her form, the fabled lifesong heard for the first time by human ears.

Abruptly, the song stopped, the pitch high, as if rising to a crescendo that never occurred. The elf stood, her form near-solid, amid the glistening grass and warm embers of a campfire. The tribal elders all waited, arms resting upon aged spears, peering inwards as their song wafted away upon the plain's wind. Lord Penance peered down at his own form, mind uncomprehending, expecting to be speaking from the Wyrding Stone yet somehow dragged into existence, though a mere shadow. Finding himself staring at his hands, he let his eyes wander over to the silent Elders, and then on to Terana Fiotir Na Partera, whose smirk caught him off guard.

She turned away from him, arms wide. "Elders, I thank you for the gift of my lifesong and my release from the Wyrding Stone. It has been too long. Thanks to Tixar Na Fiotir, I have brought High Lord Penance to speak with you."

Still taken aback by how casually she accepted being there, hundreds of miles from where her body waited, Lord Penance flinched at his name. With a gentle pulse, he felt the sigil upon his ephemeral cane affirm his God's presence, and he gathered himself, trying to ignore the fact he was a *spirit*.

"Elders of the Schenterenta tribes. Please forgive, or at least accept, any ignorance of your rites and formalities. Terana Fiotir Na Partera has had no time to prepare me for this, nor I, in truth, her." He gave a formalised bow of the head and shoulder to each of the five eldest in the circle, locking eyes as he did so. This, at least, he knew. "Being here costs me much, and I expected to be conversing from the Wyrding, rather than in – erm – spirit."

Silent stares beat him back, a confusion in his mind until he remembered there should be six.

And so the High Lord is played once again.

He turned to face the still-smirking Terana, gracing her with a bow and locking eyes. The elf returned the bow, and the tension descended into a hubbub as his name flew amid a tumble of words between the Elders. He waited, gathering himself, realising that he may well hold many of the strings in the Union, but none here. Possibly less than that.

"It is hard to say that you are welcome here, High Lord," an aged Schenterenta spoke with a husky deliberateness, eyes cast to him but not on Penance's own. "It is on Terana Fiotir Na Partera's word alone that we have allowed this. And the manner in which you are here pains us." The last two words dripped with a bitterness he had been expecting. Though little was known about their communion with ancestors, the representations he had heard and seen all spoke of a presence. And the Spirit Walkers were very real, the Unspoken's artifice dragon evidence of that, whatever the forbidden books may allude to.

"I understand." He glanced over to Terana. Her eyes glittered in the firelight and she nodded briefly, gesturing for him to begin. "I come with information you have been seeking for a thousand years. You will not like what I have to say, will spit upon my spirit, and rail against my Gods. It will hurt in the telling and is a burden I have held since first becoming a priest-in-waiting. I wish my Houses could have shared it earlier, but in this telling, I reveal much that is hidden from our own people. Before I begin, I must know that it remains within this campfire's light and goes no further until we are ready to face what is coming."

"Coming?" asked the first Elder. "*More* of your kind?"

Lord Penance could taste the bitterness riddled within the words and syllables.

"Perhaps I should start at the end, then begin again. The soul-eaters are coming, they have found our, and your, realm." He noted the confusion laced with disbelief, and felt the sigil's power writhe about him, the purple glow of his God infusing his form. Power entered his voice, and though far from solid, his spirit strengthened. "They are ravenous and unrelenting, and they take Spirit Walkers as twisted pets to ride their metal dragons. When they arrive, the soul-eaters will take your shaman, kill them, and flay their spirits until they are as evil as themselves. The Constructors will kill your people, enslaving those of mine who survive as spirit-dolls to sup from at their will." He strode out and looked each of the Elders in the eye, all contrition gone. A High Lord in the presence of a power his people needed. "And you disbelieve every word I say as a mere human trick to hide the arrival of more of our kind."

He spun, flashing out Penance's whip to crack above the campfire. Purple-tinged light coalesced, swirled, reformed, until Nathair flew above the orange flames. Sensing disbelief wash across the moot, he took his chance before it could take root. "A dragon of the veil, Nathair, risen again and returning to its masters. It murdered Sura-nista, though Terana Fiotir Na Partera tells me her spirit may still be free. If it rides anywhere, it is within this creature."

The murmurs rose, not of disbelief this time, the tone more pained and angered. Had he lost them, gone too far?

"That troubles us more than you can know," said Terana, her words spilling almost unbidden as she stared at the floor.

Penance stared at her, thoughts whirling, collapsing in on themselves.

"Why?"

She looked to the first Elder, the one the High Lord took to be the leader of the moot. He nodded curtly. "She was marked. Nista, daughter to an Elder, and a twin."

"Marked?"

"A Spirit Walker, High Lord. They are all twins, though this one riven from her calling by her brother's death. And also, Betana Refi Na Partera's daughter." Her eyes flicked to the first Elder who wavered against his spear, eyes glistening. "At least we have some awareness of what may have happened. That is, if you speak true." She lifted her chin then. Lord Penance was unsure if it was a dismissal or an affectation to hide the pain.

"Then let me start from the beginning. My time is short. My spirit cannot remain here for much longer." And he began to speak, shifting a long-held burden, wishing it could be shed rather than merely reframed as he exposed his people's deceit.

39
HE WHO WAITS

INNEALTÓIR, REALM OF THE CONSTRUCTORS

"Ecne!" Rough hands, calloused from hours gripping a sword and bow, embraced dry cheeks, beseeching the acolyte to awaken. "Girl, come on!"

Ecne coughed and rolled over, letting the phlegm hit the floor. She didn't know why, but a prickle in the back of her sore head suggested she refrain from letting it hit whoever spoke.

"Thanks. At least you missed this time."

The hands tapped at her cheek, then withdrew. Light played at the edges of her closed lids, bright, painful, but oh-so-welcome as the memories hit her. A blackness, an evil that dripped sweet promises. Her very soul under threat.

A stealer of bodies.

Her eyelids sprang open, and instant regret slammed into her brain as the brightness crashed in. "Ow," she croaked, and scrunched her eyes closed again.

She put a hand out and received a water skin in return. A sip of warm but welcome liquid eased the rawness, and she tried again, shoving fingers deep into her eye sockets and blinking away the light spots before opening them again.

"You all right in there, girl?" She glanced up. Oisin knelt at her side, tapping the side of his head.

"Since when have I been a girl, mountain man?"

"Since it annoys you, raises your hackles and gets you back with us. Learnt that from Laoch."

He stood, holding out a hand. Ecne peered behind him to catch Laoch's smirk and Keran's cross-armed spirit, standing by the throbbing heartstone. She took his hand, allowing him to pull her to her feet. Dizziness swirled and she staggered, only for Oisin to gather her in and set her right again.

"Thanks."

"Nathair says he can only sense the girl's spirit in there. No one else. Says she smells good."

"Good?" said Laoch. "As in tasty? Do you think you could have kept that to yourself?"

Keran spluttered, reddening despite his spirit form. "No, Ranger. As in, not tainted."

Oisin released her, and Ecne took an unsteady but successful step towards the scaled spirit.

"Does she know who it was?"

Keran paused, eyes distant. "She suspects."

"I've nearly had my spirit ripped from my body, Keran." Ecne replied, glowering at the spirit, anger flaring in trembles across her body.

"There's no one here who knows more about that, Acolyte, than me. Sura in death, yes. But only me in life. You will have to forgive any vagueness; I am changing, and Nathair is a thousand-year-old spirit – and a twisted one at that. Not everything is as clear-cut as in your books and scrolls."

"And most of those appear to have been lies," added Ecne, letting the anger spill into bitterness. "That spirit was old; I would say wise, but perhaps Learned would be a better term. It knew loneliness, and a depth of despair beyond my ability to comprehend. It has been without a body for a long time."

"Nathair concurs. The creatures we fought, the unalive, stir a memory of experimentation. She talks of a necromancer – an artificer of the dead – who worked with her maker, the Great Artificer Viseri. She names them Marbhleoir."

"A necromancer?" cut in Laoch. "I do not know that term."

"A raiser of the dead." Oisin uncrossed his arms, eyes roaming from Ecne to Laoch. "It is in our tales, somewhere. Those you tell around the campfire. Someone who unearths the dead and ... I don't know how to describe it. Not invested with a spirit like ..."

"Me." Sura slid out from the spear where she had been resting, eyes glittering. "And Keran. We are spirits that think, like the one Ecne and I fought. We *are* the people we once were—" She smiled at Laoch, lips tight. Laoch responded in kind. "—but the unalive were not. Not empty, but what resided in there was mindless and followed a ... a preordained path."

"Flesh artifices," Ecne's voice croaked, struggling with the words. "Yes. That was the picture in my head. Though garbled. It saw my body like a block of stone, ready to be sculpted into what it wanted. The ... that thing on the throne. That's what it saw as perfection. A crafted body." She peered at her hands, palms up, blinking back thoughts that rode in unbidden on the backs of the dead. "We need to have a look. This *necromancer* wanted my body to inhabit. Wisdom ..." Ecne spun as if suddenly remembering her God, and walked over to where her crossbow lay glowing against the wall. Placing her hands upon the sigil, she lifted it and swept the room with green eyes. "It's driven to find the emperor. The Fleshmaster. To talk of its success in *crafting* the unalive bodies. But we don't know why. There's a piece missing."

Ecne stared open-mouthed at Laoch, then spun, heading out of the heartstone room and towards the edge of Nathair's pocket. When it didn't shimmer, she looked back over her shoulder, eyes alight with Wisdom's green. "Let me out, Keran. I need to go back. Wisdom and I need to examine the throne room."

Keran peered over to Laoch, who nodded. The Ranger gathered his thoughts and let out a heavy breath before following the acolyte. Sura stepped up next to him. Her form had been weak, thin after her battle inside Ecne, yet once again she was resolved to her full form.

"No rest for the heroes, eh?" he said, then turned back to Oisin. "If you don't mind, First Ranger, could you guard the entranceway to the palace?" Laoch raised an eyebrow.

"I know I am still a risk, Laoch. Are you sure?" replied Oisin, his shoulders slumped as if the world resided on them.

"We may need someone to yank us out if it all goes to shit again. Nobody I'd rather have watching my back." Not waiting for a response, he headed towards Ecne, whose impatience seeped into the corridor.

Keran instructed Nathair, and with barely a shimmer of spiritfire, the way opened, and they exited the veil dragon to step out before the palace entrance. Ecne strode ahead, her crossbow aglow with Wisdom's light, a similar sheen across her brow. Laoch sped up, matching the acolyte stride for stride as they headed into the grand hallway with its sweeping marble stairway and the smell of burnt, ancient flesh. Ecne felt a tug – Laoch pulling her back, hand raised for calm, and using the Ranger signal for *wait*. Ecne growled in response, but he maintained a stony silence and a stare that demanded compliance. She nodded.

Laoch waited until Oisin signalled ready, and with a glance to check on Sura, he preceded Ecne along the charred, curved corridor, past the strange sculptures that inhabited it.

"These are the Fleshmaster's," Ecne said from behind. "Sculpted by him from stone. It was these visions that drove his thoughts of ... a different path."

They entered the throne chamber. Laoch scanned the room and approached the still-smoking armour. The ruin of mechanised flesh lay inside, the head shattered.

"It's uninhabited," said Sura, swirling around the body. "Empty."

Ecne slipped in beside Laoch, then knelt, a single finger raised as she was wont to do when needing silence. Or to ignore any complaints.

This time, Laoch refused to obey. "No."

The single word brought the acolyte up short, a green flare lacing her eyes.

"Tell me what you're looking for, then I will decide," growled Laoch, his body stiff. "My patience only goes so far."

Ecne crossed her arms. Laoch watched indecision play across her mind. "Wisdom suggests the necromancer needs a ... a containment of some form. Like a box, or a root."

"Or a sigil," added Sura.

"Yes. It will continue to reform there."

"Like Nathair's heartstone." Laoch glanced up to the dragon-wing throne. "I'm no Learned, and you can dig around that body all you like. But I'm fair guessing you are looking in the wrong place." He turned back to Ecne, a grim set to his mouth. The ragged beard forming, coupled with the tired circles under his eyes, struck Ecne for the first time. "So, we discount it first, slowly, and bloody carefully, aye?"

Ecne nodded and, placing her crossbow on the floor, pulled out her short sword to lay it by its side. Laoch walked over to the throne, examining the great wings, trying his best to ignore the silver-blue dragon's head, whose lifeless crystalline eyes were set upon the dais.

"Ecne?" he said, without looking away. "Anything?"

"Not that I can find," she replied. Sura had already walked away at the first slash of the short sword. "I thought there'd be a ..."

"Crystal," cut in Sura. "All their spiritfire relates to crystals – the heartstones, the spiders."

"Yes. But there's nothing in here."

"Sura. Could you take a look here? Ecne too." Laoch waited. Sura floated up next to him while Ecne wiped off her sword, then came over to stand alongside them. He pointed towards the throne's seat. "In there."

Ecne noted the wings' rainbow sheen, so familiar from Nathair – and the not-so-small matter of the curled dragon not ten yards away. She grasped the symbolism. A throne designed to remind everyone of the source of its power to rule.

With nothing to the rear of interest, she returned to the front and peered down at the seat itself, and the metal-limbed arm rests. Every instinct in her body was pulled towards Laoch being right.

The room's light flickered, and a rush of spiritfire crackled along the walls and ceiling. Weak, stretched, but roiling and crashing together. Ecne instinctively ducked, until Sura's hand fell on her shoulder. "It is ill-formed. But the *will* remains. If we wait too long, we will have to fight it again. These Constructors are hard to kill." She stared upwards. "Hurry."

Ecne turned to Laoch, who smiled in response. Justice wriggled and reformed into the God's true weapon – the great maul. Clasping it in both hands, he crashed it down upon the seat. The dent went deep and red spiritfire flared, raging as the lip of the metal rose. He drove a second blow down. The metal caved and he gripped it and tore it away, Justice wreathing his muscles.

Beneath, a clear crystal sat. The size of a double fist, it lay dead, devoid of any apparent spiritfire.

Sura took a step backwards. "Take it," she said. "We need to leave."

Laoch grabbed the stone before Ecne could move, the acolyte's weary spirit hardly having had a chance to heal after the last attack. Her sigh of relief at his choice was palpable. "Lead us out," he growled, Justice reforming into his favoured sword. "Now, Ecne."

Ecne ran down the curved corridor, crossbow up and ready as the walls rippled with whitefire. Sprinting towards the entrance-way, Oisin's cry made her look back; the ash and burnt bodies were swirling, reshaping into a travesty of a human form. Armoured plates shifted, the mishmash of placements setting her teeth on edge as the monstrous thing charged towards Laoch.

They ran onwards, Ecne stopping just outside the doorway to spin and loose a bolt to match that of Fate's bow. The air sizzled and a crackle of whitefire lashed out, wrapping Laoch's ankle and tripping him before the entrance. He hit the marble floor and threw the crystal as a trace of the whitefire flared inside it. It hit the floor, bouncing once, before Oisin bent and caught the stone just outside the entrance.

Ecne felt the air shudder, and despair overwhelmed her mind. But the pressure instantly lifted, and the whitefire burning at Laoch's ankle faded. He rolled over as the ash and shattered armour above the marble seethed. A palpable, yet unfocused anger swept the room, and then the whole, ill-formed aberration erupted.

Scrabbling back to his feet, Sura by his side, Laoch ran through the exit. The cool touch of the wind upon his face was a welcome relief.

"That has to be the last time," he said, panting. "Surely?"

"There's still a dragon in there," Oisin said drily, hand out, the crystal sat in his palm. He held it up. Fate's glow shone through it to alight on a sliver of whitefire inside. "And there's something in here."

Ecne strode over, hand out, expectant. Oisin hesitated, and caught Laoch's eye. Laoch nodded, and Oisin slapped it into the Learned's palm.

"But while you have it," he looked her straight in the eye, "you are not to be alone. Neither of us are, for that matter."

"I agree," said Laoch. "None of us should be. The dragon, Sura. What did you find when you went to look?"

"Keran agrees with me. The dragon is of no consequence. It is no more than a metal statue. There is *no* heartstone. It has been removed." Sura stepped in beside Ecne and let a touch of her spirit graze the crystal in Ecne's hand. "And nor is this it."

———

Laoch bit into the meat, juices spilling down his chin, as Oisin tore a piece from the animal he'd called a rabbit, despite its lack of a tail. He sat down, eyes on the back of Ecne's head as she toiled over the stone, the plate of meat by her side cooling after her one bite.

The First Ranger, gesturing towards the acolyte, turned to whisper to Laoch. "She seems a little obsessed. I worry."

"With good reason. Sura said the battle was intense, and what the necromancer showed her was horrific." Laoch bit in, chewing on the bone. "We are all battered and bruised, Oisin. Though she is tougher than I would ever have thought."

"You would have said that of me."

"And I still believe it. You have scars. Don't we all? They will heal. But when you feel the venom rise, you need to let us bloody know." Laoch crunched down, sipping the marrow before tossing the bone into the fire. He grabbed a second leg, tearing another for the Handren.

"And yours?" Oisin looked around, Laoch assumed for Sura.

"My scars stand with me, side-by-side. I hate the pain, Oisin. When this is done, with me in my grave, or we return to Brandshold, I fear the wave that will crash in on me." He chewed before staring into the fire, knowing Nathair was on watch and not caring a moment for his night sight. His hand absently alighted on his sword's pommel. "But I hold the grief back while Sura's presence strengthens each day."

"That I see." Oisin's eyes flicked down to the Ranger's hand before returning to his food. "I would not want Ecne to end that way, Laoch. We've seen what's coming, or a taste of it. Keran was right. We need to find a way to stop it. But at what cost?"

"When you defended your mountains from us, you stood against what you saw as wrong. Who would have died for that cause? For the freedom you lived by?" Laoch stood, cut a chunk of meat and headed towards the acolyte.

"All of us," whispered Oisin. But Laoch already knew that.

Laoch prodded at Ecne. "Eat, or I'll fetch Sura to stand over you while you do."

Ecne barely flinched, her hand upon the crystal, Wisdom glowing fiercely at her side. "She already is. Though she hides, Wisdom can sense her."

"Blame me for that." He waited, the piece of meat still steaming on the knife. Ecne tutted, reached out, and grasped the food before biting down. "Better."

Ecne swallowed, barely chewing. Then, with eyes aglow, she turned to the Ranger. "I think I have an answer. To what we seek. I need Keran."

Laoch heard Oisin rise behind him. "I'll go."

"Sura," said Laoch, "I think you've been spotted."

"A while ago," she said. "But I also hide to keep my presence from what lies in the crystal. It remembers me – as it should." With a flare of orange, a hand landed on Laoch's forearm, the glow at the tips heralding Honour's presence and a solidity to the touch as Sura coalesced.

Oisin returned, Keran emerging from Nathair as the dragon's head turned towards them, hovering above like a fearsome guardian.

Ecne swallowed, the full regard of her friends and a dragon of the veil suddenly weighing her bruised spirit down. Oisin stepped up beside her and lifted her from the cross-legged position she had sat in for the past hour.

"Erm, I speak with Wisdom's words as well as my own. The stone, we believe, is the necromancer's true root, as the heartstone is for Nathair. There's a sliver in there, just a small amount of spiritfire, that is far lesser than in our sigils. But there's enough to help me make sense of what I saw in the library when it attacked. I can't get an understanding of when, however. Once unbonded, the spirit lost all awareness of time, but it has been waiting for the Constructors' return. He was tasked with protecting the dragon while they hunted for Spirit Walkers, and with creating these *unalive*. They were necessary because the Constructors were repelled from one realm. I don't know how, just that the hunt, as he calls it, failed."

"Failed?"

"The impression is of death. True death. The necromancer finds that ... erm ... horrific yet enticing – a chance to be nothing. Many were lost."

"Then that's where we go," said Keran. "Do we know where?"

"Not in a way I understand," replied Ecne. "But Nathair?"

40
WITH TRAITOROUS INTENT

CITY OF TRANQUILLITY, REPANTI

"I said, equalise the starboard side." Admiral Incarnate Lelion bullied the Inhibitor aside, Henar watching on for a change as someone else received the woman's ire.

"This. Yes? Spin until the dual gauge marks the position. Henar, you're grinning behind my back. I can *feel* it. My chains haven't tasted blood for nearly an hour now. Would you like to be the one to check they are still well-oiled?"

"No, Admiral."

"Shame."

The admiral stepped away from the control panel, senses thrumming as her spirit mind wandered the *Kraken*'s engine room. All was in order, and finally ready for what was to come. "Stow those chains, Inhibitor Ranket, gently. And set the crew to clearing the hooks. The flesh will fester and rot."

She returned to her usual position, peering out the window, smoke and fire rising from the third city they had laid waste to over the last few days. With the Fleshmaster's remit carried out in full, the *Kraken*'s crystals were topped up, and the pleasure of death-dealing surged through Lelion's veins. The indulgence led the admiral to stroke the brass rail in front of her, the thrum of power over life and machine thrilling the admiral to the core.

"Take her down, gently. We have done this many times before, but on this occasion, it is my ire you will face, not the Fleshmaster's. Settle the *Kraken*."

The gentlest of vibration changes soothed her worries, and the Constructor soulship dropped slowly towards the earth. With chains stowed as it lowered, mechanised crystals imbued with slivers of herself sent spirit pictures of where they were and the gently approaching ground.

"Slow, slow." She grasped the curved brass and wooden device that lay close at her command chair's side. Applying a wisp of spiritfire, she spoke into it. "Brace. Though my bridge crew swear you'll hardly feel a thing. Countdown, now. Three, two, one. Landing."

The judder took her by surprise. Soft, almost playful in its intent to declare they had arrived on the surface of this realm for a second time. The first time, they had deployed the Mechanised Vanguard along with the Inhibitor army to swarm the pitiful humans of this realm. Now they were to scoop most of those remaining back up, leaving a trusted few to keep the prey breeding under the Constructors' thumb.

"Ahhhh. Now I have nothing to complain about. Fine work."

Relief washed through the bridge crew, invoking a moment of pride in the admiral incarnate that she snuffed out before they noticed and got sloppy again.

Lelion lifted the communication device to her blue, cracked lips. "Get the doors open. Take the Mechanised Vanguard first. You have a standard to match, warehouse crew. Understand? The bridge has set the quality I expect. Match it, or I shall be choosing one of your number to check how ice-cold the pathways are – from the outside."

Rumbles echoed through the *Kraken*'s corridor, and while the admiral's spirit crystals sent back the sights and sounds of her crew in action, her thoughts turned to Innealtóir and the journey home. With no veil to break, the ship could travel without the aid of the Wyrm, and finally, after countless years, they would be home once again. Yet, the hunt for Spirit Walkers continued, and the remaining dragon of the veil would be useless unless one was found. If that remained unresolved, the *Kraken* she had crafted would be no more than a work of fancy, a remnant of historic battles rather than the devastator of new ones.

And, likely, we would fall upon each other once again.

The admiral growled, teeth clenching at the thought of such waste, and the failures that had brought them to this point. Repanti had almost been too easy once the veils were broken. Perhaps the previous two campaigns had honed the revitalised Inhibitors, trained mind, spirit and body to act in unison after the debacle of Apso-Tran.

Lelion shuddered. Little caused her disquiet or fear, her eyes having witnessed and engaged in atrocities for a thousand and more years. But Apso-Tran had almost seen the death of the Constructors. Blind aggression, coupled with decadent madness. The Fleshmaster returning with a decimated army, nearly half retained in the gourds, and thousands upon thousands lost, soul-dead. To avoid a repeat of such a disaster, he had demanded two tasks. For Lelion, to build the

Kraken – the mighty soulship she had proposed before being denied the foundries and resources she so badly needed, since the Great Artificer Viseri's requirements for the Fleshmaster's precious new dragon took precedent. And Marbhleoir – the necromancer who led the Thaumaturge, those who returned Constructors' spirits to new bodies upon their physical deaths – had the second, his task to craft a weapon to lay waste to Apso-Tran and murder those spirit-splitting bastards in their sleep.

"And which of these has seen the most success, huh, Marbhleoir? Will I return to find you have carved flesh and metal? Produced what we all declared as a betrayal? A return to the decadent madness the Fleshmaster once demanded we leave behind?"

"Admiral?" Inhibitor Ranket glanced to the floor, trying to show he had not noticed Lelion talking to herself.

Lelion set her features, dispelling the anticipation of gloating that threatened to addle her thoughts. "Yes?"

"The Vanguard are aboard. The ornithopters declare the area is clear. May we stow those flying machines coming with us next, before the Inhibitors themselves?"

"Yes, Ranket. You may. And inform the Inhibitors that they are to sleep only. No hibernation."

"Admiral, I thought ..."

"We return to Innealtóir, Ranket. The journey will be relatively swift, and I would have them fed and awake when we return, yes? We have a show to put on. One I am going to enjoy. Get the orders out."

Ranket saluted and turned away, glee tainting the man's spirit. An emotion that would sweep the *Kraken* soon; a reason for the admiral to keep it quiet until now.

"Listen up, bridge crew. We are to travel the pathway home. There will be no Wyrm to lead us, but we know the way, and we have no veil to crack. Even so, I want you alert, understand? No slovenly *that'll do* attitudes. When we awaken our people back on Innealtóir, we will do so in triumph. They have slumbered, waiting for our return long enough. Some may well have perished, their spirits too weak to see them through. But the Fleshmaster has seen fit for me to lead us back in triumph, so a triumph it shall be."

And one Marbhleoir had better match, or the Kraken *will be feeding off his soul.*

41

A CLASH OF MINDS

"Halt."

Sneed peered into the morning mist, eyes watering, as the tang of the sea mingled with its slow drift across the road. Vardrin was likely still half asleep in the carriage, the ultra-smooth roads near Ridth lulling the fretting prime into slumber after a lack of rest the night before. Sneed had taken the opportunity to mount a horse, joining the guard as they entered the last valley of the foothills surrounding Ridth. Ahead, the golden livery lined with azure declared the waiting captain-to-be of the Ridth army. The helm emblazoned with the Serpent, the duke's mark, turned back to check on the soldiers milling behind before approaching the procession.

"You are Prime Vardrin's party?" the voice queried.

"We are," said the sergeant-at-arms, saluting. "And Prime Vardrin is preparing for the visit. We did not expect a welcome this far from the city."

Sneed couldn't help side-eyeing the sergeant. Not for the first time, he congratulated Mordant on his choice. This one was definitely aware of their role despite Zendril having taken the Honour Guard up north as a royal sign of her own message.

"Duke Weister has sent us ahead to ensure your safety. I am sure he will want to explain himself rather than leave it to his son, but it may be enough to say he will take little convincing of the importance of your visit."

"Son?" cut in Sneed. "Jayce, is that you under all the pomp of that helm?"

"Aye, Master Sneed, it is I. You fare well, I believe, since relinquishing your burden."

"More so for seeing you. I take it my welcome will be as frosty as ever." Sneed couldn't help but smile, his pupil and charge having grown and appearing to flourish.

"If I said the old bastard had mellowed, it would be a lie. But things have precluded his ire. The Dukedom of Ridth has seen some strange incidents over the last two days. I can say no more, or else I will have provided another whip for his barbs." Jayce Weister wheeled in next to the sergeant-at-arms, Sneed noting the decision with a little pride again. The lad had always been of solid mind and faith, a rock against his father's storm.

The Ridth cohort let them pass before taking station behind, Sneed making his excuses and entering the carriage as would be expected of one who spoke with the High Lord's voice. That, and he needed to ensure Jacka was awake and prepared.

He shook the man, the gentle snore ending as his eyes flickered open. "Sneed?"

"We are nearing Ridth, Prime Vardrin," he replied, noting Jacka picking up on the formality of his address. "And his son, Ser Jayce Weister, has ridden out to welcome us and provide protection. There have been incidents that deemed it necessary, though he could not share what."

"Could not?" Jacka sat up, straightening his jacket and pulling at the lace cuffs.

"As we know, the duke likes to be at the centre of all things. And perhaps he does not want all ears to hear what he has to say." Sneed shrugged, his thoughts wandering back to Jayce. "Though he did mention that it would help our cause somewhat."

—

Ridth's walls were no match for Erstenburgh's. Though thirty feet high, they had seen little in terms of battle in the time they had stood. The foothills provided a natural barrier, and the port a reason for the city's famed neutrality as the realm settled into a rhythm after the Journey. Despite the rise and fall of petty queens and pirate kings, the city had never fallen, and its soldiers had rarely seen an arrow in anger until they were drawn into the bitterness of the Crusade.

Jacka pulled his head back in, the clop of the horse and wheeze of the carriage echoing as they passed under the gateway and entered the city proper. Then the wave of noise hit. People shouting their wares, the full impact of the sea washing into the carriage as every edible creature from the ocean was waved at passersby.

"Home," whispered Sneed. "Or at least, it once was." He breathed in, the heavy scent firing his senses. Memories battered at his reluctance to return – of his schooling, passing his Master's exams, and eventually taking residence in the then-duke's household. On his death, with the duchess refusing the role by right of marriage to stay with the Union's army, his brother, a man embroiled in his own personal bitterness, had taken the position. Sneed had stayed to school both dukes' children, Erin Weister, and Jayce, the younger and newly adopted son of Simeon.

The carriage eased to a halt and words were exchanged before it moved on once again, at a slower pace, the crunch of familiar gravel announcing to Sneed's ears their arrival in the palace grounds. Slamming the door shut on his past for now, he redressed the mantle of Penance. Today he needed to present as a High Lord should, for his voice had to be heard.

An irony. I was never one for self-punishment, though I suspect Simeon still sees it as deserved.

The carriage halted, the door swinging open as the sergeant-at-arms stood aside. Prime Vardrin stepped out, straightening his jacket and cuffs, peering up into the clearing sky as seagulls wheeled, their cries mournful. Once Sneed had exited, Jayce led them inside. The building was far removed from the ostentatious White Palace. More a museum of its past, each wall was hung with previous dukes and duchesses, in whatever painting style held sway as they took their position. The huge fireplace on entry was adorned with the flags of the southern fleet, their mottos declaring their loyalty to Ridth and the Union. Thirty-two flags, plus that of the duke's principal ship.

"This way, Prime Vardrin. I understand the duke is impatient to see you both." The captain led them down the carpeted hallway, the weave of Meres origin – expensive, but also a welcome luxury not prevalent in Sneed's time. He remembered just how cold the stone floor was, especially in winter.

Jayce nodded to a waiting servant boy, his azure doublet marking his role, and the lad slipped inside, only to open the doors with a tight smile as the duke's high-pitched voice declared him ready.

"About time, Prime Vardrin," said the duke.

The thin rail of a man sat on an intricately carved wooden throne; the source of which was purported to be the planks from the first ship to land at Ridth. The serpent writhed about the handles, its body bent over itself to form the back before the bearded head rose above the duke. The duke sat, legs crossed, a narrow face perched on bony shoulders, a wisp of greying beard at his chin and bags beneath deep-set eyes. The cut and weave of the man's own clothes was as expensive and refined as Vardrin's, yet simpler. Elegant.

The prime approached, Sneed waiting behind as he had not been greeted. Vardrin bowed, one arm stiff at his side, the other placed upon his heart as a symbol of his queen's good grace.

"You look like you walked out of a cheap clothing emporium. Is that lace?" The thin-lipped sneer was a mummery Sneed had warned him about, as were the ill-manners, but the High Lord's servant noted Vardrin was still taken aback.

And so, you let him score the first point. Ah, perhaps he will be satisfied with that for now.

"Can't be helped in that gaudy White Palace, I suppose. Tell me of my niece, Prime. How fares the girl?"

"The *queen* is well, Your Grace, despite the trying times. She has sent you two letters." Vardrin pulled them from his doublet, and turned to eye the boy servant, who approached and collected them both, placing them on a table at the throne's side.

"Two? Our queen must have time on her hands."

"The first is personal, the second to confirm the news we bring from Erstenburgh and the Seven Houses." The prime deliberately peered over his shoulder to Sneed, announcing to the duke he'd noted the man's lack of welcome for the High Lord's servant.

"Yes. Tell me of its import, Prime, then I can read it at my leisure. We have heard rumours, but it would be good to hear what truth there is in these."

"Perhaps it would be easier to show you and then explain? We have brought evidence that it would serve you to see."

Sneed noted Vardrin was relaxing into the role, and had to credit the man somewhat for trying to highlight the duke's rudeness towards him. At the mention of the evidence, he turned and nodded to the sergeant-at-arms, who sent two of his men forwards with a chest, which they laid at the prime's feet.

"May I?" Vardrin asked, and opened the lock at the duke's agreement. He lifted out a gauntlet, its shine lost, though the material remained reflective enough and clearly of crystal form. The duke shifted to the edge of his seat before rising and walking down the steps to stare into the chest.

"And this is the Unspoken's new armour?"

"Yes," said Vardrin, tapping the gauntlet. "It is extremely light and, when we found it, acted like a mirror. Very off-putting in a fight. And this." Vardrin took out a long object wrapped in a scented cloth. "I must warn you, Your Grace, this is most unpleasant, and likely more so since it was placed in the chest." The prime responded to the duke's nod and unwrapped the burned armour plate and the charred arm within it. "We believe that this was caused by a new weapon. Though there are witnesses to the Unspoken's dragon, we think this was done using an explosive quarrel."

"I have to admit, Vardrin, when I first heard these rumours, it struck me as another of the Seven Houses' mewlings for a crusade. The appetite for which, I am sure you understand, is low in the south. Yet ..." The duke signalled to the back of the room and the doors opened. Ser Jayce approached, holding the hand of a shaking girl.

Sneed felt a tightness in his chest, knowing that what was about to be discussed was beyond Vardrin's knowledge, but not his. That his High Lord's machinations had already borne fruit took him by surprise, but the look in the girl's eye gave him no doubt about what was to be laid bare. It was the same look one of the priests had had, the one who now sat deep within the House of Penance, delivering his own painful punishments to wipe the memory of Nathair's rise.

I hope you have played this right, High Lord.

"Go on, Brenna," said Jayce, his voice low. The girl's timid glance in his direction was met with a squeeze of the hand and eyes that offered support. She began to speak, and the reality of the High Lord's actions struck Sneed as she recounted the attack on her lord's house.

Could I have done such a thing? To reap the few for a chance to save the many?

He watched as Vardrin played his innocent role, and, in turn, the duke recognised that he found this as horrifying as he did. No need for the clash of words nor the self-importance bequeathed to those in power. A simple laying down of truth – at least, the version the High Lord and the queen wanted to share – as a call to arms. The girl's recount, despite its sickened and fear-filled meanderings, undertook its role within the mummery.

"Then you understand?" said the prime, sparing no thought for the girl. No words of sympathy for her loss shared. Sneed noted it did not sit well with Jayce, though the duke cared not, ignoring Brenna as his son led her away. "That the danger is real? The Unspoken has risen in her utmost savagery. We must defend ourselves."

"I think we do," replied the duke. "Though I am loath to send any troops to Erstenburgh's aid if the Unspoken's reach can turn my own subjects to ash and blood, and take from us with impunity."

"Your Grace, that is not what the queen requests. At least, not yet. She asks for you to prepare your army for the threat and spread the fleet wide to take the news to the Isle of Meres and beyond. Get word out that the Unspoken's dragon has taken flight, and that we are all within sight of its breath."

"So, no crusade?" For the first time, the duke glanced over to Sneed. His stare was hard, but also seeking an answer to his question. Sneed gave the gentlest shake of his head. Duke Weister turned back to Vardrin.

"No, Your Grace. Though we feel the north is more vulnerable, and that the queen may need to call on support, should there be an attack from her followers, the Unbelievers."

The duke blinked once, a hand rising to stroke at the manicured beard along his jowls. "I will think on this, Prime Vardrin. Go with my son. Discuss your needs and expectations. I will speak with Penance's representative awhile."

Vardrin looked to Sneed, who raised an eyebrow in agreement, glancing back to where Jayce waited. "Thank you, Your Grace. Does your son speak with your words?"

"By the Seven, no. Nothing you agree will stand without my hand, Prime. But air it, and we will see where it leads."

Vardrin bowed, turning after the second step backwards to greet the waiting captain.

"Close the door, boy," said the duke. "And mark no one is listening."

The duke waited, Sneed's eyes on the man until he shifted in his throne as the door clacked shut.

The silence was sudden, sullen in texture, as the duke's eyes fell on him. Sneed waited. If being a priest and later the High Lord had taught him anything, it was patience. Eventually, the duke rose from his seat, turned, and walked over to the high window that looked out upon Ridth's port.

"What does it say?" he said.

"Which?" answered Sneed, still unmoving.

"The personal letter. She must have told you." The duke stared out to sea, hands clasped behind his back.

"No, she did not. But I can read it to you if you wish."

"Yes."

Sneed walked up the steps, taking the letters from the table and opening the first.

He read a while, letting the platitudes and histories of Erin's words wash over him as had been his role in the past. The words flowed, but had anyone asked, he would recall none. Such was the privacy accorded to his secondary role in the duke's Court, for despite his efforts, Duke Weister struggled to make sense of the written word, and it added a level of pain on a man who had already suffered the loss of his beloved brother.

"So, she fares well, despite having to pull the Union back from the brink after the ridiculous Crusade." It wasn't a question, and Sneed waited. "Is it true? Cut through the veneer. Does my niece stand well?"

"She has the Weister backbone through and through, Your Grace. You are rightly proud of her."

"Still telling me how I feel, Master Sneed?" The duke turned, the faintest of smiles on his lips. "Are you proud of her?"

"She is magnificent, Simeon. She has dug her way into the Gods' Council and demanded the Crown has more sway. No other could have achieved that." Sneed kept the words clipped, trying to keep the surge of emotion from the duke's ears. Memories of holding her as she wept in the Forbidden Library played themselves out in his mind.

"And she was your chosen one. That always helps." The words rasped, scraping at Sneed's nerves – the sneer he remembered so well from the months after Erin's father's funeral.

"She was the right choice, Simeon. I know you wanted to spare her the responsibility, and understand your view of the prince consort. But we all serve." Sneed folded the letter, slipping it back into the unsealed envelope for whoever read the duke's documents now. A secret he still kept by a combination of fear and paying well.

"And the second letter?"

"Much as Prime Vardrin said. There is no deceit here, Simeon. No court politics being played, nor House mummery. There is a rising threat, one we must prepare for."

The duke spun on his heel, a brief glare falling upon Sneed before he gathered it back in. "And you are here because ... why?"

"Because the High Lord wishes me to be. To reinforce Vardrin's words and prepare the Houses of Ridth for what is to come." Sneed caught the man's eye, waiting for him to bite.

"You are here as a distraction; in case the discussions went wrong. Luckily, the Unspoken has intervened, for I do not take well to being played by the High Lord's take on Crown politics. He can interfere in the Royal Court, but not mine." The last words were spat, anger causing his left eye to twitch. Sneed remembered the last time he'd witnessed that level of fury.

"You still hold the anger, Simeon. I cannot help that. Surely it is time to let this pass. I served my penance, suffered the self-blame."

"I had, until you turned up holding a prime's hand. My life ended in that moment of cowardice." The duke threw himself onto the throne, glaring back at the source of his pain.

Sneed shuffled his feet and settled on a decision. "I have no words to soothe your pain. I froze, your brother ... did not. I hold his act of bravery in the highest regard, and my own failure to act has been at the centre of my life ever since. And yours." Sneed waited for the coming tirade, the anger and hate that would spill from Simeon's lips. "As much as a master and a duke can be, we were friends once, Simeon. I mourn that, as well as your brother."

The duke leant forwards, clasping his face in ringed hands, a choking noise emanating from between the palms. "I remain bitter, Sneed. It will never leave me, understand? My life changed in that one moment. One tusk through the heart, and yet it pierced mine at the same time. I lost everything in that one act. Some say my anger lies in the loss of my brother, others in giving up the easy life of gambling and drinking. What say you?"

The stare was meant to whither, but Sneed had witnessed too much for it to work. "That is not for me to judge. Only that I have come to terms with what happened, spent my life since in service. But have I forgiven myself? No."

"Did I ... Did *I* drive you into the arms of the House of Penance?"

Sneed stared at Simeon Weister, Duke of Ridth, and for the first time in a very long time, saw the man. For all the years of servitude, self-sacrifice, the burden of the Houses' lies and deceit, nothing had prepared him for such a strike to the emotional walls he had built.

Assumptions will be the death of humanity.

"I ... I am sorry, Simeon. But you? No. The death of your brother, my failure to defend myself from the boar – and subsequently him – yes."

"A hundred times I have sat with quill in hand, wanting to ask you why you left, whether my temper and grief were the cause, but I am not even capable of that. You were my brother's friend, and my confidant in my misery with the written word. I have not forgiven you for what happened, nor for leaving when you were most needed. Nor myself."

"I cannot soothe the past, Simeon. But my time within Penance's House is something I now cherish. Do not punish yourself anymore."

"Easier said than done, as in all things."

42
ONE STEP CLOSER

PORT OF NARTET, THE REALM OF MONDREIN

Popsilin drove the knife deep into the shoulder, scoring a circle. The pain coursing through the sailor's spirit fired an urgent thrill, a desire to *feed*. She resisted, bottling the sensation, though the thrum beat at the edge of her thoughts. With practised ease, she slid the blade clear before slicing it along the man's chest, the point carving a line of blood that flowed amid the hair. The whimper almost set her hunger alight again. Only the presence of the emperor stopped her from devouring the writhing soul.

"I am holding my captain back, you understand?"

The Fleshmaster loomed at her side, the sheer power of his spirit shadowing her own. The emperor's power was ancient, and bound by walls she could not penetrate. This close, it was oppressive. She understood how the old ones had broken down as a society, unable to tolerate each others' spirit company as well as thousands of years of the same faces, lost amid their own pleasure seeking. A decadence that had led to the desperation of the hunt they were now on.

Popsilin scraped the blade's edge over the man's dimpled chin, new growth making way for the steel's path. A sliver of blood appeared between handle and tip, and she guided the edge to open his skin further. With her face in close, she remained silent, white eyes peering into those she had pinned open.

"If that is the way of it, then I will let her feed." The Fleshmaster turned around, facing the six other crew who stood manacled, foot and ankle, an Inhibitor by their side. He waited, eyes pulsing with whitefire, tongue tickling dry, blue lips. "Yes, Popsilin."

She fell upon the sailor, wrapping her legs about his stomach, teeth biting down upon his lips. Drawing back the flesh, more blood flowed, and the soul drew. The coppery taste meant little to her, a show for those watching, but the thrill of the soul-feed remained, and she dug the man's spirit free of mind and heart. She leant back, spiritfire crackling over her blood-covered face as she sucked in the soul. A murmur of ecstasy slid from her lips, no mummery required, and she rose from the empty shell, wiping her mouth clean as she stared, white-eyed, at the human crew.

The watching prisoners' eyes never left their colleague's corpse. The lip lay shredded, teeth exposed, eyes wide and unseeing, as a last breath exuded.

"As I was saying, I will let my captain feed. I have forty Inhibitors aboard. Each can smell your spirits, taste your fear through these walls. But—" The Fleshmaster sprang a clawed finger to land beneath a sailor woman's chin, her eyes suddenly wide, body shaking. "—they are nothing compared to the hunger I hold back."

"Y-you want the *Sea Pig*," said one, his cheek scarred where a hook had dug deep. "Out of Grodin. Th ... that's what I heard."

The emperor smiled; blue lips peeled back from bone-white teeth. He let the fingernail slice into the woman's chin, tasted her spirit, felt her quiver at his nip on her soul before reaching out a hand to snap open the manacle of the betrayer with the barest trace of his whitefire. Popsilin stared as the chains spilled to the floor, the use of power way beyond any she'd witnessed by one of her kind. The Fleshmaster's arm wrapped around the sailor as he led him away.

"Tell me more of this *Sea Pig*," he said, signalling Popsilin to remain patient.

She smiled at the remaining ship's crew, then lifted the dead man from the floor and flung him into a waiting corner.

—

Popsilin swore, the ornithopter dropping suddenly as the wind once again buffeted the dragonfly wings.

"For fuck's sake," she repeated under a dusty breath.

The pilot ignored her discomfort, choosing prudence and keeping them in the air, smoothing out what was already a tricky night flight. Popsilin grabbed hold of the handle bolted to the hull of the little craft – a recent addition, her personal pilot learning the captain's ways. She let that thought settle in her mind and mulled over her fated discussion with the Fleshmaster. She shuddered at her mistake, not reading the situation as well as her position demanded.

She'd kept the human crew safe until called to the bridge, where the emperor waited, stooped over a table.

"You did well, Captain, despite superseding your orders." Tarin had then waited patiently as one of the barge's bridge crew flung the corpse over their shoulder, the husked face filling the air with a swirl of dust.

And then she'd said it. "Is that admonishment or a compliment, my Emperor?" Popsilin had kicked herself. The pleasure of feeding had distracted her thoughts. Unbridled, they had stepped over a line. But she couldn't have apologised – that was weakness.

The Fleshmaster's brief smile and glance her way had bound her errant words, lashed them in place. For all the favour that had come her way, one slip could lead to her being an example, just as she had made one of her lieutenant. He'd appeared to let it pass, though it would not be forgotten, but then the barbs had slipped in as the Fleshmaster continued.

"Listen to the compliment, act upon the admonishment. In this case, it worked. Perhaps your time mired in battle with these pitiful people has you more in tune with the rhythm of their ways. But ..." Left hanging, the word had stung at her thoughts as the emperor turned to peer at the crude map splayed on the table. "Look."

She had done as ordered; the paper covered in nervous brush-strokes with a simple compass pinned to its top. It made little sense, until she focused her mind on one specific point – the word *Grodin*, scrawled in a shaky hand next to a circle she now took to be an island.

"Yes. I had to enter their mind and direct the hand. The barge captain agrees with this man, however, that a compass is useless here. The seaweed, the whole sea, oozes a very low spiritfire. If you set your mind right, it is like a constant hum in your spirit. Only the skilled would discern it, though the sailor says there are blooms when the sea is afire. The beauty of it in his mind was breathtaking, I would share, but you have already been distracted *once*."

Popsilin had winced and caught the slightest shift in the emperor's body as he enjoyed his sparring.

"So, how will we find this Grodin?"

"We are already on the way. I have ... taken his soul, Popsilin. It resides within me. Restraint has a power you would do well to learn. I can direct us, though I suspect this *Sea Pig* will not be there. They scavenge the weed beds, floating islands of seaweed, as a source of food. But we need to confirm this man's rumour before we waste time looking. He believes the *Sea Pig* transported our Repanti shamans to a Schenterenta island, though he calls them Ghosts of the Sea. The picture woven in his spirit is elven, and the fear their spirit weaving creates is palpable."

And so here she was, airborne again, with the Fleshmaster's barbs still stinging her spirit.

Over-confidence will see my spirit stripped, either to be reborn young and unthinking, or consumed and ended.

"I see light ahead," said the pilot.

Popsilin peered through the canopy into the murk beyond, to catch sight of port lights. The Constructors had never been willing seafarers, though some artificers spoke of the great metal steamships that had been one of their many fleeting passions. But it was difficult to recover a body – and more importantly, a soul – from beneath the waves.

The ornithopter sank, slower this time, and she heard the whisper of its wings change in tone. She still hated the damn things, but at least she was more in tune with it now. The pilot banked, coming in low over a rock-filled coastline before lifting the craft over a small cliff to flutter above a scrubland. A flicker of lamplight lit the ground. Satisfied, the Inhibitor pilot swung the artifice in an arc to come back around and land with a judder. By the time Popsilin had freed her straps, the others had found landing spots. They were soon following a cliff path down to the hopefully sleeping port of Grodin.

Avoiding the main town, raucous singing and the smell of shit, fish and the drying seaweed riven deep upon the wind's breath, the Inhibitors spread themselves throughout the dock. The few guards on duty, they marked as sleeping or drinking their time away. They were of little concern to Popsilin, and reflective of a people unused to war or internal strife.

With no sign of the *Sea Pig*, she chose the next path. Guard by guard, they awoke and questioned each, the stroke of her blade and a taste of their spirits urging fear-filled words from alcohol-breathed mouths. And now she stood next to the shuttered building, a sign above declaring it to be a harbourmaster's office – a new concept to her, but then, in their rampage across realms, they rarely took the time to learn as the feasting orgy took hold.

"Perhaps the Fleshmaster is right; restraint is the way."

"Eh?" answered Tenith, his buckler ready and handbow cocked.

"Never mind. Pass the order along. I need papers and likely maps. You are not to ransack the place nor kill the night watch inside, understand? This is a new way we fight. The Fleshmaster is looking for those to lead the way against the Seven. If that is to be us, we must continue to show control. Dampen the need to destroy, restrain the urge to feed until it is the right time. Understand?"

Tenith saluted, his mind already passing along the order, and Popsilin sat back as the combination of subtle strength broke through the door's lock and her team entered. A muffled cry was soon cut off. With a final glance around, she ushered Tenith to overwatch the area while she entered.

The woman knelt on the floor, a livid mark across her cheek visibly swelling, and a scowl thrown Popsilin's way until she swept back her hood. She clamped a hand down, cracked, dry fingers slamming the jaw shut.

"Not a word until I say," she hissed. "You know who I am?"

The woman shook her head.

"Good answer. See? You *listen*. You may yet live. I am looking for these." She drew out the spirit picture, the paper fizzing as an image of a Schenterenta rose from the page. A twisted body, limp and bedraggled hair, but the ears pointed up and the eyes were afire with determination. It shifted, a hale elf taking the shaman's place. The woman's eyes widened further. Popsilin couldn't judge whether it was surprise at what she saw or how she saw it. She let a wisp of whitefire weave in the air, too light to be seen, and it wheedled its way around the back of the night watcher's head, seeping inwards.

It was the most subtle use of her power she had ever used. Devoid of excitement and the thrill of causing dread, it felt unnatural.

But necessary. I do not have the Fleshmaster's control. Yet.

The memories were there, not direct, but the woman clearly had heard of their presence. Her mind flickered over images of the *Sea Pig*, a map and something akin to a written declaration of intent.

"Show me this *Sea Pig*," Popsilin said. Hoping it would be enough, she lifted the woman from the floor, but kept a hand upon her mouth, forcing a thought of quiet into her prisoner's mind that seemed to take root. She led her over to a set of boxes, and Popsilin allowed her to kneel and rifle through what appeared to be stacks of written papers. The woman grabbed a set bound by string, and dropped them on the table, eyes now on Popsilin.

"Where are they now?" she asked, and with a swirl of paper, the stack was flicked over to expose the last page. "Speak."

"They requested to harvest Muroe Weedfield. They will nearly be there by now." She grasped the paper, showing Popsilin the circled islands. "Here." She strode over to the map on the wall, pointing out the anchored islands and an area below it. "The weedfield has taken this current, so will be running south of Muroe this year. They'll be there."

"Good," said Popsilin, her mind forging the picture in her head much as the Fleshmaster had done for finding Grodin. "These papers, do they show where the *Sea Pig* went with the Schenterenta? Did they write it down?"

"No. They only have to register the harvesting."

"Thank you," said Popsilin. Lashing out, the blade along her gauntlet sliced the woman's throat clean through. She fed slowly, controlling the spirit flow so as not to overwhelm her thoughts.

She turned to the waiting Inhibitors, their eyes ablaze with the desire to feed. "Go. No witnesses. You may take one ship guard each, while another watches on. Show restraint to earn the Fleshmaster's favour." She eyed the map, tapping the island. "We are close."

43
A NEW WAY OF THINKING

THE WHITE PALACE, ERSTENBURGH, BRANDSHOLD

Queen Erin tapped her fingers against the circular table, eyes focused on the inlaid sigil of her Crown as she pondered what was to come. Time had passed swiftly, yet she felt they were no closer to being ready than when she'd first stepped onto Captain Mordant's walls. A frustration flared in her chest, the inability to get things done at speed hampering her thoughts when she needed them clear and free from dread.

With a final rap on the table, she pushed back her chair. Every set of Lord's and Lady's eyes were upon her, except one. "Where is he?"

"That is for the High Lord to answer," replied Lady Fate, her sapphire blue robe laced with a gold brocade to declare her current status on the Council, until Lord Penance returned, as promised.

"I only know that he has suffered, and as such, patience may be necessary on our part."

"And if he does not arrive?" asked Lord Justice. "Are we able to move amid the swamp of decisions we dwell in? I, for one, have things to discuss that are urgent."

"As do we all," interjected Lady Death. "Endure, Lord Justice. Use some of that famous restraint."

"Hah. I have done much to meet what is to come, martialled my priests, set them to a training regime like no other. And you? Shared a bed and ended your lover's priest-in-waiting's suffering. Seems a poor exchange of time."

Lady Death grabbed Honour's arm before she reacted to Justice's ire. She squeezed, a calming touch of her presence decrying the besmirching of Lady Honour's loss.

"That was uncalled for, Lord Justice. A step beyond the etiquette of this Council. I, as do the others who are weaponless, understand your frustration, but I will not have it lead to bickering. The straining of our weave must cease if we are to stand against the Constructors and their dragons." Lady Fate pressed her hands against the polished table. Erin assumed she forced her own grievances and frustrations through those burned and wizened fingers.

A rap at the door broke the building pressure, and it opened to the tap of Lord Penance's cane upon the marbled floor. His feet hardly left the white stone as he dragged his body over to slump into the waiting chair. Eyes lay sunken, hollow, and his hands shook.

"Forgive my tardiness," he said as the cane shone, a purple spiritfire shooting from the sigil to wreathe his newly blackened hand. "And my God's show of power. But the toll has been heavy."

Lady Honour and Lady Death looked to each other, an eagerness to talk restrained by Fate's glance towards them. She knew the High Lord needed time. Her hand rose, requesting they wait. Patience was not among Lord Justice's thoughts, and he made to speak, until he caught Queen Erin's glare. He clammed up immediately, clearly abashed.

"You are welcome to my palace, Lord Penance. I admit, I am eager to get going, but do you need some time?" she said, allowing a second glare to fall on Lord Justice.

"You are too kind, my Queen. But no. Penance will bolster me, and time is ubiquitous. We know not how long we have. We live and defend our realm in a moment that could stretch for centuries or end tomorrow. Lady Fate, lead the Council if you would, until I feel able to impart my element of the proceedings."

"Agreed. Lady Death?"

"Thank you. Council, despite Lord Justice's distaste for the loss of Nesca, it was necessary. She suffered, and while my House exists for many reasons, one is to reduce such pain. That which was Nesca had long been consumed, and that which resided within her, insane with hunger. I *fear* what it was, what it *could* do." Lady Death squeezed her blackened hand together with her healthy one, though the only tears on the Council were Lady Honour's.

"Explain, please," said Lord Hope. "We know little more than what our books tell us of the Constructors."

"I only saw death, a lost spirit screaming, wanting to spread its pain among whoever would listen. Like a plague, spread by mere touch. I could not let anyone but me near her. If it was let loose ..."

"A malaise of the spirit?" said Lord Hope.

"Worse. I fear each would become like Nesca in time, spreading this soul death."

"What purpose does it serve?" said Lord Justice.

"Purpose? I see none in this," added Lady Honour. "When the whitefire took hold of the Wyrding Stone, it had one goal: to break through the veils, to inform the horde. But it had reason. This does not."

"Then think on what you have found," added Lord Penance, "for if we encounter it again, we must know how to contain it. To destroy it before it spreads."

Lady Honour nodded in agreement, looking to Lady Fate before carrying on, a flush to her cheeks. "Also, we found something else. With Lady Fate's agreement, we healed my glyph last night."

"We?" said Lord Justice.

"We. Lady Death and I rode the Wyrding together." She held up her right forearm. "There was no pain, Lady Fate. No blackening. And the veil and glyph healed as they should, despite the spiritfire being shared by two."

"Preposterous," cut in Lord Justice. "Are you saying—"

"They are confirming something I learned, Lord Justice. Amid the Schenterenta. The power of two working in unison. Though the cost of that knowledge was high. Carry on." Lord Penance smiled at Lady Honour, his eyes less tired and skin filling out as the purple glowed from within.

"I think we need to explore this further, couple up, see where it can lead us."

"More than that," cut in Lord Hope, excitement flashing across his face. "Much more. If this is true, can it be that it just pertains to us? What if the priest-in-waiting can also act in this way?"

"Their power has not quickened, though many of us have started the process. Even when it does, it takes years to master." Lord Wisdom whispered the last few words, memories of the pain his body suffered rising to the surface.

"But if twinning works, we could specialise. Focus on what is most needed. This whitefire they use is like all our spiritfire merged. We act differently, our souls coloured by our faith. We already do this, and surely there's a need for us to develop."

Queen Erin watched Lord Hope's face drop as the others' scepticism appeared to break his resolve. She made to speak, expecting someone to shout her down in an area she had very little knowledge. But she was a Weister, and bloody-minded. She got a nod from Lady Fate.

"The crystals you use – the Wyrding Stones. You use these as a pathway? They take you somewhere?"

"Only your spirit, your awareness," said Lady Fate, eyebrows pressed together and cocking her head to the side. "If you see that as a weapon, we cannot influence what lies at the end of the pathway without an anchor – a glyph or another Wyrding Stone."

"I have learnt many things since coming to Court, the greatest of which is information. Knowledge. Sewing together the jigsaw until you get a complete picture." Queen Erin let that sink in before continuing. "My frustration lies with not being able to talk to those in need. General Zendril, Duke Weister, or those even ten miles hence. I will only know of a success or failure if a messenger arrives, and there are only so many birds or horses. Adama always said a battle was won or lost by communication, especially to those in mid-battle. The one thing he and my mother agreed upon."

"If you mean to say *we* should act as conduits, it is preposterous. We have far more important things to be doing." Lord Justice huffed, crossing his arms. The queen ignored him, her eyes alighting on Lord Hope. The man instantly caught her line of thinking.

"You mean the priests-in-waiting, yes? That we could ... That's brilliant!"

"And the type of thinking that may save us yet," added Lord Penance.

Lady Fate nodded, her eyes distant, before a nudge from Lord Wisdom brought her back into the room. "Lord Wisdom reports that the crystal development by Meister Kinst and his seneschal is seeing success."

"For storing low levels of spiritfire and the quarrel tips. Yes. But now this has me thinking that we need to switch focus. If the Council agrees." Lord Wisdom bowed his head, staring at his thick fingers. "And I, for one, would like to explore the coupling of the Wyrding. It takes a toll on me that is hard to bear. If the Constructors start an attack, will we have the strength, individually, to resist? Or to be of use once they break through?"

"Agreed," said Lord Penance, and all but Lord Justice tapped the table. With reluctance, his hand eventually reached out, palm down, to affirm his consent.

"Good," said Lord Penance. "If I may, Lady Fate? The Schenterenta ..."

44
WHEN SCIENCE EVOLVES

ERSTEN FOREST, BRANDSHOLD

"This is magnificent," said Meister Kinst, her feet set astride a rock as she surveyed the clearing. In its centre, the head of a metal dragon glinted an emerald green, metal teeth polished and menacing. Crystalline eyes peered off to the right, catching the rays of the morning sun. The refractions danced on the first buds of spring.

"A beautiful, terrifying thing," added Grand Meister Arknold, hands upon hips as she gazed at the sinuous neck that had finally been exposed – Gowan explaining Leront had been pinned there by the heaviest of the rockfall. "Can you imagine waking up to find *that* in the sky above you? Flames seething, the roar rattling your windows. And, perhaps, the true horror when you discover it is made of metal and bolts, crystal and spiritfire. An artifice of your enemy's construction."

"We would quail, but the people would run in terror." Kinst stepped down from the rock and linked arms with her friend as awe took over. "And a dragon like this, that of the Unspoken, lives on?"

"According to Gowan, the state is between life and death, but yes."

"The wings?"

"Exposed. Come and look."

Arknold strode over the last of the spring mud, breeches tucked, her excitement speeding her towards the dragon's torso. At each side, a scaffold had been built, the first of which she now clambered up using the solid-looking ladder. "Come on. It's perfectly fine unless you've been on the drink again."

"Not so much now that you seem to be consistently absent." Kinst tested the ladder and, with a modicum of distrust, clambered after the grand meister to alight upon the plinth at the top. "I hate to drink alone; you get maudlin for the old times."

Arknold stood, hand deep in a bucket of grease, before lifting out a newly forged bolt and its housing. "I've been experimenting with the smiths. It appears Lord Wisdom has a good few forbidden books on combining metals. I could have done with your opinion, but the crystals seem to have taken up your time."

"Ouch. So, what is its purpose?"

"This? To attach one of the two right-wing struts. The grease, so I can experiment with some basic movement. I can't match the strength of the sheared bolts, but if I can maintain some supported movement, then perhaps Lord Penance will have his wish. It won't fool anyone up close, however."

Kinst turned around, eyes roaming over the large pulleys similar to those Arknold had used to build the lifts along the city walls. They had been bound with living ivy to hide them, and she began to put most of the pieces together.

"A pot bomb ..." she mused. "Or Erin's Wrath."

"Eh?"

"We could lace the area with my elixirs, Arknold. And perhaps some of your ballistae. Or even the trebuchet, if its accuracy has improved." She smiled at her own barb, the wicked glance and subsequent grin from the grand meister an added bonus.

"Not your precious crystals?" Arknold slid the housing inside the raised back lug and stood back with a satisfied sigh.

"Probably not, though where that will lead with the natural crystal is going to be fascinating." She wandered over to the edge of the scaffold, peering down to where the neck stretched out and the dragon's maw welcomed anyone wishing to speak to Gowan. "Does this dragon breathe fire? Or just its artificer?"

"No." She waggled the bolt, cursing before eventually grabbing a file and rubbing away a burr. "Wood is so much easier to use."

"But it could, with enough of my Erin's Wrath."

"So why *are* you here, other than to goad me and provide more conundrums?"

"Well, I missed you, for one." Kinst let that sink in. "And secondly, I want to see the heartstone and speak to Gowan. It is clear that she, and her unwilling companion, are made of spiritfire and bound within the crystal. It would seem logical to seek out how that works."

"And Seneschal Greeth? I thought you were explicitly told not to mix her up in what I am doing." Arknold spun the bolt in place and stood back, but only just avoided wiping the grease on her robe despite the urge to place her hands upon her hips.

"While you've been closeted here, with a group of priests-in-waiting, our world is rapidly changing. The queen is rising in power, the Houses not bending the knee, but bending. They are beginning to understand the science of *pressure*. The religious dam has a leak, my friend, and they have not enough hands to block every hole."

"And you can't help but widen it so you can peer inside." Arknold lifted the huge hammer, to Kinst's surprise, the flattened head evidence of multiple strikes. "Unless you want to hold this bolt while I hammer it home, I suggest you send Priest Bentar up on your way to Gowan. Just be careful, Kinst. Don't push too far. Once this seneschal has all your secrets, what is to stop them sequestering you in Penance's cells?"

"Desperation," replied Meister Kinst as she took the first step down. "They *need* us, Arknold. And while that is the case, we strive for as much knowledge as we can. Have no doubt, if the threat ends, they will try to wrap us back up in their scripture, tighten it with a knot like never before. I, for one, aim to stop that from happening."

Arknold turned back to peer along the dragon's back, the bent and warped spines marring the mechanical beauty of the monstrosity.

"It's too late, Kinst. The dragon is out of the bag. This is the end of the Houses as they were. I think the Lords and Ladies are as pleased to shed that weight as we are to see it fall."

—

"Gowan?" Meister Kinst's cheeks glowed with the green-tinged light emanating from the crystal Seneschal Greeth held before her. "Gowan, may we speak?"

"Ah, I was having a nice dream, Meister ... ah, Kinst." The spirit flowed from the heartstone, the female Ranger presenting again with traces of scales at the corner of her slit-like eyes. A cap with the queen's sigil held back similar metallic green scales. The seneschal's gasp brought a little leap of joy to Kinst's heart; another splinter removed from the Houses' dam. To her credit, Greeth held her ground. She'd been adamant she shouldn't come, yet here she was, with no more persuasion than a cat knocking off an ornament. Just a nudge here and there.

"I would have thought spirits needed little sleep," Kinst replied, indicating for Greeth to take up one of the repaired chairs set around the large heartstone Gowan hovered alongside. "Bit of irony, eh?" she said, squeezing the seneschal's arm. "The forbidden knowledge in the hands of an old meister like myself."

"You spoke of it, but seeing it ..." Greeth reached out a hand, the tips of her fingers barely sensing the brush of Gowan's form.

"Hey. That's rude. Something Laoch would do, not a seneschal of the House of Wisdom. Talking of which, Meister Kinst, I was strictly ordered *not* to speak to *anyone* who wasn't on Lord Penance's list about *anything*."

"About the events with Leront, yes. But did the High Lord speak of crystals? For that is why we are here. We wish to know more of the heartstone and how it can hold you and Leront within it." Meister Kinst glanced over to the seneschal, not the least bit surprised to see the woman had come to terms with Gowan already. She was like a sponge, and if, as her station indicated, Greeth eventually took on the Lord's mantle, then these moments would be key to the realm's future – and that of the university.

The seneschal registered Kinst's look and unbound the backpack she'd been carrying, spilling the crystals from the queen's collection on the floor.

"I won't fit in those," quipped Gowan. "Especially when I have a nice, comfortable home." The spirit lowered itself down, letting her hands caress the stones. A variety of green-hued glows responded from each one. "These already contain spiritfire." She let a tendril of herself slide around Greeth, who didn't move, though her body tensed. "Yours. So, more of science and the Houses working together. I fear where this may lead."

"Lady Fate has heard all about our work, Ranger Gowan. And approves. I know you hold her House in your... heart."

"In my soul, Meister. Without my God, I, and the others, may not have survived the day. What do you ask?"

"We both feel," started Greeth, then checked for Kinst's agreement before continuing, "that each crystal type acts differently. But the subtleties would take a great deal of time to ascertain. The queen and Lord Hope have tasked us to find a ... I suppose you would call it a *focus* stone. A way to link one crystal to another, much like—" The seneschal glanced behind herself on both sides. Kinst was hardly able to hold back the absurdity, in the sealed belly of a dragon. "—the Wyrding Stones of each House."

"I do not know what those are," replied Gowan, now drifting over the collection of crystals, swirls of sapphire blue infusing her body. "However, there was a link to ... another that I sensed Leront use. It flowed like water, though both ways. I can be of help. It would be good to do this. Are you sure Lord Penance approves?"

"Find a way for messages to pass across hundreds of miles, Gowan, and the queen would pin a medal on your shiniest facet."

"To serve my queen and my House would be enough of a reward, Meister Kinst." And with that, Gowan's clothing shifted. The dress uniform of a First Ranger formed. The cap sat proud, the Queen's Ranger sigil prominent.

45
WHEN OLD ENEMIES MEET

THE FOOTHILLS OF RIDTH,
BRANDSHOLD

An Chéad gushed dragon's fire amid the goat herd. Flames caught their fur, and the animals screamed as he fell upon them. Metal teeth bit deep, tearing flesh from bone, releasing the creatures' measly spirits to drain down his throat and deep into the thrumming machinery that beat to the drum of his heartstone.

"Yes," said the Unspoken, eyes afire as the Spirit Walker's joy at the *taking* washed over her. "I must be careful, An Chéad. Your desires overwhelm. The taking of human spirits has ignited a past I need to lock away despite its exhilaration." Her glamour slipped in and out of focus, pulsing with the writhing of her hunger – and she glowered painfully as her unnatural needs fought her logic and reason. Squashing her spirit's urges, she hardened her resolve, attempting to force the soul-lust down.

A hand reached up, flickering between porcelain skin and withered husk, to grasp the single-jewelled necklace around her neck. Leront's eye, named Starfire by the Ridth nobility she had feasted upon. The lord's spiritfire that she had stored within spurted over her fingers, driving on up her wrist and forearm to lock the desire away. More powerful than the mere drips of the souls drained over a thousand years, it reattuned her *self*, her *being*, and let reason conquer. The glamour fixed, her mind her own again, she felt the artifice dragon respond. The wings extended to drive through the highest of the Ridth foothills, swooping, barrelling amid the mist rising from the forest below. The Unspoken let the thrill of flight, of freedom, and the memories of her beloved valley, seal the hunger; a silent thanks sent the Spirit Walker's way.

"We are as one now, An Chéad. Take us home. Our work is done here."

The beat of the mighty wings was forcing the artifice higher into the sky, the dragon containing the desire to trumpet its freedom to the realm, when the Soul Tear tore through the mechanical beast. The ripple surged along wing and scale, disrupting the heartstone. For the briefest of moments, the dragon fell. The jolt threw the Unspoken to the floor, her thigh smacking upon the brass tiles.

Angry, she shifted herself up to peer back into the stone. "What was that?"

The Spirit Walker, as mute as when it was first torn from its twin, sent a thought her way.

"Not a veil dragon? Then what? If they come, we are not ready. I will lose my valley, my world, An Chéad."

She gained her feet as a welcome thrumming of wing joints indicating the dragon caught the wind once again and had reasserted itself in the sky. The Unspoken set thin white fingers against the crystal's upper facets, breathing in unneeded air as she sent its contained whitefire out in a pulse of *seeking*. An act she had rarely used when an Inhibitor, never mind since An Chéad had first slept on a queen's floor.

A sharp pain pierced the centre of her chest, and the Unspoken was taken aback by the sudden grief enveloping a place so absent from her life for a millennium.

My heart? Did that not wither and die when the Fleshmaster cut us from our first root?

An Chéad roared, the sound pounding into the onrushing air as the *seeking* returned.

"They have come," the once-Inhibitor said, her eyes raging with whitefire, "though not in number." A thought pierced her mind, the Spirit Walker bending its will to hers as it recognised the taste of its creators upon the *seeking*'s return. "Yes, though they are different. Younger, and alone. It appears some of the Constructors are not what they once were. Whether Penance agrees or not, we must act. They will be a scouting party, and no doubt will be seeking sign of the Seven and their errant dragons. But we may also learn from them."

—

Zendril threw the remaining nettle tea over the fire, kicked the embers to spread them a little wider. She glanced over at Mander. The ex-Honour Guard was already ramming last night's sleeping blanket inside an oilcloth bag. Spitting into the guttering flame, she swirled water around her cup, before letting the remnants finish the job of extinguishing the fire.

"Well?"

"Well, what?" replied Mander, finally managing to tie the bag to the general's saddle.

"First thoughts?"

Mander sighed and turned to face the enigma who had become his entire life. "We're fucked."

"Clear. Concise. And no bloody use to me. Why?"

"No walls. Nothing but a stream between them and whatever decides to come out of the Partera Plains. Who plans a town like that?"

"You are too used to being close to the mountains, Mander. This place has never seen a battle, never mind a war. Arable land, peaceful farmers." Zendril Weister rose from her log, dragging her own bag over and attaching it to the rear of her saddle. "They are geared for peace. It's why my daughter sees fit, at Mordant's suggestion, to break me out of Death's jail."

"If the Unbelievers come here, it'll be a massacre as it stands. Human barbecues all round."

The wave washed over Zendril, her soul clinging to mind and heart as it was torn from her body. The last time the Soul Tear had come, she'd been closeted within Death's walls, as had Mander. Despite this, she knew. Mander froze, mouth wide, the flicker of his spirit visible to her eyes as the absence threatened to overtake them both. And then it ended. The fluttering of her spirit, bereft of the pain, slid back into her body as she collapsed to the floor. Heavy breaths rippled the grass before her, and she sensed, rather than felt, her soul slot back into place. It fitted, yet felt a little looser, less secure. A dread filled her mind. Rough, calloused hands fell upon her back, and a familiar, concerned face came into view.

"I'm fine," she said, grasping Mander's shoulder and squeezing before using it to help herself up. Across the small camp, her guards, and the few veterans that remained, stirred. Many had fallen, their comrades helping each other rise. All but one.

"Mander," she said, pointing towards the body that lay across a second fire, flames licking at the clothing.

Mander limped over and pulled the body clear. His eyes roamed over the wide-eyed death mask of a female veteran.

"Ansta. I liked her. Could arm wrestle a bear while taking a piss."

Zendril drew herself up to her full height, pulling in every ounce of experience, then started bellowing orders. The stunned patrol shook off their malaise, and each responded to their role as they broke camp while two of the Honour Guard stood watch.

Mander stomped his way through the milieu, directing, ordering and, above all else, checking each of the vets in turn. Rumour had it that the Tear caused hearts to fail; that at the moment it struck, the mind thought they had died, and the body responded in kind. The youngest could shake it off, perhaps the distance from an aged death gave them the belief it could not be the end. The man returned, a simple nod to suggest all was well.

A horse squealed to the north of the clearing, its whinnied shriek striking a second bout of dread through the general's mind. *No.*

"To arms," she shouted. "To arms, we are under attack."

A scream, human this time, tore through her words. A head flew across the clearing, blood spraying, half its spine attached as the almost inhuman noise continued. The Honour Guard's body crashed into the canopy of a tree to the south, the armour shredded. The whiplash of something spiked and metal slashed at branches ten yards above a man's height.

"Vets to the south, Honour Guard to the north! Rally, archers behind!" she bellowed, pushing Mander north as she grabbed her own weapon. Ignoring her lack of armour, she ran to command the defence of the veterans.

When she reached the clearing's edge, Sternath fell in by her side, the man fully armoured, a grin stretching the scar along his cheek. "By your side, General. We can't lose you this day."

The broadsword stood proud in the man's hand. With that reassurance, Zendril ordered the vets into two defensive lines. With spear and sword at the front, and the few archers they had behind, she planted her feet as the tree cracked and fell, her eyes expectant, waiting for the dragon's breath.

Huge metallic shears scythed through the saplings ahead, cutting and throwing them aside as a horror broke through the undergrowth. A tail lashed behind, high, whirling, with a single spike at its tip curled inwards, ready to strike. Dual bulbous glass eyes stared with violent intent her way. Behind them sat two sets of black, almost seamless armour.

"I'd rather a fucking dragon," she whispered. "Loose!"

The arrows rammed against the metal beast. Blunted and shattered, they fell uselessly to the ground. The tail lashed out. The sting pierced a spearman's chest and lifted him bodily upwards before the spike ripped clear. The body fell, the chest split open, as a second set of arrows slammed into the bulbous windows. Both sets of armour flinched, convincing Zendril that what lay inside at least felt fear, and was therefore killable. As a foreleg crashed down near the front defensive line, a female veteran slashed out, her sword cracking into a joint. The sword bit but, in turn, the edge sparked, tiny shards flying as metal hit metal.

"Retreat and flank," shouted Zendril, dread rising as a claw snapped out, a scissored mechanism first gripping, then shearing through, an archer's leg as they tried to back away. The snap of bone and the arterial spray set the vets into motion. None ran to the man's aid – they'd seen enough fatal injuries in their time.

Zendril estimated she had twelve soldiers left. Once they were gone, who would stand between this monstrosity and the next town? Their fear had been based on a winged dragon. Instead, a huge metal scorpion now flailed and snapped at those who remained.

They spread out, keeping as much distance as they could, using the ground and their mobility to keep clear of tail and claw. The artifice legs heaved the lumbering body, and the scorpion charged at a speed that took Zendril's breath away. This time, the claws merely swung, bashing their way through as the legs snagged at bodies, crushing ribs and smashing skulls in their urgency. Once it was within distance of the general, its tail lashed out, the sting arrowing towards Zendril. And she froze.

Zendril closed her eyes. Her thoughts were on Mander when the ring of metal shattered her prayer for him. Sparks alighted on her cheek, and she opened her eyes to see Sternath's back. The man's sword buckled under the weight of the tail, yet the sting lay, severed, upon his boot.

"Move, you fucking idiot!" he bellowed.

Zendril assumed he meant her. She shifted to one side, shouted she was clear, and the ex-sergeant stepped away, allowing the tail to finish its drive towards the ground. Zendril swung her hefty falchion. The blade bit deep, severing metal wires. The tail lashed back, its tip and top third useless, only for it to whip out behind, striking those vets who had dared close in to attack the artifice's legs.

"Go!" shouted Sternath, backing away as the scorpion finished the last of those facing it. "Run! Warn the town!"

Zendril started to back away, the cries from behind setting her heart hammering as the last few remaining veterans attacked the beast's side.

"No," she said.

Sternath spun, eyes flashing. "We need you alive, General. These …"

His voice petered out, realisation striking him as he followed Zendril's gaze into the sky.

"Fuck me," she added. "As if this day couldn't get any worse."

The scarlet dragon roared; razor-edged teeth bared within its huge maw. Red, metallic skin stretched between its wings, catching the air, steering the mechanised beast towards the battle. With talons extended proud of its metal paws, they whistled in the buffeting wind as it drove downwards.

"Fuck me too, General."

Sternath raised his sword and stood before her, ready to defend against a creature larger than the camp in which they stood. The smell of hot oil filled the air, a flicker of flame slipping from the bearded maw, and a second roar preceded a gout of searing flame. Zendril hit Sternath from behind, slamming her shoulders into the man's knees, bringing him down as the roiling flame seared overhead. The scream of her own burning soldiers met soulful ears, mixed with the pop of expanding metal and the snap of cracking wood. She rolled off, gaining her feet as the dragon's tail slammed into the burning scorpion, the wicked barbs piercing the heated armour, slicing the artifice open like a tanner's knife on leather. With a single beat of its wings, the sinuous, scarlet body rose into the air and wheeled away with a roar that shook the remaining trees.

The mechanised scorpion lay on its back, legs pulsing in a mad dance as they flailed helplessly at the air. Her soldiers lay about it, burned, skin sloughing as the dragon's breath melted flesh from bone. The screaming had stopped, only the whirr of the legs disturbing the crackle of flame. Zendril heaved Sternath up, ears listening to the clash of sword upon metal from the north. At least someone still lived.

A loud crack drew her attention back. An armoured figure had kicked one of the crystal windows out, and had their legs and torso halfway through the aperture. Raising her sword, she ignored the smouldering grass as she approached. Above, the dragon roared again, but her focus remained on the black-clad figure.

Sternath stepped in beside her, distracting her for a second. When she looked back, the armour had frozen, stock still, then began beating at the scorpion's hull in panic. Legs shook and whitefire arced across the armoured plate, lacing the air before being drawn upwards and inwards. A scream of loss and hopelessness cut through, one that petered out as the armour slid from the window to slump onto the ground. The helm cracked, and the final arcs of whitefire dissipated to reveal the white-eyed, husked face that stared back at them, mouth frozen in a rictus of terror. Bite marks shredded the cheeks, though no blood flowed, and there was no rise and fall of the chest to indicate that it lived.

A naked figure dropped from the window, dry-skinned feet landing on the dead figure's chest. Whitefire eyes stared their way as it knelt, animal-like, upon the body. Its head was bare, scarred and raw, matching its starved body, along which the veins pulsed a sickly white. Sternath's sword rose, and the creature ran, skittering through the burning debris, screeching as it dived into the woods.

"I—" started the ex-sergeant, but Zendril slapped the man's shoulder.

"We have others to worry about."

She pivoted and headed north as the dreaded artifice in the sky glinted red in the sun's light. "Retreat! Break off! Follow my voice!" She knew it was hopeless. If they faced another mechanised scorpion, it would strike as they ran. But it was that or burn, for the red glint closed in with wings narrowed, the Unspoken's dragon cutting through the air on its dive towards them. "Run!"

This time the flame roared from the west, the rush of wind and fire crashing into the clearing ahead of them. A metal scorpion's tail swung in the air, spiralling as heat poured through its joints. The pop and squeal of expanding metal was lost amid the screams of a woman enveloped by the flame.

Zendril caught sight of two Honour Guards running her way, dragging someone between them as flames billowed behind. The heat hit them, engulfing their armour, and they threw their charge to the ground, smothering the body as fire tore above. Sternath shoved her aside and dived the other way as the roiling heat passed them by.

As she rose, a glance told her Sternath was fine. She ran to the two guards and beat at their leather and plate armour. Realising the futility, she pulled a boot knife out and ripped hot buckles open. Sternath soon copied her. Rolling the guards clear, stinking of sweat and ash, skin raw but alive, she swore at the bloodied figure beneath. Mander lay there, a heavy cut across his brow. She was searching his body for more wounds when he reached out a hand and grasped her wrist.

"I'll live," he whispered. "The others?"

Zendril tapped him on the cheek, her eyes briefly sparking, before nodding. She rose, only to stumble as the ground shook, the beat of four heavy feet hitting the earth causing her to stagger.

"Well, if this is how it happens, at least it's by a dragon's bite and not a fucking scorpion's sting." She gathered herself and strode out, booted feet kicking smouldering grass aside as she headed through black smoke towards the clamour of battle ahead.

Within three steps, she was no longer alone, Sternath and one of the Honour Guard by her side. It galvanised her heart, reminded her why she fought. As they cut through the smoke, the lash of tail and talon filled the air high and wide with distressed metal. They emerged as the artifice scorpion, wrapped in the barbed tail of the scarlet dragon, rose into the air, its own tail whipping at the crystalline eyes that stared into its open top. The dragon's forked tongue rasped into the scorpion's torso, dragging out an armoured figure much like the others. The tongue flicked its feast into the sky and the mouth crunched down. A second bite swallowed the treat whole as whitefire arced between metal teeth.

Gauntleted hands pulled at the serrated metal of the scorpion's shell, and a second figure threw itself out to fall a good ten yards to the earth below. The thud was punctuated by the snap of bone, but the figure rose and scrambled along the ground, half-running towards Zendril. All three acted as one; Sternath and the guard stepped to one side each, leaving Zendril at the tip of the triangle.

As the armour closed, the guard struck first, his blade biting into the armoured knee. Sternath followed in, his sword slamming into its back as the armour hit the smouldering ground. Zendril drove her blade's tip between helm and neck guard, and waited for a spurt of blood that never arrived. Whitefire sparked briefly along her weapon as a huge, taloned foot drove deep into the shattered leg, grasped the body, then pulled it back before the dragon's mouth snapped around the torso and crunched down. The sinuous neck writhed, and the huge head pulled back. A severed leg tumbled to the ground, ignored, as the beast swallowed.

Zendril stared up, her gaze returned by crystalline eyes. "Fuck me. Maybe I would settle for a metal scorpion."

The bearded head pulled back to expose the dragon's chest, almost as if it readied a final surge of dragon's breath. The general braced, waiting for the end, when the metallic scales shimmered. Zendril's first thought, of it being a heat haze, was confounded as a figure emerged. It stood six feet tall, with skin of porcelain, its hair flame-red. Each stride held a grace that belied the threat her aura radiated – a barely veiled menace beyond the mere sense of sight or touch.

"General Zendril." The words were soft, yet carried above the crackle of flame and complaining metal. "I thought you a thorn pulled and cast far away. And you have found your errant king. A busy day." She turned to cast an eye at the squealing scorpion behind her, before returning her gaze. "Not one of my making. Your people *will* be mine, General, and no *other* shall have you. Yet you appear to have a new enemy, and I will not be here to help another time. Mark this beast, for there will be more."

The Unspoken turned away. Zendril found herself unable to tear her eyes away until the shimmer returned, and a God entered a dragon's chest.

The scaled neck lifted the mighty head and the mouth split wide, trumpeting victory. With two beats, the dragon leapt back into the air, and as the third drove it upwards, the powerful tail wrapped around the artifice scorpion.

Zendril tore her eyes away to alight on Sternath, who gawped as the dragon took to the sky. "Errant king?"

"And I'd like it to stay that way," replied Sternath.

"Fuck that, Your Majesty," she said. "Nobody gets to hide from what's coming."

46
AN ETERNAL LIE

INNEALTÓIR, REALM OF THE CONSTRUCTORS

Laoch pulled the bag across the grass, the weight of the meat inside reassuring as he eyed the water barrel Oisin was rolling towards him.

"Keran says there's no need," said Ecne, checking over the variety of materials, including rope and string, she had gathered together. "He can put us to sleep while we shift between realms."

"You say that as if it's almost natural," said Oisin, hands on the barrel's top as he propped it against the palace steps. He began to heave it upwards. Laoch came over to lend his strength. "But after arriving here with little or no preparation, I'd like to make sure we're okay, if you don't mind, Learned."

"And we had no choice last time," added Laoch. "We were all sorely burned or injured."

"Or dead," said Sura, not an ounce of irony in her words.

Laoch stopped and stared back at her. Sura remained oblivious to his reaction, wrapped in communing with Honour's sigil, the spear lying on the grass where she sat. He shook his head, put his shoulder back behind the barrel and helped to heave it upright.

"I agree. I was just saying it." Ecne rose, gathered up the skin on which her things lay and wrapped it together, tying it off with a knot. She felt her pouch, lips a little tight, before taking it off her belt and checking the contents. The mechanical spiders lay there still. Devoid of their crystals, they appeared dead. The acolyte looked up to Oisin and back again before shaking her head. "There must be some way I can help him," she whispered.

Keran appeared, the shimmer of Nathair's chest heralding his arrival. The spirit almost looked like his old self, with fewer scales and his eyes clear. He kept the pocket open, standing aside as Oisin nodded and spun the barrel along its bottom edge and into the dragon. Laoch followed, lifting the heavy bag up and disappearing through the metallic scales.

Nathair murmured, the brief sound slipping out as the split tongue lolled, tasting the air. Sura's head snapped up, almost in response, eyes flaring with Honour's light. Her head jerked and caught Keran's gaze as he steadied his spirit form against Nathair's suddenly heaving chest.

"What is it?" she asked, rising. Her hand solidified and she grabbed the spear. "It felt ... different. Ecne? Did you feel anything?"

Ecne closed a second pouch, tying it off on her belt. "Felt? I didn't feel anything at all. Why?"

Keran's eyes were distant, and then his lips began to move with no sound. Sura watched and waited until his spirit body relaxed from its rigid posture. "Nathair does not know, but tastes something on the wind. Of spirit and oil. Powerful."

"Constructors?" asked Ecne.

"Undoubtedly. But not something she knows. Nor a dragon. More than that, but lesser. She can't put it in words or thoughts. I think we should leave. We know where we are going."

Sura strode towards Keran and threaded her arm through Ecne's, trying to hurry her along. The acolyte resisted, staring up into the sky where dark clouds swirled. Sura had to add a sliver of Honour's will into her form to yank Ecne towards Nathair.

"We are going," she stated.

They were one stride from the pocket when Ecne pulled herself clear, eyes locked on the white glow now billowing along the edge of the maelstrom above.

"Look," she said, "it's coming through. But there was no Soul Tear."

"There are no veils here. The Constructors consume spiritfire. Surrounding their world with it would send them insane. Well, more insane. And they have no reason to hide."

Keran followed Ecne's gaze, hand over his eyes as if on his ship of old, staring out to sea. A huge brass bulge, wreathed in whitefire, broke through the cloud, pulsing as it slowly dropped. The middle section emerged to reveal rows of windows five storeys high above a band of smooth brass of a similar height. The domed shape was almost familiar, something that whispered at the edge of his mind.

Laoch and Oisin reappeared, eyes wide at the sight of the huge ship as its top finally broke through the swirl of clouds. It pulsed, and a visible wave spread outwards in ripples that swathed the city. Wave upon wave of weak whitefire. Nathair balked, her neck quivering before turning its crystalline gaze on Keran.

"They awaken," Keran spoke, his voice imbued with a sibilant hiss. "The city and itsss inhabitantsss."

A howl broke from the shattered palace entrance, mournful and pained. It shook Ecne, its pull recognisable and hated, though devoid of the honeyed words. The palace walls came alive, shining with a whitefire to match that filling the air from above. Inside, the crack of stone and metal echoed.

"Who awakes?" asked Laoch.

"The sleepers. Nathair can only sense them now. Thousands, left amid crypts and basements. Sleeping until the Fleshmaster returns. Conserving what little energy they have left. They awaken to *feed*."

"Then we leave." Sura shoved Ecne towards Nathair. The acolyte finally responded to the spirit's demands. "Laoch?"

He nodded and quickly checked the area, ensuring they had everything, as a low moan rose from the surrounding city. He strode towards Nathair's chest, allowing Sura and Ecne to enter before stopping next to Keran.

"Will she …?"

"I can only go by what she senses. At the moment, they are all distant from her. Young. If she met the emperor or her creator, perhaps we would have a problem."

Laoch grimaced, and ducked his head as he always did to enter through the dragon's metallic chest.

"At least, that is my hope," added Keran, and faded into the belly of the beast.

Nathair rose up onto all four legs, then sat back to leap into the air. Two beats of her wings saw her rise above the palace, orange metal gleaming amid the sparkle of white streaking down from the Constructor ship. The dragon swooped behind a set of tall chimneys, power surging into her wings as the heartstone mapped the pathway. As the connection formed, Keran and the Spirit Walker acted as one, urging the artifice upwards, towards escape.

"Please," whispered Keran. "For my people."

47
A TASTE OF THE FUTURE

PORT OF GRODIN, MONDREIN

Popsilin adjusted her soulreaver, sliding the restraining strap over. She did the same with her handbow. Assuring herself that the quarrels were stowed safely, she worked through each section of her armour. Once satisfied, she peered along the line of her Inhibitors. In pairs, they ran through the same routine. And now, under her careful watch, their efforts stumbled. She flicked her helm up, white eyes demanding perfection. Giving no other sign of displeasure, expecting her regard to be enough, they redoubled their efforts to complete the checks. Popsilin pushed the visor down again and sent a thought to the team.

"You will be working in pairs, and in silence. The spiritfire seeps strongly from the sea and the weed, blocking thoughts. So, hear this now. We need the ship's captain and any officers, alive, or the Fleshmaster

will flay your spirit and feed on each morsel over a thousand years. Hear me?"

Each helm nodded as one, gauntlets thumped chests. She peered down into the spiritfire mist that rolled across the waves. Three masts peeked above its swirl, anchored to a floating bed of thick, bloated seaweed. Nodding to herself, she looked through the hatch. The clank of chains and hooks announced they were almost ready for the assault.

A thought washed over her. Glancing towards the Inhibitor at the barge's bow, she received the signal to descend.

"Now."

The Inhibitors dropped through the hatchway and plummeted, only for their harnesses to pull them up ten yards short of the ocean below. She tasted their fear; dropping into those depths would be an eternity in the void. Yet, still far better, in her mind, than riding an ornithopter onto a swirling bed of seaweed.

When the last Inhibitor had passed through, she took up her station at the barge's rail, eyeing the approach. The sailing ship's crew was in disarray as they watched the brass and wood barge floating in the sky towards them. Whitefire crackled along the hull, the arcs mingling with those sparking within the mist her Inhibitors swung through. An eerie sight to greet anyone at sun's rise. She imagined just how the ship's crew would react when they spotted her armoured soldiers swinging from the chains, glowing wildly.

Blinded by the rising spiritfire, she smiled to herself. How far she'd risen in Emperor Tarin's favour since the last time she had thrown herself onto hooked chains. Choosing practicality and restraint over the ocean's depths, she dropped through, her wrist harness catching onto the hooks as the chains clanked against the sailing ships' hull. Her Inhibitors were dropping onto the ship now, arms wide, bucklers and their favoured weapons ready as they hit the deck.

The first thwack brought her up short, one of her team's shields split in two by a long sea axe wielded by a hugely muscled human. The second blow never came, as the Inhibitor's partner smashed their maul across the back of the seaman's skull. The head caved in, blood and brains showering them both. More fighting ensued as she dropped, the membranes between her chest and arms catching the air.

Landing on her feet amid the fighting, she rolled, unclipping her soulreaver and handbow. Thus armed, she loosed a quarrel into the knee of a female sailor who, roaring in defiance, swung a massive two-handed axe down in an arc designed to split Popsilin in two. The crystal tip exploded, whitefire shattering the sailor's knee. Her assailant toppled to the deck. Issuing a swift kick to the head, Popsilin swivelled to check on her Inhibitors. With one wounded, their arm shattered by the blow that had destroyed their buckler, she let the dismay pass. Of the ten crew who had fought back, all lay or sat, moaning, upon the deck.

A quarrel smashed into her helm. The whitefire explosion shattered the visor, sending her flying across the deck to crash into the rail. For a second, she hung there, white eyes peering at a veil of mist and the long, slow death the sea beyond promised. A surge of spiritfire raged through her body, electrifying the pathways of long-dead nerves, and she shoved herself backwards and to the deck. A second quarrel flew over her shoulder. With the protective helm in pieces upon the floor, the rush of wind set her on edge. The scuffle of feet told her the Inhibitors were on the move. She rolled to her feet, soulreaver up as a woman on the ship's upper deck reloaded her crossbow. With greying hair wrapped tight behind her neck, and steely eyes solely on Popsilin, she recognised a leader when she saw one. Two of her Inhibitors were already at the stairs. The ship's captain was clearly torn between targets, and had settled on Popsilin.

A backbone too.

The quarrel flew. Popsilin gorged her muscles with whitefire and leapt over it. The rail behind her exploded. Large wooden splinters peppered her armour, sending her flying into the mast. She soaked up the blow, her arms saving her head from impact. The armour absorbed the rest.

Then Popsilin hit the deck again. Swearing, she rose to find the woman backing away from the two Inhibitors, batting at their mauls with the crossbow as she edged towards the rail. Popsilin ran, leaping to place one foot on the lower deck's balustrade before jumping over the upper one to land next to the retreating woman. She lashed out with her fist. The punch crunched into hip and kidney, and her follow-up blow cracked against the woman's neck. The woman collapsed.

"No!" she bellowed as the two Inhibitors closed. "This may well be the captain. I want the ship searched, and then the weed island. Everyone rounded up, now!"

Catching her urgency, they ran down the ladder. Popsilin peered over the balustrade to ensure her team did as ordered. With injured crew restrained, and the clatter of inner doors being broken open, she turned back to the unconscious captain lying prone on the deck.

"Nearly," she said as she knelt. She used the keening sword's tip to move the captain's hair to one side. "I shall not underestimate your people again."

The younglings shouted, anger and fear not quelling their voices; rather, it gave them a fury Popsilin admired. It matched the strong spirit of the captain who knelt before them, head manacled to her feet via a hooked chain and neck brace. Within a breath, the children fell silent, eyes widening as they stared over her armour-plated shoulder. The thrum of the barge's engines told her all she needed;

they were watching the Fleshmaster descend upon twin chains. The emperor wanting to question the ship's captain personally.

The clank of metal links was briefly accompanied by the splintering of wood as the hooks gripped. Sensing Tarin's approach, she yanked the woman's bowed head up to face the Fleshmaster as he strode across the deck.

"Ah," said Tarin. "Yes. Your spirit tastes ... delightful." A single finger alighted beneath her chin, and he lifted the woman's gaze to meet his white-eyed stare. Her weather-beaten face remained stern, only a twinge of fear at the corner of her eyes betraying the dread her spirit displayed. "Delicious. But not as tempting as one younger, more innocent." The emperor did not remove his gaze nor gesture towards the children, but the spike of his words still drove home.

"No," she whispered, low and hard.

"Perhaps I should consume one now. Speed things up a little so you know I speak true when I say my patience is thin." He let his finger drop, and turned to eye the three teenage boys, who had wrapped arms around each other. "Which should I choose?"

"No," she repeated.

The Fleshmaster turned back to her, the twist of his blue lips mirroring his pleasure as he closed in on what he needed. "Do not resist me, Captain. Let me in and, on my word, no harm will come to your precious children's bodies."

He caught the faint nod, and his smile broadened. Kneeling, he cupped the woman's chin and the back of her head in his hands. A sliver of his *self* slid into her mind, cutting through muddied thoughts, seeking the one thing that had driven him to this realm. Filtering through useless memories of happiness and joy, hard work and sweat, the pleasure of harvest and loss of those close to her, he came upon those he sought.

"Yessss," he said, the words sliding between aged teeth.

Three twisted Schenterenta, aboard this very ship, stowed below against the fiercest of storms as Surena steadied her crew, driving the ship towards a rocky isle.

"Yesss," he repeated, squeezing the memories further, hooking the sliver deeper into her mind. "Show me."

The ship pitched and yawed its way through the turbulent ocean before reaching the shelter of a rocky reef. The lagoon beyond led them towards a grey sandy beach covered in dead, rotting weed. He tasted the woman's bitterness. It thrilled him. A distant memory, of her first visit to this place, just beyond his reach and teasing at the Fleshmaster. Letting it go, he focused on the rowboat that made its way to the shallows, and the Schenterenta that greeted them.

"You know," he said.

The Fleshmaster let go and stood to regard the children. "They are to be kept unharmed, Popsilin. Not a hair upon their heads shall fall, understand? This captain knows where we must go, and for that, I will keep my bargain. Bring them all aboard. The hunt nears its end."

48

OF OLD FRIENDS IN NEED

WEISTER CASTLE, RIDTH,
BRANDSHOLD

Sneed pushed himself up from the bed, mind swirling, his spirit sore from the Soul Tear, and fumbled for the letter the queen had given him. It lay sealed upon the table at his bedside. He let a sigh slip from his lips. "Your foresight, my Queen, matches my High Lord's at times."

He rose and stretched his aged body, feeling the crack of each joint and protest of muscle and tendon. A brief look in the mirror told him all he needed to know. After a splash of water, he donned his purple robe and entered the castle's corridor. A few yards along, Death's priest stood, hands clasped before her, eyes peering through an open door as low moans echoed out.

Sneed rubbed a healed hand against the back of his neck and nodded in greeting before clasping hands with Hertina. Her eyes bore bad news.

"No change?"

She shook her head. "His heart," she said, head dipping to the stone floor. "I heard of some whose heart failed on the first Tear. But they were aged, old. He is still young."

Sneed nodded and risked a glance into the darkened room. Only a single candle lit Jacka's sweat-covered face; pain was etched into the newly formed wrinkles about his mouth and eyes. "Then he cannot be moved. I will ask the duke to maintain him here until the queen decides what comes next. Do you ...?"

"I do not fear his death, no. But it will take time. His heart is wounded and will need to heal."

Sneed nodded, then thanked the priest.

Entering Jacka's sleeping chamber, he took the chair next to the prime. Placing one hand upon his brow, he let a little of his spiritfire wheedle its way inwards. He left a message there, one he hoped Jacka would recover in time to hear. With a squeeze of the man's hand, he rose and returned to his chamber, and the letter that awaited him.

—

Simeon sat hunched over the ornate table, the display of fruit, cheese and bread before him hardly touched as he sipped at the hot tea. Sneed squirmed in the wooden chair opposite, though it wasn't the seat that he found uncomfortable.

"A change. You should be used to that after the last few years," said the duke, eyeing Sneed over the cup's lip.

"I think you are enjoying this too much. A man lies gravely ill in your castle's chambers." Sneed picked at the grapes on the plate before him, combining them with a little cheese before biting down.

"And I will care well for him, Prime Sneed."

The High Lord's servant squirmed in his seat. "Temporary, Simeon. How did she know?"

"She's a Weister. And, as you said on arrival, a damn fine one too. I suspect, however, that Vardrin will bear a similar letter somewhere among his things should you have fallen to a malady of some kind." Simeon placed the cup on the table, an unhelpful grin upon his thin lips. "But the question is, what to do next?"

"It is already clear. Prime Vardrin was to go on to the isles of Meres and Khund, though she had kept that from him until arriving here. To prepare the people for what is to come. I was to accompany him, make contact with the Khundish Priesthood."

"They are the strangest of the strange, Sneed. Not an easy task."

"But allied to us. And though their practice bends scripture, it does not break it. You have witnessed what the Unspoken can do. I cannot see water being a barrier to her ire, so the High Lord's and the queen's reasoning is sound. Yet ..."

"Now you go alone, with only the queen's letter as proof of her word." Simeon reached for the cup before changing his mind and raising his hand so he could set his chin upon it. "There is an alternative. I can send a fast horse, with word for the queen."

"And?"

"We are to ready the fleet. My seneschal is competent and can protect the city alongside the militia as well as I. General Mandrich is already preparing the standing army for what is to come. I can leave orders that he is to follow the queen's oversight."

"You propose to come?"

"I would have the status you require, and taking a third or so of the fleet with us would demonstrate its import. Yes, I believe I am."

Sneed considered the duke's words, running over the reasons he'd outlined. Though the past was a confusion of emotion and misalignment, he could see the benefit.

"You ponder on whether there is an underlying reason. Perhaps there is. But do not take this as a mellowing, or forgiveness. In truth, I would not offer if I did not believe in the threat. Word comes of a village that was attacked a few nights past. One we had not heard from for a while – though this wasn't unusual. Death comes on dragon's wings, Sneed."

"That it does."

But far more than you think.

"I agree with your assessment." Sneed took another bite of grape and cheese, and chewed before continuing. "Yes. If this is my task, then the joining of the Houses and the Crown as prime is an honour that would be doubled by your company. A servant, I remain."

"Though one of a higher calling, *Prime*."

49

A SPIRIT'S SACRIFICE

Above Innealtóir, Realm of the Constructors

Nathair roared, the thud of her wings against the wind defiant as she rose. Keran felt the pull, the demand in the pulse emanating from the Constructor ship. Shaped by spiritfire, he sensed Nathair respond, the Spirit Walker tasting age upon its waves. Within the leviathan was someone whose touch she recognised, the demand to serve bound by the chains of venom wrapped about the spirit.

Like Oisin. But deeper, poured into the wound where the twin was consumed, leaving this half in madness and despair. Such evil.

The great dragon lurched, wings twisting as the venomous chains pulled and hardened inside the heartstone. Keran felt the dragon's loyalty waver, knowing well it both hated and needed to serve. The

Constructor's control had evolved into habitual responses, driven by the hunger for spiritfire to heal the wound of loss. It sickened Keran. His own memories of being unbound, separated from the love he'd shared before despair took him, drowning him over and over again along with his brother's family.

The metal-limbed wings curved, turning the dragon away from the clouds, its roar now an answering call as it flew towards the Constructor ship.

"No."

'I mussst.'

"My people."

'Will be consumed, or enslaved. It issss the way.'

"I cannot let that happen, Nathair."

'You have a choicccce?'

One, he thought, and sent out a calling. "Sura? Can you hear me?"

"Yes, Keran. What is happening? I can feel the change, is Nathair ...?"

"She is about to return to her creators. Taken by the pulse. I may not survive what is to come. If I fall, you and yours will be the last thing that stands between the Constructors and my people. If there is but a chance, I beg of you to take it." He sent out a thought, a mere wisp of his being, framing a woman with great strength in her eyes. A babe was swaddled on her back, while two more stood at her hip.

"Surena," he whispered.

"If you fall, we will be in the belly of the beast."

"Where there is life, there is always hope."

Keran let the last of his touch fade, then peered inwards, to where the swirling mass of a twisted Spirit Walker roiled under the venomous chains of the Constructor's control.

He narrowed his *self*, became a lance of pure spirit, and drove through those links, deep into the centre of madness. Chaos assailed his spirit mind, a thousand fractured thoughts of pain and agony, of servitude and a longing for freedom, all stirring at once. The sacrificial knife plunged into a twin's heart, lips purple stained, eyes etched in spiritfire. Their last breath smoked the air with a violet hue that writhed and curled in upon itself before plunging down between Nathair's lips, immersing nerves in ecstasy and pain. Fusing, spirit within spirit, twin upon twin. Keran shuddered, his honour railing against his invasion as he witnessed the most intimate of connections as a voyeur. It sat heavy. Yet the memories flowed, as if something within Nathair wanted him to see, to understand.

Nathair lay pinned to muddy ground, elven limbs twisted, joints screaming in pain. Her outer shell was an ugliness that belied the beauty of the connection within. A hand appeared in her view, dried, ancient, skin flying off. The mechanical spider it held raised its forelegs, displaying fangs dripping black venom. It leapt to land upon Nathair's exposed chest, and the rib cage with its paper-thin skin. It bit down, fangs penetrating deep, injecting Nathair between the ribs, into the heart below. The cry was silent, yet filled Keran with an agony beyond measure.

He flailed and turned away, only for a warm embrace to pull him back. He watched the black, the streaks of evil, tear into the entwined souls. It burned with hate and control, overwhelming both spirits as they fought. Then one parted from the other, wrapping itself in sacrifice, giving itself up to the venom lest they both be consumed. It said nothing, thought nothing, but love, and passed into the void after alleviating much of the venom's bite. All that remained was a keening spirit, that which was Nathair, and the suppurating wound that the remains of the venom bound and chained.

Keran flinched, the agony too much. Yet, the warmth remained, a love lost, and he felt himself pressed towards Nathair and the wound that bound. Then an understanding held him in thrall. A moment of stillness. An awakening and an ending, combined. He poured himself upon the wound, soothing, calming – entwining.

———

Sura sensed the shift. The heartstone missed a beat, matching the stutter to the dragon's metal-skinned wings. Nathair dropped, though the protective pocket squeezed tight to hold her companions in a safe embrace. Reaching out, she sensed that Nathair's anger and desperation – the need to supplicate to her masters – had slipped from the Spirit Walker's thoughts. Awe swept over her at the touch of a new spirit. Not Nathair, nor the suffering Keran. No. This one had shed its chains, shattered the binding through a joining of souls.

She glanced over towards Laoch, lips twisting, her mind lost in thoughts of the future and the choice she had made.

Nathair broke her reverie, wings swinging and dipping to bring the dragon about. Yet the Constructor ship still loomed, the boiling mass of whitefire at its heart hurting her senses. How many had died to feed that machine? What agonies had they suffered so the Constructors could live to fall upon their prey like locusts, ravaging the realms?

A thick, foul arc of power lashed out from its brass base, striking their dragon of the veil between its shoulders. Nathair roared with pain, and that which was both Spirit Walker and Keran writhed in agony as the whitefire seeped between scales and metal skin, along wire and cog, to wreath the heartstone in its evil.

Sura's spirit mind seemed to be wading through treacle, the atmosphere thick with power, slowing everything about her except those with physical form. Her eyes widened as Laoch drew Justice and held the sword high, its crimson light casting about the room in battle with the white. A leader with people to save, his face was set. A dread pierced her heart as she realised what he would do next.

"Laoch, no."

And the most stubborn man she had ever met ignored her. Justice swung down towards the crystal that danced with the viscous, dreadful whitefire. She saw what was to come, Honour flashing the future through her mind's eye. Justice's recklessness, Laoch's acquiescence. The metal's edge melted beneath the onslaught, the sigil overwhelmed and consumed. As Justice, or the sliver that remained, faded into the past, so would Laoch be burned from the inside out. Ash and bone were all that would remain of the maddening man she loved.

Sura slammed into Laoch's brain, the fullness of her denial triggering him into a seizure. Muscles twitched, fingers splayed. As he writhed in the pain, Justice clashed against the metal floor. Hating herself, she drew back, the briefest of kisses left upon the now still lips.

"My warrior of bone and heart," she whispered in his ear, breathless.

A last caress of his cheek, and Sura, Nista of Betana Refi Na Partera, a Spirit Walker split asunder by happenstance, poured herself into the whitefire.

50
THE RETURN OF A KING

THE WHITE PALACE, ERSTENBURGH,
BRANDSHOLD

Lord Penance eased himself into the curved back of the wooden chair, cane propped between his legs, both hands resting on the sigil set in its cap. The queen stared back at him from across the breakfast table, her eyes sunken and tear-stained.

"Death's priest says he will survive the heart failure, though recovery will be long. His body is weakened by it." The High Lord watched Erin's reaction, expecting perhaps a release of guilt somewhere from the iron skin she wrapped herself in.

"Suffice to say, I have complete trust in House Death's ministrations, High Lord. But the distance makes it … difficult." Queen Erin wiped away the hot tear threatening to roll down her cheek. "Somehow, I feel this is my fault by sending him away."

"A penance for someone who worships at the House of Fate? I think not, my Queen. Just the failings of a body. Others have passed, or been weakened, by the Soul Tear. Jacka is no different. I thank the Seven we have not lost more." He raised an eyebrow, waiting for a tumble of words to fill the void.

But no. Maybe, when she has saved the realm, they will come. Guilt for her consort, and for her prime, whose attention she pushed away. Sacrifices for her people.

"I believe Prime Sneed has sent word?" he continued.

"I am sure he sent it to us both. Yes, and he has accepted the post of prime in this hour of need." Erin brushed away another tear, then pulled her back straight, taking a slice of cheese to distract herself.

"How did you know? I pride myself, whether it be foolish or not, on being prepared, my Queen. But you foresaw issues beyond my own sight." He scrunched both hands on the cane top, feeling the reassuring warmth of his God's touch.

"Foresaw? No. But my father always said to prepare for the worst. Distance will be the death of the realm, Lord Penance. The frustration of not being able to direct the pieces in play is a difficulty I did not foresee when I—" The queen caught herself, causing Lord Penance to smile in delight despite himself.

"When you challenged the Houses? Yes? Do not fret. I think you have already seen I have been swept along by the changes you have forced upon us. We have witnessed traditions dashed, prides knocked. And we are all the better for it. And yes, you see what we do not. I have set Meister Kinst with a task alongside Lords Hope and Wisdom. If we can utilise scrying stones across the realm, then we have more chance to survive what is to come. A pity we could not ready this for, heh, *Prime* Sneed, before his journey."

"I agreed to the duke's request to accompany the new prime as my representative. It makes sense. If, between them, they can rally the Khundish, then at least our realm is not going forward blindly into battle." The queen dabbed at her mouth, removing a few imaginary crumbs before placing both hands on the table to rise.

Before she could, the chamber door echoed with a servant's knock.

She looked to Lord Penance. "I am not so used to all this secrecy, though. Sending the servants out and talking of new Court protocols has raised the hackles of my palace. I believe you must start to spread rumours you can control about what is really coming, High Lord. With Jacka ill, and Sneed halfway across the realm, it falls to you – to us – to prepare the people. Nothing raises dread more than not knowing. They see the army muster, weapons adorn the city walls, yet no word of when or whom. I believe the way would be easier should the people believe in the cause. Fear of the Unspoken's dragon may not be enough to assuage the pious when spiritfire is in play."

She turned towards the door. "Enter."

The servant promptly pushed the door wide enough for him to slide through, before closing it as was the queen's new demand prior to speaking.

"We have two visitors, my Queen," he said, looking directly towards her and then to Lord Penance. "An elf, here at the High Lord's request, and a man called Sternath who carries General Zendril's mark with an urgent message."

Queen Erin looked to the High Lord, whose face was suddenly bleak.

"No doubt the recent Soul Tear had a source, Queen Weister. Perhaps that is something the general wishes to speak of?"

"And the Schenterenta?"

"Terana Fiotir Na Partera. A tribal chief. Here because ... well, because I need to protect the realm's greatest asset." He let that sit until the queen's patience faded and she made to speak. He eyed the servant and whispered, "You. Should the city fall, or the realm be overrun, we need you and the Lords and Ladies of the Houses safe. Rallying points."

And if they hide you, the Spirit Walkers will also be hidden from the Constructors' eyes. Two birds.

"Send the general's representative in, would you?"

As the servant turned to open the door, she leaned forwards, eyes on the High Lord. "If the realm falls, Lord Penance, I will fall with it – whether it be with sword in hand or from the taste of poison. I will not be a spirit-doll, nor watch my people become so."

The door opened wide. A dirtied and bloodied soldier strode through, scabbard empty, with a sealed letter in hand. He came to a standstill, waiting at the very point expected of him with head bowed, before the servant spoke.

Lord Penance felt his stomach churn as he caught sight of the scar upon the man's cheek. It failed to hide, from such knowing eyes, just who stood before them.

He made to rise when the soldier looked up. Ice-blue eyes held the High Lord in place, a familiar grimace and nod settling him back down.

Queen Erin looked from soldier to High Lord, feeling the tension. "I am no fool, High Lord," she said as the servant bowed and left. "Speak."

"I'm not sure it is my place," he replied, letting another wisp of spiritfire seep into his palms. "Is it?"

"My Queen." The man bowed, a perfect posture that set the queen's curiosity raging. "I have General Zendril's mark, and message." Again, he waited, the perfect protocol from a commoner scraping at her nerves.

"Approach," she said, angrily side-eyeing the High Lord.

The soldier presented the letter's seal before handing it to the queen, a piece of cloth present between grubby fingers and the envelope's edge. She slit it open and read the first few lines before letting her hand drop to her knees.

"I ..." She rose, protocols whirling, unsure of what to say.

"Please ignore your mother's descriptions, my Queen. I am once again at the service of the realm, under the general's direction."

"King Panset, I—"

"I forsook the crown due to the madness of the Crusade. I am no longer king, and the crown fits your head far better than it ever did mine. I would wish to maintain my anonymity, but your mother is ... Forgive me. I do not think I can repeat the words. However, the message carries much of import. Few survived the attack, but rumour will be rife of what we fought, and who intervened."

Queen Erin nodded, reading on, eyes widening, before handing the letter over to the High Lord. "You say *something* escaped?"

"Something monstrous, yes. And on my way here, there were rumours of its sighting. A farmhouse was attacked, the family murdered."

Lord Penance rose from his chair, a tremor running through him. "Murdered? How so?"

"I did not see the bodies, but there is talk of them being beaten and bitten. There was a fancy among all this. They say the skin was dry, sunken and shrivelled."

"No. Are you sure? Where are these bodies? They *must* be burnt."

51
THE PREY

The Whispering Isle, Mondrein

Popsilin rode the chain once again, the taste of fear upon her dried lips as the Fleshmaster's barge flew low over the reef that protruded above the raging waves. Wind rasped at her grip, urging her fingers to let go, to plummet down and break upon the rocks, or sink below the ocean's surface.

She forced the rising tremor to stop, whitefire lacing muscles that threatened to return to their atrophied state as her spirit drew inwards in response to her thoughts. Angry at herself, she wrapped her hand a little tighter, glancing ahead at the Inhibitors who waited for the chains to touch the island ahead. The storm bucked and tore at her soldiers, but everyone thanked their captain that they rode the chains and not the ornithopters circling above. It had been her insistence that the flying artifices would struggle to land, and one crash could give their presence away too early. A decision met with their gratitude, and her relief.

The first chains dug into the ravaged beach, weaving patterns in the sand and snagging ocean-spawned detritus. The first pair of Inhibitors dropped, eschewing the wings at the lower altitude and with the rising threat of the storm. They hit the beach rolling, pulling their crystal slingers out to eye the dunes. The second and third pairs hit the sand. Satisfied, Popsilin followed, rolling to come up with her soulreaver drawn. The beach grass rippled in the wind, and she sent the second pair up the nearest dune to watch from the top. With a thought of 'All-clear' reaching her, she surveyed the beach, glad she wasn't going to be anywhere nearby when the ornithopters attempted to land.

"Tenith, stay here and signal them in. Once the first has landed, lead them to my position."

The Inhibitor saluted and jogged out to the centre of the beach as the Mechanised Inhibitor captain headed to join her team.

"Slingers, stay here. Cover our approach to the next dune, follow on my signal, and we'll track inwards until we hit the village edge. By Surena's description, it is in the lee of a rocky outcrop. A high fence constructed from driftwood serves as another wind block, and may prevent eyes on us. There will be *magi* here, but not like you've faced before. These wield the spirits, not spiritfire. Understand? Attacks will be subtle. Watch out for the green shit they spit."

Popsilin sent the lead pair down the dune, and the next. As they reached the valley between, she followed.

On attaining the next rise, she signalled the slingers over, then brought her paired eyeglasses up to stare across an outcrop to the village walls. Beyond them, fires lit the sky, their flames straight in the lee. Popsilin caught a whiff of cooking fish.

She sent the slingers out separately, each accompanied by another Inhibitor as guard and watcher. Connected, she was able to sift between the spiritfire pictures they sent, obtaining a view of the entire village of Schenterenta as they prepared an evening meal.

"A perfect family scene," she muttered. "For now."

'Hold, keep watch until the second team arrives.'

She didn't have to wait long. Tenith sent thoughts of five bedraggled Inhibitors staggering up a dune her way. She'd expected fewer – a testament to the skill of the pilots rather than the robustness of the infernal machines.

"Give me a Vanguard Scorpion any day."

The wind whipped up, blowing harder, driving a haze into the sky and infuriating Popsilin. Blinded, she received the complaints of the slingers – and then lost contact completely.

A block. Spirits, not wind! Shit.

She sent a thought Tenith's way as she knelt and brought the paired eyeglasses to her eyes. Scanning to her right, she caught sight of the first pair. A Schenterenta stood above them both. A wicked-looking spear had been driven through the back of the Inhibitor carrying the slinger, while the other was chopping at the elf's knee. A spurt of blood brought her a little joy, but then a second elf emerged from the sand to drive a curved knife into the Inhibitor's back. Not a killing blow, but severed muscles and tendons were just as detrimental to a Constructor until healed.

'Tenith! Hurry!' she bellowed, the thought winging its way to her second as hands rose from the surrounding sand to claw at her feet. She jumped backwards, only to sense a blade slashing towards her heel. It bit into the boot, her quick movement enough to blunt the blow. Spinning away, she slashed downwards. The soulreaver cleaved hands and drew the spirit in. With muscles spurred by tasteless spiritfire, she flipped forwards, dodging the first of the Schenterenta warriors to pull clear of the sand. His short sword slashed air, only its tip catching her black armour. A spark of whitefire leapt, lashing at her, but the plate reflected the power away harmlessly. Thanking the artificers, she landed, soulreaver before her as the elf charged. A crystal-tipped quarrel smashed into the elf's shoulder. The explosion

shattered bone, and flesh speared through the air, accompanied by a scream of pain. Popsilin drove her sword deep, drinking the soul before it departed, and spat on the warrior's body.

"The other slinger pairing got lucky," said Tenith, reloading his handbow as he hurried to her side. "We were closer. They expected us, yes?"

"Of course they fucking did," she replied.

The sand spun, whirling into a dervish of searing grit, and Tenith slapped her back, shoving his captain down the dune. She rolled, tumbling to crash into the edge of the outcrop. Angry, she rose and stared back up as Tenith dissolved before her eyes, his armour shredded, merging with the sand as it flayed his husked flesh from the bone. Mouth wide, teeth bared, skull stripped back, his body disappeared into the maelstrom. The whirlwind dropped as swiftly as it had arisen. Popsilin sent her fearful thoughts skywards.

———

"The barge is yours, Captain," stated the Fleshmaster. "Await my signal."

Thumping a spiked gauntlet against his armoured chest, Tarin, Fleshmaster and emperor, dropped through the hatch. His hand caught upon the first chain, and spun him about to grab another lower down, before spiralling to the beach below. Heavy prints drove into the sand. The Fleshmaster was unable to resist a huge grin that spread his blue lips wide. His sword flared, white flame searing into the night sky.

Tarin strode, his pace rising to a run as he arrowed in on Popsilin. The clash of artifice and spirit roared ahead of him. With the wind unable to stop his passage, he sensed the spirits shift in focus to aim for his captain. Reducing the odds before facing their nemesis. He couldn't help but laugh, life thrilling his being.

'I have so missed this. Popsilin, move!'

Sending that thought, he leapt the dune ahead and tore towards the outcrop, and the pathetic wooden fence beyond. He sensed Popsilin react, and called upon the Inhibitor pilots to abandon their artifices and join the fray. Fodder, perhaps, but there were enough gourds in the barge above to recover the fallen.

On reaching the outcrop, a spirit barrier rose, the swirl of a Spirit Walker's power rising to draw in and solidify their ancestors. But this was magic he knew, had beaten a time before. The soulreaver might draw upon the living, but they were designed for the dead.

"Build your veils, hide yourselves away. But you fracture your knowledge, stagnate, and fail to learn, while *I* empower and grow."

Tarin sensed the pilots' movements, handbows cocked, running up the second dune. Roaring defiance, he leapt the nine feet to the edge of the rocky outcrop, joining Popsilin as she scrambled up to stand by his side. The scene below had changed. Torches doused, the village was in darkness. But to the Fleshmaster's eyes, the elven spirits within glowed. Three were entwined in the embrace of Spirit Walkers.

He sent a thought Popsilin's way. As the remaining Inhibitors clambered up, he took two steps forwards and drove his sword deep into the shimmer of the spirit shield. White flame flared bright, the sword's edge slicing spirit and air, withering the souls that resisted his demand. Yanking the sword out, he drove it in again horizontally, sawing away the spirits that shrivelled at its touch.

"Now, Popsilin. Leave none but those marked, alive."

She nodded, dived through, and cut down any Schenterenta that stood in her way – or those that ran, in equal measure. The explosions of crystal quarrels were greeted by the elves' own, a battle in which the Schenterenta held the numbers advantage, and the Constructors, a toughened armour the likes of which these elves had never seen. Amid the chaos, the emperor strode, a smile upon his face. He was the Master of the Flesh, and death rode upon the wind to thrill his detached soul.

The lash of a spirit ward whipped at his face, tearing a flap from his cheek. The skin flaked, lifting upon the heat of whitefire as he healed the wound. Without missing a beat, he strode towards the doorway and the glow of the twinned souls within. A second ward reared up, a spirit of tooth and claw. The Fleshmaster dodging the first blow before driving the soulreaver deep to draw the spirit from within. It shrank, withering beneath his power, and his booted foot crashed into the doorway. The Fleshmaster immediately sensed danger and threw himself to one side. A pain spirit rushed by, wreathing the poor Inhibitor that battled behind him. It slammed into the protective armour, but this was not spiritfire. Digging itself between the plates, it imbued the husked flesh beyond, coursing through dead nerves. The Inhibitor shrieked, her body alive once again with a hundred years of pain delivered in one blow.

The emperor swore. "Something new," he added, and crashed through the open doorway to spear the Schenterenta beyond.

The warrior writhed on the floor as Tarin slashed the spear tip up through chin and skull. The quiver of ancient spirits in the air tasted weak, the Spirit Walkers spent.

He laughed with a thousand years of relief.

"Pin them," he whispered, letting whitefire carry his thoughts to their ears. Their eyes widened in response. His command of the soul magic was far beyond any written in their histories.

Popsilin stepped in behind. Two of her surviving team grabbed the three withered, twisted Schenterenta and dragged them through the splintered door. The emperor followed them out and scanned the village, smiling at the smell of blood and pain that rode the wind, and the scattered remnants of whirling spirits. The taste thrilled him near as much as the anticipation.

Suppressing the excitement lest he fall foul of a mistake, he waited until the iron spikes had been driven between wrist and ankle, the cries of pain suppressed by the gags rammed into stretched elven mouths. Then the Fleshmaster knelt, husked fingers bared, and let them play along each of the three Spirit Walkers, touching ears and cheeks, tasting their entwined souls.

"Yes," he let slip.

Reaching to unclip a panel of his armour, he brought out a silver metal box. He nodded to Popsilin, and the captain tore open the woven shirts of the prone elves, her eyes full of anticipation as the Fleshmaster flipped open the lid. Inside sat a mechanical spider. It flared its legs once, before hopping onto the box's edge. There, it skittered from side to side, then leapt onto the chest of the first Spirit Walker.

Tarin shook, the ecstasy of what was to come almost stymying his reason before he wrested back control.

The spider's front legs rose again, baring its black-tipped fangs. And with a future reborn, it pierced the skin and flesh between ribs, pouring evil deep into the racing heart.

"Yesssssssssss," cried the Fleshmaster of Innealtóir, Emperor of the Constructors, future conqueror of the Seven.

52
A DECISION MADE

ABOVE INNEALTÓIR, REALM OF THE CONSTRUCTORS

"What is happening?" bellowed Lelion, the admiral's anger incandescent amid the bridge. The crew gripped their levers and wheels, focusing on their roles as an armoured foot crashed into the brass floor. "Tell me!"

"Nathair resists," replied a lieutenant. The woman's spirit wrapped itself around heart and mind, awaiting the blast that would surely come.

"You lie!"

Lelion slapped the woman hard across the face, brass fingernails tearing flesh from cheek and jowl. The Inhibitor officer hit the deck, hands spread on the floor, head down lest the admiral caught her eyes again.

"Nathair cannot escape! Draw the whitefire back! Attack again!" shouted Lelion.

"There will not be enough for our people," said the lieutenant, the words spitting between the flaps of her cleaved cheek. "They will awaken and starve, or they will live, and the *Kraken* will never fly again."

Lelion's foot lashed out. The brass tip of her boot caught the second beneath her chin, driving the jaw up to shatter against the Constructor's skull. Bone cut into her brain, severing the spirit's root. The admiral struck again with her heel, this time shattering the gourd the officer carried. Anger spilled upon the deck. Spent, she stared at the body, reality finally overcoming her murderous rage.

"Ranket, your gourd!" she said through clenched teeth.

The Inhibitor nodded, slipped the soul container from his uniform's belt and flipped the lid next to the officer's body. He felt the shift, the moment when the Constructor spirit disengaged from the broken body, its need to survive driving it to the sanctuary of the gourd.

The admiral stared, though not at Ranket's actions. Instead, she stared into the distance, her violent shaking subsiding. Turning, she grasped the rail before the bridge window, her eyes piercing the sky as Nathair's wings beat a steady rhythm up into the swirl of dark clouds.

"Sever the connection. Take us down. Let our people feed," she said, blue lips stretched tight against her metal teeth.

53
A SOUL LOST

ABOVE INNEALTÓIR, REALM OF THE
CONSTRUCTORS

Laoch's muscles shook, the remnants of Sura's attack upon his mind still surging through his nerves. On tingling lips, he felt her last kiss and, on his rough cheek, the caress of her fingers. A tear fell unbidden as he watched her soul be rent and torn by the whitefire wreathing the heartstone.

"Keran!" bellowed Oisin. Ecne reached out for the heartstone before the mountain man slapped her hand down. "No, Ecne! This is not our battle."

Ecne swore, turning away as Sura's face stared outwards, mouth wide in a silent pain. Lightning arced, wrapping her spirit body, drawing her back into the maelstrom. Ecne's eyes dropped, unable to watch her friend suffer.

"Keran, by Fate's weave, where are you? Sura dies for you!" the Handren howled at the crystal, anger at his own impotence coursing through him. His hand reached for Fate's bow as the sigil pulsed in the whitefire's light. Face set, he pulled, expecting the bow's string to flare into life.

Only absence responded.

"Fate?" he said, his words barely a whisper.

'No. She weaves her own path; we would only hinder. If she falls, we stitch the hole and move on.'

Oisin snarled and let the bow drop, pointing it towards the floor. The only sign he held a God's weapon was the soft glow at his thumb. He turned, eyes searching Laoch's agonised face for some form of forgiveness, but the man was absent, his soul withering inside. Oisin could see him dying by degrees, trembling fingers reaching out, feet dragging him towards the evil that wrapped the stone.

"Laoch," he said, taking a step. The next placed him between the Ranger and Sura's agony. "No, Ranger." He opened his arms wide and pulled the grief-stricken man in close.

Oisin sensed the spider's venom rise inside him as it finally responded to the whitefire at his back. And only then did Fate act, pulsing, her warmth sliding down his spine to form a shield.

Helping him moments after refusing to come to Sura's aid.

"Oisin." Keran's voice, layered upon Nathair's as if the two spoke in unison, echoed throughout the room. "It endsss."

Keeping one arm wrapped around Laoch, the First Ranger looked back at the heartstone. The scaled face of dragon and man peered out from the large crystal, locked in by the whitefire battling their comrade. A keening struck up, a pulse, wavering within the arc of energy, and its grip upon the heartstone loosened. For a second it paused, tendrils of power hanging in the air. As he watched, Sura stretched, her too-thin spirit form extricating itself, pulling clear like rubber sap from an ancient tree.

Laoch moved, too fast for Oisin, his arm grasping for her. Fingers cut through her wisp-like form, ripples the only sign of contact, and her cat-like eyes fell upon Laoch for a final time. Nathair lurched and the whitefire lashed out, wrapping itself about Sura before ripping her backwards, up and out between the scales of the artifice dragon. A strangled cry emanated from Laoch, and the Ranger fell to his knees. Before him, Justice throbbed, but its refusal to act hit Laoch far more than the power it held.

"We mussst leave," echoed about the room.

A second lurch shook the mechanical dragon, its wings beating against thinner and thinner air as it rose above the cloud and the realm. "We mussst follow the path, be true to our caussse. Save our people."

Oisin watched as Laoch wept, griefs old and new pouring from the man who had led them through the terrors and madness of the Constructor's realm. His hands were held tight on his lap, stayed from Justice's grip. So often he'd watched Laoch's fingers alight on its pommel in times of pain, seeking the sigil's touch. Finally, perhaps, needing to release the grief rather than have it soothed yet again. To endure the reality of the loss before facing what was to come.

"I do not think this bodes well," whispered Ecne at his side.

"For us, or for him?"

"For everything. He has held us all together." She looked to Oisin, her eyes full of tears. "And I am torn apart. Losing Sura again, it is too much. Before, it felt like she had not passed. That she had remained her."

"SSSura," said Keran, emerging from the heartstone, his naked body scaled and reflecting the room's glow. "The whitefire consss-sumed her, took her back to the ... the *Kraken*."

"And why did you not stop it?" raged Laoch, rising to his feet, hand now grasping Justice. "Why let it take her?"

Keran grimaced, sharp metallic teeth glinting from between the bulbous lips. "I wasss imprisoned, Laoch. I could not."

"Or would not. Reduce our numbers, make taking us out one by one easier. Or perhaps, in doing so, you would fail to escape to save your own precious people. *She was one of us!*" Laoch raised Justice above his head. Oisin once again moved towards the maddened Ranger.

"She saved me. All of usssss," replied Keran, double eyelids blinking as he turned to face Laoch. "It was not a choice. But if it had been, I would have still chosen my people, and Ssssura would have rejoiced in that honour."

"Stand down, Laoch." Oisin raised both hands, palms out, though he kept Fate's bow hooked around one thumb. "We need Keran, and Nathair."

"We are one now, Oisin of the Handren. We – *I* am Nathair. Two as one. The sssame venom that burns inssside you, and rendered the Spirit Walker in half, hasss been purged. We are joined – *my* sssacrifice to keep you sssafe."

As Nathair spoke, the scales shifted, its face shadowed by constant change as if it couldn't settle.

"And to save your people over ours," spat Laoch, though Oisin could see the rage had begun to dissipate. The spirit's words had, perhaps, not so much taken the wind from his sails, more reminded him of why it blew.

"I would hope to sssave us all. Marbhleoir has provided the path to this new realm, this Apso-Tran, and a hope that the Conssstruc-tors have a weakness that the people there exploited." Nathair's eyes glazed, then the dragon spirit turned back to Oisin. "I mussst direct the mechanism, be itsss guide. You will need to sssleep as before, for the journey isss long in your time."

Oisin nodded, and turned to find Laoch slumped against Ecne. The young woman's inner strength still surprised him.

"Let us grieve awhile. When we first sleep, take us then. And wake us before we arrive, K ... Sorry, Nathair." Oisin looked back to the spirit. "We must act with one goal, or we will fail. And both our realms will burn under that ... that *Kraken*."

54
THE PLEDGE OF A SHRIVEN SOUL

"You are an obnoxious prig," shouted Lelion. The admiral incarnate was slumped across the Fleshmaster's throne. The chamber swirled with old ash, the smell of burnt flesh still lingering in the air.

The faded spirit before him had barely formed, yet incandescent rage swirled within it. "How dare you." The words, hardly audible in the huge chamber, were carried on a wisp of whitefire. "I sacrificed my body to remain alive for my work, while you ride in that ridiculous contraption as if you are the emperor himself."

"Yet I live on in the same body, and your work is in the ashes that taste bitter on my tongue, Marbhleoir."

"It was Nathair. Its Spirit Walker must have eradicated my spirit venom. Perhaps it fades over such time." The necromancer winced at the thought, and waited for Lelion's next tirade.

"No matter. Despite your failings—" The admiral peered up at the huge silver-blue dragon that loomed over them. "—I suspect the Fleshmaster will still have need of your talents."

The curved doors to the chamber sprang open, and two Inhibitors dragged a female human across the floor, pinning her before Lelion. Her eyes were wild, face mud-caked, hair tangled with the detritus of their overgrown city. Lelion could make out the howls of her kin echoing through the palace doors, the feeding entering its second day as their people arose from whatever crypt or cellar they had slept in for the last few hundred years.

If the intruders aboard Nathair had known of them, how many would have died unaware, heads crushed or cut free from bodies?

"What is this?" whispered Marbhleoir.

"Your new body. And you should be grateful. Our kin have consumed any life they came across on awakening. This one, my Inhibitors found hiding inside a foundry. One Nathair must have entered."

"It is …"

"Get it done while she's still fresh. We have work to do."

Lelion, ignoring the moaning, strode down the steps to draw back the woman's head to expose the neck. With a flicker of her gauntlet, a razor-thin slash filled with blood, and she watched with glee as life departed from the woman's eyes. The spirit rolled through Lelion's fingers, infusing her ancient body, easing a hum that nagged at the edge of her hearing. The sound had started when the *Kraken* released its whitefire to invigorate the sleepers, always on the cusp of being audible.

A sated hunger, perhaps.

The admiral shuddered, and a deep thrum resounded through the palace walls. At first she wondered if Marbhleoir had hidden his true power, playing the lost soul when, in truth, he had stored his might within the crystal shards of the walls. But no. The sound coalesced into a familiar tone, and Lelion rolled her neck, letting her ancient body's vertebrae crack and settle.

"Hurry, Marbhleoir. Our emperor returns." She peered back to the dragon-wing throne, the briefest of smiles flickering at the memory of its touch.

A forlorn hope, though is that really what I want? A thousand years ago, I would have torn Tarin's body apart to sit upon it. But now?

She counted the steps echoing through the chamber. The Fleshmaster appeared through the doors. Behind walked his new pet, Popsilin, arms wrapped about a heartstone whose inner surface roiled with a welcome sight.

"Oh," said Lelion, her expectations of Tarin's success having been extremely low.

"Yes," replied the Fleshmaster, eyes roaming the wind, tasting the loss and dread within it. "We have it. Where is my promised army, Marbhleoir? Is it they I can taste upon the air?"

"It is," replied the admiral, trying to hide the glee from her voice. But it still brought the Fleshmaster's gaze upon her. "Marbhleoir is rebirthing. He is too weak in his current spirit form, though he assures me his soul imprint will remain intact. He used the palace to store himself."

"And my army? How are we to take Apso-Tran without them? Not even a dragon of the veil nor the *Kraken* would last long." The growl of the Fleshmaster's voice set Lelion's mind racing.

He still reels at the loss, despite it hastening the change amongst our people.

"Ashes. Nathair—"

"Nathair? What do you speak of, Lelion?" growled the Fleshmaster.

"The necromancer has shown me the memories of her attack, and those that ride within her. They bore weapons that had the Seven's taint upon them. Nathair burned the army, and they cut Marbhleoir's avatar down and near shredded his spirit."

The admiral's creeping unease grew, and she turned to peer at the convulsing body that lay at the base of the throne's dais. "Oh no. A thought."

"Speak."

"Marbhleoir said he was attacked when he invaded one of them, attempting to sever their spirit and take the body. He says they have a piece of him. What if?"

"If?"

"Marbhleoir knows of Apso-Tran. It's location, and what the realm holds."

"That, I worked out for myself."

The Fleshmaster peered up at Tabharthóir, the dragon's silver-blue scales gleaming, crystalline eyes vacant. "That realm is full of insanity. They will not welcome Nathair, nor these servants of the Seven. That our own dragon has turned against us pains me more, but Tabharthóir will be the stronger. And we have the *Kraken*, do we not? Popsilin." The Fleshmaster indicated for the Mechanised Inhibitor captain to follow. Together, they faced the metallic sheen of the dragon's chest. The emperor placed his hand upon the scales.

"Thank you, Viseri, though its construction took the last of you from us. You will be remembered." With one hand resting on the seething heartstone, the other upon the scaled chest, a shimmer rose – the first his eyes had witnessed in a thousand years. Blue lips split into a smile and, ignoring the captain's dread, he stepped in, pulling Popsilin through with him.

Lelion peered upwards, watching, waiting. Tarin's desire to activate Tabharthóir had haunted his people for the last few hundred years. Their success with the *Kraken* was now at risk, with the Wyrm fading or dead, its children too young to cut a path for the mighty soulship. That, and the need to crush the Seven who had brought them so low.

A squeal of metal upon metal broke through the groans emanating from the necromancer's new body as it writhed upon the floor, his spirit taking root in its brain. A crystalline eye burst into whitefire, followed by the next, and then the huge, bearded head swivelled to stare down at the admiral incarnate. Hot, oiled breath filled the space between them, and the mechanised legs heaved the beast up from the floor. The admiral stepped aside, old memories assailing her thoughts. A glance over to the necromancer caused a little glee to seep into her mind.

The awakening feast.

"And there will be so many more," Lelion whispered.

The teeth bit deep, penetrating chest and back, slicing the newly arisen body in two. Whitefire wreathed the razored edges, lancing its way up to fill the dragon's maw. A scream pierced the room, and the waiting Inhibitors took a step back as realisation struck. One of the ancient ones had fallen, their soul consumed. Another that would not see the death of the Seven.

But the young witness the emperor's ruthlessness towards those who fail him.

She peered across at the dragon-wing throne, and back to the newly imbued artifice dragon. And with a rueful smile, Lelion, admiral incarnate, dropped to one knee.

And Tabharthóir, the newly arisen dragon of the veil, roared her defiance.

The End of A City of Ashes

THE WARRIORS OF SPIRIT AND BONE SERIES

Thank you for reading the second book in this series of dark fantasy novels. My mother always asks why I didn't choose fantasy when I first started to write. I spent much of my late teens and early twenties exploring the worlds of the Eternal Champion with Michael Moorcock, one of my early literary heroes, along with Ursula K. Le Guin, and I agree, it seemed the logical thing to do. However, I needed to cut my authorship teeth on something a little less layered, hence my sci-fi series, Weapons of Choice. However, I found there was so much within those books that I develop further, and it was that temptation that led to the writing of A Dragon of the Veil. This follow up, A City of Ashes, is heavily influenced, however, by the worlds devised by Michael Moorcock. The macabre past of the Constructors and their fall into decadence and rise from the Sundering is a theme that plays out in many of his books. However, the arcane punk aesthetic was the driving force behind the ensuing story arc and taking a race of soul-vampires and running with them as my counterpoint had to be done.

The third and final book in the trilogy, A Queen in Blood, is a

humdinger. It was a challenge to write because I had to pack everything in to give the series the ending it deserves. There were a lot of
pieces to fit together – I am not a fan of loose ends – but I haven't
compromised. The book is nearly as long as the other two combined
as you, the reader, need to see just how far the Constructors will go
to retrieve their escaped slaves and spirit-dolls.

I hope you like your fantasy more than a little dark!

If you enjoyed this and other books in the series, please consider
leaving a review or a rating. There are readers out there who might
just enjoy my take on fantasy.

Thank you

About the Author

If you have read my previous books, you will know that most of my work has been in the action/military science fiction genre with the Weapons of Choice and Wrecking Squad series. These are not your usual action series as they delve into aspects of the human condition and have a reputation of being surprisingly thoughtful in their emotional depth and social conscience.

However, I have also released two standalone books in The Scorching science fiction/climate fiction series, with one more book to follow. Just Press Play is a daring take on a mystery thriller from a first-person point of view. It was a real joy to write, and though full of humour, it retains a dark undertone that will surprise. The World in My Hands is also a standalone novel exploring the Drathken who arrive to help as the Earth dies, and the humans who leave the planet to seek new worlds with a dark, secret history of their own.

You can view all my books, sign up for a newsletter and receive free books related to the Weapons of Choice and Wrecking Squad Series on my website below:

www.nicksnape.com

AUTHOR BIO

Nick Snape has been steeped in Science Fiction and Fantasy since his friends first dragged him from his schoolwork and stuck a book under his nose. Lost to the world of imagination, he became a teacher by accident, though he thoroughly enjoyed developing the joy of reading and writing in his pupils. Having retired after thirty years, he thought it was high time to practise what he preached. Nick's books feature everything from all out, heart-pounding, fast-paced action to thoughtful, character driven twists on the fantasy and sci-fi genres. Genetics to artificial intelligence, artifice dragons to soul-eating enemies, nothing is off the menu.

BOOKS BY NICK SNAPE

Weapons of Choice Series

(Amazon Only)

Hostile Contact

Return Protocol

Zuri's War

Finn's War

Alien Rebirth

Invasive Species

Legion Earth

Nemesis Earth

Weapons of Choice Box Set Vol.1 Bks 1-8

The Wrecking Squad Series

(Amazon Only)

The Wrecking Squad

Butcher's Folly

Warmonger's Wrath

Acknowledgements

As with all authors, this book and my other series would never have existed without the dedicated friends and family who were there by my side throughout the entire process. The least I can do is give them a mention for their patience with my obsession! My Beta readers, supporters and fiercest critics for this book have been Pak and Julie. Amazing people who put that aside to make sure whatever I put out there was something they wanted to read. I have also had great support from Martin Lejeune – an author who has given generously of their time during my trials and tribulations. I would also like to thank Laurel C Kriegler, who took on the editing duties – little did she know!

Very much appreciated, and the book would not be where it is without you all.

Julie, my wife, needs a special mention. Over the past few years, she has kept me going, being there at every step through the dark and joyful times. I can't believe how lucky I am. Finally, the New Year, Ceres Station and Pub Night Crews. Wouldn't be here without you.

Thank you all.

PRAISE FOR THE AUTHOR

'*A masterful storyteller.*' **SPR**

'*Nick Snape's creative storytelling, rich world-building, and engaging characters make this book an unforgettable journey.*' **Literary Titan**

'*Stunning series. Very highly recommended.*' **Goodreads**

'*Wildly creative*' **Self-Publishing Review**

'*I haven't enjoyed a series this much in along time. The twists and turns keep me constantly surprised.*' **Amazon Customer**

'*A truly immersive story.*' **Amazon Customer**